W9-DEO-851

COGNITIVE BASES OF MUSICAL COMMUNICATION

Edited by

Mari Riess Jones
Susan Holleran

Published by
American Psychological Association
1200 Seventeenth Street, NW
Washington, DC 20036

Copies may be ordered from
APA Order Department
P.O. Box 2710
Hyattsville, MD 20784

Designed by Grafik Communications Ltd., Alexandria, VA
Cover artwork by Grafik Communications Ltd., Alexandria, VA
Typeset by Harper Graphics, Waldorf, MD
Printed by Braun Brumfield, Inc., Ann Arbor, MI
Technical editing and production coordinated by Linda J. Beverly

Library of Congress Cataloging-in-Publication Data

Cognitive bases of musical communication / edited by Mari Riess Jones and Susan Holleran. — 1st ed.
p. cm.
Proceedings of a conference held in Columbus, Ohio, Apr. 5–9, 1990, sponsored by the American Psychological Association and The Ohio State University.
Includes bibliographical references and index.
ISBN 1-55798-127-2 : $40.00 ($32.00 to members). — ISBN 1-55798-127-2
1. Music—Psychology—Congresses. 2. Music—Performance—Psychological aspects—Congresses. 3. Cognitive psychology—Congresses. I. Jones, Mari Riess. II. Holleran, Susan.
III. American Psychological Association. IV. Ohio State University.
ML3830.C58 1991
781′.11—dc20 91-23245
CIP
MN

Printed in the United States of America
First edition

Contents

Contributors

Jamshed J. Bharucha, Department of Psychology, Dartmouth College
Helen Brown, Division of Music, Purdue University
David Butler, School of Music, The Ohio State University
Diana Deutsch, Department of Psychology, University of California, San Diego
Robert O. Gjerdingen, Department of Music, State University of New York at Stony Brook
Susan Holleran, Department of Psychology, The Ohio State University
Ray Jackendoff, Progam in Linguistics and Cognitive Science, Brandeis University
Mari Riess Jones, Department of Psychology, The Ohio State University
Robert Kraut, Department of Philosophy, The Ohio State University
Carol L. Krumhansl, Department of Psychology, Cornell University
Fred Lerdahl, School of Music, Columbia University
Eugene Narmour, Department of Music, University of Pennsylvania
Caroline Palmer, Department of Psychology, The Ohio State University
Diana Raffman, Department of Philosophy, The Ohio State University
L. Henry Shaffer, Department of Psychology, University of Exeter (U.K.)
John A. Sloboda, Department of Psychology, University of Keele (U.K.)

Foreword

Federal research agencies stopped regularly supporting investigator-initiated state-of-the-art research conferences in scientific psychology over a decade ago. During this period, however, scientific psychology has continued to grow, as well as to diversify into many new areas. Yet there have been relatively few opportunities for investigators in new and promising research areas to convene in special settings to discuss their findings.

As part of its continuing effort to enhance the dissemination of scientific knowledge in psychology, the American Psychological Association (APA) has undertaken a number of initiatives designed to foster scientific research and communication. In particular, the APA Science Directorate established in 1988 the Scientific Conferences Program, from which this publication resulted.

The APA Scientific Conferences Program provides university-based psychological researchers with seed monies essential to organizing specialty conferences on critical issues in basic research, applied research, and methodological issues in psychology. Deciding which conferences to support involves a competitive process. An annual call for proposals is issued by the APA Science Directorate to solicit conference ideas. Proposals from all areas of psychological research are welcome. These are then reviewed by qualified psychologists, who forward substantive suggestions and funding recommendations to the Science Directorate. At each stage, the criteria used to determine which conferences to support include relevance, timeliness, comprehensiveness of the topics, and qualifications of the presenters. From its inception in 1988 to mid-1991, 19 conferences have been funded, with a total outlay of more than $250,000. We expect to support several conferences annually in the future.

This program has two major goals. The first is to provide, by means of the conferences, a broad view of specific topics and, when appropriate, to encourage interdisciplinary participation. The second goal is to assure timely dissemination of the findings presented, by publishing carefully crafted scholarly volumes based, in part, on the conferences. The information thus reaches the broader psychological and scientific communities as well as the audiences at the conferences. Psychology and related fields thereby benefit from the most current research on a given topic.

This volume is the result of the "Cognitive Bases of Musical Communication" conference held in April 1990 and cosponsored by APA and The Ohio State University. The conference brought together some of the major names among the multidisciplinary scholars and theorists active in the field of music psychology to discuss how music communicates. This relatively new area of study of the cognitive bases of musical communication (most of the research has occurred within the past decade) invites the comparison of music with other forms of communication, particularly natural languages. Conference presentations provided perspectives on the role of affect and meaning in musical communication, listeners' interpretive responses to musical structure, approaches to pitch perception, the representation and acquisition of musical knowledge, and the issues of performance.

The American Psychological Association is pleased to have supported this conference and now to make the research presented there available in book form. We hope you will enjoy and be stimulated by this volume and others to come.

A list of the conferences funded through this program follows:

Research Community Psychology: Integrating Theories and Methodologies, September 1988

The Psychological Well-Being of Captive Primates, September 1988

Psychological Research on Organ Donation, October 1988

Arizona Conference on Sleep and Cognition, January 1989

Socially Shared Cognition, February 1989

Taste, Experience, and Feeding, April 1989

Perception of Structure, May 1989

Suggestibility of Children's Recollections, June 1989

Best Methods for Analysis of Change, October 1989

Conceptualization and Measurement of Organism-Environment Interactions, November 1989

Cognitive Bases of Musical Communication, April 1990

Conference on Hostility, Coping/Support, and Health, November 1990

Psychological Testing of Hispanics, February 1991

Study of Cognition: Conceptual and Methodological Issues, February 1991

Cardiovascular Reactivity to Psychological and Cardiovascular Disease: Conference on the Evidence, April 1991

Developmental Psychoacoustics, August 1991

Maintaining and Promoting Integrity in Behavioral Science Research, October 1991

The Contributions of Psychology to Mathematics and Science Education, November 1991

Lives Through Time: Assessment and Theory in Personality Psychology from a Longitudinal Perspective, November 1991

Lewis P. Lipsitt, PhD
Executive Director for Science

Virginia E. Holt
Manager, Scientific
Conferences Program

Preface

On April 5–9, 1990, the American Psychological Association and The Ohio State University sponsored the conference "Cognitive Bases of Musical Communication." This book is a result of that conference. The meeting in Columbus, Ohio, brought together a group of scholars and theorists active in the field of music psychology to discuss and debate how music does what it does: communicate.

Although a relatively small group of psychologists is currently involved in research in music psychology, its number is constantly growing, and the over the past decade the field itself has developed rapidly. Important new journals, books, and conference series have appeared on the scene. But given the multidisciplinary nature of the field, researchers have tended to remain within their own specialties; crossing disciplinary boundaries is difficult because of differences in terminology and theoretical perspectives. By inviting a small group of speakers and observers from different fields to discuss a focused theme in which they share theoretical interest and research experience, the Ohio State conference organizers hoped to lay foundations for increased understanding of terms and constructs of common concern, and for longer term collaborative projects as well.

We believe the conference succeeded in doing this. While this book cannot reproduce the lively discussions and debates that erupted as these issues were being raised, we hope it can achieve another goal of the conference: to bring some of the insights concerning communication via musical events into mainstream psychology. Issues related to this topic have interesting implications for prevailing theories of comprehension, mental representation, memory, and affect, among others.

Conference Plan

The conference was a 3-day meeting of 19 participating speakers, who came from various disciplines (psychology, music, philosophy, linguistics, and artificial intelligence), and 18 invited observers, who included interested faculty and graduate students from around the country. Faculty members associated with The Ohio State University Center for Cognitive

Science, directed by Professor Peter Culicover, served as hosts for the conference. Funding was provided by the American Psychological Association as well as the Center for Cognitive Science, the College of the Arts, the Departments of Psychology, Computer and Information Science, and Linguistics, and the Office of Research and Graduate Studies of The Ohio State University.

During the conference, each speaker presented a 40-minute talk, followed by 20 minutes of open discussion. Talks were grouped into sessions that lasted approximately 3 hours. The first 2 days of the conference consisted primarily of talks and discussion and were closed to the public. A final closed session was held on the morning of the 3rd day. The afternoon of this day featured a panel discussion of major issues that had emerged from the conference, followed by a guest lecture by Professor Jean-Jacques Nattiez of the Université de Montréal. Entitled "*Répons* and the Crisis of 'Communication' in Contemporary Music," this talk was the first in an annual lecture series honoring the late William Poland of The Ohio State University's School of Music, a pioneer in the psychology of music. The panel discussion and the Poland lecture were held in the Wexner Center for the Arts and were open to the public.

All of the events of the 3-day meeting, from scheduled sessions to breaks to the panel discussion, provided valuable opportunities for animated exchanges of points of view. The conference especially benefited from the lively insights of one of its most distinguished invited observers: Leonard B. Meyer.

Organization of the Book

This book follows the organization of the conference. Following this section, there are five parts, each preceded by a brief summary of the pertinent issues raised in the chapters that follow. Part 1 introduces various perspectives on the role of meaning and affect in musical communication. Part 2 presents three different approaches to listener's interpretive responses to musical structure as a musical event unfolds in real time. Part 3 describes a variety of approaches to pitch perception and its role in determining a listener's sense of tonality. In Part 4, important new perspectives on the representation and acquisition of musical knowledge are presented. Part 5 considers some provocative work on performance that explores how performers convey one of several interpretations of a score to listeners.

Mari Riess Jones
Susan Holleran

Acknowledgments

The editors and conference organizing committee are deeply indebted to a number of departments and programs at The Ohio State University for support both tangible and intangible: the Center for Cognitive Science; the College of the Arts; the Departments of Computer and Information Science, Linguistics, and Psychology; and the Office of Research and Graduate Studies. The conference would not have taken place at all without the enthusiastic support of the American Psychological Association's Scientific Conferences Program.

We are also very grateful to many individuals at our university who, in large and small ways, and on a daily basis, contributed to the success of this conference. Their diligence and good cheer were sustaining: Sylvia Andromeda, B. Chandrasekaran, Mary Darr, Hope Huntzinger, Julia Mills, and James Naylor.

Finally, the editors wish to acknowledge the faculty from diverse areas of The Ohio State University who conceived and delivered this conference. Their enthusiasm, commitment, and hard work in preparing and carrying through this conference were critical. All are linked by common interests in music perception and cognition, a fact which makes Ohio State a special place to be. This was never more evident than at the April 1990 conference. We thank our friends and colleagues of the conference organizing committee:

David Butler, School of Music
Peter Culicover, Center for Cognitive Science
Osamu Fujimura, Division of Speech and Hearing Science
Richard Jagacinski, Department of Psychology
Robert Kraut, Department of Philosophy
Caroline Palmer, Department of Psychology
Jordan Pollack, Department of Computer and Information Science
Diana Raffman, Department of Philosophy.

CHAPTER 1

Cognitive Bases of Musical Communication: An Overview

Mari Riess Jones and Susan Holleran

The topic of the conference "Cognitive Bases of Musical Communication" is central to the field of music psychology. It invites comparison of music with other forms of communication people use, particularly natural languages. This comparison is a theme that recurs in many of the chapters in this book. The topic also raises new issues, which, to some degree, echo trends in the psychology of language concerning the function of various speech patterns in communication. But in the field of music cognition, systematic exploration of these issues is just getting under way.

Communication is central to many influential theories of cognition. However, mainstream psychology typically relies heavily on models of text comprehension, word recognition, lexical decision-making, and speech perception to develop a perspective on communication. Communication via other stimulus materials (ones not so explicitly rooted in natural language) is less commonly studied. Yet music is a powerful communicative medium. Its prevalence in numerous guises in contemporary society tells us this. But what exactly does music communicate and how does it do this? These are important questions that have been ignored by mainstream theory and research in cognitive psychology. And yet, as researchers in the field of music psychology agree, answers to such questions can have profound implications for thinking about the general problem of communication.

Background of Music Psychology

Only in the past decade has the psychology of music moved from the status of an isolated research topic more or less independently pursued by a few scholars (e.g., Seashore, 1938; Francès, 1958/1988) to a full-fledged field of research in which an increasing number of experimental psychologists participate and interact. Of course for centuries, music has been the primary domain of study for musicians and musicologists and has sparked important debates among philosophers. Nowadays, as these various disciplines coalesce to form a new field, each contributes a distinctive background of theory and methodology.

Psychological Perspectives

The legacy of early researchers such as Seashore (1938), Mursell (1937), Francès (1958/1988), and Fraisse (1956) provides an important backdrop for current research in this area. Indeed, many of the issues which occupy us today were foreshadowed in their writings. Nevertheless, in spite of their pioneering contributions, in the last quarter of this century their direct impact on psychological theory building about music cognition has been modest.

Contemporary psychological approaches which began to emerge a little over a decade ago reflect the current tenor of the times. Experiments on perception of interleaved melodies (e.g., Dowling, 1973a) have extended principles of auditory pattern streaming (Bregman, 1990; Jones, 1976); those on melody recall have appealed to chunking and coding principles (Deutsch, 1980; Dowling, 1973b); and those concerned with tonality have taken mental geometry into new realms (Krumhansl, 1979). New theoretical approaches to accommodate these findings have blossomed. These range from coding theories which outline rules for mental representations of musical grammars (e.g., Deutsch & Feroe, 1981), for memory of scale and contour information (Dowling, 1978), and for guiding expert productions of meter and tempo (Clarke, 1985; Handel, 1989; Shaffer, 1982) to models that elegantly portray knowledge of tonal music in terms of multidimensional tonal pitch spaces (Krumhansl, 1990; Shepard, 1982), networks (Bharucha, 1987), or dynamic expectancies and prototypical musical patterns (Jones, 1981, 1982).

More recently, largely under the increasing influence of other disciplinary perspectives, attention is shifting from the study of music-like events and their mental representations to questions about their function in the activity of musical communication. Does the act of communication place constraints on a description of what the performer or listener knows? Recent research on the way in which artists actually interpret and perform a score to achieve a certain level of comprehension in the listener suggests provocative answers to such questions (e.g., Palmer, chapter 15; Shaffer, chapter 16, this volume; Sloboda, 1983). This inevitably reverberates back to theoretical descriptions about the listener's understanding of a performed piece of music. Does a rule system which describes the listener's mental representation have to incorporate performance characteristics, or is it enough to pose grammatical rules implied by the score? This relates to a larger question which loomed in the background of the "Cognitive Bases of Musical Communication" conference: Does music have a "grammar" (in a conventional linguistic sense) and, if so, do its rules derive from relations suggested by the score, by the auditory sound pattern, or both?

Perspectives From Music Theory

Two significant influences on current music psychology come from music theory: the work of Heinrich Schenker (1935/1979) and Leonard B. Meyer (e.g., 1973). Schenker, a prominent music theorist from the turn of the century, has exerted a powerful influence on contemporary musicological analyses. His approach to the structure of tonal music is hierarchical, emphasizing that any tonal composition is structurally decomposable to reveal a higher order background level of structure, the Ursatz, based on a certain arrangement of notes in a single critical chord, the tonic chord (Schenker, 1979). The surface structure of a piece, the *foreground*, recurrently implies these background harmonies, according to Schenker's system. Meyer's approach (1973) is less explicitly hierarchical, placing greater emphasis on unfolding melodic and harmonic structures in the musical surface. Meyer argues that certain critical musical configurations carry implications of their future course for a listener and these implications and their ultimate realizations (or denials) form the basis of our affective response to music.

The work of both Meyer and Schenker has had a strong influence on the cognitive approaches to the question of musical communication exemplified in this book. One of the most influential current theories about tonal music, that of Lerdahl and Jackendoff (1983), has a Schenkerian flavor: It proposes various hierarchical descriptions of prominent musical structures (meter, phrasing, etc.), while remaining explicitly rooted in psychological principles (e.g., Gestalt laws). At this conference, Jackendoff and Lerdahl separately pursued aspects of their original approach which showed interesting convergences with experimental and theoretical analyses in psychology (e.g., Krumhansl, 1979;

Deutsch & Feroe, 1981; Bharucha, 1984) and with current thinking in the semantics of music (e.g., Kraut, chapter 2, and Raffman, chapter 3, this volume).

Meyer's approach has been extended in different ways by both Narmour and Gjerdingen. Narmour (1977, 1990) has sought to show that theorizing about the psychologically salient aspects of musical structure should go "beyond Schenkerism" to include ideas about melodic rules and prototypes and to provide a richer analysis of the listener's response to continuing conflicts and surprises in music as it unfolds in real time. Gjerdingen has extended the study of prototypical style structures both in historical studies (1988) and in connectionist models (1990; chapter 14, this volume). The perspectives of both Narmour and Gjerdingen reflect themes pertinent to the research of psychologists at the Musical Communication conference (e.g., Jones 1981, 1982; Sloboda, 1985).

Contemporary Convergence: Music Perception and Cognition

Against these broad perspectives, music theorists and psychologists have been joined by scholars in philosophy, linguistics, and artificial intelligence to craft a new multidisciplinary field. This book, guided by a thematic orientation, selectively samples from this field.

The theme, cognitive bases of musical communication, encourages questions that can be addressed by scholars from all of the constituent disciplines. As we shall see, it raises important issues of indeterminacy that are not unfamiliar to linguists, philosophers, and psycholinguists. The problem of multiple meanings or interpretations is clearly a fundamental one in any attempt to understand the communicative act. Communication, virtually by definition, assumes a low level of uncertainty with respect to some shared idea of speaker and listener or, in the case of music, of performer/composer and listener. Multiple analyses of the musical structure of a given piece are possible, and this fact has important implications both for formal theories of musical grammar and for psychological approaches that strive to explain aspects of the acts of perceiving, representation, and expressive performance. Thus, one of several issues weaving through the chapters presented in this book concerns the ways in which listeners arrive at one or another interpretation of some potentially indeterminate sound pattern. It is evident that memory load, affect, artistic device, attention, and learning are all relevant. We believe that conference authors and observers have acquired a greater appreciation of both the complexity of this problem and the benefits of raising it in the musical domain, and we hope that readers will come to share this appreciation.

References

Bharucha, J. J. (1984). Anchoring effects in music: The resolution of dissonance. *Cognitive Psychology, 16,* 485–518.

Bharucha, J. J. (1987). Music cognition and perceptual facilitation: A connectionist framework. *Music Perception, 5,* 1–30.

Bregman, A. S. (1990). *Auditory scene analysis.* Cambridge, MA: MIT Press.

Clarke, E. F. (1985). Structure and expression in rhythmic performance. In P. Howell, I. Cross, & R. West (Eds.), *Musical structure and cognition* (pp. 205–236). London: Academic Press.

Deutsch, D. (1980). The processing of structured and unstructured tonal sequences. *Perception & Psychophysics, 28,* 381–389.

Deutsch, D., & Feroe, J. (1981). The internal representation of pitch sequences in tonal music. *Psychological Review, 88,* 503–522.

Dowling, W. J. (1973a). The perception of interleaved melodies. *Cognitive Psychology, 5,* 322–337.

Dowling, W. J. (1973b). Rhythmic groups and subjective chunks in memory for melodies. *Perception & Psychophysics, 14,* 37–40.

Dowling, W. J. (1978). Scale and contour: Two components of a theory of memory for melodies. *Psychological Review, 85,* 341–354.

Fraisse, R. (1956). *Les structures rhythmiques* [Rhythmic structures]. Louvain, France: Editions Universitaires.

Francès, R. (1988). *The perception of music* (W. J. Dowling, Trans.). Hillsdale, NJ: Erlbaum. (Original work published 1958)

Gjerdingen, R. O. (1988). *A classic turn of phrase: Music and the psychology of convention.* Philadelphia: University of Pennsylvania Press.

Gjerdingen, R. O. (1990). The categorization of musical patterns by self-organizing neuronlike networks. *Music Perception, 7,* 339–370.

Handel, S. (1989). *Listening.* Cambridge, MA: MIT Press.

Jones, M. R. (1976). Time, our lost dimension: Toward a new theory of perception, attention, and memory. *Psychological Review, 83,* 323–355.

Jones, M. R. (1981). Music as a stimulus for psychological motion. Part 1. Some determinants of expectancies. *Psychomusicology, 1,* 34–51.

Jones, M. R. (1982). Music as a stimulus for psychological motion. Part 2. An expectancy model. *Psychomusicology, 2,* 1–31.

Krumhansl, C. L. (1979). The psychological representation of musical pitch in a tonal context. *Cognitive Psychology, 11,* 346–384.

Krumhansl, C. L. (1990). *Cognitive foundations of musical pitch.* New York: Oxford University Press.

Lerdahl, F., & Jackendoff, R. (1983). *A generative theory of tonal music.* Cambridge, MA: MIT Press.

Meyer, L. B. (1973). *Explaining music.* Berkeley: University of California Press.

Mursell, J. L. (1937). *The psychology of music.* New York: W. W. Norton.

Narmour, E. (1977). *Beyond Schenkerism: The need for alternatives in music analysis.* Chicago: University of Chicago Press.

Narmour, E. (1990). *The analysis and cognition of basic melodic structures: The implication-realization model.* Chicago: University of Chicago Press.

Schenker, H. (1979). *Free composition* (E. Oster, Trans.). New York: Longman. (Original work published 1935)

Seashore, C. E. (1938). *The psychology of music.* New York: McGraw-Hill.

Shaffer, L. H. (1982). Rhythm and timing in skill. *Psychological Review, 89,* 109–122.

Shepard, R. (1982). Geometrical approximations to the structure of musical pitch. *Psychological Review, 89,* 305–333.

Sloboda, J. A. (1983). The communication of musical meter in piano performance. *Quarterly Journal of Experimental Psychology, 35,* 377–390.

Sloboda, J. A. (1985). *The musical mind: The cognitive psychology of music.* Oxford: Clarendon.

PART ONE

Communication, Meaning, and Affect in Music

Introduction

Any exploration of the issue of musical communication must deal with the difficult question of what it is that music actually "communicates." It is natural that attempts to answer this question often include appeals to the best studied communication system, natural language. But the debate is long standing over the degree to which this parallel can be pushed: Is there a semantics of music, and can it be compared to well-established semantic systems for natural language? Music seems to lack the capability of natural language to convey explicit referential "information" about external states, but at the same time few can deny that music is somehow "meaningful" and that a sense of meaning can be communicated between composer, performer, and listener.

The philosopher W. V. Quine has argued that the semantic content of natural language is indeterminate—that it is possible for several hearers of the same utterance to have nonequivalent interpretations that are nevertheless equally correct. Robert Kraut, in chapter 2, claims that this kind of argument, when advanced to explain the fact that different listeners have different responses to the same musical work, does not recognize that there are indeed "correct" ways to hear a piece. Arriving at a "determinate" semantics of music can be achieved only by studying the possibilities for objective correctness in musical judgments, as determined by the genre of the piece as well as its intended audience.

In chapter 3, Diana Raffman further explores the role and behavior of listeners: Their understanding of a musical work can be thought of as consisting of the experiencing of appropriate "feelings," which are specific to music, in response to specific musical structures (e.g., experiencing a particular chord sequence as a cadence). These feelings can act to constrain possible musical structures, much as a linguistic semantics can be said to constrain the syntax.

Another viewpoint on the relationship of musical structure and listener response is offered by John Sloboda, whose recent work has begun to provide a much-needed body of empirical data on the relation of emotion to music. In chapter 4, he identifies specific structural features in music that evoke classes of physical responses characteristic of emotions typically elicited by nonmusical stimuli. He sees some of these reactions as being provoked in part by different levels of analysis carried out on the same musical event, a viewpoint in many ways complementary to the perspectives of Eugene Narmour (chapter 6), Ray Jackendoff (chapter 5), and Leonard B. Meyer (1973).

CHAPTER 2

On the Possibility of a Determinate Semantics for Music

Robert Kraut

We are prone to talk of meaning, or content, or significance, or semantics, in connection with music. Theorists of various persuasions are led to talk this way for various reasons. For example, given the prevalence of "syntactic" considerations about music, one might ask whether a "semantic" dimension is somehow presupposed. My focus here is different: I am led to countenance musical semantics because of a concern with the phenomenon of *understanding music.* I want to know what it is to understand a musical event, and how musical understanding relates to other varieties of understanding—for example, to the varieties of understanding at work when a native speaker (or a translator) understands a grammatical sentence, or when a scientist understands experimental data, or when a person understands another person's actions or mental states. What must I be able to do, or say, or feel, or what must I believe, in order to qualify as understanding—for example—Stravinsky's music? The question matters to those interested in architectural and computational aspects of the human mind. It also matters within the art world. After all, some of us understand John Coltrane's music and some of us do not; New Wave aficionados view traditional critics as not understanding their music, and thus as ill-equipped to provide legitimate criticism. Jazz enthusiasts of the 1960s regarded Sonny Stitt's rejection of Eric Dolphy's music as based, in part, on a failure to understand it. Many of us are willing to talk this way, but it is not clear what such talk amounts to, or the conditions under which ascriptions of musical understanding are true. We need to know what it *is* to understand a musical event.

Semantics of Music

We should be careful with analogies and borrowed paradigms. Musical genres are not, in any straightforward way, natural languages: Understanding music may or may not involve the processes and achievements involved in attaining linguistic competence. Inquiries into the semantics of music are usually puzzling: After all, musical phrases do not have truth conditions, and no matter how you twist the logician's concepts of reference, extension, and satisfaction, music simply isn't a phenomenon for which one wants to seek a Tarski-style recursive theory of truth. "Expressivist" semantics, according to which music is somehow a vehicle for the expression of emotion, is implausible in connection with a wide range of music. Here the issue is perhaps terminological (what precisely is an emotion?); but caution is nevertheless required. Seasoned listeners rarely experience joy, jealousy, indignation, envy, love, fear, or other stereotypical emotions in response to uptempo Ornette Coleman performances. Not every phenomenological episode corresponds to an emotion; there is more to emotion than feeling. The complex experiences and intricate sensory-perceptual states associated with such music cannot be assumed, pending further discussion, to constitute emotions.

But there are additional options; there is more to linguistic meaning than truth conditions or the expression of emotion. Words are artifacts. They subserve complex social-institutional functions; they play roles in the games of gathering evidence, theorizing, communicating, deliberating, and countless other activities. Semantical roles are thus multidimensional, involving relations between word use and parameters such as perceptual evidence, appropriate behavior, and inferential transformations. The analogy between music and natural language appears irresistible; for, although natural language and music might subserve very different roles, musical phenomena are nonetheless located in a complex system involving many of the parameters relevant to linguistic meaning. Musical event-types (i.e., repeatable, reidentifiable musical events) are implicated in "inference-like" practices (e.g., certain temporal orderings of pitches imply specific tonal centers); and musical events are often thought to warrant certain affective and/or behavioral reactions rather than others. Facts of this kind provide the resources for characterizing a dimension of musical significance, and thus provide help in understanding musical understanding.

Quine's Indeterminacy of Translation

Having gone this far, a certain question appears tantalizing. One of the more hotly disputed issues in metaphysics and the philosophy of language concerns W.V. Quine's claim that natural language meaning is indeterminate (Quine, 1960). The claim, enshrined in Quine's Indeterminacy of Translation thesis (hereafter IT) is this: For any given language L, it is possible, in principle, to construct incompatible translations of L, all of which are equally correct. As Quine puts it, "manuals for translating one language into another can be set up in divergent ways, all compatible with the totality of speech dispositions, yet incompatible with one another" (p. 27). The envisaged manuals are "incompatible" or "rival" insofar as they assign distinct and nonequivalent interpretations to the same expressions. Quine dramatizes the point by considering a context of "radical translation"—the activity of translating a totally unfamiliar and hitherto unknown alien language into one's home language. A translation scheme is a general recursive function whose domain is the set of all sentences of the alien language and whose range is a subset of the home language, and which satisfies certain conditions (preservation of stimulus meaning, commutation with truth functions, etc.) Quine claims that it is possible to have rival translation manuals which fit the totality of speech behavior equally well, but which nonetheless diverge in the meanings they assign to individual expressions. This is possible because there is, intuitively, far more to meaning than is captured in Quine's notion of stimulus meaning. Consider English expressions which are stimulus-meaning-equivalent (i.e., prompted by the same nonverbal stimuli) but which, intuitively, differ in their meanings. Quine offers the expressions 'rabbit,' 'undetached rabbit part,' and 'instantaneous time-slice of a rabbit' as examples: any English speaker judges these expressions to differ in meaning and extension. But despite the obvious semantic divergences, these expressions are stimulus-meaning-equivalent, and are thus equally suited to serve as translations of some native expression routinely volunteered in the presence of rabbits. Manuals which differ in assigning one or another of these expressions as translations of a native expression would perforce differ in other ways as well: Differences in the interpretation of one expression require compensatory adjustments elsewhere in the translation scheme. But Quine is confident that such global translational alternatives can be constructed, all of which would conform equally well to the empirical data. This is linguistic behaviorism:

Quine casts doubt on the determinate reality of those aspects of meaning not fixed by stimulus meaning. Given the existence of alternative manuals that conform equally well to the requirements of translation, he urges that there is no "fact of the matter" as to which translation scheme provides the correct translation; in an absolute sense, there is no such thing as correct translation, because there is nothing over and above stimulus meanings for a translation to be right or wrong about. Note that Quine's claim is not epistemological: He is not saying that, because of the underdetermination of theory by data, there is no way to be certain which translation scheme is correct; such epistemic slack between evidence and theory is present in any theoretical endeavor, and shows nothing special about translation. Quine's claim is rather ontological: Within certain constraints, there simply is no fact of the matter as to what an expression means.

It takes time and work to formulate IT properly, and to provide the kinds of examples that render the thesis even remotely plausible. For the present, note that IT bears on varieties of understanding which involve *interpretation*: In claiming the existence of rival translation manuals, IT entails that two agents could lay equal claim to understanding the same linguistic phenomenon despite serious disagreements with one another (assume for the present that achieving a translation is sufficient for achieving understanding). Thus IT underwrites a kind of *pluralism* about semantic meaning: Over and above what is captured in stimulus meaning (and that is not very much), there is no such thing as the unique meaning of a word, given the availability of alternative global translation schemes. Moreover, there need be no consensus, beyond the point of stimulus meanings, between those who understand a native utterance.

There is little agreement about the correctness of IT, the cogency of the arguments for it, or its precise consequences; one can hold IT to be importantly true, importantly false, a trivial consequence of too minimal a set of constraints on proper translation, self-refuting, or even unintelligible. It takes a few months to sort out the options and even longer to make up one's mind. Prima facie, the thesis is profound: It tells us that if there is one way to correctly translate a linguistic item, there are many ways. Some ways might seem more natural than others (e.g., translating a native expression typically volunteered in the presence of rabbits as "time-slice of rabbit" or "undetached part of a rabbit" rather than simply as "rabbit" seems bizarre and unnecessary); but this, according to Quine, is a fact about our own parochiality, our own provincial sense of what counts as a natural kind, and does not point toward the "incorrectness" of the apparently bizarre translation schemes. IT does not entail that "anything goes" in translation: There are indeed incorrect translation schemes. But there also exist a multiplicity of translations which, though distinct (and in some sense incompatible) are equally correct. That is just a consequence, according to Quine, of the kind of thing that linguistic meaning *is*. In this dispute, Frege and Carnap are the traditional enemies outside Quine's gates.

It is important to note that IT is, prima facie, totally bizarre; philosophers motivated by common sense, as well as those unimpressed by behavioristic arguments against the possibility of a "science of intention," thus join forces in rejecting it.

Hearing With Understanding

Quine's goal is to undermine certain traditional views about linguistic meaning; as noted above, his arguments bear on our very understanding of what it is to understand a linguistic phenomenon. For if translation is a sufficient condition for understanding, then disagreement among translators is itself no indication that any of them fail to understand the natives' utterances; perhaps none of the translators, despite their disagreements, are in error. This is an exciting possibility—so exciting that we begin to wonder whether it can be generalized to those forms of understanding which do not involve (or, more cautiously, do not *obviously* involve) translation or interpretation (we must be careful here, since 'interpretation' means different things to different theorists). For example, understanding music is a matter of experiencing appropriate qualitative states in response to it—a matter of hearing it in certain ways. As Roger Scruton puts it, "musical understanding is a form of hearing. The content of music is a heard content, and it is heard *in* the tones." Moreover, "if a work of music means something ... this is a fact about the way it sounds" (Scruton, 1987, p. 171). In this chaper, I want to reflect upon whether "those who hear with understanding" do so only by virtue of having precisely the same perceptual experiences, or whether, owing to some musical correlate of translational indeterminacy, musical understanding tolerates quite distinct (and in some sense incompatible) perceptual experiences of the same musical event.

By *musical significance* I mean whatever is grasped in musical understanding; it is best thought of as a syndrome of experiences correlated with the musical stimulus—experiences of stability and tension, of metrical groupings, of tonal centers, of variations on harmonic, melodic, or rhythmic structures, and the like. The question is this: For each musical phenomenon, is there a unique, *correct* syndrome of experiential responses corresponding to it? Or are there many ways of hearing the piece, such that each way is as "legitimate" as any of the others? Is there even any basis for distinguishing *proper* from *improper* experiences of the music?[1] This is, I think, a close correlate of questions about the indeterminacy of semantical meaning.

Having discussed these matters with both lovers of music and lovers of language, my impression is this: IT flies in the face of common sense and seems wrong; but its musical counterpart, once articulated in the terms I recommend here, tends not to offend. There are—I am told—facts of the matter as to what a natural language sentence means, but there are no facts about the significance of a musical event (and thus, there is no single syndrome of perceptual-phenomenal experiences of the musical event which, to the exclusion of others, is "correct"). This is an interesting set of intuitions: Either (a) it signals a profound difference between music and natural language; or (b) we should side with Quine (and the "semantic pluralists") and insist that linguistic meaning is indeterminate; or (c) we should insist, against the musical pluralist, that musical significance is determinate.

Indeterminacy of Musical Significance

But is there any *argument* for the indeterminacy of musical significance? One such argument might be this: A person understands a musical event M if and only if that person has appropriate (i.e., correct) qualitative experiences of that event; moreover, a syndrome of qualitative states is an *appropriate* response to M if and only if it is a response provided by enough members of the relevant community. But (the argument proceeds), such criteria provide no foothold for the uniqueness of musical significance, because there are no facts of the matter as to which people constitute the relevant community.

This argument provides no basis for distinguishing linguistic meaning from musical significance vis-a-vis determinacy. To see this, recall that linguistic behavior is norm governed: inferences can be warranted or unwarranted, uses of expressions can be correct or incorrect, patterns of behavior can be justified or unjustified in light of antecedent verbal performances, and so on. (Quine is often accused, wrongly I believe, of excessive preoccupation with causal considerations to the neglect of these normative dimensions).

[1]*It is sometimes urged that feelings and other qualitative phenomenal states cannot, unlike propositional attitudes, be assessed for correctness or incorrectness; they are not the types of states to which such evaluations apply. R.G. Collingwood, for example, in discussing the differences between cognition and experience, says that "There is nothing in the case of feeling to correspond with what, in the case of thinking, may be called mis-thinking or thinking wrong" (p. 157). His claim is not merely that feelings, unlike propositional thoughts, are neither true nor false; he seems to embrace the stronger view that feelings cannot be assessed for appropriateness (see Collingwood, 1938). The origins and plausibility of this cognitivist prejudice are discussed in Kraut (1986).*

Natural language translation must reflect the relevant norms: The fact that an expression has a certain range of appropriate uses bears on the proper translation of that expression. So there is an obvious relation, however we explicate it, between the meaning of these words in this speaker's repertoire and the roles of these words in the community to which this speaker belongs. We say "it is the word's usage in *this* population that constitutes its meaning," thereby signaling the relevance of *this* collection of communal practices rather than some other. A speaker's overt verbal behavior involves the use of utterance-types which are, so to speak, the property of the group with which that speaker engages in fluid dialogue. Word-types are community property; semantical interpretation takes this into account by attempting to discover the role played by a speaker's utterance-type *relative to that class of speakers by whose semantical norms the speaker is constrained.* Because of a need to distinguish semantical differences from differences in collateral information, circumscribing this class is often difficult. But working translators inevitably make the assumptions and idealizations necessary to oil the wheels of smooth translation; none of this tells against the determinacy of linguistic meaning.

Relevant Populations

Musicians also belong to communities: people they work with, people who have influenced them, and people to whom they defer. Why not take the experiences prevalent among *that* community as constitutive of the significance of a musical event?

Herein lies a difference between our concepts of natural language and our concepts of artistic phenomena like symphonies: We balk at designating any particular population as the one in which "property rights" for a piece of music (and thus its significance) reside. We are willing to insist that native discourse belongs to the natives—or, more broadly, to those with whom the natives would be willing to converse. But Beethoven's Fifth Symphony belongs to the world. *No* population enjoys privilege over any other in fixing the musical-perceptual facts constitutive of the "real significance" of a musical piece. And this spells doom for strict analogies between linguistic meaning and musical significance.

Most musicians with whom I have discussed these matters find this sort of pluralism intuitively objectionable. They usually urge that Beethoven's sophisticated peers constitute the relevant population vis-a-vis attributions of "proper experience" of his work. If there are serious disagreements as to which population is relevant, there are corresponding disagreements about who does, or does not, understand the music. What matters for the present discussion is that the latter disagreements derive from the former. Attributions of understanding rest, for their semantical force, upon decisions about relevant population. For it is that population by which the standards of appropriate experiential response are constituted.

Consider dialectically clever musical novices. They wish to ensure that their own musical responses are as legitimate as anyone else's; they regard strategies of the kind just outlined as self-serving elitism. They treat the "expert's" remarks about designated populations as mere parochiality—simple manifestations of a prejudice in favor of the relative significance of a specific population. These novices see no reason to dignify any particular population as the tribunal against which the correctness of musical experiences is measured.

I do not see that any further discovery or argument can resolve this dispute. The one side—call it the *egalitarian* side—insists that, within certain constraints, one experiential response to a piece of music is as good as another. The other side (which I prefer to call the *informed* side) flatly denies it, insisting on the primacy of a specific population and the primacy of a procedure for determining it. This latter strategy, in itself, does not ensure uniqueness of appropriate experience: Depending on the details, establishing a reference population might not thereby fix a single syndrome of correct responses to the piece. There might be room to maneuver, even among the experts; there might be more than one equally acceptable syndrome of experiential responses to a work even within a designated population. But this "population-fixing" strategy nonetheless provides a basis for rejecting certain responses as inappropriate. Any adequate understanding of musical understanding requires some decision as to which side—the egalitarian or the informed—embraces the more plausible position.

Musical Indeterminacy

Let me quickly sketch another argument for musical indeterminacy, suggest that it fails , and then worry about how this issue could possibly be resolved. The philosopher Kendall Walton (1970) stresses the distinction between correct and incorrect perception of an artwork. He argues that the kinds of experiences requisite for a proper understanding of a work are determined by the *category* to which the work belongs, and he spends considerable time trying to specify a set of conditions which determine, for any given work, the artistic category to which it belongs. But sometimes one cannot specify the rules for deciding how works are correctly perceived, because the stated conditions determine *no unique category.* In discussing situations of this kind, Walton considers a possible critical dispute concerning Giacommetti's thin metal sculptures. He says:

> To a critic who sees them simply as sculptures, or sculptures of people, they look frail, emaciated, wispy, or wiry. But that is not how they would strike a critic who sees them in the category of thin metal sculptures of that sort (just as stick figures do not strike us as wispy or emaciated). He would be impressed not by the thinness of the sculptures, but by the expressive nature of the positions of their limbs, and so forth, and so no doubt would attribute very different aesthetic properties to them. Which of the two ways of seeing these works is correct is, I suspect, undecidable .... So perhaps the dispute between the two critics is essentially unresolvable. The most that we can do is to point out just what sort of a difference of perception underlies the dispute, and why it is unresolvable. (p. 362)

If there is any foothold for the indeterminacy of musical significance, it surely involves cases such as this. But there exists a simple strategy for restoring determinacy, a strategy actually employed in attributions of artistic understanding. Suppose that a simple diagram can be seen either as a duck or as a rabbit, and that Walton's conditions point to *neither* perceptual experience as more correct than the other; in such a case, we say that the person who "genuinely understands" the diagram is the one who alternately sees it as both. A viewer incapable of, or unaware of the possibility of, both sorts of perceptual experience is likely to be treated as lacking in understanding; anyone who sees only a rabbit has fallen short of the mark, and has only partial understanding. So it is with musical experiences. It is, for example, extremely important to hear Led Zeppelin's "The Crunge" (from *Houses of the Holy*) not only as a more-sophisticated-than-usual instance of Heavy Metal, but also as a sarcastic commentary on James Brown's more involuted performances. This is not simply collateral knowledge about the piece: It involves hearing certain modulations and syncopations in quite special ways. One who does not hear this has yet to totally understand the piece.

There is, then, no reason to believe that musical significance is any less determinate than word meaning. Ambiguous words do not, by mere virtue of ambiguity, lack determinate meaning; *ambiguity is not indeterminacy.* When confronted with an alleged case of indeterminacy, it is easy enough to invoke duck-rabbit analogies and claim that each of the touted rivals is merely *part* of the total syndrome of appropriate responses, and that both responses are requisite for proper understanding. Determinacy restored.

As restorations go, this one is suspicious and disappointing; it was too easy. Recall that we were seeking a basis for the possibility of genuinely rival interpretive stories, or—in musical cases—rival, equally appropriate perceptual responses. Our present rejoinder is that the touted rivals are not rivals at all, but rather parts of the single correct story (or of the single correct syndrome of experiential responses). It is no longer clear, then, how anyone who countenances the indeterminacy of musical significance can win; no sooner is an example provided than we urge that it is not really an example at all. It is no longer clear what the excitement is about.

Indeterminacy and Pluralism

There is excitement because indeterminacy and pluralism were born twins: Friends of indeterminacy insist on the legitimacy of distinct syndromes of experiential response to musical events. Those repulsed by such pluralism seek a basis for judgments of objective correctness. Walton, for example, eschews accounts of aesthetic perception which "do not allow aesthetic judgments to be mistaken often enough." (p. 355).

It is interesting, and perhaps even profound, that we still do not know how to settle this dispute. Perhaps there are further constraints, as yet unarticulated, that would resolve the matter. Or perhaps the entire dialectic between "pluralism" and "monism" is less a disagreement about a matter of fact and more a clash between disparate commitments concerning music and musical understanding. I have tried to demonstrate that pluralism about musical understanding (as codified in a doctrine of indeterminacy of musical significance) is mistaken. But it might have been a mistake to proceed this way.

We imagined a musician who demanded that Beethoven's peers—his knowledgable peers—constitute the "reference population" for attributions of appropriate experience of Beethoven's work. The existence of this reference population provides a ground for the objectivity of musical significance; for it provides a standard against which to assess musical experiences for correctness. I suggest that this insistence on determinate musical significance is the expression of a commitment: a commitment to the explanatory importance of the musical perceptions and standards of taste upheld within the particular population which is *responsible for the musical event* in question. The monist believes that it is only in terms of such perceptions and standards that various key aspects of the piece can best be explained. Thus, to insist upon objectivity in the domain of musical significance is to manifest a commitment to the norms upheld in a particular population—a commitment to seeing oneself as a member of that population. The significance of a symphony is as much an artifact of social/institutional forces as the meaning of an utterance; to insist upon the objectivity of that significance is to manifest an unwillingness to divorce the artifact from the very population that consitututes its significance.

The novice, we may suppose, is unimpressed with such considerations. He or she may agree, should the issue explicitly arise, that the designated population does indeed occupy a special position relative to the kinds of explanations with which the musician is preoccupied. But lacking any urgent drive to provide such explanations, the novice is willing to cut the piece loose from its causal-historical ancestry and let a thousand equally legitimate audiences bloom. The novice insists that music is just the *sort* of thing from which people should derive whatever experiences they can, none being any more or less correct than any other.

The musician, repulsed by this sentiment, insists upon objectivity. It is precisely this insistence which I am trying to understand; I want to know why it persists despite the pluralist's preoccupation with the population relativity of semantical phenomena. My suggestion is that population relativity does not undermine the objectivity of musical significance, for the same reason that the social character of linguistic behavior does not determine the objectivity of linguistic meaning. There are facts about how a word is used in a given population; and there are, similarly, facts about how a musical event is "used" in a given population. The trick is to choose the right population, and to defend one's choice against the charge of arbitrariness. The musician is confident that this can be done. Thus, like the translator of natural language, the musician has decided to treat certain populations rather than others as relevant to the determination of semantic content. Such decisions are subject to evaluation; in the linguistic case, they might render translation more, rather than less, difficult; in the musical case, they might render the explanation of musical phenomena more, rather than less, difficult. But beyond a point it seems miguided to assess such decisions for factual correctness or incorrectness.

Conclusions

If this is right, then we should not have asked whether musical significance is, like linguistic meaning, objectively determinate; for there is room to maneuver in either direction. We should instead have asked about the purposes subserved by insisting on objective determinacy, and whether those purposes are worth achieving.

Musical understanding, like natural language understanding, is attributed against a backdrop of several parameters, foremost among which are the relevant community and standards of normalcy within that community. Every attempt to specify a procedure for determining unique values for these parameters invites charges of arbitrariness. Musical significance, like linguistic meaning, *can* be made to appear indeterminate if we dwell on this; alternatively, we can specify enough constraints as to rule out all but one community and one coherent class of musical experiences within that community as relevant. This, joined with additional constraints, might restore the appearance of determinacy. I opt for the latter strategy; the deeper question is whether anything can be said in its defense.

References

Collingwood, R.G. (1938). *The principles of art.* London: Oxford University Press.

Kraut, R. (1986). Feelings in context. *The Journal of Philosophy, LXXXIII, 11,* 642–652.

Quine, W.V. (1960). *Word and object.* Cambridge, MA: MIT Press.

Scruton, R. (1987). Analytical philosophy and the meaning of music. *The Journal of Aesthetics and Art Criticism, XLVI,* 169–176.

Walton, K. L. (1970). Categories of art. *The Philosophical Review, 79,* 334–367.

CHAPTER 3

Proposal for a Musical Semantics

Diana Raffman

Cognitive theory has it that perception, among other things, is a matter of mentally representing the world in certain ways. According to one popular view, perception consists of the computation of a series of increasingly abstract mental representations of the environment which proceeds from raw sensory responses to full-blooded conscious percepts (Fodor, 1983). Elaborating this computational story for music perception, composer Fred Lerdahl and linguist Ray Jackendoff have borrowed techniques from standard Chomskyan linguistics to develop a so-called *generative grammar* for tonal music. By analogy with its linguistic cousin, the musical theory is designed to model "the largely unconscious knowledge which the [experienced] listener brings to music and which allows him to organize musical sounds into coherent patterns" (Lerdahl & Jackendoff, 1977; p. 111).[1] Very roughly, the musical grammar is a set of recursive analytical rules that you, the experienced listener, have stored unconsciously in your head. As you hear the incoming musical signal, you mentally represent it (i.e., you recover the score, more or less) and then analyze it according to the grammatical rules; that is to say, you compute a *structural description* of the piece. In this way, the grammar takes as input a "mental score" and produces as output an analysis or structural description of the sequence of pitch-time events specified therein. Having the right sort of structural description in your

[1] *The experienced listener is one familiar with an idiom, though not necessarily schooled in its theory.*

head is what hearing the piece as tonal consists in; as Lerdahl and Jackendoff put it, that's what understanding the piece consists in, just as having the right sort of linguistic structural description in your head is what understanding a sentence consists in.

Two sets of grammatical rules parse the music into rhythmic and metrical groups, and then two further sets, the time-span rules and prolongational rules, generate hierarchical orderings of the pitches within these groups according to their structural importance or "stability." As previously observed, the operations of the musical grammar are unconscious, but the final results of those operations are accessed consciously: An event structurally analyzed as a downbeat will be consciously *felt* or *experienced* as the strongest beat in the bar, a sequence analyzed as an authentic cadence will be consciously *felt* or *experienced* as a resolution, a chord analyzed as a tonic triad consciously *felt* or *experienced* as the most stable chord in the key. Thus, certain rule-governed mental operations structurally analyze the acoustic stimulus in a way that accounts for the character of conscious musical experience.

Despite their prima facie plausibility, music–language parallels have received some harsh criticism in the philosophical literature. Roger Scruton speaks for many in his assessment that "[c]urrent theories of music tend to go wrong [insofar as] they describe musical understanding in terms of some theory whose primary application is in a field (such as linguistics) which has nothing to do with music" (1987, p. 17). Indeed, Lerdahl and Jackendoff (1983) themselves are rightly and emphatically wary of forced analogies:

> Many previous applications of linguistic methodology to music have foundered because they attempt a literal translation of some aspect of linguistic theory into musical terms—for instance, by looking for musical "parts of speech," deep structures, transformations, or semantics. But [this] ... is an old and largely futile game .... [T]here are no substantive parallels between elements of musical structure and such syntactic categories as noun, verb, adjective [and so forth, and] no musical counterparts of such phonological parameters as voicing, nasality, tongue height, and lip rounding .... [Furthermore,] whatever music may "mean," it is in no sense comparable to linguistic meaning. (pp. 5–6)

It's this last claim, about a musical meaning, that concerns me here. I am sympathetic to its negative spirit; scholars writing about music have often simply *assumed* that music is "meaningful," and the specific characterizations of musical meaning typically supplied are, to my mind, unsatisfying. Nevertheless there is, I think, a compelling argument to show that the grammarian's postulation of musical structure, if it is to have any explanatory force, must be motivated by an appeal to semantic considerations or something very much like them. Apart from such an appeal, I shall contend, there would be no obvious reason to postulate one musical structure rather than another. In what follows I lay out the argument and then nominate what seems to me the most plausible candidate for this semantic or quasi-semantic role.

Linguistic Parallels

Typically we envision the linguistic meaning as doing a number of things for which there would seem to be no musical analogue, substantive or otherwise. In particular, it forges a tie to the "extra-linguistic" world, enabling its bearers to refer, describe, command, and assert. Music, on the other hand, does not seem to do any of these things—or, at least, it does not do them *autonomously*, you might say.[2] Granted, if we set things up right we can lend the music a certain intentionality: to the listener armed with a glossary of Wagnerian leitmotifs, a given theme may mean "Here comes Siegfried"; to the listener well-versed in Greek mythology and the intended allusion, the descending Phrygian scale that opens Stravinsky's *Orpheus* may mean "There goes Orpheus, down into the underworld." Perhaps there are also various "pragmatic" musical meanings attending the performances (particular "utterances") of a work—imitating Isaac Stern's playing style while performing Ravel's *Tzigane* in honor of Stern's birthday might be an example. But these are not the sort of musical meaning that have generated such interest and controversy in philosophical circles. These types of musical meaning are wholly parasitic on linguistic or otherwise nonmusical meanings. That *Orpheus* opens with a descending scale and closes with the same scale in ascent is, of course, a stroke of genius; but those scales do not, *taken by themselves*, mean anything about Orpheus at all.

Perhaps the disparity between language and music in this respect can be brought out by a thought-experiment. Suppose an arbitrarily chosen, competent English speaker is left alone in a room with nothing but a passage of text in English—say, an article from the day's *New York Times*—and asked to read it. Left entirely to his own devices, he will understand the text. Lacking various contextual cues, he may miss some of the article's so-called pragmatic meanings; nevertheless, in a very straightforward (indeed, paradigmatic) sense of 'understand,' if he does not understand the article then we shall want to say that, contrary to hypothesis, he is not competent in English. My present claim, then,

[2] *There are those, of course, who would disagree; Deryck Cooke (1959) is a case in point.*

is that no understanding of that autonomous sort exists in the *Siegfried* and *Orpheus* examples. To put this another way, the thing about language, as Chomsky has famously observed, is that it's *creative*; competent speaker/hearers can produce and understand indefinitely many novel utterances (i.e., utterances they've never heard before). Let's put this by saying that linguistic understanding "passes the novelty test." The variety of musical understanding involved in the *Siegfried* and *Orpheus* examples, by contrast, fails the novelty test.

Underwriting reference, assertion and the rest is not the only role played by the linguistic meaning however. It has other, more architectural roles to play, and it is to one of these that a musical parallel can, and indeed must, be drawn. Specifically, understanding, the recovery of linguistic meaning, is the *explanandum* of the grammatical theory. The central goal of the theory is to explain the competent speaker-hearer's ability to (produce and) understand indefinitely many novel utterances. We might put the point by saying that the goal of explaining understanding motivates the postulation of grammatical structure; specifically, it motivates the hypothesis that competent speaker-hearers understand their language in virtue of assigning structure to incoming acoustic strings. Not surprisingly, that explanatory goal then constrains just which structures (phonemes, morphemes, nouns, verbs, etc.) the theory postulates. Thus the goal of explaining understanding has the dual role of motivating the postulation of linguistic structure and constraining the particular kinds of structure that get postulated. A few examples will help to clarify what I have in mind.

Perhaps the most vivid illustration is provided by ambiguous strings. Consider the well-worn example, "They are frying chickens." Presumably any adequate grammatical theory will assign the sentence (at least) two distinct structural descriptions, one classifying "frying" as an adjective, the other classifying it as a verb. Why is that? Why else but because the sentence can be *understood* in two different ways—has two different meanings—and the postulation of those two structures is supposed to explain that duality of understanding and meaning. Imagine the linguist attempting to explain the understanding of the sentence. Which of the two structural descriptions will be assigned to the sentence inevitably depends on further contextual considerations. If, for example, the sentence is uttered as a description of poultry at the grocer's, then 'frying' is an adjective; whereas if it's uttered to describe the activity of a team of chefs at the stove, 'frying' is likely to be classified as a verb. Thus, the structures assigned by the grammatical theory depend on contextual considerations having to do with the character of the speaker's behavior in a given set of circumstances, the sort of activity the speaker is engaged in, and what the speaker wants to accomplish by making the utterance in question. This is because those structures are postulated in order to explain—to make sense of—that behavior; the theory hypothesizes that certain of the speaker-hearer's verbal and nonverbal behaviors—symptoms of linguistic understanding—are underwritten (i.e., made possible) by tacit knowledge of the postulated structures in question. The crucial point is this: These contextual considerations are, of course, among the very factors that determine the *meanings* of the utterances at issue; it is largely owing to the context in which a given sound is emitted that the grammatical theory assigns it the interpretation it does. Thus it seems fair to say that the theoretical assignment of structure is motivated and constrained by semantic factors, factors that also serve to determine the meanings of utterances. From the viewpoint of grammatical theory construction, the assignment of structure and the assignment of meaning are, at many junctures anyway, mutually dependent.

Ambiguous strings are only the most obvious illustration. Imagine the linguist confronted with the vast array of acoustically different objects (sounds) that can constitute utterances of the English word "car." If the linguist's theory is adequate it will classify these many sounds as structurally identical (i.e., as instances of the same word). Why? On what grounds? The answer is that classifying them in that way provides the best explanation of observed similarities in their contexts of utterance. For example, individuating the sounds as 'car' tokens provides the best explanation of the fact that speakers emit them when in the presence of cars (I'm greatly oversimplifying, of course), emit them in response to such questions as "What is your favorite mode of travel?" and so forth. As before, the theory's assignment of structure goes hand in hand with its interpretation of the items to which the structure is assigned. Apart from an appeal to such contextual, ultimately semantic considerations, the grammatical theorist would have no reason to regard the various utterances in question as tokens of the same word type; that is, there would be no reason to regard some acoustic differences as grammatically relevant, others as mere noise.

Let me be quite clear. I do not mean to claim that the language *user* must have access to semantic factors in order to assign structure (phonemic, morphemic, syntactic, lexical) to an acoustic string, nor even that the grammatical theory must explicitly mention matters semantic. I am not advocating a so-called generative semantics over a theory of autonomous syntax. Rather, my claim concerns what might be called the *logic of theory construction*: There is no theoretical motivation for the postulation of grammatical structure (*a fortiori* certain particular grammatical structures) apart from the explanatory considerations I have been discussing. Indeed, the very idea that linguistic understanding is underwritten by the unconscious assignment of such structure is itself a *hypothesis* of the grammatical theory. On any realist interpretation of the linguist grammar, after all, speaker-hearers' representations of structure are just states of their brains, and there is no reason for the theory to regard those neural states as phonological, morphological, or syntactic analyses except insofar as regarding them that way serves to explain why speaker-hearers say and do what they say and do in the circumstances in which they say and do it.

Explanandum for the Musical Theory

I want to suggest that a closely analogous scenario obtains in the musical domain. That is, there must be an explanandum for the musical theory, something that motivates and constrains the postulation of musical structure in the way that ultimately semantic considerations motivate and constrain the postulation of linguistic structure.

An obvious candidate is the behavior of performers—their production of various dynamics, speeds, phrasings, and articulations—in short, their interpretations of the music, as well as the bodily motions that make for a compelling performance. Then there are the various verbal and nonverbal behaviors of listeners (trained and otherwise), such as foot-tapping, anticipatory applause as the final cadence nears, weeping, indeed listening itself, and the making of statements such as "The climax occurs here," "That was a wrong note," "It is being played too slowly," and so forth. The list is virtually endless.[3] My point, in any case, is that all of these behavioral phenomena require explanation, and that is what the grammarian's postulation of unconscious structural analyses is supposed to provide.

If we stop there, however, we will be leaving out the crucial element of the musical story. The various verbal and nonverbal behaviors just described are but symptoms of what we're *really* interested in explaining—namely, our conscious musical experience. What we seek to explain is the kaleidoscopic sequence of peculiarly musical feelings we experience on hearing a performance. As I observed at the outset, our conscious access to our underlying structural descriptions consists in the experience of feeling certain events as points of instability, feeling certain progressions as increases in tension, feeling

[3]Because the musical grammar has so far been developed only for audition, and not, in particular, for composition, I do not cite compositional behaviors here. But of course the grammatical theory will ultimately be invoked to explain some of those as well.

certain events as the most important beats.[4] Our conscious *knowledge* or *understanding* of the music consists in experiencing these types of feelings.[5]

What I'm suggesting, then, is that the feelings that constitute conscious musical experience (aka musical understanding) are, along with the aforementioned verbal and non-verbal behaviors, the explananda of the musical grammar and serve to constrain the particular structures postulated by the theory. It is in large measure because listeners consciously *feel* a sequence of musical events as moving from relative instability to relative repose that those events are analyzed as a cadence, or because a chord is consciously *felt* as the most stable chord in the key that it is analyzed as the tonic, and so on. To that extent, then, the musical feelings play the same role vis-à-vis the musical grammar that the contextual-semantic factors play vis-à-vis the linguistic grammar; to that extent, in other words, it is plausible to regard them as semantic factors.

Objection and Reply

These feelings may play the motivating and constraining role described above, but why call them "semantic"? Is not classifying something as a downbeat or a cadence on a par with classifying something as a consonant or a verb phrase? In other words, do not such classifications lie solidly within the realm of formal structure? Why muck up the works with talk of musical *meaning*? I do not propose to expend too much energy rebutting such doubts, because in the end they are perfectly reasonable; nothing I have said requires any commitment to so-called musical meaning. My claims about the influence of contextual factors on the theoretical postulation of structure should apply in any domain, whether or not it makes sense to talk of meaning. For example, we analyze the human heart as having four chambers because analyzing it that way provides the best explanation of its "behavior" in the context that interests us (viz. its pumping blood throughout the human body). Of course, it is not plausible to suppose that these contextual factors serve, however indirectly, to endow the heart or its activities with meaning—at least not

[4] *Whether conscious linguistic understanding has a so-called phenomenology is an interesting question on which pretheoretic intuitions divide. Be that as it may, it seems safe to say that linguistic understanding lacks a phenomenology with the salience of conscious musical understanding. At the very least, the need for an explanation (of the character of the experience) is obvious in the latter case and not so in the former.*

[5] *Here I mean to include whatever feelings are invoked by the explanatory machinery of the best grammatical theory. In particular, I would not expect emotions to be among them; so far as I am aware, no music theory or model of musical competence includes emotions among the referents of its theoretical terms. In other words, it does not seem necessary to include any mention of emotions in a theory of musical understanding. I think there are excellent reasons for this, but I cannot go into those here.*

in any sense of 'meaning' remotely akin to that in which linguistic utterances are meaningful. Rather, I shall make a conditional claim: To the extent that talk of musical meaning is warranted at all, the feelings cited above are the best candidate. And even if we ultimately deny the existence of musical meaning as such, it will have been important to recognize the explanatory considerations that motivate and constrain the postulation of musical structure.

There are, however, several features of the musical case, over and above those cited so far, that enhance the plausibility of our proposal to regard the musical feelings as a semantics or a semantic analogue, and I shall conclude by briefly mentioning two. First, the proposal gets a boost from the fact that, alone in her room with Wagner and Stravinsky, the experienced listener cannot help but understand. This kind of musical understanding passes the novelty test. The experienced listener can no more fail to understand her native music than her native tongue. Moreover, if she does fail to feel the tonic triad as the most stable, or a 4–3 suspension as moving from a point of tension to a point of rest, or a major seventh as more dissonant than a major third, then she is liable to censure and we will be justified in saying that she has misunderstood the music—that she ought to listen again, and more carefully. And meaning, whatever else it may be, is the sort of thing you can be right or wrong about.

Second, the proposed view serves up a plausible account of the communication of musical meaning. According to Fodor (1975), verbal communication is possible because

> when [an acoustic object] U is a token of a linguistic type in a language [both speaker and hearer] understand, the production/perception of U can effect a certain kind of correspondence between the mental states of the speaker and the hearer.... [T]his sort of account has a quite natural interpretation as a *causal* theory of communication. For if, as I have supposed, the utterance of a wave form can bring about a certain correspondence between the mental states of the speaker and the hearer, this is presumably because, in the relevant cases, the utterance is causally sufficient to initiate the sequence of psychological processes in the hearer which eventuates in his coming to be in a mental state that corresponds to the one that the speaker is in. (pp. 13–14)

One can imagine the communication of musical feelings proceeding in much the same way, underwritten by a correspondence of musical structural descriptions in the minds of composer, performer, and listener.

I have done little more than gesture in the direction a thorough treatment of musical meaning might take, and a proper defense of my view will require, among other things, showing why the cited feelings are to be preferred over other contenders for the role of a musical semantics. Here I have tried to show that, though there may be no musical semantics in the ordinary "intentional" sense of the term, something akin to a semantics, in its explanatory role, may well be required by a grammatical theory of the kind Lerdahl and Jackendoff have developed.

References

Cooke, D. (1959). *The language of music.* Oxford: Oxford University Press.

Fodor, J. (1975). *The language of thought.* Cambridge, MA: Harvard University Press.

Fodor, J. (1983). *Modularity of mind.* Cambridge, MA: MIT Press.

Lerdahl, F., & Jackendoff, R. (1977). Toward a formal theory of tonal music. *Journal of Music Theory, 21*(1), 111–171.

Lerdahl, F., & Jackendoff, R. (1983). *A generative theory of tonal music.* Cambridge, MA: MIT Press.

CHAPTER 4

Empirical Studies of Emotional Response to Music

John A. Sloboda

There is a general consensus that music is capable of arousing deep and significant emotion in those who interact with it. In a study of autobiographical memories of musical events (Sloboda, 1989a), one subject recalled the following event from the age of 7:

> I was sitting in morning assembly at school. The music formed part of the assembly service. . . . The music was a clarinet duet, classical, probably by Mozart. I was astounded at the beauty of the sound. It was liquid, resonant, vibrant. It seemed to send tingles through me. I felt as if it was a significant moment. Listening to this music led to me learning to play first the recorder and then to achieve my ambition of playing the clarinet. . . . Whenever I hear clarinets being played I remember the impact of this first experience. (p. 37)

This study asked a wide variety of adults to recall any memories from the first 10 years of their lives that involved music in any way. There was no attempt by the experimenter to suggest particular types of memory. Forty-four out of 113 memories so produced (39%) shared an important characteristic with the aforementioned example: a valued emotional experience that was derived from an awareness of some aspect of the musical sound itself. Although there were other memories in the sample where the emotional tone of the experience (positive or negative) derived from the context in which the music took place, the study showed that sustained involvement with music was more likely in those subjects who could recall a musical event of the positive type.

Because such experiences are widespread and seem to be important motivators for engagement with music, the study of these experiences deserves a more central position in the psychology of music than it currently enjoys. The purpose of this chapter is to explore how empirical science may study this type of phenomenon and to summarize some of what is known about it.

The Cognitive Content of the Emotional Experience

Free Verbal Response—Adult Experience

In a previously unpublished study, I asked 67 regular listeners to music to describe in their own words the nature of their most valued emotional experiences of music. Although every account was different in detail, some common themes emerged. The most commonly mentioned concept was that of music as *change agent* ($n = 41$). Some common comments were:

- "Music relaxes me when I am tense and anxious";
- "One feels understood and comforted in pain, sorrow, and bewilderment";
- "Involvement in music detaches me from emotional preoccupations";
- "Through hearing emotions in someone else's music, it is possible to feel that emotions are shared and not your burden alone"; and
- "Music motivates and inspires me to be a better person (e.g., more agreeable and loving)."

Common to these examples is the characterization of music as offering an alternative perspective on a person's situation, allowing him or her to construe things differently.

A second cluster of responses focused on the notion of music as promoting the *intensification* or *release* of existing emotions ($n = 34$). These responses included:

- "Music releases emotions (e.g., sadness) that would otherwise be bottled up";
- "Music helps me discover what I am actually feeling";
- "Music reconnects me to myself when my emotions are ignored or suppressed through sheer busyness";

- "Music makes me feel more alive, more myself"; and
- "Music can provide a trigger for the outlet of my emotions concerning memories of pleasurable or painful experiences in my past."

Common to these examples is the notion that music does not create or change emotion; rather it allows a person access to the experience of emotions that are somehow already "on the agenda" for that person, but not fully apprehended or dealt with. Gabrielsson (1989) reports a similar finding in a study where he asked 149 people to describe the "strongest (most intense, deep-going) experiences" they ever had to music. A significant number of respondents reported "feelings that this music deals with myself; it reflects or clarifies my feelings and situations."

Free Verbal Response—Childhood Experience

Gardner (1973) has demonstrated an age progression in the kind of adjectives children spontaneously use to describe the character of music they hear. Children aged 6 to 14 were asked to say whether or not two musical extracts came from the same composition and were then asked to verbally justify their choices. The 6-year-old children tended to base their justifications on such simple dimensions as fast/slow or loud/soft. Eight-year-olds used metaphors drawn from outside music, such as 'peppy,' 'dull,' 'churchy,' and so forth. Neither this study nor any other known to the author has directly asked children to describe their emotional experiences to music.

The previously mentioned retrospective study of Sloboda (1989a) provides some indirect evidence of an age progression in the nature of emotional response to music. For each memory, adults were asked to describe the nature and significance of the event and also to recall the age at which the experience had occurred. Many subjects spontaneously used emotion words or concepts to describe their experiences. The emotion words were divided into three broad categories: an *enjoyment* category (including love, like, enjoy, excited, elated, and happy), a *wonder/surprise* category (including enthralled, incredulous, astounded, overwhelmed, and awestruck), and a *sadness* category (including melancholy, sad, and apprehensive). There was a significant difference in the mean age associated with the recalled experiences relating to these categories. For enjoyment experiences the mean age was 6.2 years, for wonder/surprise experiences the mean age was 8.1 years, and for sad experiences 8.7 years.

This study also provided independent corroboration of Gardner's (1973) results. Descriptions of the music in terms of simple characteristics (e.g., fast, loud) were associated with experiences at a mean age of 4.8. Descriptions in terms of metaphor and character (e.g., liquid, funny, romantic) came at a mean age of 8.0. Gardner's results may have been partly due to the expanding vocabulary of the children he tested rather than a fundamental change in experience. However, the Sloboda data—coming as they do from adults with sophisticated vocabularies—are less plausibly explained in a similar way. It appears increasingly likely that there is a fundamental change in the experience of emotion to music and in its cognitive construal between the ages of 6 and 8. At the heart of this change is a heightened response to aspects of music which strike children as surprising or unexpected. This may be related to a widely reported increase in sensitivity to aspects of tonality at about this age (Dowling, 1982; Imberty, 1969; Thackray, 1976; Zenatti, 1969). The more one has understood and internalized the implicit "grammar" or "rule system" of a musical language, the greater the possibilty for surprise at novelty.

Forced Verbal Response—Adult Experience

The great majority of studies on emotional characteristics of music have asked subjects to ascribe such characteristics to pieces of music by choosing an adjective from a checklist (e.g., Hevner, 1936; Scherer & Oshinsky, 1977; Wedin, 1972). These studies show that, by and large, adults in a given musical culture agree on the broad characterization of a musical passage. The relevance of these studies to emotional *experience*, however, is not proven. It is possible to make character judgments on the basis of conventional characteristics without experiencing any emotion whatsoever.

A study by Waterman (personal communication, March 1990) approached the issue more directly by asking 76 college students to indicate on a checklist of emotions which ones they have actually experienced to music. The checklist consisted of 25 emotion words or phrases, each representing a major emotion type in the theory of Ortony, Clore, and Collins (1988). This theory proposes that experienced emotion arises through cognitive appraisal of situations construed as either *events*, *actions of agents*, or *objects*. Until such construal takes place, no emotion is possible. The most undifferentiated emotion arises from simply placing a positive or negative valence on a situation so appraised. The basic event-related emotion pair is PLEASED–DISPLEASED. The corresponding pair for actions of agents is APPROVE–DISAPPROVE, and that for objects is LIKE–DISLIKE.

Within the theory, other emotions are produced by appraising the situation to finer levels of differentiation. For instance, within the event branch, an event can be appraised as relevant to oneself or relevant to someone else. It can be further appraised as a present event or one in the future. Each level of differentiation is achieved by the consideration of an additional variable: The more variables added, the more specific is the emotion and the more specific the eliciting situation. A relatively unspecific event-based emotion is that of being DISPLEASED at the occurrence of an event judged UNDESIRABLE. A typical word for such emotion would be SADNESS. A more specific event-based emotion is that of being DISPLEASED at the nonoccurrence of a event whose PROSPECT was judged as DESIRABLE for ONESELF. A typical word for such an emotion would be DISAPPOINTMENT.

Waterman found that the emotions reported most often did not fall under any one appraisal category (events, actions of agents, or objects). People frequently experienced emotions relevant to appraisals of music as event (for instance, 72% of the subjects reported experiencing HOPE in response to music), action of agent (53% experienced ANGER), and object (92% experienced LIKING). However, there was a significant negative correlation between the proportion of subjects experiencing an emotion and its specificity in the theory, in terms of the number of cognitive variables requiring appraisal. Less specific emotions such as JOY (71%) were experienced more often than more specific emotions such as RESIGNATION (33%). The full list of emotion labels used in the study is given in Table 4.1, together with the percentage of respondents experiencing that emotion and the number of local appraisal variables relevant to that emotion in Ortony et al.'s theory.

Waterman's data demonstrate that most adults have experienced a range of emotions to music and that frequency of response is less a function of the type of cognitive appraisal underlying the emotion than of its cognitive specificity. There are, however, major problems with any empirical approach which limits subjects' responses to a set of experimenter-determined categories. A more direct way of eliciting data would be to ask subjects to specify a nonmusical situation in which they have experienced the same emotion as during a particular episode of music listening. It may then be possible to map formal characteristics of the nonmusical situation directly onto formal characteristics of musical events without any need to employ the vocabulary of emotional terms at all. This approach is currently being explored.

The Antecedents of Emotional Experience to Music

Factors External to the Music

It is clear that the same event, be it musical or otherwise, does not always result in the same emotional experience. For example, I can listen to the same recording on two

TABLE 4.1

Proportion of subjects who have felt each emotion to music, and the number of local variables influencing the intensity of each emotion, according to Ortony, Clore, and Collins (1988). Data are from Waterman (personal communication, March 1990).

		Number of Local Variables Influencing Emotional Intensity			
Emotion	**%**	**1**	**2**	**3**	**4**
Sadness	96.2	■			
Joy	93.4	■			
Liking	92.1	■	■		
Appreciation	86.8	■	■		
Dislike	81.6	■	■		
Satisfaction	78.9	■	■	■	■
Suspense	77.6	■	■	■	
Hope	72.4	■	■		
Anger	52.6	■	■	■	
Hopelessness	52.6	■	■	■	
Disappointment	52.6	■	■	■	■
Pride	51.3	■	■	■	
Relief	50.0	■	■	■	■
Sympathy	48.7	■	■	■	■
Happiness for	46.1	■	■	■	■
Resignation	43.3	■	■	■	
Fear	42.1	■	■		
Remorse	39.5	■	■	■	■
Gratitude	32.9	■	■	■	
Resentment	30.3	■	■	■	■
Self-satisfaction	30.3	■	■	■	■
Fears confirmed	23.7	■	■	■	■
Shame	17.1	■	■	■	
Reproach	15.8	■	■		
Gloating	13.2	■	■	■	■

different occasions and be moved to tears on one of them, while remaining completely detached on the other.

There are several possible reasons for this inherent variability. One is that the same piece of music may be appraised on different criteria. A musical passage appraised as event may incline a listener to an event-based emotion such as sadness. The same piece appraised as the action of an agent may incline a listener towards an emotion such as gratitude.

Another possibility is that one's prevailing mood determines the extent to which a piece of music will lead to strong emotional experience of particular sorts. It may be hard to experience grief or sadness in response to music when one's prevailing mood is cheerfulness, even though one is carrying out the relevant cognitive appraisals of the music, which in other circumstances would lead to sadness.

A third possibility is that there may be some emotional or mood states which simply preclude any relevant appraisal-based emotion to the music from occurring at all. One of the most striking features of the Sloboda (1989a) study was the almost complete absence of differentiated responses to the music itself when the context was being appraised as negative. The most typical negative context was a situation of threat, anxiety, or humiliation, brought about by being placed in a situation where one's performance was being assessed. Such situations included singing or playing in front of an audience or a teacher. They often included fear of verbal or physical punishment (and sometimes its realization). For many subjects these contexts had long-lasting effects, leading to "refusing to have anything to do with music" or "considering myself completely unmusical."

The evidence of the study is that the likelihood of experiencing positively valued emotional responses from music is a direct function of the degree to which the subject feels relaxed and unthreatened. If someone is feeling frightened, anxious, or under threat, this usually means that there are factors in the environment which are dominating the appraisal system, probably because they impinge on significant personal goals (e.g., preservation of self-esteem). Under these circumstances the music itself will not be likely to yield appraisal-based emotions. This may be because the appraisals are not undertaken at all (the attention is on the threat-provoking context) or because the appraisals are in some way "blocked" from access to the system which produces emotional experience.

Factors Intrinsic to the Music

Although it is well established that people respond emotionally to music, little is known about precisely what it is in the music that they are responding to. A recent study (Sloboda, 1991) attempted to establish something about the specific types of musical events that are associated with physically based concomitants of emotional response to music. Physical reactions such as crying, shivering, a racing heart, and so forth avoid some of the problems associated with verbal emotion labels that were discussed previously. It is very difficult to be mistaken about whether you cried or not to a piece of music. Such reactions are stereotyped, memorable, distinct from one another, and shared by all humans regardless of culture and vocabulary. They are arguably more closely connected to the experience of emotion than verbalizations which may be infected with rationalizations.

In a study by Sloboda (1991), subjects were asked to specify particular pieces of music to which they could recall having experienced any of a list of 12 physical manifestations commonly associated with emotion. Having identified such pieces, they were then asked to specify the location within the music that provoked these reactions. They were encouraged to do this, where possible, with reference to a score or a recording, but since this was a postal questionnaire study, no direct check on method was made. Surprisingly, and in contradistinction to Meyer's (1956) misgivings, a significant proportion (about one third) of the people were able to locate their reaction within a theme or smaller unit. Those specific segments for which a published score was available (i.e., the classical citations) were classified according to the musical features they contained, and according to the emotional reaction they provoked.

Table 4.2 shows the main results of this analysis. Twenty musical passages provoked the cluster of responses labelled TEARS (i.e., crying, lump in the throat). The

TABLE 4.2

Music–Structural Features Associated With Physical-Emotional Responses

Feature	Number of musical passages provoking a response		
	TEARS	SHIVERS	HEART
1. Harmony descending cycle of fifths to tonic	6	0	0
2. Melodic appogiaturas	18	9	0
3. Melodic or harmonic sequence	12	4	1
4. Enharmonic change	4	6	0
5. Harmonic or melodic acceleration to cadence	4	1	2
6. Delay of final cadence	3	1	0
7. New or unprepared harmony	3	12	1
8. Sudden dynamic or textural change	5	9	3
9. Repeated syncopation	1	1	3
10. Prominent event earlier than prepared for	1	4	3
Total number of musical passages	20	21	5

From "Music Structure and Emotional Response: Some Empirical Findings," by J. Sloboda, in press, *Psychology of Music, 19*(2). Copyright 1991 by Society for Research in Psychology of Music and Music Education. Adapted by permission.

majority of these passages contained melodic appoggiaturas and melodic or harmonic sequences. Twenty-one passages provoked the cluster of responses labelled SHIVERS (i.e., goose pimples, shivers down the spine). The majority of these contained a new or unprepared harmony. Only 5 passages provoked HEART reactions (i.e., racing heart and pit-of-stomach sensations). These were associated with repeated syncopations and prominent events occurring earlier than prepared for.

A more recent unpublished analysis of the popular and jazz citations (by transcription from audio tracks) has confirmed this basic picture. The same features tend to be operative, although the picture is somewhat obscured due to the fact that combined physical reactions are more common in these passages than in classical music. That is to say, subjects frequently reported TEARS, SHIVERS, and HEART reactions simultaneously to the same segment of music.

Figure 4.1 shows an example of an excerpt that provoked TEARS. It is the opening passage from Albinoni's *Adagio for Strings*. Note that the first 7-note melodic phrase contains 3 consecutive appoggiaturas, C–B♭, A–G, G–F♯. The phrase is then repeated in sequence form (exact repetition at one higher scale step). This is followed by a second phrase which is repeated twice more in sequential fashion. What seems to characterize this, and other TEARS-provoking passages, are the successions of harmonic tensions or dissonances which are created and resolved within a structure which has a high degree of repetition and implication-realization (see Narmour, 1977). In general terms, an implication is set up when a musical segment contains within it some parameter, such as a pitch movement. The implication is realized if the parameter is repeated. For example, in Figure 4.1 the initial scalar movement D–C sets up implications for further downward scalar motions, which are realized. A sequence realizes implications that a theme, once stated, will be repeated. If the first repetition is at a certain pitch distance from the first statement, then the implication is that a second repetition will repeat this pitch jump. Psychologically, passages with strong implication-realization are to some extent predictable. In cases like that of Figure 4.1 it is possible that the predictable but repeated appoggiaturas, which "tease" the sense of consonance, are responsible for the particular form that the emotional response takes.

Figure 4.2 shows an example similar to an excerpt that provoked SHIVERS (copyright restrictions preclude citing the actual example). It is characterized by a sudden key shift from E to C♯ in the context of a rising sequential pattern based on E, then F♯, and then G♯. In terms of music analytic theories of

FIGURE 4.1 Opening theme from Albinoni's *Adagio for strings.*

expectancy/implication (see, for instance, Meyer, 19 56, 1973; Narmour, 1977; Schmuckler, 1989), the sequential progression E–F♯ sets up an implication for a progression G♯ (which is fulfilled). At the same time the harmonic progression (successive chords within E-major tonal space) sets up an implication for further chords within this tonal space (which is violated). This dual characteristic of an event being both expected (at one level or according to one criterion) and unexpected (at another level or on another criterion) seems to be shared by several of the SHIVERS-provoking passages. For example, an enharmonic change fulfills one expectancy (melody note stays the same) while violating another (harmonic function of

FIGURE 4.2 An example similar to an excerpt that provoked SHIVERS.

melody note changes). In other cases, the response seems to be associated with a significant change in some characteristic of the music at or near a major structural boundary (e.g., new phrase or verse in a 32-bar song). If there is some psychological dissociation or independence between the various mental analyses that may be carried out on music, then it could well be that some emotional responses come about when there is a mismatch between the output of two processing units or "modules." The boundary may be expected according to the computations of one "module" (e.g., a rhythmic/metrical analyzer assigning events a hierarchical position within a phrase-structure tree), but the specific parameter change can still "surprise" another "module" (attuned to, say, texture or dynamic).

Figure 4.3 shows a passage provoking HEART reactions. This is bar 191 from the last movement of Beethoven's *Piano Concerto No. 4* in G major, op. 58. Here the phrase structure of the whole movement is built on multiples of even numbers of bars (2, 4, 8, etc.). The piano solo starting at bar 184 reinforces this. A new phrase starts at 188, and there is an implication that the next phrase will commence at bar 192. Instead it arrives at 191 with a sudden increase in dynamic. Each phrase beginning functions as an accent within the phrase structure. Here, then, is a case of an expected accent arriving earlier than it "should." This is also the principal feature of syncopation, another provoker of HEART reactions.

In each case, it is clear that expectancies and violations of expectancy are playing a major part in the promotion of emotional reactions to the music. These results are an empirical vindication for the music-theoretic tradition whose main inspiration is L. B. Meyer. However, what the data demonstrate is that the nature of the emotional experience depends on the particular character and pattern of an interlocking set of implications and their realization or nonrealization. A major task for the future is therefore the specification of the precise way in which emotions map onto different kinds of musical events. A theory providing at least the differentiation of Ortony et al.'s will be necessary.

Conclusions

The empirical study of emotional responses to music is in its infancy, despite several recent attempts to construct a theoretical framework for considering emotions in music (e.g., Dowling & Harwood, 1986; Sloboda, 1989b). The subject poses serious methodological and theoretical problems. Since there is no generally accepted theory of the emotions and how they interact with cognition, I believe that open-ended empirical investigations

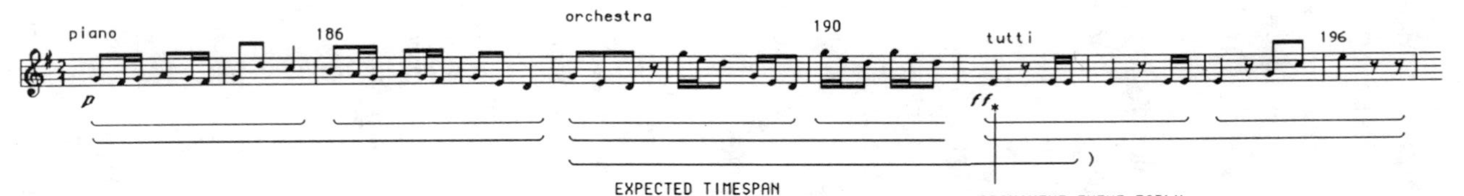

FIGURE 4.3 Main features surrounding bar 191, last movement, in Beethoven's *Piano Concerto No. 4* in G major, op. 58. From *Eulenberg score no. 705.* Copyright by Ernest Eulenberg, Ltd. Adapted by permission.

with a strong element of natural history continue to be the most profitable way of exploring this area at this time. Music psychology is already a successful interdisciplinary study, with major advances at the junctions of music theory and cognitive science. A satisfactory incorporation of the study of emotion into this work will require methods and theoretical approaches drawn from a wider range of subdisciplines. I hope this chapter has given at least a hint that this is a promising area ripe for further development.

References

Dowling, W. J. (1982). Melodic information processing and its development. In D. Deutsch (Ed.), *The psychology of music.* New York: Academic Press.

Dowling, W. J., & Harwood, D. L. (1986). *Music cognition.* New York: Academic Press.

Gabrielsson, A. (1989, October). Intense emotional experiences of music. In *Proceedings of the First International Conference on Music Perception and Cognition* (pp. 371–376). Kyoto, Japan: The Japanese Society of Music Perception and Cognition.

Gardner, H. (1973). Children's sensitivity to musical styles. *Merrill-Palmer Quarterly of Behavioural Development, 19,* 67–77.

Hevner, K. (1936). Experimental studies of the elements of expression in music. *American Journal of Psychology, 48,* 246–268.

Imberty, M. (1969). *L'acquisition des structures tonales chez l'enfant* [The acquisition of tonal structures in the child]. Paris: Klinksiek.

Meyer, L. B. (1956). *Emotion and meaning in music.* Chicago: University of Chicago Press.

Meyer, L. B. (1973). *Explaining music.* Berkeley: University of California Press.

Narmour, E. (1977). *Beyond Schenkerism: The need for alternatives in music analysis.* Chicago: University of Chicago Press.

Ortony, A., Clore, G. L., & Collins, A. (1988). *The cognitive structure of the emotions.* New York: Cambridge University Press.

Scherer, K. R., & Oshinsky, J. S. (1977). Cue utilization in emotional attribution from auditory stimuli. *Motivation and Emotion, 1,* 331–346.

Schmuckler, M. A. (1989). Expectation in music: Investigation of melodic and harmonic processes. *Music Perception, 7,* 109–149.

Sloboda, J. A. (1989a). Music as a language. In F. Wilson & F. Roehmann (Eds.), *Music and child development.* St. Louis, MO: MMB, Inc.

Sloboda, J. A. (1989b). Music psychology and the composer. In S. Nielzen & O. Olsson (Eds.) *Structure and perception of electroacoustic sound and music.* Amsterdam: Elsevier.

Sloboda, J. A. (1991). Music structure and emotional response: Some empirical findings. *Psychology of Music, 19,* 110–120.

Thackray, R. (1976). Measurement of perception of tonality. *Psychology of Music, 4,* 32–127.

Wedin, L. (1972). A multidimensional study of perceptual-emotional qualities in music. *Scandinavian Journal of Psychology, 13,* 1–17.

Zenatti, A. J. (1969). *Le développement génétique de la perception musicale* [The genetic development of musical perception]. (Monographies Françaises de psychologie No. 17). Paris: Centre National des Recherches Scientifiques.

PART TWO

The Influence of Structure on Musical Understanding

Introduction

Musical structure is so rich, multilayered, and complex that it inevitably defies simple answers to broad questions about its influence on musical understanding. The chapters of Part One underscore the challenges to understanding that indeterminacy poses. Yet musical understanding remains at the heart of musical communication. Performers must understand the musical ideas and their forms in a to-be-performed score if they are to convey those ideas and a corresponding understanding to listeners. And, of course, while performance molds these ideas, in essence their beginnings are found in the composer's score. The relational structure of music as it exists in the score is the basis for understanding a musical idea.

The three chapters in this section address parts of the larger issue of musical understanding and structure from the viewpoints of different disciplines (music, linguistics, psychology) and theoretical perspectives. However, all are concerned with the influence of different levels of musical structure on the way a listener "makes sense" of the piece as a whole. What each theorist means exactly by "level" is different, depending on his or her theoretical perspective. But there are commonalities in that each acknowledges the complications posed to both listener and theorist by multiple levels of musical structure and the corresponding possibilities of multiple interpretations (i.e., indeterminacy).

In chapter 5 Ray Jackendoff directly confronts multiple interpretations of musical structure as an indeterminacy problem for the listener. The listener is shown to actively seek a clear interpretation of meter, key, and other aspects of tonal structure as outlined in Lerdahl and Jackendoff's influential book (1983). In fact, Jackendoff extends the grammatical analyses of this earlier work to describe the act of perceiving musical structure in real time. He outlines the uncertainties posed for the listener as a musical pattern unfolds and examines three different models of psychological processing. The most parsimonious, a parallel processor that assesses multiple interpretations simultaneously, lays the groundwork for hypotheses about expectations and affect which he contrasts with those of the implication-realization model of Leonard Meyer and Eugene Narmour.

Eugene Narmour (chapter 6) finds, in the wealth of relations offered by respectively different levels of structure, a basis for an enlarged understanding of music. Indeterminacy implies richness in this account. He reviews the elements of the melodic implication-realization theory, which involves a formal analysis of melodic structure at several different levels. Melodic structures at different levels are shown to yield either similar implications, thus displaying mutuality, or dissimilar implications, displaying conflict. Finally, musical understanding, in part, entails sensitivity to the richness of these sorts of interactions.

Mari Riess Jones, in chapter 7, sees the musical changes which transpire over different levels of melodic structure as outlining different times within the event. Different time levels, in turn, have the potential to support different time-bound levels of attending, allowing the listener to selectively monitor one or another level of structure. A future-oriented attending model reflects expectancies about "when" certain higher order melodic/temporal levels should end. In this view, musical understanding comes with the listener shifting attending over different time levels to achieve different perspectives on its structure.

CHAPTER 5

Musical Processing and Musical Affect

Ray Jackendoff

What Is Musical Perception?

Following the approach of Lerdahl and Jackendoff's (1983a) *A Generative Theory of Tonal Music* (GTTM), the perception of music parallels the perception of language: it involves the unconscious construction of abstract musical structures, of which the events of the musical surface are the only audible part. The abstract musical structures so constructed are what account for one's musical understanding.

The theory of music developed in GTTM takes the form of a *grammar* of tonal music: a set of principles that (a) define the abstract structures of tonal music available to a listener experienced in the tonal idiom and (b) relate these structures to musical surfaces of pieces in the idiom. GTTM shows that these principles provide a formal account of many aspects of musical understanding discussed in more traditional approaches to musical analysis.

This chapter was originally conceived as part of a larger undertaking in collaboration with Fred Lerdahl; for reasons of geographical distance, it proved more convenient to develop our ideas separately. Still, there are many aspects of this chapter for which I am grateful for Fred's influence. I am especially in his debt for risking his reputation by agreeing to compose several of the musical examples.

As stressed in GTTM, the grammar proposed there is intended as an account of the experienced listener's "final-state" understanding of pieces—the structures that the listener can attain, given full familiarity with the idiom and with the piece and no limitations of short-term memory or attention. A theory of musical processing based on this theory must show how the principles of the listener's internalized musical grammar can be deployed in real time to build musical representations. In particular, it must show that the rules used for idealized final-state analyses can actually be used to account for listeners' experiences as they hear a piece over time. This chapter will work out some of the aspects of such a processing model.

Assumptions About Musical Structure

For present purposes, we can assume that the following aspects of musical structure are essential to musical understanding (see GTTM for justification):

1. a *grouping structure* that partitions a piece into motives, phrases, and sections, arranged hierarchically;
2. a *metrical structure* that associates a piece with a hierarchical grid of strong and weak beats;
3. some sort of *reductional structure* that marks events of a piece in a hierarchy of relative importance, such that some are relatively "structural" and some are relatively "ornamental."

In any theory of reduction, the sense of tonality, of "being in a key," plays a crucial role. The reason for this is that a pitch-event's reductional importance is determined primarily by its rhythmic position and its relative "consonance," where consonance is defined by the principles of tonality for the idiom. Different tonal contexts (i.e., different keys) may change the relative consonance of two pitch-events, resulting in different relative structural importance. For example, the sequence of an A♭ major triad followed by a D♭ major triad is heard as I–IV in A♭ major but as V–I in D♭ major. Other things being equal, a I chord is more consonant relative to the tonality, hence more important in the reductional structure. Hence the A♭ triad is primary on one hearing and the D♭ on the other. In short, a prerequisite to deriving a reductional structure in real time is deriving a sense of tonality.

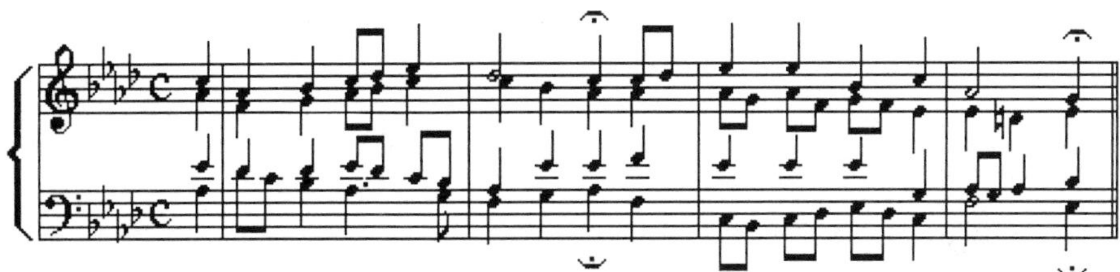

FIGURE 5.1 Beginning of J. S. Bach's "Ich bin's, ich sollte büssen" from the *St. Matthew Passion.*

A Sample Analysis

Let us work through an example, asking how a listener might assign structure to the beginning of a piece as it is heard. The piece we will examine is "Ich bin's, ich sollte büssen" from the *St. Matthew Passion,* the first few bars of which are given in Figure 5.1.[1]

I assume that what the listener hears is the sequence of pitches with durations; that is, the key signature, time signature, bar lines, and beams play no role in the musical surface. I also assume, somewhat counterfactually, that the musical surface is presented without any surface accents that would bias interpretations of meter. Such an idealization is probably realized only in computer-generated performances and perhaps performances on the organ, but it is useful for purposes of exposition.

After hearing just the first event of the musical surface (Figure 5.2A), the listener has very little information, except that this event is the beginning of a group (or phrase), that it falls on some metrical beat, and that the piece is likely to be in a key whose diatonic collection includes the pitches C, A♭, and E♭.

FIGURE 5.2 The first and second events of the chorale in Figure 5.1.

[1]*A full analysis of this piece in GTTM terms appears in Lerdahl and Jackendoff (1983b).*

Adding the second event (Figure 5.2B) provides more substantial information. At least three questions must be asked immediately by the listener (not consciously, of course: a better locution would be "by the listener's unconscious processor," as will be seen more clearly in the next section):

1. What are the relative metrical weights of the two events? Using the GTTM notation, the three possibilities are notated as in Figures 5.3A, 5.3B, and 5.3C. In this notation, an event with more dots under it is considered metrically stronger. Hence the first event is stronger in Figure 5.3A, and the second in Figure 5.3B; alternatively, the two events may be metrically equal, as shown in Figure 5.3C.
2. What key are we in? The pitches so far are consistent with the pitch-collections of at least A♭ major, D♭ major, and, much less plausibly, their relative minors.
3. Is the first event structurally stronger than the second, or is it weaker, that is, which of these events is more structural and which is relatively ornamental? We can represent this choice by using the GTTM notation for time-span reductions, which encodes relative structural importance as a tree structure. The two possibilities appear in Figure 5.4A and 5.4B. In Figure 5.4A, the branch associated with the second event terminates on the branch associated with the first, so the first event is structurally more important and the second relatively ornamental. This analysis suggests a I–IV progression in A♭. In Figure 5.4B, the roles of the two events are reversed, suggesting a I–V progression in D♭.

Given just these two events, the answers to all three questions are indeterminate. One can hear the initial event as a downbeat or as an anacrusis to the second event. One

FIGURE 5.3 Three metrical possibilities for the first two events of the chorale in Figure 5.1.

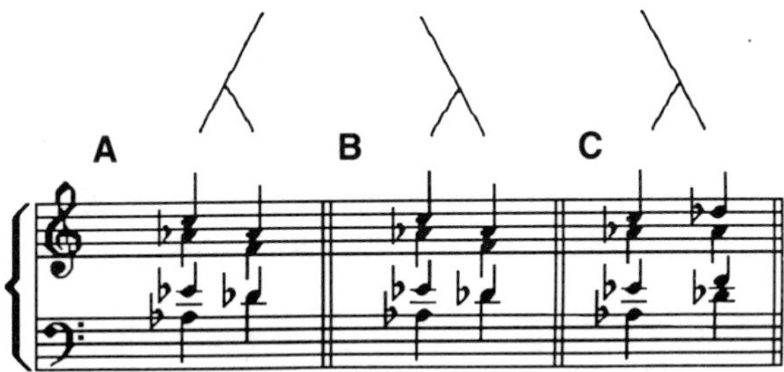

FIGURE 5.4 Figure 5.4A shows the first event of the chorale in Figure 5.1 as structurally stronger than second. Figure 5.4B shows the second event as structurally stronger than first. Figure 5.4C shows the same structure as Figure 5.4B, but with different voice-leading in the soprano.

can hear the key as A♭ or D♭. Linked with the key, one can hear the harmonic progression in either of the ways suggested in Figure 5.4A or 5.4B. However, the second possibility is undermined to some degree by the voice-leading of the soprano: as a V–I progression, it would have an unresolved leading tone. The V–I interpretation becomes much more salient if the voice-leading is changed to the configuration in Figure 5.4C. In other words, grammatical principles of voice-leading have an effect on judgment of tonality (see the discussion in Butler, 1989, for experiments with similar effects).

To show that the meter and key are at this point indeterminate, we can invent alternative continuations of Figure 5.2B that present different possibilities than Bach's. Figure 5.5 presents one in which the first event is heard as a downbeat rather than as an anacrusis and in which the key proves to be D♭ instead of A♭.

We can also construct a continuation in which the first two events are heard as metrically equal. Within the constraints imposed by the principles of metrical structure, this can occur only if the two events constitute a two-beat anacrusis in a triple meter. Figure 5.6 illustrates this possibility.

Even after the third, fourth, and fifth events arrive, the metrical structure is still highly indeterminate. Figure 5.7 gives five possibilities: (a) the first event is the strong beat in a duple meter; (b) the first event is the weak beat in a duple meter; (c) the first event is the strong beat in a triple meter; (d) the first event is the second weak beat in a triple meter; and (e) the first event is the first weak beat in a triple meter. All of these

FIGURE 5.5 A continuation of the first two events of the chorale in Figure 5.1 that is heard with an initial downbeat, in D♭ major.

possibilities can be realized with fairly plausible music. Consider Figure 5.8, in which the dashed bar lines indicate the point up to which the passages are identical. Structure A in Figure 5.7 is the most likely interpretation of Figure 5.8A; structure B is of course Bach's choice (Figures 5.1 and 5.8B). Structure C in Figure 5.7 is the most likely interpretation of Figure 5.8C; structure D is the most likely interpretation of Figure 5.8D (whose musical surface is moreover identical to Figure 5.8A except that the final event probably receives less stress); and structure E appears in Figure 5.8E. Of these five, only the last structure is relatively hard to hear.

The metrical uncertainty can even be continued a few events further into the piece. Figure 5.9 is identical to the musical surface of the Bach chorale up to the dashed bar line, at the eighth event of the piece.

FIGURE 5.6 A continuation of the first two events of the chorale in Figure 5.1 that is heard in triple meter with a two-beat anacrusis, in A♭ major.

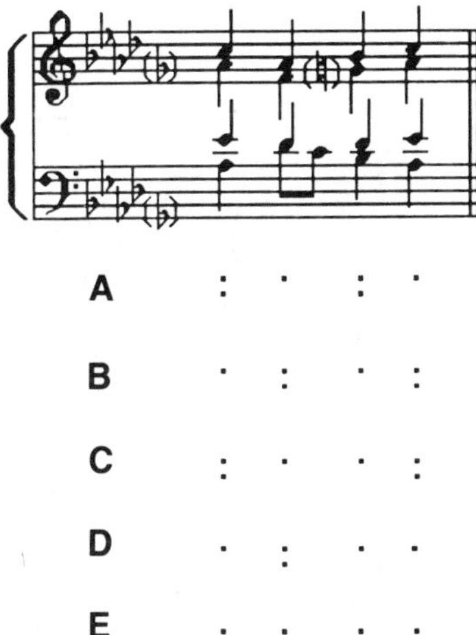

FIGURE 5.7 Five possibilities for metrical structure in the first five events of the chorale in Figure 5.1.

What finally settles the meter in the Bach chorale is a combination of factors that have accumulated up to this point:

1. The dotted quarter note A♭ in the bass and the root position harmony above it should begin on a strong beat (Metrical Preference Rules 5 and 6 of GTTM);[2]
2. The suspension in the soprano and alto in measure 2 should begin on a strong beat (Metrical Preference Rule 8);[3]
3. The long soprano D♭ in measure 2 should begin on a strong beat (Metrical Preference Rule 5).

These factors determine that strong beats should fall two beats apart, requiring a duple meter. Projecting this pattern backwards through the musical surface heard up to this

[2]*Metrical Preference Rule 5 (Length Rule) states: "Prefer a metrical structure in which a relatively strong beat occurs at the inception of either (a) a relatively long pitch-event, . . ., [or] (f) a relatively long duration of a harmony in the relevant levels of the time-span reduction (harmonic rhythm)" (Lerdahl & Jackendoff, 1983a, p. 84). Metrical Preference Rule 6 (Bass Rule) states: "Prefer a metrically stable bass" (Lerdahl & Jackendoff, 1983a, p. 88).*

[3]*Metrical Preference Rule 8 (Suspension Rule) states: "Strongly prefer a metrical structure in which a suspension is on a stronger beat than its resolution" (Lerdahl & Jackendoff, 1983a, p. 89).*

A B

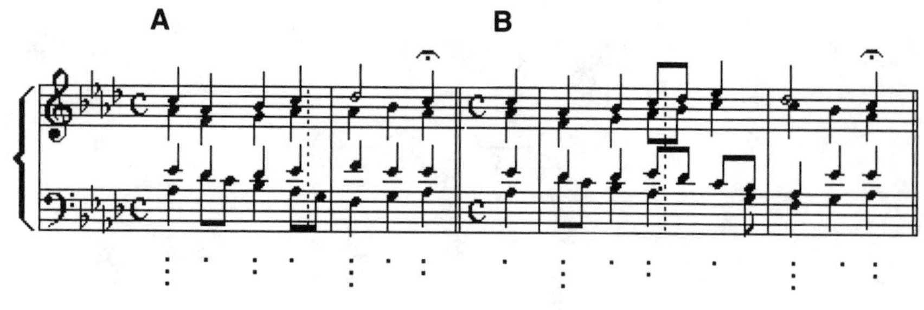

C

D E

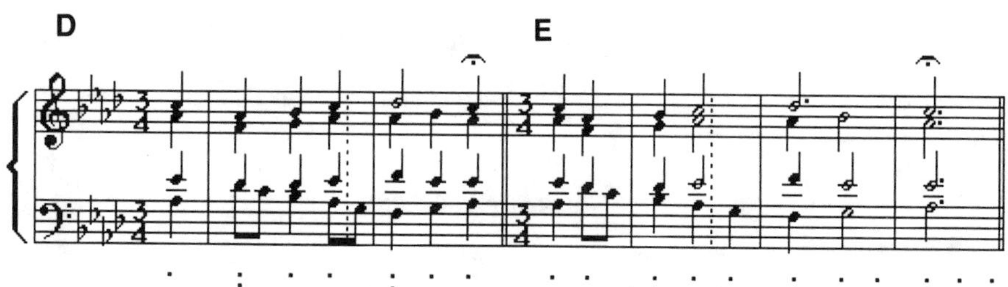

FIGURE 5.8 Continuations of the first five events of the chorale in Figure 5.1, heard with structures corresponding to Figure 5.7.

point, we see that the first strong beat must fall on the second event. By contrast, in Figure 5.9 the suspension and long soprano D♭ are displaced one beat to the right. This forces a distance of three beats between strong beats, hence a triple meter. Projecting this pattern backwards results in the first event falling on a strong beat.

Next consider the tonality of the piece. This cannot be determined with certainty without taking into account complex factors. In Figure 5.5, the pitch collection presented in the first measure is most consistent with an interpretation of A♭. However, the

FIGURE 5.9 A different continuation of the first eight events of the chorale in Figure 5.1.

cadence in the second measure fixes the key as D♭ and forces the G♮ in the first measure to be heard in retrospect as a chromatic alteration. (I will explain what I mean by "in retrospect" shortly.) In the actual Bach chorale, the tonality is fixed by the continuing consistency of the presented pitch collection with completely diatonic A♭ and by the full cadence in A♭ at the end of the phrase.

This exercise of analyzing the information available to the processor at any point in time, though exhausting, has hardly been exhaustive. Moreover, I have dealt with only the briefest portion of a relatively simple piece, for which the listener has no sense of any processing complexity. What is the point of going through all this trouble? We will now examine the implications of this exercise for a theory of musical processing.

Three Models of Processing

The first section of this chapter claimed that the processing of a piece of music as it is heard amounts essentially to deriving the abstract structure of the piece in real time. We have just seen that one of the fundamental problems facing the processor is the indeterminacy of the analysis at many points—an indeterminacy that sometimes cannot be resolved until considerably later in the music. This section proposes three models of increasing complexity that attempt to do justice to these observations.

Serial Single-Choice Model

The first model might be called a *serial single-choice* processor. Such a processor computes only one analysis at a time for a piece. Confronted with a potential indeterminacy among multiple analyses, it chooses the most likely alternative as the one to continue with. If what is chosen at one point as the most likely analysis proves later on not to be viable, the processor must back up to the choice point, choose the next most likely possibility, and pursue that as far as possible. If the processor can reach the end of the piece, the resulting analysis is selected as the correct one. This basic mode of operation is a feature of one popular breed of linguistic parsers (e.g., the ATN parser described in Wanner & Maratsos, 1978), so it is worth considering for music processing as well.

There are at least two serious problems with this model. The first is in deciding which of a set of alternative analyses should be tried. In order to choose among alternative possibilities, all of them must first be formulated. So, for example, consider the point after the second event of the Bach chorale (Figure 5.2B), where the processor must decide which single metrical structure to pursue. Should it initially assign the second event a metrical weight greater than, less than, or equal to that of the first event? In order to make this decision on other than an arbitrary basis, all three alternatives must be formulated and tested on the evidence of the music up to this point. Similar choices with respect to both meter and key arise at every point in the music up to at least the fifth and even possibly the eighth event. Therefore, at each of these points, the processor must have access to the available choices and their relative likelihoods, in order to be able to decide which single analysis it will try first. Thus there is a basic logical difficulty in the conception of this processing model: In order to compute only the single most likely analysis, it must first compute at least fragments of all possible analyses.

A second difficulty with this model has to do with the way it putatively recovers from incorrect analyses. If at some point it is forced to backtrack, it must pass through and reanalyze all the music between the choice point and the most recent event, while at the same time new events are occurring inexorably as the piece goes on. Given the amount of indeterminacy we have seen just in a very short passage, one would expect that this sort of processor would spend a great deal of its time backtracking. For example, in the Bach chorale, suppose it begins by trying a downbeat-first analysis after the second event—according to the musical grammar,[4] this structure is inherently most stable. After the fourth event it would probably choose a duple meter,[5] resulting in the structure in Figure 5.7A. But this possibility would be disconfirmed three events later by

[4] *Metrical Preference Rule 2 (Strong Beat Early) states: "Weakly prefer a metrical structure in which the strongest beat in a group appears relatively early in the group" (Lerdahl & Jackendoff, 1983a, p. 76).*

[5] *Metrical Preference Rule 10 (Binary Regularity) states: "Prefer metrical structures in which every other beat is strong" (Lerdahl & Jackendoff, 1983a, p. 101).*

the A♭ in the bass continuing beneath the eighth notes, for reasons detailed at the end of the previous section. It would then go back to the fourth event and try a triple meter, as in structure C in Figure 5.7; this would be disconfirmed by the suspension in the soprano and alto five events later. Having tried successively the two possibilities with an initial downbeat, it would erase everything it had done and backtrack again to the second event, assigning it a strong beat this time. At the fifth event a decision would have to be made between a strong beat (implying duple meter) and a weak beat (triple meter). We can suppose that it would choose the duple meter and finally come up with the correct analysis. However, if the input were Figure 5.8D instead of Figure 5.8B, it would have to backtrack once more before hitting on the correct meter.

In order for the processor to accomplish all this backtracking in real time without a sense of effort or loss of information, one must attribute to it considerable speed in comparison to the speed of the music. The processor will often have to perform many analyses one after another, fast enough to keep up with the flow of the musical surface in real time.

Serial Indeterministic Model

Let us next consider what might be called a *serial indeterministic* model. The basic characteristic of this model, like the previous model, is that it computes only a single analysis at a time for a piece. However, when confronted with an indeterminacy, it does not make a commitment as the previous model does; rather, it bides its time and collects evidence, without making a decision until such time as a unique analysis can be settled on. The idea behind this sort of processor appears in linguistic parsers such as those of Marcus (1980) and Frazier and Fodor (1978). Such parsers compute preliminary analyses of local parts of a sentence, but do not connect them up into a global analysis until a single correct structure can be determined for the whole.

This sort of processor avoids the onerous backtracking of the serial single-choice model. But it does not escape the basic logical difficulty. In order to decide when it is appropriate to commit itself to an analysis, the processor must have available to it all of the possible candidate analyses, plus an evaluation of the evidence that decides among them. But it is precisely the defining characteristic of such a processor that it does not have the analyses available: it puts off any analysis until it can make a decision.

A second problem with this sort of processor is that it makes the wrong sort of prediction about musical experience, suggesting that up to the eighth event of the Bach chorale we should have no experience of metrical structure at all, since none has been adopted by the processor. But this is patently wrong, since we certainly have metrical intuitions long before the definitive evidence arrives.

Parallel Multiple-Analysis Model

Since both serial models have entailed the computation of multiple analyses, let us consider a *parallel multiple-analysis model.* The idea behind this theory is that when the processor encounters a choice point among competing analyses, processing splits into simultaneous branches, each computing an analysis for one of the possibilities. When a particular branch drops below some threshold of plausibility, it is abandoned. Whatever branches remain at the end of the piece then contain viable structures for the piece as a whole.

In the Bach chorale, such a processor would develop three concurrent metrical analyses after the second event is heard, corresponding to the three possible distinctions in metrical weight shown in Figure 5.3. After the fourth event, two of these analyses would branch further; hence five analyses would be active at once, corresponding to the five structures in Figure 5.7. As observed in the previous section, the long A♭ in the bass is inconsistent with three of these (Figures 5.7A, 5.7D, and 5.7E), so the processor will abandon them when the A♭ is heard. Of the remaining two, only Figure 5.7B is consistent with the suspension, so Figure 5.7C will be abandoned upon encountering the suspension, leaving only one viable metrical structure. In short, this processor proceeds more or less in the same manner as our informal analysis in the previous section.

A processor of this sort overcomes the logical problem of the other two: Alternative hypotheses are always formulated and available to be compared with one another. It also overcomes the problem of backtracking in the serial single-choice model. In the parallel model, increased complexity in the music requires increased numbers of analyses proceeding in parallel; hence processing load demands not more speed but more space. It is hard to evaluate this trade-off, as we know little about space limitations in the brain. However, the speed required for backtracking in the serial model does seem implausible.

One important difficulty in developing a parallel multiple-analysis model lies essentially in data management: How many hypotheses can the processor entertain at once, and how long does it let a "wrong" hypothesis continue before abandoning it? If this model is on the right track, these questions should be susceptible to experimental techniques such as memory load tasks and priming tasks. Whatever the upshot, the complexity of the Bach analysis puts a surprisingly large lower bound on the number of hypotheses the processor must be able to entertain at one time without appreciable stress.[6]

Another difficulty with the parallel model as stated so far lies in its prediction about musical experience. If indeed five analyses are being pursued simultaneously after five events of the chorale, why do we not experience all five at once? Such a prediction is at odds with intuition. Rather, as in other cognitive domains, it is generally the case that one perceives only one interpretation at a time. This observation lies behind the appeal of the single-analysis models of musical processing. However, it is not inconsistent with a parallel model either, given the proper interpretation of the phenomenology. It is true that one is only *conscious* of one analysis at a time, or that one *can attend to* only one analysis at a time. But this leaves open the possibility that other analyses are present unconsciously, inaccessible to attention. This is the position I adopt.

To flesh this position out slightly, I propose that the processor contains a *selection function*, a device that continuously evaluates the currently active analyses for relative plausibility and designates one of them as the currently most salient. This selected analysis will be the single one that appears in awareness as *the* structure of the music at this point. (See Jackendoff, 1987, for discussion and justification of a selection function in the faculties of linguistic and visual processing.)

The only major difference between the parallel model and the serial ones is in how they decide among competing analyses. In the serial single-choice model, the decision is made before exploring the consequences of each possibility for the subsequent music; in the serial indeterministic model, the decision is made before making a commitment to any analysis in particular (a notion that proves computationally incoherent); in the parallel model, the selection function chooses among analyses as they are being derived. In fact, the parallel model is, in a sense, the simplest of the three in this respect: The problem never arises of deciding when to make a commitment to a particular analysis, when to give up on a particular analysis and backtrack, or which analysis to backtrack to. Rather, all analyses are undertaken, and they are abandoned independently of each other, leaving the field to whatever analyses remain active.

Parallel models are hardly unprecedented in language perception. A widely cited program of experimental research in psycholinguistics (Swinney, 1979, 1982; Tanenhaus, Leiman, & Seidenberg, 1979) has shown that, for a brief time after presentation, all senses of a word are active, regardless of preceding semantic and syntactic context.

[6] *Fred Lerdahl has suggested (personal communication, April 1990) that cadenced group boundaries are points when less stable analyses are "pruned," a hypothesis that probably needs to be settled by experimental research.*

During this period all senses, of whatever part of speech, are capable of priming (speeding up recognition of) semantically related words. Syntactic parsers with this organization are discussed (although not endorsed) by Berwick and Weinberg (1984). Bever, Garrett, and Hurtig (1973) give experimental evidence that multiple unconscious syntactic analyses are indeed computed in parallel, and that the clause boundary is the point at which all analyses but the most salient one are discarded. This parallels Lerdahl's suggestion for music perception (see footnote 6).

Implications and Realizations in the Processor

An intuition shared by many people (musicians and nonmusicians alike) is that understanding or appreciating music has something to do with expectation. To put this intuition roughly, each fragment of music, as it is heard, builds in the listener expectations of what is to come. Either these expectations are fulfilled by the succeeding music, with an accompanying positive affect or satisfaction in the listener, or else they are not fulfilled, with an accompanying negative affect such as surprise or disappointment.

This intuition becomes more fully fleshed out in the 'implication-realization" approach of Meyer (1956, 1967a, 1967b, 1973) and Narmour (1977), developed as a theory of melody. (Experimental work based on this theory includes that of Rosner & Meyer, 1986, and Schmuckler, 1989.) Its basic premise is that particular melodic elements set up expectations or implications (Meyer changes from the former term to the latter over the years) about the melody's completion. Meyer argues that such "musical implications" are not just superficial associations to past experience but rather the product of musical cognition—the construction of abstract musical structures by the listener on the basis of a multitude of internalized principles of musical form.

The theory of musical processing sketched above makes possible a stronger notion of musical expectation or implication, or what might be called *prospective hearing*. The theory claims that the listener is using principles of musical grammar to assign multiple possible analyses to the fragment of music heard thus far. Among these principles, there are many that can project structure for parts of the music that have not yet been heard. For example, one of the principles of grouping (Grouping Preference Rule 5 in GTTM) creates a preference for symmetrical organization. When a single group is heard, this principle leads the processor to create a potential structure in which this group is balanced by a second group of the same length—that is, there is an "expectation" that the music will continue in a way that fills in a symmetrical structure. Similarly, the strong preference for a constant meter (Metrical Well-Formedness Rule 4) projects the existing metrical structure beyond the portion of the musical surface that has already been heard, and the principles of cadences (Time-Span Reduction Well-Formedness Rules 3 and 4, Time-Span Reduction Preference Rule 7) project closed harmonic patterns at the (projected) ends of phrases. Notice that these rules need not anticipate exactly what notes will appear in the musical surface (as Narmour's rules appear to). Rather, they project the abstract structures that are to be associated with the actual notes of the musical surface as they occur.

In addition to prospective hearing, the present model of processing permits us to describe a phenomenon that may be called *retrospective* hearing. This accounts for various sorts of "satisfaction," "shock," or "surprise" associated with the hearing of music. Here are three representative cases:

1. The processor is computing multiple analyses in parallel, but the selection function settles the indeterminacy among them on the basis of straightforward evidence in the musical surface. This results in the listener hearing the music with the proper structure and projecting this structure backward to the point where the indeterminacy arose. This is the case we encountered in the Bach chorale; phenomenologically, this case is experienced as "hearing the music without effort."
2. The processor is computing multiple analyses in parallel, and enough evidence has accumulated for one of these to be chosen as most plausible by the selection function. However, subsequent events in the musical surface lead to a relative reweighting of the analyses being computed by the processor. The selection function thereby "changes horses in midstream," jumping to a different analysis. The phenomenological effect of such an occurrence will be a "retrospective reanalysis" of the passage as it is heard. An example of this case might be Figure 5.5, where a phrase initially heard as being in A♭ is suddenly heard as being in D♭.
3. The processor is computing multiple analyses in parallel, and subsequent events are not consistent with *any* of the existing analyses. All must be abandoned and the processor must start over. This case is experienced as a sense of bewilderment, "losing one's bearings" musically. An instance of this might be the passage for which Mozart's "Dissonant" Quartet, K. 465, is named.

Memory and the Expectation Theory of Affect

There is, however, a fundamental difficulty with basing a theory of musical *affect* on the notion of expectation. If one is listening to a piece one knows very well, one knows exactly how the music is going to continue. Hence there should be no occasion whatsoever for shock, surprise, or disappointment at the way the piece turns out (unless the performer on this occasion happens to make a mistake)—only for continuous satisfaction at the fulfillment of one's expectations. Thus a familiar piece should present no possibilities for distinctions of affect. In short, according to this approach, all pieces should approach the very same affect as they become familiar: total satisfaction.

In fact, quite the opposite is the case, at least for what we call "good music"—music that we (or the culture as whole) have come to consider as being of lasting value. Such music continues to engage us more deeply as we get to know it better; we find more and more distinctions of interest in it. This would seem to be a fatal flaw in an expectation-based theory of affect. (This problem is ruminated on at some length by Meyer [1967a].)

To push this point home, notice that it is possible to derive distinctions of affect from musical imagery—from replaying a piece in one's head. In this case nothing can be unexpected, since everything experienced comes from one's own memory.

Still, there is a germ of insight in the expectation theory of affect, which can be recovered and built upon within the approach to musical processing proposed here. The solution comes in two parts.

The first is that expectation is not the only source of musical affect. Certain aspects come from very local sources in the musical surface. For instance, it is a longstanding (even ancient) observation that tempo affects the musical response. Other things being equal, fast music will tend to be exciting and slow music will tend to be soothing. Sheer volume, too, has an effect. In addition, musical affect is a result not just of hearing (and predicting) the musical surface of a piece, but of the activity of deriving in real time all the details of abstract musical structure. The musical structure has intrinsic points of instability or tension, which require resolution and therefore produce affect. In addition, when alternative analyses are being processed concurrently, the points of tension in each individual analysis may or may not coincide with those of its cohorts. This tension among the conflicting analyses may also surface in the listener's experience as affect, even if only one of the analyses is experienced at the moment as "the" structure of the music.

The second part of the answer has to do with the character of the processor. The idea is that the music processor, like the language and visual processors, is a *module* in the sense of Fodor (1983). As such, it is "informationally encapsulated" from long-term memory of pieces: It has only the rules of musical grammar at its disposal to develop an analysis. Moreover, its operation is obligatory: In response to any plausibly musical signal, it tries its best to develop a musical structure.[7]

Under this conception, even if the listener consciously knows that, say, a deceptive cadence is coming, the processor itself is innocent of this knowledge. The selection function therefore projects as most salient the stablest continuation of the current musical surface: a full cadence, in which the conclusion of the phrase is a harmonic relaxation. As a result, when the deceptive cadence actually arrives, the selection function has to re-evaluate the relative salience of its analyses, creating a retrospective reanalysis. Because of the organization of musical grammar and the independence of the processor from long-term memory for the piece, the processor will be taken in every time by a deceptive cadence, and it will produce its characteristic affect, as long as one is attending to the music.

Because of the obligatory operation of the processor, it will apply even to music that is being imaged (i.e., being "heard in one's head"). Whatever musical structure is retrieved from memory in the course of producing a musical image, the processor goes dumbly to work on it, recreating the structure already being stored in and retrieved from long-term memory. Hence the music can potentially be experienced as though one is hearing it externally.

To sum up, the expectation theory of musical affect does not make much sense if we think in terms of conscious expectations or a processor that has full access to one's musical memory. But it does make sense if the processor is conceived of as being parallel to that for language, using the rules of grammar to construct abstract structures that analyze the musical surface and operating autonomously with at best limited access to musical memory. However well one knows a piece, then, expectation, suspense, satisfaction, and surprise can still occur within the processor. In essence, the processor is always hearing the piece for the first time—and that is why affect remains intact.

References

Berwick, R., & Weinberg, A. (1984). *The grammatical basis of linguistic performance.* Cambridge, MA: MIT Press.

[7] *This point is also suggested by Bharucha (1987).*

Bever, T. G., Garrett, M. F., & Hurtig, R. (1973). The interaction of perceptual processes and ambiguous sentences. *Memory and Cognition, 1,* 277–286.

Bharucha, J. (1987). Music cognition and perceptual facilitation: A connectionist framework, *Music Perception, 5,* 1–30.

Butler, D. (1989). Describing the perception of tonality in music: A critique of the tonal hierarchy theory and a proposal for a theory of intervallic rivalry, *Music Perception, 6,* 219–242.

Fodor, J. A. (1983). *Modularity of mind.* Cambridge, MA: MIT Press.

Frazier, L., & Fodor, J. D. (1978). The sausage machine: A new two-stage parsing model. *Cognition, 6,* 291–325.

Jackendoff, R. (1987). *Consciousness and the computational mind.* Cambridge, MA: MIT Press.

Lerdahl, F., & Jackendoff, R. (1983a). *A generative theory of tonal music.* Cambridge, MA: MIT Press.

Lerdahl, F., & Jackendoff, R. (1983b). An overview of hierarchical structure in music. *Music Perception, 1,* 229–252.

Marcus, M. (1980). *A theory of syntactic recognition for natural language.* Cambridge, MA: MIT Press.

Meyer, L. (1956). *Emotion and meaning in music.* Chicago: University of Chicago Press.

Meyer, L. (1967a). On rehearing music. In L. Meyer (Ed.), *Music, the arts, and ideas.* Chicago: University of Chicago Press.

Meyer, L. (1967b). Meaning and music in information theory. In L. Meyer (Ed.), *Music, the arts, and ideas.* Chicago: University of Chicago Press.

Meyer, L. (1973). *Explaining music.* Berkeley: University of California Press.

Narmour, E. (1977). *Beyond Schenkerism.* Chicago: University of Chicago Press.

Rosner, B., & Meyer, L. (1986). The perceptual roles of melodic, process, contour, and form. *Music Perception, 4,* 1–40.

Schmuckler, M. (1989). Expectation in music: Investigation of melodic and harmonic processes. *Music Perception, 7,* 109–150.

Swinney, D. (1979). Lexical access during sentence comprehension: (Re)consideration of context effects. *Journal of Verbal Learning and Verbal Behavior, 18,* 645–659.

Swinney, D. (1982). The structure and time-course of information interaction during speech comprehension: Lexical segmentation, access, and interpretation. In J. Mehler, E. Walker, and M. Garrett (Eds.), *Perspectives on mental representation.* Hillsdale, NJ: Erlbaum.

Tanenhaus, M., Leiman, J., & Seidenberg, M. (1979). Evidence for multiple stages in the processing of ambiguous words in syntactic contexts. *Journal of Verbal Learning and Verbal Behavior, 18,* 417–440.

Wanner, E., & Maratsos, M. (1978). An ATN approach to comprehension. In M. Halle, J. Bresnan, and G. Miller (Eds.), *Linguistic theory and psychological reality.* Cambridge, MA: MIT Press.

CHAPTER 6

The Influence of Embodied Registral Motion on the Perception of Higher-Level Melodic Implication

Eugene Narmour

The theory of melodic implication and realization holds that, given a melodic stimulus, our cognitive systems simultaneously generate two types of expectations.[1] The first type of expectation depends on a prior reservoir of learned style structures—representative plans, forms, prototypes, and so forth—in other words, schemata. The listener's mapping of such schematic expectations onto the input is thus top down in orientation. In musical analysis, such stylistic invocation comes from both within and without the piece under inspection. I call such repetition or replication in a piece of music *intra-* and *extraopus style* (see Meyer, 1989; and Narmour, 1977, 1990). Since one can demonstrate whether, and the extent to which, conformance between any two given patterns exists, such invocation of style is an empirical phenomenon.

The second type of expectation emanates from an automatic, mandatory system. Rationalistic in concept, this reflexive, preprogrammed, hardwired system operates from the

[1] *"Implication" is an objective term referring to demonstrable analytical patterning in a piece of music, whereas "expectation" is a subjective term denoting the listener's psychological response to such patterning. In other words, from the listener's point of view, one could call the implication-realization model the "expectation-confirmation model."*

bottom up on the stylistic primitives (i.e., pitches, intervals, registral directions, durations, etc.) of various parameters (i.e., melody, harmony, durational patterning, meter, etc.). Thus, we can analyze any given parameter in terms of the primitive elements that constitute it. With reference to expectation and implication, the parameter of melody, for example, is composed of registral direction, intervallic motion, and pitch specificity.

A number of researchers in music cognition (Deutsch, 1982; Deutsch & Feroe, 1981; Francès, 1958, 1988; and Serafine, 1988) have argued for the perceptual necessity of positing bottom-up systems operating on incoming primitives, and Fodor (1983) has presented the general philosophical and psychological evidence for our believing in them. In sum, the theoretical model of melodic implication and realization treats the top-down schema system and the bottom-up parametric system as hypothetical constants that are at root independent (Krumhansl [in press] and Krumhansl & Schellenberg [1991] have gathered some preliminary experimental evidence supporting the implication-realization model). In this chapter, I shall concentrate on the parametric system.

The Parametric System

In the bottom-up parametric system, I hypothesize, ceteris paribus, that small initial intervals generate implications of continuation and that large intervals generate reversals. Within this theory, the concept of continuation rests on the bottom-up Gestalt laws of common fate and similarity (Pomerantz, 1981), whereas, philosophically, the concept of reversal constitutes a symmetrical construct.

The concept of continuation refers to a small melodic interval that causes listeners to expect (a) registral direction to be maintained and (b) a motion of intervallic similarity. As to the former cause, three possible continuations of registral direction exist: up followed by up (e.g., C–D–E), down followed by down (E–D–C), and lateral followed by lateral (C–C–C). As to the latter cause, I define intervallic similarity (A + A) to be when registral direction is maintained (up/up, down/down, lateral/lateral) as a difference of a plus/minus minor third. Thus, an ascending pattern like C–D–F♯ satisfies the definition of intervallic similarity (M2 − M3 = M2 = A + A), whereas an ascending pattern like C–D–A does not (M2 − P5 = P4 = A + B).

The concept of reversal refers to a relatively large interval that implies (a) a change in initial registral direction and (b) an intervallic motion of differentiation.[2] I define intervallic

[2]It should be emphasized here that, in addition to intervallic motion and registral direction, melodic implication also has a durational (time), metric (place), and pitch-specific aspect (see Narmour, 1990).

similarity when registral direction changes (up/down, down/up, up/lateral, down/lateral, lateral/up, lateral/down) as a plus/minus major second. Thus, an ascending/descending pattern like C–G–F♯ satisfies the definition of intervallic differentiation (P5 − m2 = T = A + B), whereas an up/down pattern like C–G–D does not (P5 − P4 = M2 = A + A).

The Intervallic Scale classifies the bottom-up hypotheses of continuation and reversal with reference to the kinds of intervallic implications found in Western music:

Intervallic Scale (I)

u m2 M2 m3 M3 P4 A4/d5 P5 m6 M6 m7 M7 (P8) m9

sameness ....similarity ....differentiation ....

($a^0 + a^0$) ($a^0 + a^1$) ($a + b$)

continuation implied....................(threshold).....reversal implied ....

As can be seen in this display (adapted from *The Analysis and Cognition of Basic Melodic Structures*: *The Implication-Realization Model* (p. 78) by E. Narmour, 1990, Chicago: University of Chicago Press), I define the unison (u), minor second (m2), major second (M2), minor third (m3), and major third (M3) as small intervals, implying continuation, whereas I define large intervals, like sixths (m6, M6), sevenths (m7, M7), and ninths (m9) as implying reversal. As one moves from left to right, from sameness between pitches ($a^0 + a^0$) making up the unison (u) to similarity between pitches ($a^0 + a^1$)—making up seconds and thirds (m2, M2, m3, M3) to clear difference between pitches ($a + b$) making up the larger intervals (m6, M6, m7, M7, m9)—note that a gradual change in implicative function occurs, the perfect fourth (P4), tritone (A4/d5), and perfect fifth (P5) occupying a threshold position between continuation and reversal. In other words, near the middle of the octave, context will come into play in determining the precise implication of the threshold intervals. For example, listeners tend to hear diminished fifths (e.g., an ascending C–G♭) as implying reversal, whereas they tend to hear augmented fourths (e.g., an ascending C–F♯) as implying continuation.

The next display (the Registral Scale; from *The Analysis and Cognition of Basic Melodic Structures: The Implication-Realization Model* (p. 284) by E. Narmour, 1990, Chicago: University of Chicago Press) shows how concepts of sameness (lateral + lateral), similarity (e.g., up + up), and difference (e.g., up + down) are applied to the three possible registral directions:

Registral Scale (V)

lateral to lateral	ascent to ascent	ascent to descent
	descent to descent	descent to ascent
		ascent to lateral
		descent to lateral
		lateral to ascent
		lateral to descent
(sameness)	(similarity)	(differentiation)
continuation signified		reversal signified

Notice that any two pitches will cause the perception of lateral, ascending, or descending motion—and thus continuation—whereas the perception of reversal requires three pitches. Although the perception of ascent and descent without the perception of interval is possible (as in a rising or falling siren), when one encounters incremented pitch, as in all common melodic styles, the property of interval always emerges. For this reason, any change of registral direction involving a small interval always carries with it an implication of continuation of direction. That is, in an up/down reversal pattern like C–A–G, the descending major second of A–G would, in terms of the basic hypothesis of the Intervallic Scale (I), also imply a continuing descent. This is why the Registral Scale (V) uses the term "signified" in connection with continuation and reversal rather than the term "implied" (as in the Intervallic Scale). Thus, the descending A–G reverses the initial ascending C–A, but A–G is also immediately subject to the Intervallic Scale (I), as an initial interval of a major second ($a^0 + a^1$) implying continuation of both intervallic similarity (A + A) and registral direction (down + down).[3]

Thus, in melody, implication of registral direction always maps onto interval. Note that although a crossover in implicative function occurs on the Intervallic Scale at the point of the tritone (A4/d5), the classes of sameness, similarity, and differentiation are absolute with reference to the Registral Scale. That is, registral direction either continues or reverses. No threshold area exists on the Registral Scale.

The Basic Structures

Since melodic implications entail both registral direction and intervallic motion, one must also evaluate realization of implication in the light of these two variables. For instance,

[3]Realizations of continuation following reversal are, in fact, what give rise to gap-filling melodies (Meyer, 1973).

when the hypothesized registral direction (continuation) and the intervallic motion (sameness or similarity) are realized from a small interval, we say we have a *process* [P] or a *duplication* [D], as shown in the musical snippets of Figure 6.1 (registral direction in P is either up or down, and in D it is lateral). Likewise, when both implied registral direction (change) and intervallic motion (differentiation) are realized from a large interval, we say we have a *reversal* [R], like the one shown in Figure 6.1C. Such patterns [P, D, R] characterize complete realizations of implication in that both the expected intervallic motion (similar in P or D; differentiated in R) and the expected registral direction (continued in P or D; reversed in R) are realized.

With reference to syntactic function, realizations of continuation [P, D] emanating from the bottom-up parametric system are ongoing; that is, they create nonclosure (the ≻→ in Figures 6.1A and 6.1B). In contrast, realizations of reversal [R], also emanating from the bottom-up system, create closure (the ≻— in Figure 6.1C) to some degree (whether that closure is articulative on the level of its occurrence or is transformational and thus emergent on higher levels).

Implications of process [P], duplication [D], and reversal [R] can, of course, be suppressed. By suppressed, I mean that a given melodic implication is weakened, sometimes so severely that no further, low-level expectation arises in the mind of the listener. There are two basic ways such suppression of melodic implication may come about. First, closure in other parameters (i.e., in duration, meter, dynamic stress, and harmony) may so weaken a melodic implication that the listener will focus attention on the emergent higher level and not search for further realization on the low level. When this happens, the two pitches of the suppressed interval create a dyadic relation on the level of their occurrence—that is, on the durational-metric level at which they function in the musical hierarchy.[4]

The second way for suppression of melodic implication to occur is when the top-down system interferes with implications emanating from the bottom up. For example, if the second pitch of a melodic interval moves to a stable scale step—to, say, the tonic—then melodic implication may be suppressed. (Scale-step relations clearly constitute a top-down schema in tonal music, as Krumhansl, 1979, has shown.)

[4] *This is so because melodic implications are durational specific and metric specific; thus, for a realization to take place, such implied specificities must be satisfied. This is why I say "weaken" rather than "prevent." In the theory, both bottom-up and top-down systems are independent and thus always generate implications. As to definitions, closure occurs in the parameter of harmony when a strong dissonance goes to a strong consonance; in the parameter of duration, closure occurs when a short note goes to a relatively long one (cumulation); and in the parameter of meter, closure occurs when a weak beat goes to a strong one. Nonclosure in these parameters, of course, results from the opposite conditions (consonance/dissonance; long/short durations [countercumulation]; weak/strong beats), conditions which produce the possibility of structural combining and chaining.*

A

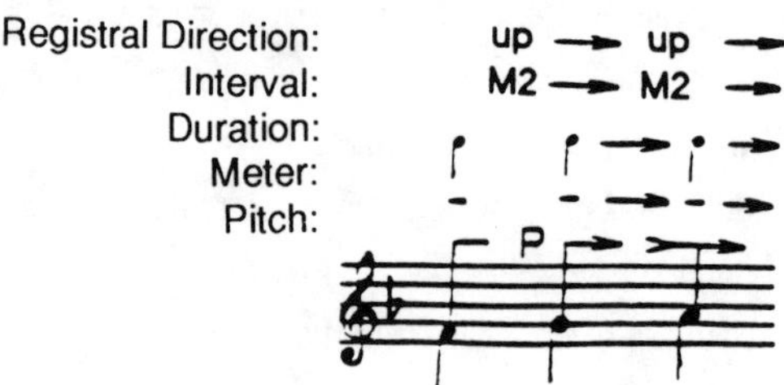

B

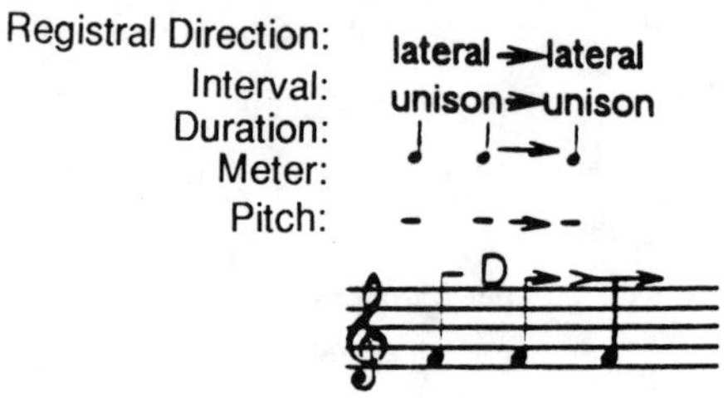

C

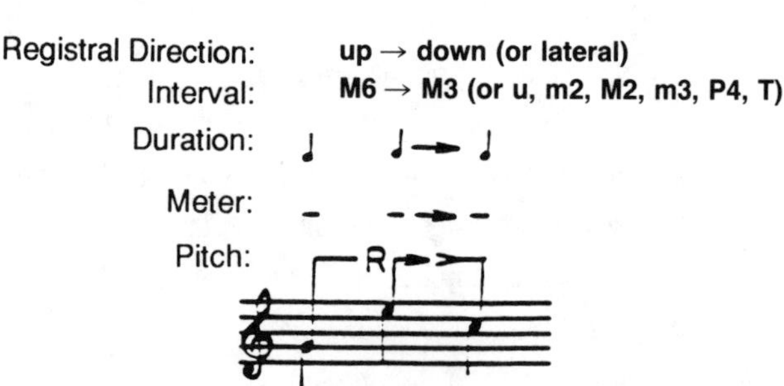

FIGURE 6.1 In Figure 6.1A, P = process (similar intervals, same registral direction); → = implies; and ≻— = realization. In Figure 6.1B, D = duplication (iteration; same intervals, same registral direction); → = implies; and ≻— = realization. In Figure 6.1C, R = reversal (different intervals, large to small, different registral directions); → = implies; and ≻— = realization.

Partial Realizations

Because melodic implication has both registral-specific (V) and intervallic-specific (I) properties, it follows that either one or the other of these may be realized. As we saw in Figure 6.1, P, D, and R realize the implications of both registral direction and intervallic motion. But denial of implied intervallic motion simultaneous with realization of registral direction from a small interval may occur. And vice versa: Realization of intervallic motion may accompany denial of registral direction from a small interval. Of course, the same two possibilities are also obtained when the initial interval is large. Figure 6.2 illustrates these kinds of melodic structures.

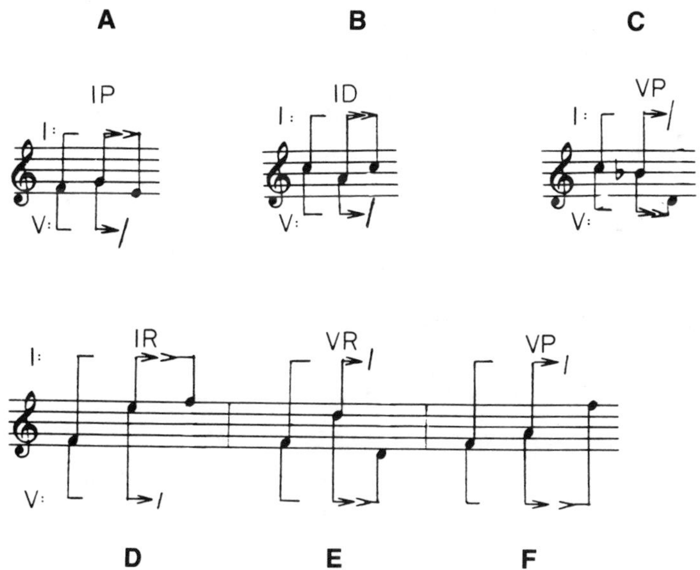

FIGURE 6.2 IP = intervallic process (similar intervals, different registral directions); ID = intervallic duplication (same intervals, different registral directions); VP = registral process (different intervals, small to large, same registral direction); IR = intervallic reversal (different intervals, large to small, same registral direction); VR = registral reversal (different intervals, large to larger, different registral directions).

In Figure 6.2A, the small initial interval of the major second implies an ascent with continuing intervallic similarity; but, as can be seen, the implied registral direction is denied (V, →/) even while the intervallic similarity is realized (I, →≻—). F–G–E thus realizes what I call an *intervallic process* [IP]. Figure 6.2B is similar except that the intervallic motion is exact. Hence, C–A–C creates what I call an *intervallic duplication* [ID]. In Figure 6.2C, implication to descend from the initial small interval is realized (V, →≻—), while intervallic motion is differentiated and thus denied (I, →/). I call this kind of structure a *registral process* [VP].

With reference to large initial intervals, the implication in Figure 6.2D—that a small interval is to follow a large one—is realized (I, →≻—), but the implication to change registral direction is denied (V, →/). Thus, we have an intervallic reversal [IR]. In Figure 6.2E, what I call registral reversal [VR], the intervallic and registral realizations are the opposite.

Altogether then, the bottom-up system theoretically generates eight, and only eight, types of prospective realizations:[5]

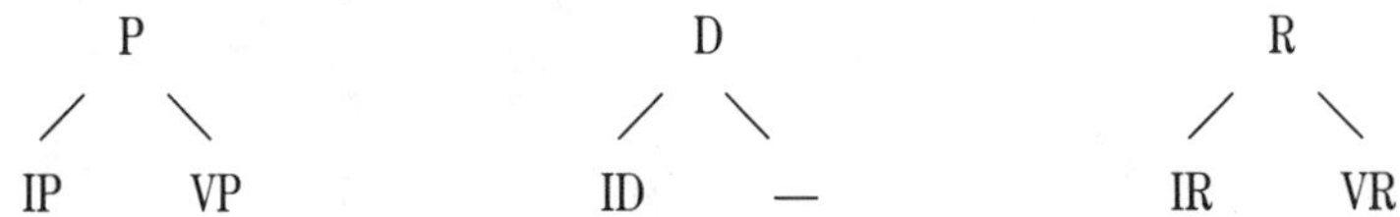

In the "parental" display shown here, process [P], duplication [D], and reversal [R] realize both implied intervallic motion and registral direction according to the bottom-up hypotheses of the I-scale and V-scale, whereas intervallic process [IP], registral process [VP], intervallic duplication [ID], intervallic reversal [IR], and registral reversal [VR] realize only one or the other.

The patterns shown in Figure 6.2 are all prospective realizations—where the theory says that the listener subconsciously projects certain kinds of realizations from the onset of small or large intervals. Thus, a "partial" realization such as IP, VP, ID, VR, or IR would produce a partial surprise (all other things being equal). However, eight retrospective realizations are also possible. For example, a large interval, which initially implies a reversal [R], could go on to create a retrospective process [(P)] if it were followed by a similarly-sized large interval in the same registral direction (e.g., C^1–A^1–F^2, M6 + m6). In

[5] *There is no remaining structural type for the symbol VD to represent; hence its absence in the display. For a discussion why, see Narmour (1990).*

this case, both the initially implied registral direction and the initially implied intervallic motion are denied (the parentheses around the P denote the retrospection). Similarly, an initial large interval followed by an even larger, differentiated interval in the same registral direction (e.g., C^1–A^1–C^2, M6 + m10) would create a retrospective registral process [(VP)]. Likewise, a retrospective intervallic process [(IP)] would take place if two large intervals in opposite registral directions occurred (e.g., an up/down pattern like C–A–B, M6 + m7). And by extension, an up/down pattern like C–A–C would create a retrospective intervallic duplication [(ID), M6 + M6]. Note, however, in (IP) and (ID) cases that the listener would expect registral change but not intervallic similarity.

Initial small intervals also have the capability to create retrospective realizations. For instance, a small interval could retrospectively realize a retrospective reversal [(R)] if, for example, an ascending F–A went to a descending G♯. Since here the implication that the registral direction should continue upward is denied, and since the intervals involved (M3 + m2) are not similar but differentiated (according to the rules of the theory), both implied registral direction and implied intervallic motion in (R) are denied. Small intervals can also retrospectively realize registral reversal [(VR)], an up/down pattern like F–A–C (M3 + M6) being a case in point. Here, too, both the initially implied registral direction and the implied intervallic similarity are denied. Retrospection is symbolized with parentheses around the letters:

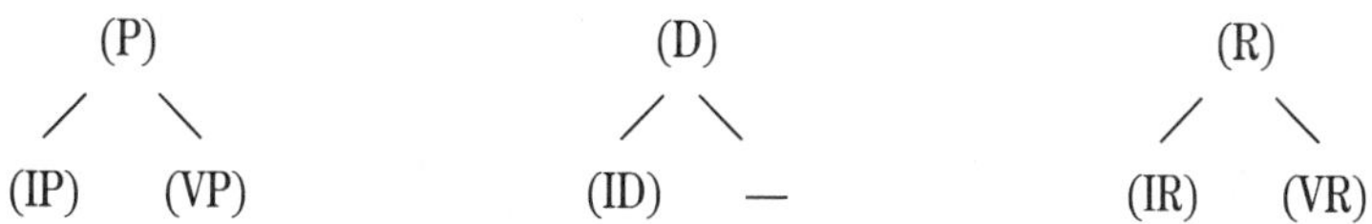

In this chapter, we shall encounter only (VR), (R), and (IP).[6]

Dyads

In addition to the 16 prospective and retrospective possibilities, the only other basic structures that concern us are dyads and registral returns.[7] As mentioned earlier, dyads

[6] *Because of the limitations of space, I have not illustrated retrospective duplication [(D)] because its occurrence involves stylistic repetition. The reader interested in further discussions of retrospective realization may consult Narmour (1989a, 1989b, 1990).*

[7] *One other structure is necessary for the analysis of melody—the single-note structure, which I call monad (M). For a discussion of this, see Narmour (1990).*

are two-note structures; they come about when suppression of melodic implication occurs, usually when closure in other parameters obtrudes on the second tone of the implicative interval in question. In an ascending interval like C–D, for example, if the first tone were dissonant and the second tone strongly consonant (resolving the dissonance), then the implication of C–D to continue processively to, say, E would be greatly suppressed. We would be left, in other words, with C–D functioning as an independent melodic pattern whose ordinary implication was closed by the parameter of harmony. I symbolize such dyads, such permanently denied implications, with the number representing the size of the interval (e.g., 2 for the major second).

Registral Return

Registral return, the last structure to concern us, is a nonimplicative, discontiguous structure between isolated pitches. In an up/down pattern like C–F–C, the listener hears the second C to be an exact return to the initial pitch, quite apart from the intervallic similarity present (P4 + P4). Likewise, in an up/down pitch sequence of C–F–B (P4 + d5), the listener perceives the B as a near registral return of the initial pitch (nearness occurs when any two discontiguous pitches fall within a major or minor second). In Figure 6.3, the exact registral return is symbolized by "aba" and the near return as "aba^1", with the small letters standing for the individual pitches (registral return is a perceptual result governed by the bottom-up gestalt law of proximity). As an independent melodic phenomenon, exact registral return [aba] almost always overlaps intervallic duplication [whether ID or (ID)], whereas near registral return [aba^1] and intervallic process [whether IP or (IP)] frequently go together.

Figure 6.3 shows two synthetic melodies representing the eight basic types of prospective structures, as well as numerous registral returns and a couple of dyads.[8] Horizontal brackets outline the beginning and ending points of each kind of structure, while the capital letters, small letters, and numbers denote the kinds of realizations that occur. As we shall see, such initial and terminal anchor points between tones spanning the brackets constitute the structural tones of each type of realization, tones which transform and create higher levels that generate their own implications and realizations.

[8] *Near registral return [aba^1] can create simultaneous, networked processes [P] among discontiguous pitches; note how this networking differentiates Figure 6.3A from Figure 6.3B even though each melody is a nearly perfect inversion of the other.*

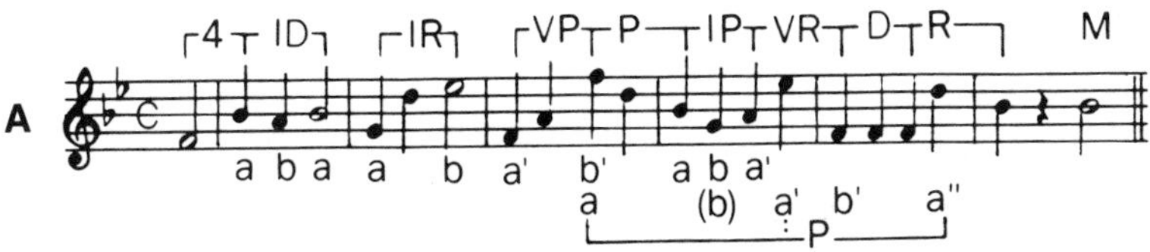

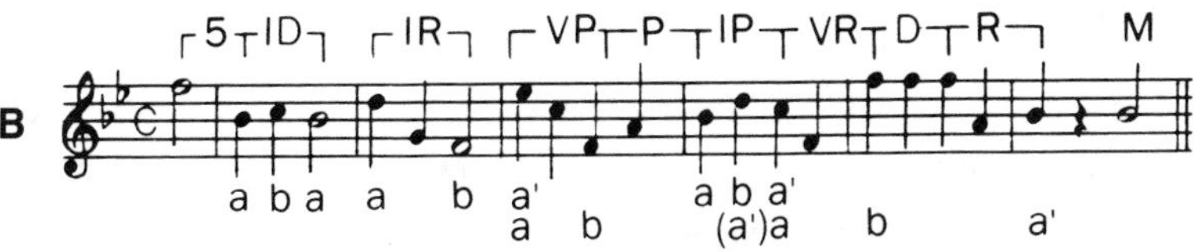

FIGURE 6.3 Two synthetic melodies illustrating the basic structures generated by the theory. 4, 5 = dyads (unrealized implications); ID = intervallic duplication; IR = intervallic reversal; VP = registral process; P = process; IP = intervallic process; VR = registral reversal; D = duplication (iteration); R = reversal; M = monad (single-tone structure); aba = exact registral return; aba^1 = near registral return. From *The Analysis and Cognition of Basic Melodic Structures: The Implication-Realization Model* (p. 7), by E. Narmour, 1990, Chicago: University of Chicago Press. Copyright 1990 by University of Chicago Press. Reprinted by permission.

Because the bottom-up system of intervallic motion and registral direction is context free (independent of style-structural learning),[9] these basic structures will, in some sense, account for all melodies ever written or ever to be written. Such a sweeping statement is tenable only because the melodic structures represented by the capital letters have the potential to combine and chain together in an indefinite number of ways, just as letters and words have the capacity to create an infinite number of different sentences.

[9] *This is not style-primitive learning because the syntactic items filling up the slots of the Intervallic (I) and Registral (V) Scales come from the style (e.g., the fixed set of intervals and registral directions found in Western music).*

We shall encounter a few chains and combinations in Figures 6.3–6.10.[10] The basic bottom-up structures, however, can account for the world of melodic structuring only if we consider the complexity of hierarchical interactions between melodic implications and realizations, the central emphasis of this chapter.

Implicative Mutuality Between Levels

First consider the possibility of implicative mutuality between different levels. According to the theory, hierarchical structuring of the realizational possibilities is a matter of next-level transformation at points of initiation and termination. In measure 1 of Figure 6.3A, for example, the initial and terminal B♭s of the closed ID would constitute the structural tones, and, recursively, these tones would form a melodic interval of B♭–B♭ (a unison) on a higher level, thus creating a new, bottom-up implication there. However, unlike foreground melodic intervals on the note-to-note level, the unison on the new level would not be a "pure" melodic interval, like a unison on the note-to-note level. For the implicative meaning of the second B♭ on the higher level would be shaped by the lower-level A–B♭ that fed into it in the first place. As an ascending minor second, the lower-level melodic implication of A–B♭ to continue upward therefore does not support the higher-level melodic implication of B♭–B♭ to continue laterally. Of course, we would also, at some point, have to take into account the top-down influence of scale step—that A is a leading tone and B♭ a tonic. But the important issue for our purposes is to observe that lower-level, note-to-note realizations can conflict with higher-level, recursive implications created by the transformed structural tones on the new level. To be sure, feedback from a higher-level implication will also shape a listener's expectation of melodic implication on a lower level, and this too has to be accounted for.

When higher-level feedback and lower-level feedforward promote the same registral implication, we say that implicative mutuality exists between levels. Terms such as "conflict," "support," and "mutuality" are justified in the description of interlevel relations because in musical systems higher-level melodic structuring embodies to some extent the

[10] *There are four low-level conditions that cause combining and chaining: (a) the occurrence of dissonance on a metric accent (regardless of level); (b) the presence of ongoing meter (e.g., nonaccents in triple grouping, regardless of level); (c) the envelopment of metric accent by melodic or harmonic process [P] in additive (isochronous) or countercumulative durations (long to short); and (d) the envelopment of metric accent by duplication [D] in additive durations. Figure 6.4 and 6.6 illustrate combinations and chains (see, for example, the RP in Figure 6.4B, or the PIDP chain between mm. 5–7 and the IDP combinations between mm. 7–8 and 9–10 in Figure 6.6). What is important to remember about combinations and chains is that the musical context causes the terminal interval of one basic structure to become the initial interval of another. In short, combinations and chains result from interval-sharing.*

implied registral direction of the lower-level structure that creates it (see Narmour, 1983). In other words, higher levels store some of the implicative registral information found on lower levels.[11] But it is only the registral implication of the last interval of the lower-level pattern that the higher-level structural tone embodies. That is, no higher level incorporates all the details of the lower level beneath it since that would lead to a perceptual problem of infinite regress.[12]

Consider, for example, the processes in Figure 6.4A. In the beginning, the transformed half-note A terminates the initial dyad (symbolized by a 2, a result of durational cumulation and metric emphasis) and embodies the implied ascent of the dyadic, anacrustic G–A. Thus, the continuation of the ascent to the transformed, half-note C in measure 2—the metrically emphasized, durationally cumulative tone closing the A–B–C process on the low level (m. 1)—is not a surprise. The point, however, is that the realized, lower-level process of A–B–C enhances the ascending implication of the half-notes A–C at the higher level.[13]

The same kinds of remarks could be made about the ensuing C–D–E process in measures 2–3. This process supports the continuing ascending registral implication at the higher level. The process composed of A–C–E at the level of the bar (mm. 1–3; the dashed lines trace the transformations to the higher level) illustrates that closure occurs in the parameter of duration when a short note goes to a relatively long one (cumulation) and in the parameter of meter when a weak beat goes to a strong one.[14] Of course, the emergent, similar motivic form encompassing measures 1–3 also contributes to the ascending processes, on both levels (A–B–C, C–D–E; A–C–E).

For another case of implicative mutuality between levels, consider now the reversals on levels 1 and 3 in Figure 6.4B (the lone R in m. 1 and the R of the RP). In this case, the higher-level F (m. 2) embodies the descent of the lower-level G–F, the last interval of the B♭–G–F reversal on level 1 (mm. 1–2). That is, as a small interval, the G–F connecting measure 1 to measure 2 implies a continuing descent. Hence, on the level of the dotted half note, the structural tones B♭–F create another reversal implication (the R

[11] *Higher levels may also embody, to some extent, implication of intervallic motion.*

[12] *In my earlier article on hierarchies (1983), I asserted that higher levels embodied all the details of lower levels. However, as Professor Eric Clarke rightly reminds me (private communication, September, 1990), that is not cognitively tenable.*

[13] *Since the quarter-note B on the third beat in measure 1 belongs to the lowest level, it does not form a direct realization of the implication embodied in the anacrustic G–A, where the A transforms, creating a new level at the duration of the dotted half. In other words, in a strict hierarchical sense, no G–A–B pattern exists in this example even though A occurs over a six-four chord, the reason being that the theory elevates the closural durational cumulation on the A over the instability of the six-four.*

[14] *For those unfamiliar with the concept of levels in musical analysis, it should be pointed out that music theorists refer to pitches taking place at a given durational level (here the "level of the bar") because the higher-level, transformed structural tones represent the time span of the notes of the lower-level structures lying beneath them.*

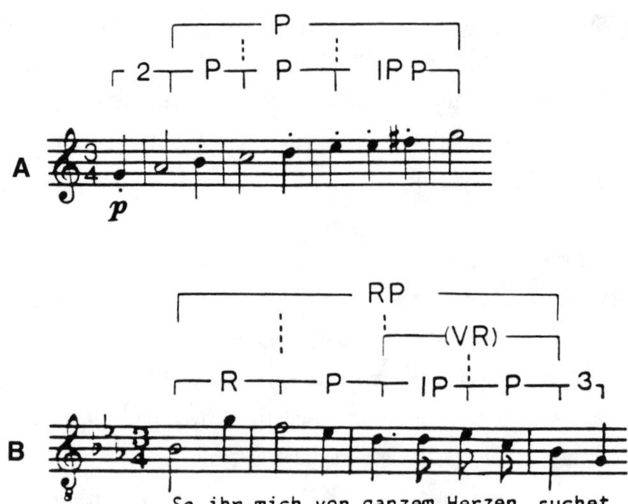

FIGURE 6.4 Figure 6.4A comes from Beethoven: Symphony No. 1, 3rd movement (*Allegro molto e vivace*), measures 1–4. 2= dyad of a major second; P = process; IPP = combination of intervallic process and process; dashed vertical lines trace tones transformed to higher levels. Figure 6.4B comes from Mendelssohn: *Elijah*, Aria No. 4 (*Andante con moto*), measures 1–3. R = reversal; RP = combination of reversal and process; (VR) = retrospective registral reversal; P = process; IP = intervallic process; 3 = dyad of a minor third. From *The Analysis and Cognition of Basic Melodic Structures: The Implication-Realization Model* (p. 162) by E. Narmour, 1990, Chicago: University of Chicago Press. Copyright 1990 by University of Chicago Press. Reprinted by permission.

of the RP). In turn, the ensuing low-level implication of F–E♭ (m. 2) supports the processive realization of F–E♭–D to measure 3. On level 3, the overall higher-level structure from measure 1 to measure 4 realizes one RP combination (B♭–F–D–B♭). The R dovetails with the P because the motivic forms of each bar are differentiated (the B♭–G in m. 4 creating a closed dyad [3]); observe again that dashed lines track the transformation of lower-level tones to higher levels. Thus, in Figure 6.4B both the lower-level reversal of

B♭–G–F (mm. 1–2) and the lower-level process of F–E♭–D (mm. 2–3) support the higher-level process of F–D–B♭ (the P of the RP, mm. 2–4).

Finally, note in both these examples that each level of implication and realization separately specifies the time and place that its realization must occur. That is, melodic implications on whatever level specify a durational property (time) and a metric position (place) concerning the registral direction and the intervallic motion that "ought" to take place (as the items of duration and meter in Figure 6.1 showed). See Jones (1981, 1982) for the importance of the time dimension to melodic expectation.

Implicative Conflict Between Levels

Implicative mutuality between hierarchical levels (like that seen in Figure 6.4) is common, and its occurrence gives the listener a sense of cognitive "control" over the path that the melody is to follow. But, as we have seen, the opposite syntactic possibility—that of cognitive "conflict" between levels and, thus, aesthetic arousal—frequently occurs as well. By conflict I mean that the registral implication of the higher level goes against the implication embodied from the lower level. Conflict between a melodic implication on one level and a different one on another level is, however, rarely proportionally equal. For the melodic implication on the higher level will frequently tend to dominate the implication on the lower level. This is a result of the inherent nature of syntactic hierarchies. That is, because it is closure on the lower level that gives rise to the higher level in the first place, emergent nonclosure on the higher level will often demand most of the listener's attention. In Figure 6.4A, for example, the emerging ascent of the A–C–E–G on the second level causes the listener to evaluate the repeated E on the second beat in measure 3 as a minor foreground deviation. In other words, this E is a low-level feature lacking the strength to thwart for more than a passing moment the assimilating strength of the processive A–C–E–G ascent [P] underscored by the motivic repetition.

As one might imagine, conflicting asymmetry between melodic implications on lower levels and those emerging on higher levels creates considerable aesthetic interest. Such cognitive asymmetry raises the issue of control versus freedom—a struggle between the higher level's attempt to govern and suppress foreground melodic implication and the lower level's striving to break free of that suppression.

For the listener who prefers governance and control, the continuing melodic deviation of the lower level bucking the higher-level implications it establishes to begin with will seem cognitively "boisterous." Alternatively, if a listener finds individuality attractive, then overriding order and lower-level suppression will seem cognitively unappealing. I anthropomorphically characterize the aesthetic syntax of melody this way because it appears that many composers, like many listeners, stylistically prefer either the "control mode" or the "anarchy mode." Whatever the case, the "war" between conservation and originality is probably a syntactic necessity, a permanent and desirable feature of the aesthetic landscape.

To see further how low-level implications can go against emergent higher-level ones, consider Figure 6.5. Here, the ascending escape-tone patterns at the sixteenth-note level (the IPs [B♭–C–A, A–B♭–G; F♯–G–E, E–F♯–D] appear to be under the thumb of the higher-level descending linear processes [P; D–B♭–A–G, G–F♯–E–D]). Such talk, however, is purely metaphorical. For low-level implications always retain some inherent independence—without which higher levels would largely lack aesthetic-syntactic purpose. Indeed, if all low-level implications were not inherently independent, then a composer would gain nothing in writing deviant melodic tones, and listeners would have no reason to attend to them. Deviant melodic tones occur because within the bottom-up parametric system they always generate independent implications and thus carry with them the aesthetic potential to escape from the influence of emerging structures at higher levels.

Of course, in analyzing the syntactic possibilities of mutuality or conflict between levels, one must always consider the influence of scale step, a factor of extraopus learning in tonal style. Yet even scale step, as a top-down impingement of style, is an influence that can be, and frequently is, denied. Take the melody of Figure 6.6. Following a closed intervallic reversal [IR] at the beginning, the sudden, continuing ascent to the high B♭ [R] achieves aesthetic power because it denies the descent implied by the transformed

FIGURE 6.5 Bach: Organ Fugue, *BWV* 452, measures 1–2. 3 = dyad; IP = intervallic process; P = process.

FIGURE 6.6 Brahms: Sextet, op. 36 (*Allegro non troppo*), measures 2–13. IR = intervallic reversal; R = reversal; PIDP = a chain of process, intervallic duplication, and process; IDP = combination of intervallic duplication and process; (R) = retrospective reversal; aba = exact registral return.

higher-level structural tone on the altered scale step of E♭. That is, according to the listener's invoked scale-step learning, the structural tones of G–E♭ (mm. 1, 3) on the two-measure level should have reversed since the flatted sixth (E♭) implies a descent. Thus, when the high B♭ occurs instead—significantly at the apex of the crescendo—the listener experiences a moment of considerable aesthetic effect.[15]

To sum up, we see that in melodic hierarchies either mutuality or conflict of implied registral direction between adjacent levels may occur. Level enhancement via mutual registral implication between levels can take place when the implicative class of intervals differs (Figure 6.7A shows how the implication of the ascending G–E reversal interval [R] supports the continuation of the higher-level, descending structural tones of E–D) or when the class is the same (Figure 6.7B shows how the low-level B–D continuation underpins the rising structural tones of C–D on the next level). It is also the case that registral implication of same-class intervals (whether continuation or reversal) can conflict (see, for example, the conflicting descending implication in Figure 6.8A and the conflicting ascending implication in Figure 6.8B).

As Figure 6.9 shows, no type of realization is immune to such conflict. Indeed, it is the potential implicative conflicts between same-class and different-class intervals (according to the Intervallic and Registral Scales) that partly account for the ways that the parameter of melody generates a syntax of great perceptual richness and vitality. Otherwise, generating a perceptual universe of syntactic melodic asethetic from only a few kinds of basic structures would not be possible.

[15]*Scale step is not the only aesthetic influence affecting feedback and feedforward between levels. One must also take into account forces such as near registral return (aba*[1]*), not to mention discontiguous realization of process (see Narmour, 1990).*

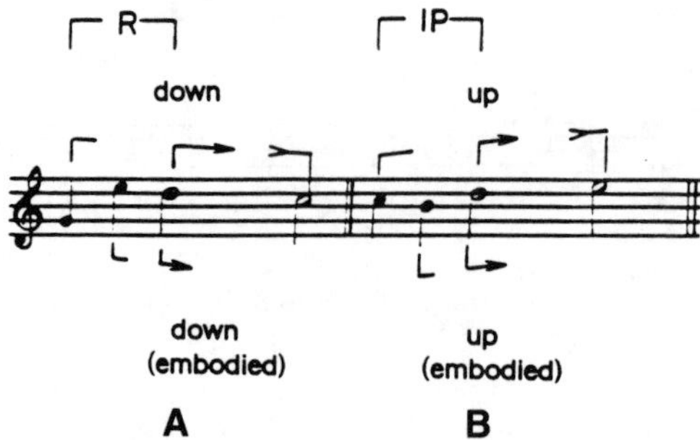

FIGURE 6.7 Figure 6.7A shows that both the embodied implication from the E–D of the low-level reversal [R] and the implication from the transformed structural tones on the higher level (G–D, also implying a reversal) are the same (down). Figure 6.7B shows that both the embodied implication from the B–D of the low-level intervallic process [IP] and the implication from the transformed structural tones on the higher level (C–D, implying processive continuation) are the same (up).

Recursion, Isomorphism, Reductionism: A Suggested Experimental Hypothesis

At this juncture, an important conclusion presents itself. For, if the theory here is correct, it means that concepts like recursion and isomorphism do not mechanically obtain in melodic hierarchies. That is, the idea that one invariant set of generative rules and one set of interpretations uniformly apply to similar shapes between different levels appears to be false. For the strength of, say, a reversal implication on a higher level depends on the registral direction that the transformed interval embodies from the foreground level. The initial and terminal transformed structural tones of an intervallic reversal like C–A–B [M6 + M2, IR], for example, may outline on the next level the implication of a plain reversal [R, C–B], yet the low-level registral direction embodied in the terminal structural tone (B) may perceptually also specify a continuation of registral direction (A–B implying C). Conversely, a strong reversal implication [R] stemming from the realization of an intervallic reversal [IR] on a lower level is also possible if, for instance, scale-step style intervenes (e.g., an ascending G–E–F,

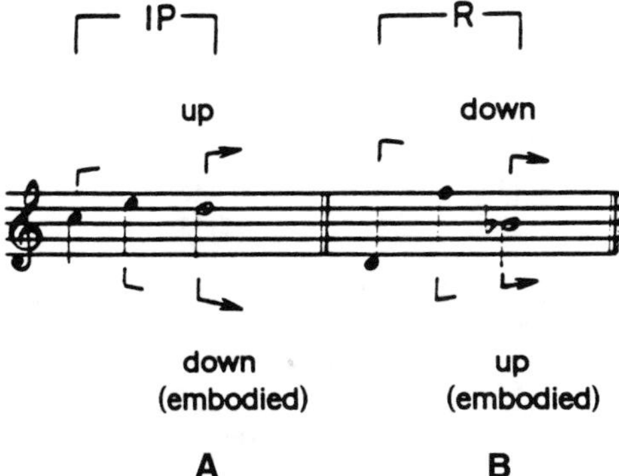

FIGURE 6.8 Figure 6.8A shows that the embodied implication from the E–D of the low-level intervallic process [IP] and the implication from the transformed structural tones on the higher level (C–D, implying a continuation) conflict (up versus down). Figure 6.8B shows that the embodied implication from the F–B♭ of the low-level reversal [R] and the implication from the transformed structural tones on the higher level (D–B♭, implying a downward reversal) conflict (down versus up).

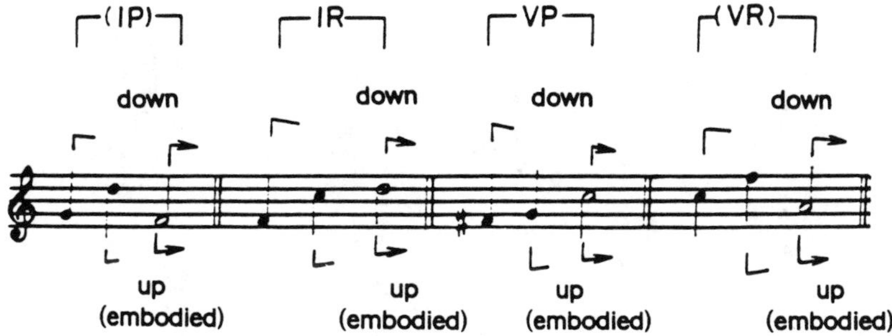

FIGURE 6.9 Implied registral conflicts between embodied implication and implication on a higher level. (Similar to those discussed in connection with Figure 6.8.)

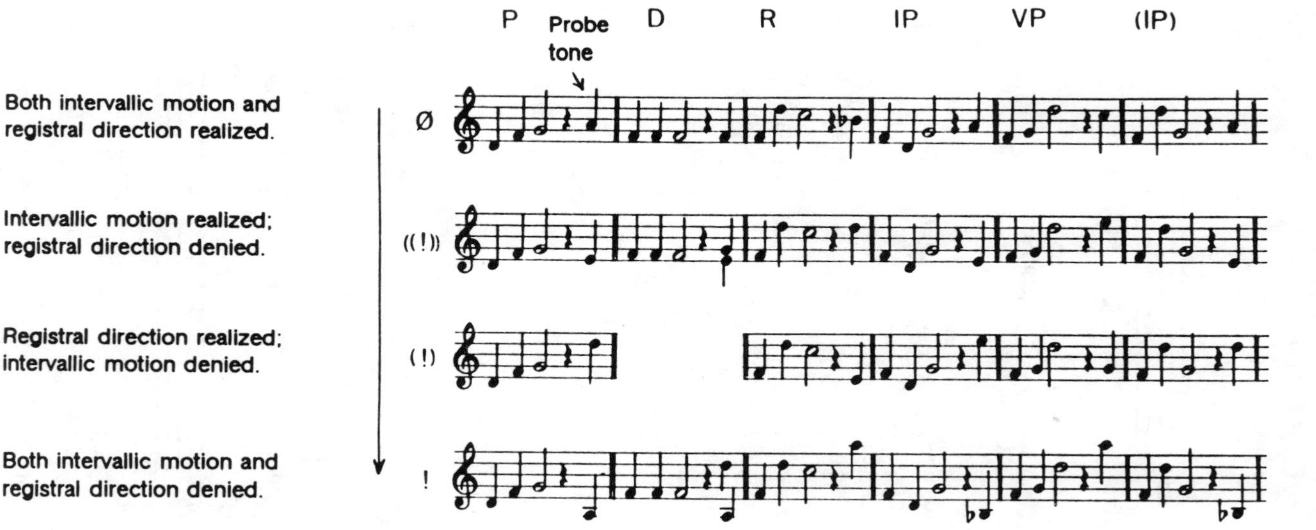

FIGURE 6.10 A suggested experimental hypothesis based on the theory. On the top row, the probe tone following each structure realizes both the embodied implication and the implication emerging from the transformed structural tones (hence, a null and no surprise). On the second row, the probe tone realizes only the implied intervallic motion from the embodied and transformed implications, therefore denying the implied registral implications (hence, a mild surprise). On the third row, the probe tone realizes only the implied registral motion, therefore denying the implied intervallic motion (hence, more of a surprise). And on the fourth row, the probe tone denies both the implied intervallic and registral motions from the embodied and transformed implications (hence, a complete surprise).

where the F is, say, the fourth degree of the key). In sum, the nature and strength of higher-level melodic implications always depend on what structurally lies beneath them and not just on a mechanistic application of a recursive set of rules.

To be sure, the extent to which a reductionistic application of the rules of the theory operate in any given melodic context is a matter for psychological experiment. For, since this model specifies degree of realization and thus degree of surprise inherent in the various types of melodic configurations, one should be able to determine whether listeners actually evaluate embodied implications on higher levels in the precise ways predicted by the theory. Using a probe-tone technique, I have illustrated in Figure 6.10 how one such experiment might be devised. Note that the half-notes here function to prepare the listener for the probe tone and to strengthen the closural cumulation of the quarter notes moving to the long notes.[16] The horizontal dimension shows six structures [P, D, R, IP, VP, (IP)] whose terminal structural tones (the closed half-notes) embody suppressed implications from various terminal intervals of realization. In each case, embodied implications are congruent with higher-level implications generated by the transformed structural tones.[17] The vertical dimension tracks degree of surprise, based on the extent to which probe tones realize or deny the embodied and transformed registral implications. As the vertical dimension shows, degree of surprise is theoretically predictable, depending on whether implication of registral direction, intervallic motion, or both are denied. Observe that denial of intervallic motion is ranked as more of a surprise than denial of registral direction (! = total surprise; (!) = partial surprise [two levels]; Ø = no surprise [one level]).

Whatever the results of such an experiment, aesthetic syntax must stem directly from the realization or denial of registral implication between adjacent levels. For the profound aesthetic syntactic experience that one has in listening to melody must cognitively depend, at least in part, on a hierarchical exchange of information.

[16] *Conflicting embodiment between registral implications of levels produces eight degrees of change instead of four (V in both low and higher levels can never be a Ø or a !). Of course, in devising examples for such an experiment, one would have to control the scale-step value of both the terminal tone of the pattern and the probe tone (whether leading tone, tonic, dominant, etc.). Virtual registral direction (up versus down) may also be a factor that would have to be considered in evaluating the results. In addition, the influence of implied harmony (stylistically invoked) must be taken into account.*

[17] *Duplication [D] is blank on the third line because both up and down deny its implied registral direction. That is, both up and down following duplication entail surprise, whether intervallic motion is similar [((!))] or differentiated [!]. Thus, duplication admits only three possibilities of denial instead of four.*

References

Deutsch, D. (1982). Grouping mechanisms in music. In D. Deutsch (Ed.), *The psychology of music* (pp. 99–134). New York: Academic Press.

Deutsch, D., & Feroe, J. (1981). The internal representation of pitch sequences in tonal music. *Psychological Review, 88,* 503–522.

Fodor, J. (1983). *Modularity of mind.* Cambridge, MA: MIT Press.

Francès, R. (1958). *La perception de la music* [The perception of music]. Paris: J. Vrin.

Francès, R. (1988). *The perception of music* (W. J. Dowling, Trans.). Hillsdale, NJ: Erlbaum.

Jones, M. R. (1981). Music as a stimulus for psychological motion. I. Some determinants of expectancies. *Psychomusicology, 1,* 34–51.

Jones, M. R. (1982). Music as a stimulus for psychological motion. II. An expectancy model. *Psychomusicology, 2,* 1–13.

Krumhansl, C. L. (1983). The psychological representation of musical pitch in a tonal context. *Cognitive Psychology, 11,* 346–74.

Krumhansl, C. L. (in press). Melodic structure: Theoretical and perceptual aspects. In J. Sundberg, L. Nord, & R. Carlson (Eds.), *Music, language, speech, and brain.* London: Macmillan.

Krumhansl, C. L., & Schellenberg, E. G. (1990, September). An empirical test of the implication-realization model. Paper presented at the conference on Music and the Cognitive Sciences, Cambridge, England.

Meyer, L. B. (1973). *Explaining music.* Berkeley: University of California Press.

Meyer, L. B. (1989). *Style and music: Theory, history, and ideology.* Philadelphia: University of Pennsylvania Press.

Narmour, E. (1977). *Beyond Schenkerism: The need for alternatives in music analysis.* Chicago: University of Chicago Press.

Narmour, E. (1983). Some major theoretical problems concerning the concept of hierarchy in the analysis of tonal music. *Music Perception, 1,* 129–99.

Narmour, E. (1989a). The 'genetic code' of melody: Cognitive structures generated by the implication-realization model. In S. McAdams & I. Deliège (Eds.), *Music and the cognitive sciences* (pp. 45–63). London: Harwood.

Narmour, E. (1989b). L'implication et la réalisation mélodique dans "La terrasse des audiences du clair de lune" de Debussy [Implication and melodic realization in "La terrasse des audiences du clair de lune" of Debussy]. *Analyse Musicale, 16,* 44–53.

Narmour, E. (1990). *The analysis and cognition of basic melodic structures: The implication-realization model.* Chicago: University of Chicago Press.

Narmour, E. (in press). *The analysis and cognition of melodic complexity: The implication-realization model.* Chicago: University of Chicago Press.

Pomerantz, J. R. (1981). Perceptual organization in information processing. In M. Kubovy & J. R. Pomerantz (Eds.), *Perceptual organization.* Hillsdale, NJ: Erlbaum.

Serafine, M. L. (1988). *Music as cognition.* New York: Columbia University Press.

CHAPTER 7

Attending to Musical Events

Mari Riess Jones

Communication is something that occurs among living things. In music at least three people can be involved: composer, performer, and listener. In this interactive setting, one prevailing aspect of artistic communication is the self-conscious way in which an artistic creation, here a musical event, reflects an artist's attempt to control the point of view or perspective of a listener. I suggest that an important and basic aspect of communication involves the way any musical or linguistic interaction effectively controls the attending of the parties involved and in so doing establishes for them a shared perspective from which to assess the event itself.

In this chapter I focus on a few aspects of attending and the ways these may be controlled by the structure of Western tonal music. The ideas that I offer are a direct outgrowth of a theoretical orientation that has motivated my research for more than 15 years. But they are new ideas that we are just beginning to evaluate.

Attending to Three-Dimensional Objects

Imagine inspecting a three-dimensional object such as Donatello's *David.* A viewer can examine this graceful statue from a variety of positions, each supporting a unique spatial perspective or point-of-view on the figure.[1]

The author is indebted to Marilyn Boltz, Helen Brown, and Susan Holleran for comments on earlier versions of this chapter.

[1] *I have in mind here Donatello's* final *statue of David, the most graceful in my mind.*

A viewer can draw close to the statue and inspect its detail. Surface changes in local curvature often compel us to move still closer or to advance in one direction or another to attend to additional details. I have called this sort of attending *analytic attending* (Jones & Boltz, 1989).

Alternatively, one can move farther away from the statue (keeping a fixed angle) and thereby achieve a perspective that includes the object's entire contour. In fact, if one moves far enough away, global shape dominates. In painting, French Impressionists exploited this fact to great effect. This sort of attending focuses on larger structural relations that specify form and overall shape. We might call this global attending, but when I take it into the time domain I call it *future-oriented attending.*

Analytic and future-oriented attending yield different perspectives on the same object. In many cases, they reflect mutually exclusive attending states: One cannot attend to the big picture (i.e., overall form) as one attends to detail. By the same token, it is difficult to attend to fine detail when one is focusing on an object's broad contours.

The structure of the object itself may determine our attending mode. Its shape and contour influence the times we move about it as well as the speed and proximity with which we encircle it. It also constrains what we "expect" to see at each successive view because it is a coherent whole. Nevertheless, at different times in interacting with this object we are attending to different parts of its structure and ignoring others. I hope to show that this idea of modes of attending has implications for model building in psychology. Specifically, it speaks to problems of structural ambiguity and mental representation. I argue that attending is flexibly selective, not only in space but in time, and that because this is so there may be no "right" and enduring mental representation of an object, musical or otherwise. Instead, I will suggest we are left largely with questions about different ways in which the structure of an artistic object controls our attending in space and time.

Attending to Musical Objects

I suggest that the structure of a three-dimensional visual object, such as a statue, can affect the movements and scanning patterns of an attender. But clearly there is a good deal of freedom for the viewer as well. The object is stationary and the attender is free to speed up, slow down, and move in and out to gain various perspectives on it. Gibson would love this setting (Gibson, 1979).

In music, the reverse is true. The object itself changes in time and the attender, the listener now, is stationary. But for this listener, composer and performer together offer up a series of perspectives on musical objects. The structure here is musical structure and it controls attending more directly than in the preceding example; it invites listeners to assume different perspectives on the same object as it turns, twists, deforms, expands, and transforms throughout the whole composition. The objects that I refer to here are melody-rhythm objects. These are musical events where the configurations based on relations in pitch and time with "shadings" offered by loudness and timbre form serially coherent integrated patterns.

The primary framing dimensions for musical perspectives involve time and pitch, the latter in part through its tonal functions.[2] Just as a viewer studies a statue close up, far away, or by encircling it and so on, so may a listener attend to a melody-rhythm configuration from different pitch-time perspectives. But the point I wish to emphasize is that an important part of perspective-taking in attending to music involves time and temporal relations (Jones, 1987a, 1987b). I will argue that attending is inherently temporal (Jones, 1976; Jones & Boltz, 1989).

In the context of music, attending to local detail involves attending over relatively small time periods. This is analytic attending. Attending over relatively large time periods is future-oriented attending. The latter permits attending to global changes in form and supports anticipating of longer range future events such as endings of phrases and movements. Furthermore, following the previous example, this distinction suggests that it is possible for a listener to attend to the local details of note-to-note changes but at times miss some larger aspect of form (e.g., an ABA structure) as well as the reverse.

Figure 7.1 clarifies why I emphasize the relative nature of this temporally based attending. By relative, I mean the size of some time interval taken with respect to a *referent* time period. The referent is called this because it is a temporal regularity in a musical pattern that entrains some anchoring time level in the listener, an implied beat or some optimal tempo. Relative to this time level, future-oriented time spans are large and analytic ones are small. Thus, in Figure 7.1 the referent level is depicted as sort of a middle-level time period. It serves as an anchoring and more-or-less stable recurrent periodicity for the attender, who is temporally sensitive.

Relativity here implies that other time intervals are gauged with respect to an anchoring time frame (the referent level). These other time intervals can figure in a more stable overall structure such as a time hierarchy, where the referent level assumes some middle level. By time interval, I mean any time period that is marked within an auditory

[2] *In tonal music the referent pitch is taken as the tonic. I do not consider tonality issues in this chapter.*

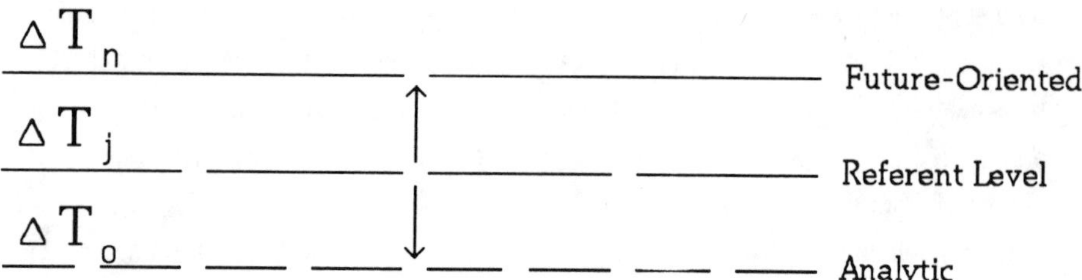

FIGURE 7.1 Three different levels of time which support different modes of attending. A long time span, ΔT_n, supports future-oriented attending; a medium time span, ΔT_j, is a referent level; and a relatively brief time span, ΔT_o, supports analytic attending.

event by some significant changes in pitch (including key), loudness, duration, and so forth. In any case, the type of change that outlines an interval is important and it varies with the level. For example, key and harmonic changes are more likely to mark relatively large time levels whereas simple loudness changes (tone onsets) tend to mark smaller levels.

The notation for time intervals shown in Figure 7.1 is standard (Jones, 1976, 1981; Jones & Boltz, 1989). An interval is ΔT with its level in some time structure subscripted by n ($n = 0,1, \ldots, j \ldots, n$) : ΔT_n. Relatively small time intervals correspond to smaller values of n. Because smaller intervals are systematically nested within larger time spans, this represents a recursive temporal embedding structure.

I suggest that in music there exist relations among the different embedded time levels that listeners come to rely on and which can be said to control attending. Indeed in auditory events, these embedding relations offer ways in which time structure controls attending. Such relations influence how and how effectively a listener engages in one or another attending mode. I am referring to the temporal nesting properties that characterize metric and phrasing relations in much of Western tonal music. In Figure 7.2, for example, a simple folk tune realizes a rather straightforward relation between the relatively long time spans of phrases and groups of phrases (here coincident with metric structure) and lower order time spans. The embedding structure here is expressed within a time hierarchy. Melodic phrases are marked by temporal (t) and tonal/harmonic (h) accents. Together all four phrases span a time level lasting 32 beats if we take the quarter note as a beat.

As shown in Figure 7.2, we can denote this higher level as ΔT_6 and the lower or beat note level as ΔT_1. The longer time spans such as ΔT_4 and ΔT_6 offer temporal perspectives for future-oriented attending while the shorter ones support analytic attending. But in addition to identifying these levels, because this tune embeds various time levels in a simple recursive structure I maintain that listeners should have little difficulty shifting attending between levels to acquire different temporal perspectives. One may effortlessly shift attending from relatively small time levels to phrase levels (i.e., from analytic attending to future-oriented attending).

This idea can be expressed more formally. If we assume that control of temporal attending is responsive to certain embedding properties in the event itself, then we can identify simple and complex event embedding structures (Jones, 1987; Jones & Boltz, 1989). Such embeddings can be expressed in a general recursive form where the value of the generator linking different time levels is also an index of embedding simplicity. This generator is a ratio rhythm generator and has been denoted C_t. In principle, it can take

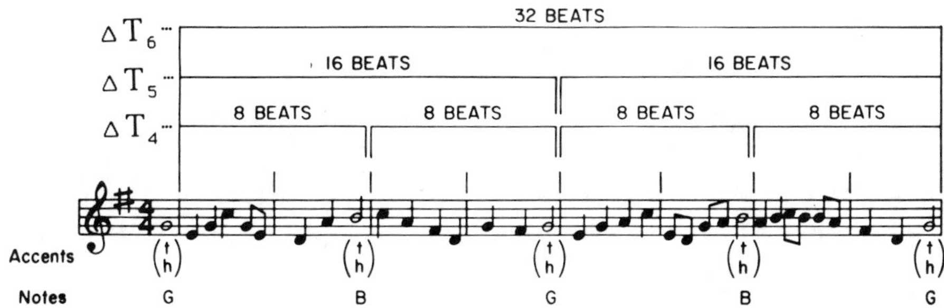

FIGURE 7.2 A hierarchical time structure associated with a simple folk tune. Assuming the beat period, a quarter note, is ΔT_1, longer time periods at higher levels, ΔT_4, ΔT_5, ΔT_6 are marked by different accents. Temporal accents are denoted t and harmonic accents h. From "Dynamic Attending and Responses to Time" by Mari Riess Jones and Marilyn Boltz, 1989, *Psychological Review, 96*, p. 469. Copyright 1989 by the American Psychological Association. Reprinted by permission.

on integer and noninteger ratio values, but small integer values of C_t reflect simpler and more coherent embeddings. With this rationale the relation between any level, j, and some other level, n, is $\Delta T_n = \Delta T_j\, C_t^{n-j}$.

The simplest embedding scheme has a C_t value of 2. An example of such a scheme is the time hierarchy in Figure 7.2. To illustrate, the time span of the highest time level, ΔT_6, can be determined from the one beat level by this expression: $\Delta T_6 = \Delta T_1 2^5$ or 32 beats. Any time interval, ΔT_n, becomes a time level that can potentially support attending. The generator, C_t, suggests how various embedded time levels are recursively linked.

In summary, two parameters describe the way musical structure might control attending. These involve, respectively: (a) the time interval that realizes some attending mode (analytic or future-oriented), ΔT_n; and (b) the ratio time generator that expresses embedding relationships in the surrounding temporal context, C_t. Together, these parameters reflect two basic ideas about time-based attending to music. The first is that attending itself can realize different temporal perspectives (future-oriented or analytic) with future-oriented attending focusing on melodic structure at the phrase level and analytic attending opening up pitch changes over the individual note level. The second is that musical contexts differ in the extent to which they support shifts in attentional perspectives, with temporally complex contexts discouraging attentional flexibility. Both of these ideas have been developed more extensively elsewhere (e.g., Jones & Boltz, 1989). My purpose here is to demonstrate how the idea of attending modes relates to earlier theory and research and at the same time points to new directions for the future.

Relationship to Prior Theory and Research

In the context of a rhythmic attending analysis, I suggested in 1976 that there is a psychological dependency between pitch structure and time (Jones, 1976). This was expressed, in part, as an expectancy hypothesis about the way people abstract relational invariants of pitch change and time in some ongoing (music-like) pattern. I assumed that a listener abstracts certain invariant relations present in the unfolding melody-rhythm context of a tune and uses these relations generatively to extend attending in pitch space and time. The gist of this idea is that listeners "use" pitch/time relationships to anticipate the "where" of pitch and "when" of time in an ongoing event.

A second and closely related idea was that of a serial integration region (SIR). In 1976, I argued that not only do people effectively target attending to particular regions in pitch-space and time, but that in fact there is a space-time neighborhood that defines boundaries of the most expected events. In music, a SIR is a neighborhood in pitch-space and time that reflects the most coherent extensions of current pitch/time relations unfolding in a pattern. Its boundaries are measured in terms of pitch distances and time intervals. I assumed those events (tones) realizing simple extensions of current structure would be more readily integrated into an ongoing pattern structure, whereas events outside such boundaries would be less readily incorporated. Indeed, it would be surprising if an event fell outside a SIR.

Let me first enlarge on the concept of expectancy in light of ideas about modes of attending. Let us assume that an expectancy depends on the listener's current mode of attending; that is, it depends on the time level over which a listener is selectively attending. This suggests that multiple expectancies are possible depending on the particular time level within a pattern to which a listener attunes. Beyond this it also acknowledges that at each level of an embedding structure, pitch and time relations co-constrain one another. An expectancy reflects the psychological abstraction of such pitch/time constraints at a given level of musical structure. Thus, in Figure 7.2, if one is engaged in future-oriented attending one can expect the tonic at the ends of certain phrases, namely after 16 or 32 beats. On the other hand, over smaller time periods different kinds of expectancies about pitch relations obtain.

An example taken from Narmour (1977) illustrates this idea. Figure 7.3 is a simplified version of implications (which I take to be expectancies) proposed by Narmour for a fragment of *Soldier's March* by Schumann. Notice that two different expectations are outlined for the first note in the second measure, namely G and E. According the present analysis, I suggest that each of these extrapolations of the ongoing pattern is time bound, tied to respectively different time frames. The former expectancy is based on a larger time span than the latter. Thus, if a listener is relying primarily upon the larger time span, then extrapolated pitch relations will depend on the tonic triad, namely B to D to G; but if a listener is analytically attending at the note-to-note level, or relying on the smaller time period to target attending in time, then the expected pitch will be based on a timed extrapolation of B to C to D and finally to E. In principle, it should be possible to bias a listener in such situations to attend over one or another time level and so manifest one or another expectation by manipulating the time structure of the surrounding context.

One consequence of linking the potential for multiple pitch expectancies to different time bases is that it not only forces a theorist to incorporate time into formal descriptions of event and attentional structure but also has implications for approaching the

FIGURE 7.3 Two different time levels associated respectively with different levels of melodic structure. From *Beyond Schenkerism* (p. 190) by E. Narmour, 1977, Chicago: University of Chicago. Copyright 1977 by the University of Chicago. Reprinted by permission.

problem of mental representation and structural ambiguity. It suggests that listeners can attend to the same event from different perspectives and so arrive at different expectancies about the same object. One's evaluation of a given pitch event is predicated on one's mode of attending.

This enlargement of the idea of expectancies leads readily to the second way in which I connect the 1976 framework to the present one. With regard to the SIR, I simply maintain that its size is proportional to the event time level that currently controls attending. This hypothesis was implied by the SIR concept in 1976 but not developed. Here I make explicit the idea that the size of the SIR increases with level in a temporal embedding structure so that, all other things equal, the SIR is larger for future-oriented attending than for analytic attending. Figure 7.4 shows two different SIRs, one based on a relatively small time interval, ΔT_1, and one based on a slightly larger one, ΔT_2, both derived from different ways of attending to the preceding context. The circled "E" stands for an expected pitch-time event based on extrapolated pattern relations.

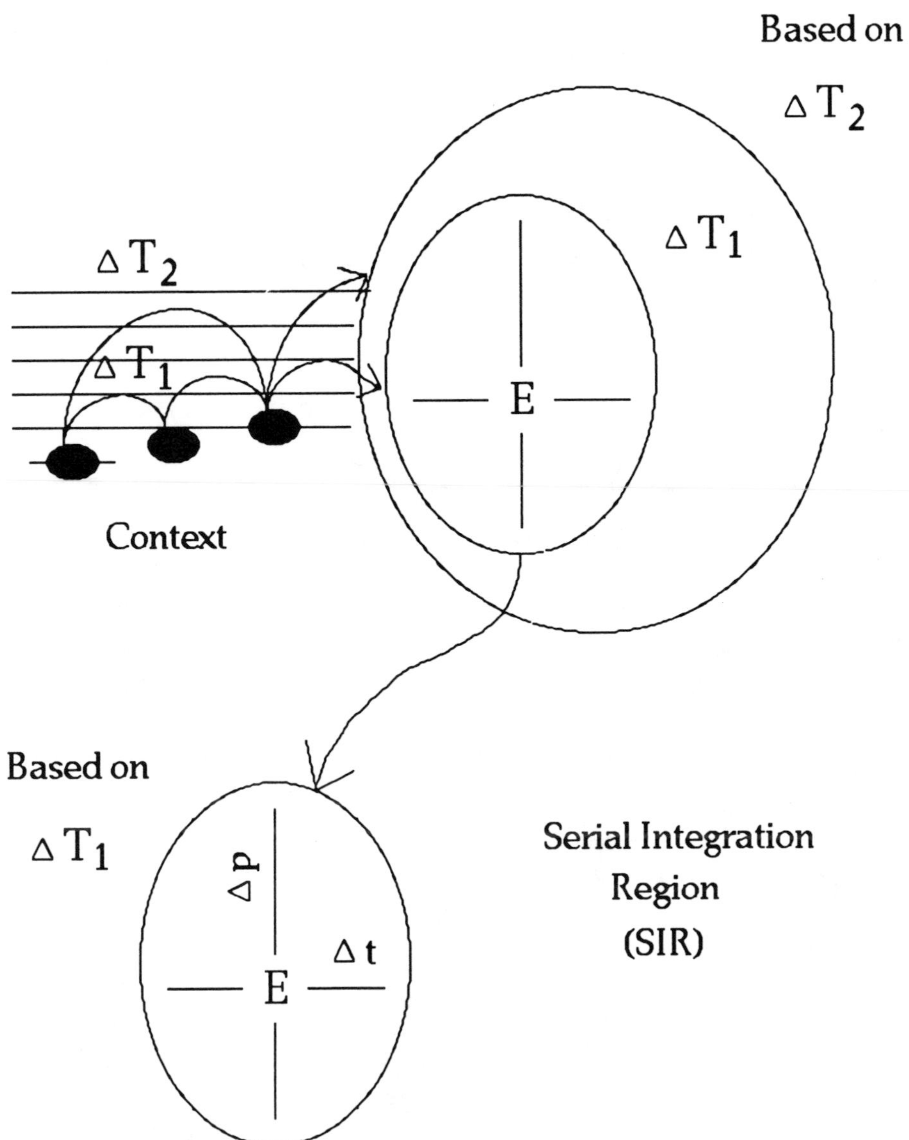

FIGURE 7.4 Two serial integration regions, determined respectively at time periods ΔT_1 and ΔT_2. Encircled "E" stands for an expected point in pitch space and time.

Extending this idea to the three different time levels already discussed, we find in Figure 7.5 that the size of the SIR increases as we move from analytic through referent level to levels of future-oriented attending. Similarly, because the SIR changes with level, this means that what can be integrated into the ongoing pattern and what constitutes a "surprise" changes with level and mode of attending.

Suggestive evidence for this sort of analysis of music-like events is selectively summarized in Table 7.1. This is a sample of studies pertinent to the supposition that expectancies and SIRs may exist at different attending levels.

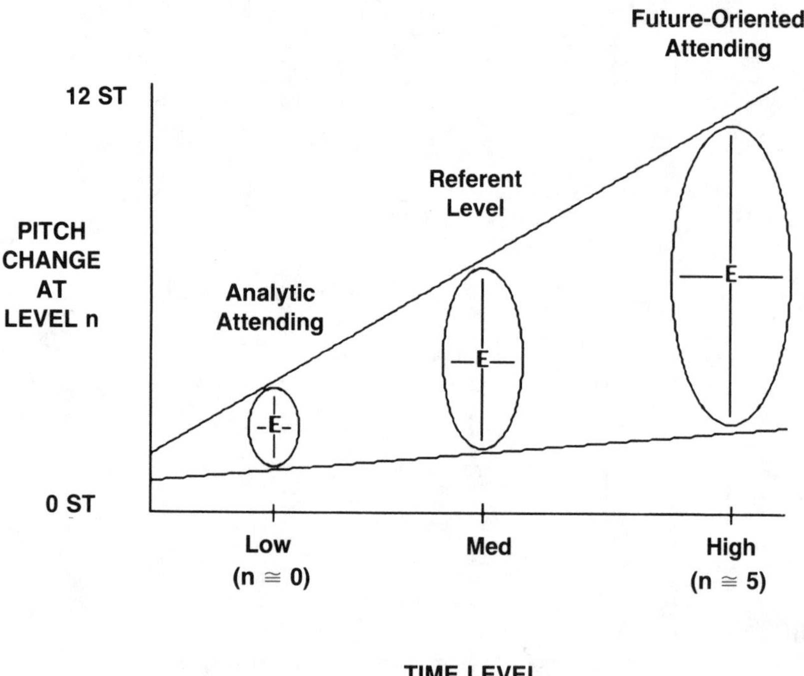

FIGURE 7.5 Serial integration regions associated with time levels underlying three different attending levels, future-oriented, referent level, and analytic attending.

TABLE 7.1
Evidence For Serial Integration Regions

Time Level	Attending Mode	Evidence
Low	Analytic	Auditory streams • Bregman & Campbell, 1971 • van Noorden, 1975 • Jones, Maser, & Kidd, 1978
Medium	Referent	Captor effects • Bregman & Rudnicky, 1975 • Jones, Kidd, & Wetzel, 1981 • Dowling, Lung, & Herrbold, 1987
High	Future-oriented temporal	Extrapolation • Jones & Boltz, 1989 • Boltz, 1989

Let's begin by reviewing some evidence for expectancies at the level of analytic attending. This comes from work on auditory pattern streaming. The classic work here is that of Bregman (e.g., Bregman & Campbell, 1971; Bregman, 1990) and van Noorden (1975). With smaller time intervals, namely those typically associated with the onset to onset time intervals of adjacent melodic tones, it is common to find that streaming is more likely at faster rates and when the pitch intervals between these tones are large. *Streaming* refers to the phenomenal breakup of a series of tones into two or more seemingly co-occurring serial patterns. For example, if one listens to a serial pattern consisting of tones from two different pitch sets, xi and yj, ordered serially as $x1$ $y1$ $x2$ $y2$ $x3$ $y3$ $x4$ $y4$ ... it is more likely to be "heard" as two overlapping streams, namely, $x1$ $x2$ $x3$ $x4$ ... and $y1$ $y2$ $y3$ $y4$ ... if the two pitch sets are separated by many semitones and if it occurs at a rapid rate. In general, the streaming research indicates that a listener's ability to integrate successive pitches to form a single coherent melody declines as the magnitude of ΔT decreases.

Research on the captor effect is related to streaming. The *captor effect* refers to the observation that certain tones from one stream will be phenomenally assimilated (captured) into another stream. This research suggests that an important factor in capture involves the relative time properties of the two streams; in particular tones are more likely to be integrated into a captor stream if they fall on implied beats of the captor stream. This speaks to the role of time periods that hover around some referent level. In 1981, my students and I (Jones, Kidd, & Wetzel, 1981) showed that people are better at detecting similar pitch relations among tones when the tones involved are predictable in time (i.e., on a beat implied by the larger context). This technique has been used more recently by Dowling and his colleagues (Dowling, Lung, & Herrbold, 1987) to provide corroborating evidence for a SIR. They used interleaved melodies that occurred at rates of 6 to 8 tones per second. Listeners had to detect/identify familiar target tunes like *Frère Jacques* that were hidden in larger tonal contexts as shown in Figure 7.6. Here every other tone functions as a distractor; solid circles form the target tune whose notes occur at rates of four per second. Most importantly, target melodies were presented so that their tones occurred either *on* or *off* the implied beat (i.e., at the expected time or not).

In one study, Dowling and his colleagues also varied the pitch of distractors to be close (hence in the SIR) or far (outside the SIR) from the target's pitches as shown in Figure 7.6. The tonality of distractors was also varied factorially, but it did not affect performance (consistent with the idea that SIR boundaries reflect pitch interval not tonal distances at these levels), and so I focus on their results concerning joint effects of pitch and time intervals.

If the serial integration region concept is a reasonable one, then people should be best at identifying hidden target tunes when: (a) distractors are far from the targets in pitch; and (b) target tones fall on the implied beat. Table 7.2 shows that this is precisely what Dowling et al., found, thus confirming earlier findings of Jones et al., and supporting the idea of a SIR.

At the referent level if we consider the idea of implied beat level, we must acknowledge that this level is defined in part by the larger context a listener is experiencing. Is there any converging evidence for the influence of context on captor effect results? There is and it is instructive. In the Jones, Kidd, and Wetzel (1981) studies as well as many others in our lab we have found that the extent to which listeners display clear pitch/time expectancies depends on temporal properties of the entire experimental context! Specifically, it depends on the way one experimentally manipulates a temporal variable (tempo, meter, or rhythm). When a temporal variable is treated as a within-subjects variable so that, over the course of a session, a listener experiences many different levels of, say, arbitrarily related tempi or rhythms, and so forth, then his or her attentional entrainment to any one time level appears to fail; in these cases clear-cut expectancies about pitch relations also wash out. On the other hand, when a temporal variable is manipulated as a between-subjects variable so that the listener experiences

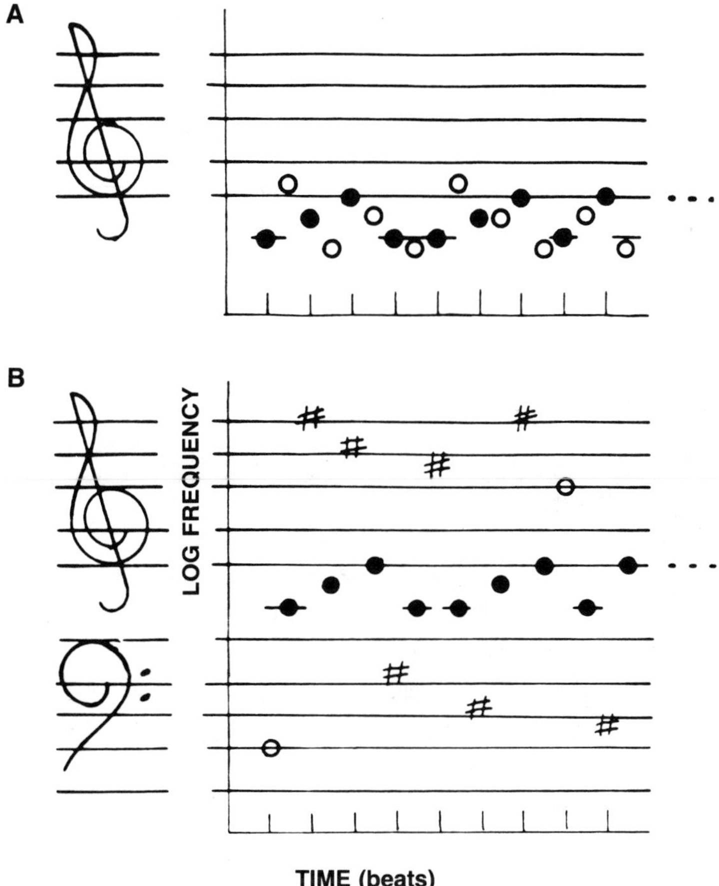

FIGURE 7.6 Sample stimuli from Experiment 1 of Dowling, Lung, and Herrbold (1987) illustrating some of their conditions. Implicit beats are indicated on the abscissa. (Figure 7.6A represents target notes [•] *on* the beat, with tonal distractors [○] *off* the beat interleaved in the same pitch range as targets. Figure 7.6B represents target notes *off* the beat with nontonal distractors [○ and ♯] in separate pitch ranges.) From "Aiming Attention in Pitch and Time in the Perception of Interleaved Melodies," by W. J. Dowling, K. M. Lung, and S. Herrbold, 1987, *Perception and Psychophysics, 41*, p. 646. Copyright 1987 by the Psychonomic Society, Inc. Reprinted by permission.

TABLE 7.2
Performance as a Function of Target Timing and Pitch Range of Distractors in Experiment 1 of Dowling, Lung, and Herrbold (1987)

	Target Timing	
	On Beat	**Off Beat**
Distractor Range:		
Inside Target Range	.84	.71
Outside Target Range	.90	.88

.50 = chance
1.00 = perfect

Note. From "Aiming Attention in Pitch and Time in the Perception of Interleaved Melodies" by W. J. Dowling, K. M. Lung, and S. Herrbold, 1987, *Perception and Psychophysics, 41*, p. 647. Copyright 1987 by the Psychonomic Society, Inc. Reprinted by permission.

only a single recurrent tempo or rhythm, and so forth, then entrainment of attending rhythms is facilitated. Predictably, given a rhythmic attending account, specific expectancies about pitch changes also become more evident. It was only in the latter conditions, for example, that Jones et al. found strong evidence for the captor effect. Intuitively all of this makes sense. Just as listeners rely on a more global context to get some sort of a reference beat in music, so in an experimental session it is impossible for them to ignore the timing implications of stimuli presented on neighboring trials in an experimental session (see also Kidd, Boltz & Jones, 1984; Jones, 1984). The complexity of a larger temporal context can determine how effectively a listener attunes to any one time level.

Finally, as we move up the temporal embedding hierarchy to relatively long time levels we find less research directly concerned with the structure and function of time levels on attending. At these levels, the distinctions suggested by the SIR and its boundaries are less critical because the SIR has been defined with respect to pitch interval differences. Instead, issues of temporal context and of prior pitch relations that control attending become more important. Investigations here remain to be done.

Directions for Future Research: Future-Oriented Attending

Traditionally, the concern of theorists and experimentalists with higher levels of structure have focused on descriptions of mental representations of musical events, often with the aim of determining which grammar and what set of pitch relations might explain the listeners' encodings of whole phrases or passages of a musical event. But I would maintain that without a corresponding concern for the time structure of the event and the way a temporal context guides a listener's attending over one or another time level, the search for the "right" mental representation of a musical creation will be in vain. If listeners do shift attending to acquire different perspectives on the same event, then what is THE correct mental representation?

In both the 1976 framework and the current one, I assume that attending involves a synchroncity between graded attending rhythms and various time levels in the event itself. At different points in a composition we can synchronize one or more of these rhythms to relevant time levels within a musical event in order to track relationships at that level (this synchronicity has also been called *attunement*, Jones & Boltz, 1989). Given these assumptions, a number of preliminary questions arise that are related to future-oriented attending and attending modes in general.

Marilyn Boltz and I have recently addressed two of these questions. This is the research indicated in Table 7.1 as support for the future-oriented attending mode, the least studied temporal level of attending. We formulated our questions in terms of the two parameters of temporal event structure mentioned earlier:

1. Do listeners have a sense of the time properties associated with the more global musical structure involving phrases and groups of phrases, namely of longer time span values of ΔT_n?
2. Does temporal context, as indexed by the relative durations of phrases, and hence by C_t, affect the listener's sense of these larger temporal spans?

The first question addressed the psychological reality of future-oriented attending and in particular a listener's attunements to higher order time intervals associated with whole musical phrases. We aimed to show that people do in fact attune to these time intervals in a way that is consistent with the hypothesis of synchronization of attending rhythms over relatively large event time spans. To answer this question experimentally we asked listeners to essentially "complete" certain higher-order time spans associated with final phrases in simple folk tunes.

The second question addressed the extent to which listeners might actually be able to anticipate accurately the duration of some phrase in a melody as a result of its larger temporal context. A number of factors might influence whether listeners engage in future-oriented or analytic attending, among these structural predictability, familiarity, tempo, arousal level, and listening goals (Boltz, 1991). But structural predictability or coherence provided by the temporal context is an important one, one that composers undoubtedly rely on to control the listener's shifts in attentional perspective, and this is directly related to the recursive time structure of a musical event. If recursive time structure controls attending, it should be more difficult to anticipate temporal "completions" in events where embedded time levels are related in a complex fashion. There is already evidence that polyrhythmic events with complex time ratios are more difficult in certain perceptual-motor tasks (Handel, 1984; Klapp et al., 1985). For example, Klapp et al. found that people were less accurate in predicting "when" a cycle of a polyrhythm will end when the event was based on a complex time ratio.

So to address the second question, Marilyn Boltz and I attempted to systematically manipulate future-oriented attending by varying temporal context. We attempted to manipulate temporal context in such a way as to induce people to expect melodic phrases to end on time, early or late. If listeners are tracking relations at the phrase level, then we reasoned that adjusting the relative timing of phrases would change expectancies about when a subsequent melodic phrase should end.

Figure 7.7 shows some of the modified folk tune segments we used. The Original tune (Figure 7.7A) displays fairly simple temporal embeddings throughout. However, we complicated its time structure in other conditions shown in Figure 7.7B (Early) and 7.7C (Late). Notice that while the temporal structure of phrases is the same in the first half of all three melodies (the rhythm generator has a ratio of 2; i.e., $C_t = 2$), they differ with respect to durations of third and fourth phrases. If this rhythm generator is applied to the third phrase of each tune, then it generates three different predictions for the expected length of the final (fourth) phrase in Original, Early, and Late conditions, respectively. These predictions are shown in Figure 7.7; E denotes the predicted (expected) time of the final tonic that completes the last phrase. Thus, listeners should expect the final tonic to occur on time in the Original tune, early in the Early tune, and late in the Late tune.

To test these predictions, we presented musical segments to musically sophisticated listeners, but we lopped off the final three tones in all cases. Subjects never heard any of these tunes intact. We asked them to tell us when the final tonic should occur by pressing a hand-held button at precisely the time they expected the tonic to occur. This means that they were required to extrapolate (complete) relatively long time spans, in the neighborhood of 1,000 ms or more. We recorded their extrapolation times as a measure of future-oriented attending.

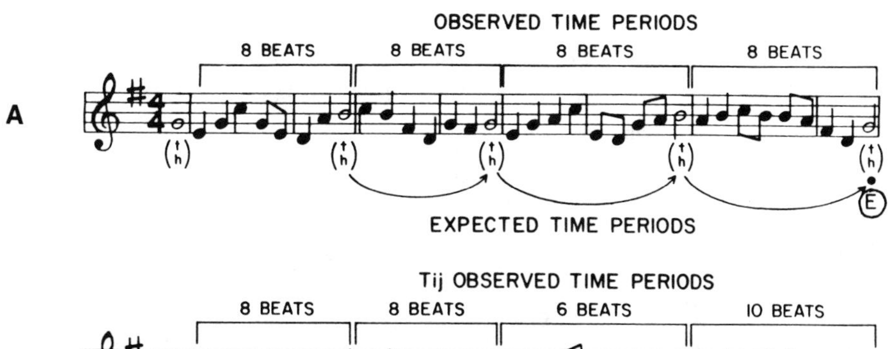

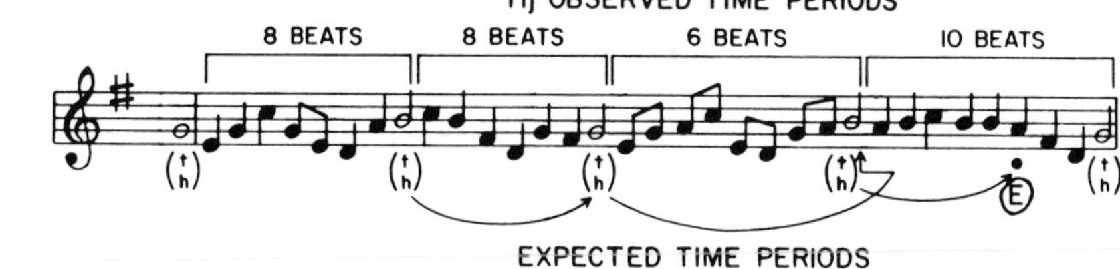

FIGURE 7.7 Samples of stimulus patterns used in Experiment 2 of Jones and Boltz (1989). Temporal (t) and harmonic (h) end accents mark musical phrases. E denotes expected time of final tonic as a function of temporal context (i.e., relative timing of phrases for each of three conditions) (Figure 7.7A represents the original stimulus pattern. Figure 7.7B represents the early stimulus pattern. Figure 7.7C represents the late stimulus pattern.) From "Dynamic Attending and Responses to Time" by Mari Riess Jones and Marilyn Boltz, 1989, *Psychological Review, 96*, p. 478. Copyright 1989 by the American Psychological Association. Reprinted by permission.

The results are shown in Table 7.3. In terms of median accuracy listeners were best, and indeed quite good, with the Original tune. And as predicted, listeners anticipated a short final phrase with the Early condition and a long final phrase with the Late condition. These and related findings that we have recently collected (e.g., Boltz, 1989) suggest tentative answers to questions posed earlier:

1. People do have a sense of the more global time structure of a musical event that is fairly precisely synchronized with the event itself as suggested by the future-oriented attending mode; and
2. People are responsive as well to the relative time constraints among phrases in the context of these events and this larger context systematically influences when they expect future events to occur.

Conclusions

I have suggested that an elementary aspect of musical communication involves establishing a perspective. In music, this perspective involves the time structure of an event, and it may be possible for listeners to achieve different temporal perspectives by relying on different attending modes (e.g., analytic or future-oriented). Implied in this analysis is the idea that attending is flexible, meaning that a listener can attend alternately over relatively short and relatively long time spans to track different sorts of relations in an unfolding composition. A listener's acceptance of one or another perspective may be partly under the control of the composer, via the score, and partly modulated by artistic devices of the performer, but ideally it is a *shared* perspective and this is the essence of communication.

TABLE 7.3
Judged Time to Ending*
(Extrapolations)

	Original	Early	Late
Median Accuracy (MS)	−46	−301	+309

*Relative to true ending time

Note. From "Dynamic Attending and Responses to Time" by M. R. Jones and M. Boltz, 1989, *Psychological Review, 96,* p. 484.

If this is so, then theories that posit a single psychological representation of a musical piece are incorrect. We have seen that music, as with language, may be indeterminate, affording multiple interpretations (e.g., see Kraut, chapter 2, and Palmer, chapter 15, this volume). In fact, often we can identify multiple descriptions and expectancies associated with the same musical event. While these may shrink to a very few when we consider the constraints imposed by time level, a prevailing context that shapes attending, it remains true that at different times or for different listeners the effective structure becomes determined by the particular attending mode. This being so, the real questions then, that should concern us involve the way musical structure guides attending.

References

Boltz, M. (1989). Perceiving the end: Effects of tonal relationships on melodic completion. *Journal of Experimental Psychology: Human Perception and Performance, 15,* 749–761.

Boltz, M. (1991). Time estimation and attentional perspective. *Perception and Psychophysics, 49,* 422–433.

Bregman, A. S. (1990). *Auditory scene analysis.* Cambridge, MA: MIT.

Bregman, A. S., & Campbell, J. (1971). Primary auditory stream segregation and perception of order in rapid sequences of tones. *Journal of Experimental Psychology, 89,* 244–249.

Bregman, A. S., & Rudnicky, A. (1975). Auditory segregation: Stream or streams? *Journal of Experimental Psychology: Human Perception and Performance, 1,* 263–267.

Dowling, W. J., Lung, K. M., & Herrbold, S. (1987). Aiming attention in pitch and time in the perception of interleaved melodies. *Perception and Psychophysics, 41,* 642–656.

Gibson, J. J. (1979). *The ecological approach to visual perception.* Boston: Houghton-Mifflin.

Handel, S. (1984). Using polyrhythms to study rhythm. *Music Perception, 1,* 465–484.

Jones, M. R. (1976). Time, our lost dimension: Toward a new theory of perception, attention, and memory. *Psychological Review, 83,* 323–335.

Jones, M. R. (1981). Only time can tell. *Critical Inquiry,* Spring, 1981, 557–576.

Jones, M. R. (1984). The patterning of time and its effects on perceiving. *Annals of New York Academy of Science, 423,* 158–167.

Jones, M. R. (1987a). Perspectives on musical time. In A. Gabrielsson (Ed.), *Action and perception in rhythm and music* (pp. 153–175). Stockholm, Sweden: Royal Swedish Academy of Music.

Jones, M. R. (1987b). Dynamic pattern structure in music: Recent theory and research. *Perception & Psychophysics, 41* (6), 621–634.

Jones, M. R., & Boltz, M. (1989). Dynamic attending and responses to time. *Psychological Review, 96,* 459–491.

Jones, M. R., Kidd, G. R., & Wetzel, R. (1981). Evidence for rhythmic attention. *Journal of Experimental Psychology: Human Perception and Performance, 7,* 1059–1073.

Jones, M. R., Maser, D. J., & Kidd, G. R. (1978). Rate and structure in memory for auditory patterns. *Memory and Cognition, 6*, 246–258.

Kidd, G., Boltz, M., & Jones, M. R. (1984). Some effects of rhythmic context on melody recognition. *American Journal of Psychology, 97*, 153–173.

Klapp, S. T., Hill, M., Tyler, J., Martin, Z., Jagacinski, R., & Jones, M. R. (1985). On marching to two different drummers: Perceptual aspects of the difficulties. *Journal of Experimental Psychology: Human Perception and Performance, 11*, 814–827.

Narmour, E. (1977). *Beyond Schenkerism.* Chicago: University of Chicago.

Van Noorden, L. P. A. S. (1975). *Temporal coherence in the perception of tone sequences.* Unpublished doctoral dissertation, Eindhoven University of Technology.

PART THREE

Pitch and the Function of Tonality

Introduction

Pitch and the way listeners respond to its multiple relationships in music have been the focus of the vast majority of theoretical and experimental investigations in music cognition. This fact notwithstanding, the very concept of "tonality" itself is a difficult construct to define and has been the subject of some disagreement.

In general, tonality in Western music reflects musical conventions which play on special sets of pitch relations, especially those established by three chords, the tonic, dominant, and subdominant. The result is a highly relativistic pitch system in which one note somehow functions as a reference frame for others.

In this section we find different perspectives on this relativistic system. In chapter 8, Diana Deutsch raises some fundamental questions about our percepts of pitch and pitch intervals themselves. Chapters 9, 10, and 11 are concerned with tonality, its discovery, and its psychological shape in music.

The essence of Deutsch's claim and supporting research is that competent listeners may disagree profoundly about what they are hearing when presented with exactly the same stimulus. Using the tritone interval, outlined by Shepard tones, Deutsch shows that one listener will hear it as an ascending interval, while another will hear it as descending. This "tritone paradox" presents difficulties for mental representations of pitch that assume two orthogonal dimensions of tone height and tone chroma (e.g., as in helical descriptions). Deutsch provocatively suggests that these perceptual differences relate to a listener's speaking voice frequency.

Helen Brown (chapter 9) and David Butler (chapter 10) both address theoretical problems inherent in moving from pitch descriptions at this fundamental level to those associated with tonality. Indeed, they ask how listeners, without the aid of a visual score, discover the key of a piece of music to which they are listening. They, too, raise questions about static descriptions of pitch because these fail to incorporate important information on which listeners rely to disambiguate an aural sound pattern with respect to its tonality. Both the presence of rare intervals, such as the tritone, and the temporal ordering of these intervals in the unfolding piece are critical tonal information.

Using a tonal hierarchy representation as a foundation, Fred Lerdahl (chapter 11) offers a pitch-space model to extend the conditions for tonal stability first mentioned in his 1983 book with Ray Jackendoff. Combining this with pitch reduction analyses, he shows the paths through pitch space, defined at three different levels, which are implied in the musical events of two Chopin preludes.

CHAPTER 8

The Tritone Paradox: Implications for the Representation and Communication of Pitch Structures

Diana Deutsch

Much has been written concerning strategies employed by composers and performers to communicate their musical ideas. A substantial body of music analysis and criticism is concerned with the stylistic strategies used by composers to convey a sense of completion, surprise, confusion, and so on (see, for example, L. B. Meyer, 1973, 1990). Another body of literature concerns devices used by performers to emphasize the composer's intentions, such as deviations from exact reproduction of the notated score (see, for example, Palmer, chapter 15, and Shaffer, chapter 16, this volume).

This chapter is concerned with musical communication at a different level. It is generally assumed that competent listeners will agree as to what musical sounds are being presented; disagreements are considered to be based on differences in reaction to, or interpretation of, these sounds. This assumption is an eminently reasonable one. However, we here document the case of a simple musical pattern for which substantial perceptual differences between listeners emerge. This pattern, together with its properties, is known as the *tritone paradox* (Deutsch, 1986, 1987; Deutsch, Kuyper, & Fisher,

1987). Although work on this pattern has so far been performed only with artificially contrived tones, it serves to illustrate that we cannot assume that perceptual agreement always exists.

A further issue raised by findings on the tritone paradox concerns the ways in which pitch structures are represented by the listener. In particular, the model of pitch as a geometrically regular helix is discussed, and it is shown that perception of the tritone paradox cannot be accommodated in this model.

Finally, it is shown that perception of the tritone paradox is related to the speech characteristics of the listener. First, a significant correlation has been found between the way the pattern is perceived and the range of fundamental frequencies of the listener's speaking voice. Second, a significant difference in perception of the pattern has been found between a group of listeners who grew up in the south of England and those who grew up in California. These findings indicate that the same, culturally acquired pitch template influences both speech production and perception of this musical pattern.

Pitch Class and Perceived Height

It is generally agreed that tones that are separated by octaves (i.e., whose fundamental frequencies stand in the ratio of 2:1) have a strong perceptual similarity (Babbitt, 1960, 1965; Demany & Armand, 1984; Deutsch, 1969, 1973; Forte, 1973; Humphreys, 1939; Shepard, 1964, 1965, 1982; Ward & Burns, 1982; Westergaard, 1975). The system of notation for the Western musical scale acknowledges this similarity, in that tones that are separated by octaves are given the same name (F, G♯, A, and so on). Tones with the same name are regarded as being in the same pitch class (for example, D3, D4, and D5 are all regarded as being in pitch class D).

Given such considerations, it has been proposed that pitch varies along two separable dimensions. First, the monotonic dimension of height defines its position on a continuum extending from high to low. Second, the circular dimension of pitch class defines its position within the octave (Bachem, 1948; Charbonneau & Risset, 1973; Demany & Armand, 1984; Deutsch, 1969, 1973, 1982; M. Meyer, 1904; Nakajima, Tsumura, Matsuura, Minami, & Teranishi, 1988; Ohgushi, 1985; Revesz, 1913; Risset, 1971; Ruckmick, 1929; Shepard, 1964, 1965, 1982; Ueda & Ohgushi, 1987; Ward & Burns, 1982). This proposal has, in turn, led to the characterization of pitch as a geometrically regular helix, in which the entire structure maps onto itself by transposition (Figure 8.1; see, in particular, Shepard, 1964, 1965, 1982, and earlier work by Drobisch, 1952).

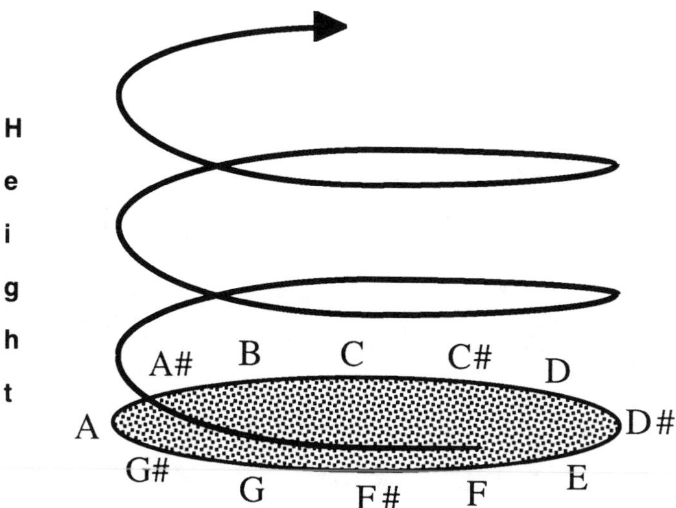

FIGURE 8.1 Representation of pitch as a geometrically regular helix.

Now, as Shepard (1964) noted, this model leads to a very interesting possibility: By suppressing the monotonic component of height, leaving only the circular component of pitch class, one should be able to map all tones that are an octave apart onto the same tone, which would then have a well-defined pitch class of an indeterminate height. In this way, the tonal helix would be collapsed into a circle, and judgments of pitch would become entirely circular.

To produce a formal demonstration of this orthogonality, Shepard generated a specially contrived set of tones. Each tone was composed of 10 sinusoids which stood in octave relation, and their amplitudes were determined by a fixed, bell-shaped spectral envelope. The pitch classes of the tones were then varied by moving the sinusoidal components up or down in log frequency, keeping the position and the shape of the envelope constant. It was argued that since the spectral center of gravity remained fixed, the perceived heights of these tones would remain constant in face of variations in pitch class.

To test this prediction, Shepard presented subjects with ordered pairs of such tones, and they judged whether each pair formed an ascending or a descending pattern. He found that when the tones within a pair were separated by one or two steps along the pitch class circle (Figure 8.2), judgments depended almost entirely on proximity. So when, for example, D♯ was played followed by E, subjects heard the pattern as ascending, since the shorter distance here was clockwise. And when instead G♯ was followed by G, subjects heard the pattern as descending, since the shorter distance here was counterclockwise. Thus when the pitch class circle was traversed in semitone steps, judgements of height were indeed completely circular: C♯ was heard as being higher than C, D as higher than C♯, D♯ as higher than E, . . . , B as higher than A♯, C as higher than B, and so on. Later work, by researchers such as Burns (1981), Nakajima et al. (1988), Pollack (1978), Risset (1971), Schroeder (1986), and Ueda and Ohgushi (1987) have further explored and qualified this proximity effect.

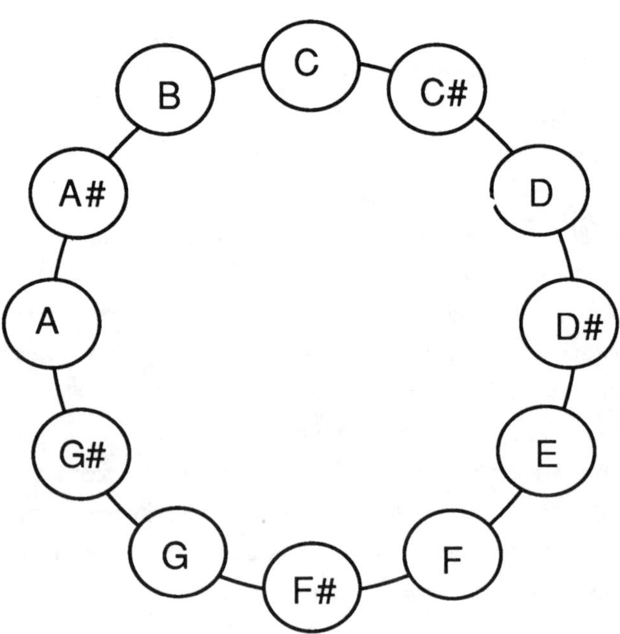

FIGURE 8.2 The pitch class circle.

Shepard (1964) also found that as the distance between the tones along the pitch class circle increased, the tendency to follow by proximity lessened, and when the tones within the pair were separated by a half-octave, ascending and descending judgments occurred equally often. He concluded that the dimensions of pitch class and height were indeed orthogonal. As he wrote: "As anticipated, then, diametrically opposed tones are ambiguous and the second tone is judged to be higher about as often as it is judged to be lower" (1964, p. 2351).

And further:

> tonality [meaning pitch class] seems quite analogous to the attribute of being clockwise or counterclockwise. One of two nearby points on a circle can be said to be clockwise from the other; but it makes no sense to say how clockwise a single point is absolutely (1964, p. 2351).

However, certain problems of interpretation arise here. First, where judgments were largely determined by proximity, any influence of pitch class on perceived height could have been overwhelmed by the proximity factor. In other situations, proximity has been shown to be a very powerful cue in the organization of pitch materials, often overriding other cues (see, for example, Bregman, 1978; Butler, 1979; Deutsch, 1975a, 1975b; and van Noorden, 1975). Second, since the data here were averaged across pitch classes, any influence of pitch class on perceived height would have been lost in the averaging process. The issue of orthogonality was therefore left unresolved in Shepard's study.

The Tritone Paradox

Given these considerations, we may ask what happens when two tones are presented that are separated by a half-octave (or tritone), so that the same distance between them along the pitch class circle is traversed in either direction. In this case we shall not average across pitch classes, or across subjects, and shall ask specifically what happens when, for example, C is played followed by F♯, or D followed by G♯, and so on. Will the circle of pitch classes be found to be flat with respect to height, as predicted from the assumption of orthogonality, or will an interaction between the two dimensions emerge?

In the first experiment to examine this issue, Deutsch (1986) presented subjects with just such tone pairs in random order, so that each of the 12 tones within the octave served equally often as the first tone of a pair. Subjects judged whether each pair of tones formed an ascending or a descending pattern.

The sounds used to generate these patterns were octave-related complexes, similar to those used by Shepard, except that the shape of the spectral envelope was slightly different,[1] and there were 6 sinusoidal components rather than 10. Figure 8.3 shows one such pair of tones. It can be seen that the components of the second tone were exactly equidistant from those of the first along the log frequency continuum, since the two tones were related by a half-octave. Each tone was 500 msec in duration, and there were no gaps between tones within a pair.

The tritone pairs were generated under envelopes which were placed at six different positions along the spectrum. The peaks of the spectral envelopes were C6, F♯5, C5, F♯4, C4, and F♯3, so that the envelopes were spaced at half-octave intervals, with peaks spanning a 2½ octave range. The envelope positions were varied in this fashion to control for interpretations based on the relative amplitudes or loudnesses of the components, and also to determine how well the phenomenon generalizes over the frequency spectrum. The 12 possible pitch-class pairings (C–F♯, C♯–D, . . . , B–F) were presented equally often under each of these six spectral envelopes.[2]

Figure 8.4 displays the results from one subject, averaged over two sessions. Judgments are plotted separately for tones generated under each of the six envelopes. It can be seen that for this subject the tones C♯, D, D♯, and E were heard as lower members of the tritone, and the tones F♯, G, G♯, A, A♯, and B were heard as higher members, for all positions of the spectral envelope. Thus if we envision this pattern as successively transposed up in semitone steps, beginning with C as the first tone of a pair, followed by C♯ as the first tone, and so on, the pattern was first heard ambiguously, then it was heard as ascending, and finally when F♯ was reached as the first tone, the pattern was heard as descending.

Figure 8.5 displays the results from a second subject, and it can be seen that these were virtually the converse of the first. Tones B, C, C♯, D, and D♯ were heard as higher

[1] *The general form of the equation describing the envelope is as follows:*

$$A(f) = 0.5 - 0.5\cos\left[\frac{2\pi}{\gamma}\log_{\beta}\left(\frac{f}{f_{min}}\right)\right] \qquad f_{min} \le f \le \beta^{\gamma} f_{min}$$

where (f) is the relative amplitude of a given sinusoid at frequency f Hz, β is the frequency ratio formed by adjacent sunusoids (thus for octave spacing, $\beta = 2$), γ is the number of β cycles spanned, and f_{min} is the minimum frequency for which the amplitude is nonzero. Thus the maximum frequency for which the amplitude is nonzero is $\gamma\beta$ cycles above f_{min}. Throughout, the values $\beta = 2$ and $\gamma = 6$ were used, so that the spectral envelope always spanned exactly 6 octaves, from f_{min} to 64 f_{min}.

[2] *Tones were generated by a VAX 11/780 computer, interfaced with a DSC-200 Audio Data Conversion System (16-bit, 48K sampling rate). The sounds were recorded and played back on a Sony PCM-F1 Digital Audio Processor, and the output was passed through a Crown D-60 amplifier and delivered to subjects binaurally through headphones (Grason-Stadler TDH-49, calibrated and matched) at a level of approximately 72 dB SPL.*

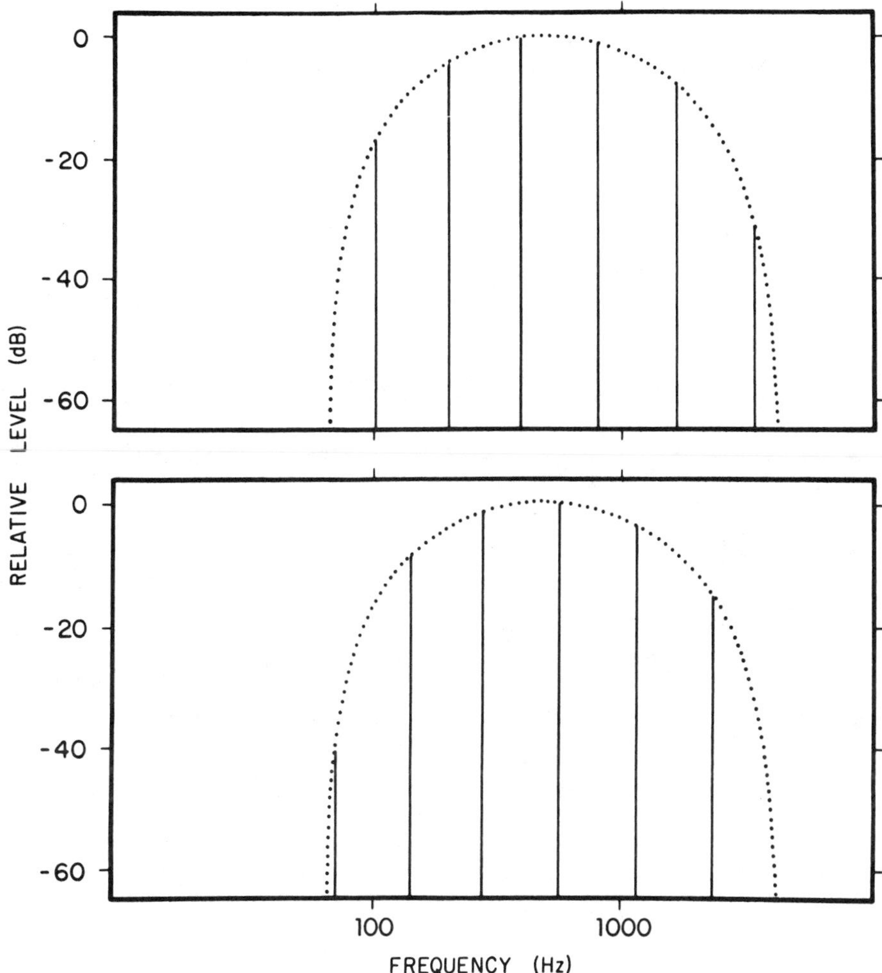

FIGURE 8.3 Spectral representation of a tone pair giving rise to the tritone paradox. The spectral envelope is here centered on C5. Upper graph represents a tone of pitch class D, and lower graph a tone of pitch class G♯.

members of the tritone, and tones F♯, G, G♯, and A as lower members, again for all positions of the spectral envelope. Thus if we envision the pattern as successively transposed up in semitone steps, it was first heard as descending, then when F♯ was reached as the first tone of the pair it was heard as ascending, and finally when B was reached it was heard as descending again.

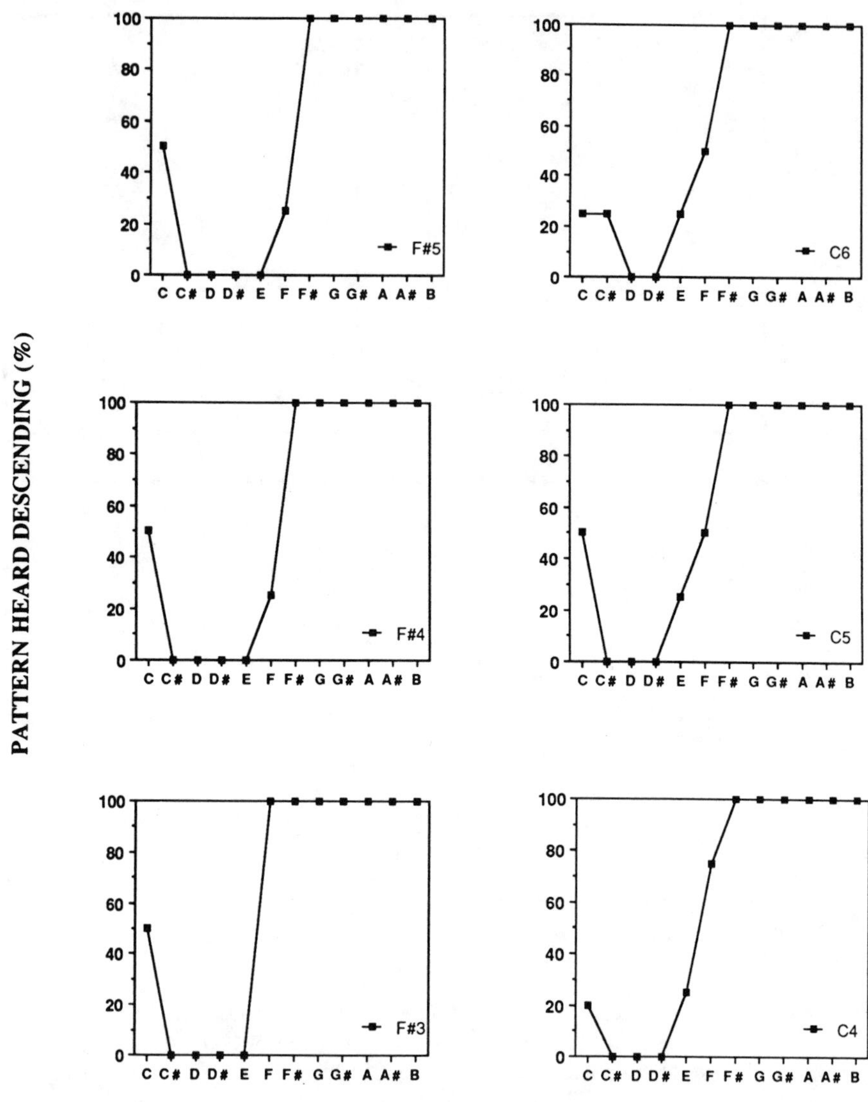

FIGURE 8.4 Percentages of judgments that a tritone pair formed a descending pattern, as a function of the pitch class of the first tone of the pair. Data from a first subject are shown, for tone pairs generated under six different spectral envelopes, and averaged over two sessions. Symbols C6, F♯5, C5, F♯4, C4, and F♯3 indicate peaks of spectral envelopes. (Data from Deutsch, 1986.)

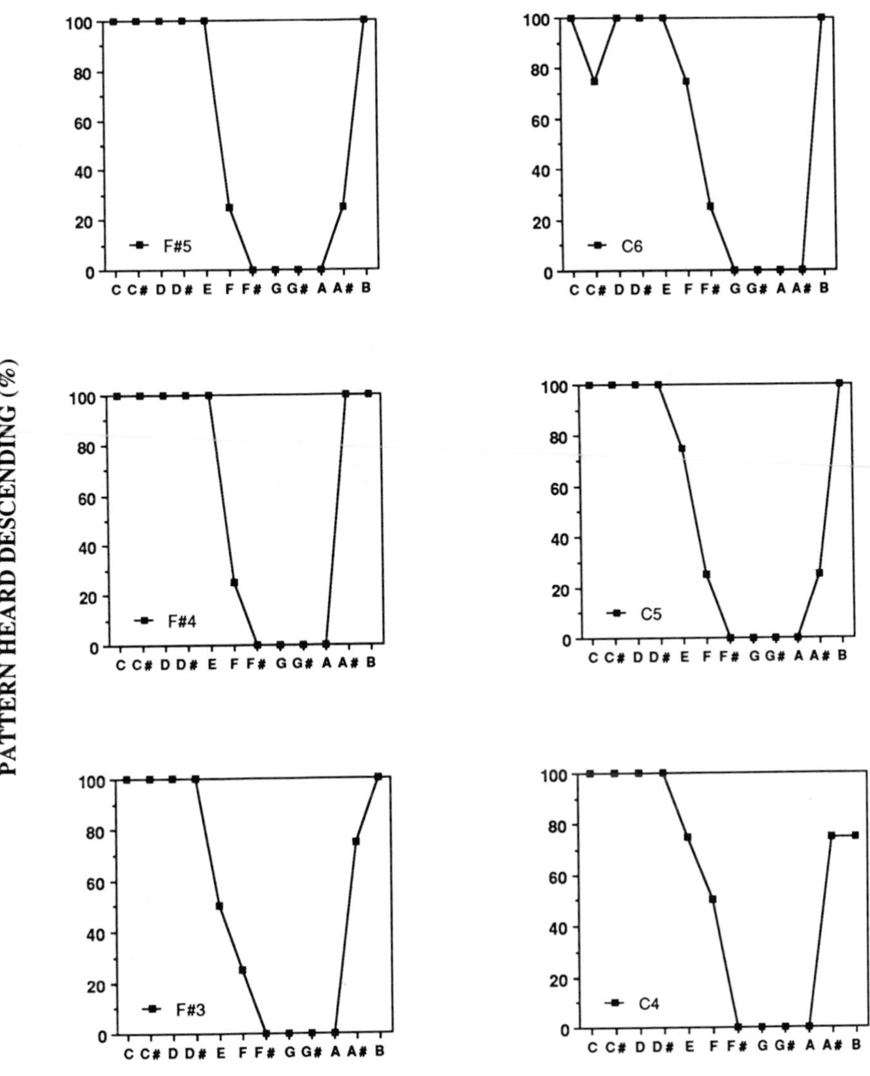

FIGURE 8.5 Percentages of judgments that a tone pair formed a descending pattern, as a function of the pitch class of the first tone of the pair. Data from a second subject are shown, for tone pairs generated under six different spectral envelopes, and averaged over two sessions. Symbols C6, F♯5, C5, F♯4, C4, and F♯3 indicate peaks of spectral envelopes. (Data from Deutsch, 1986.)

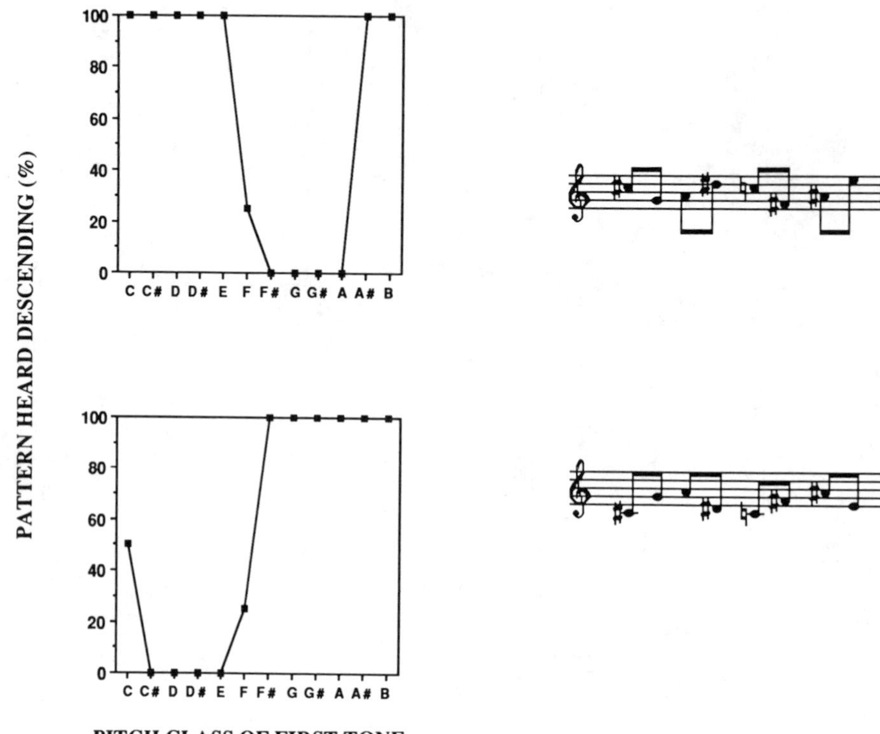

FIGURE 8.6 Graphs on the left show percentages of judgments that a tone pair formed a descending pattern as a function of the pitch class of the first tone of the pair. Data from the first and second subjects are displayed, for tone pairs generated under the spectral envelope centered on F♯4. Musical notation at the right indicates how these two subjects perceived the identical series C♯–G; A–D♯; C–F♯; A♯–E. (Data from Deutsch, 1986.)

Figure 8.6 displays the judgments from these two subjects together, taking those with the envelope centered on F♯4. It can be seen that for both subjects, as the pattern was transposed up in semitone steps, it was heard as moving first in one direction and then the other. However, for the most part, when the first subject perceived an ascending pattern, the second subject perceived a descending one, and vice versa. Thus extended patterns formed of such tone pairs were perceived by these two subjects as forming entirely different melodic contours. An example is given on the right hand part of Figure

8.6. (Indeed, a block of 12 trials can be regarded as an extended pattern of this general type.)

Figure 8.7 displays the results from another study, in which the percepts of four subjects were examined in detail. The data presented here were averaged over 12 spectral envelopes whose positions varied in ¼-octave steps over a 3-octave range and over nine experimental sessions. It can be seen that for each subject, judgments depended in an orderly fashion on the positions of the tones along the pitch class circle. However, the direction of this dependence varied from one subject to another. When the effects of envelope position were explored, the judgments of some subjects showed an interaction between pitch class and the relative amplitudes of the sinusoidal components, and others

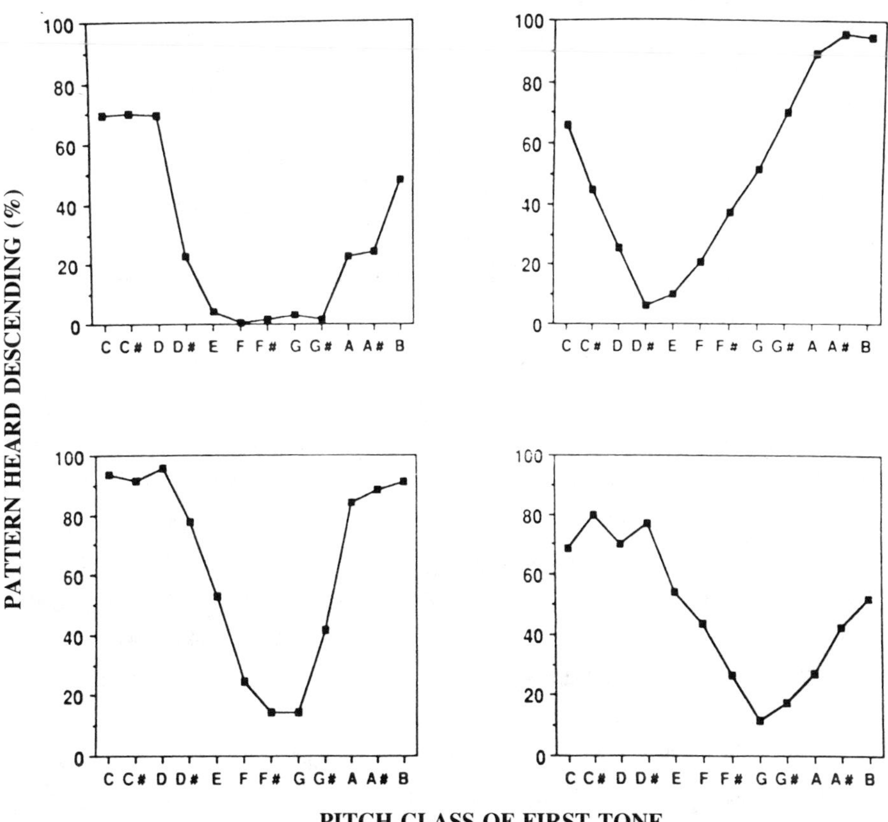

FIGURE 8.7 Percentages of judgments that a tone pair formed a descending pattern as a function of the pitch class of the first tone of the pair. Data from four subjects averaged over 12 spectral envelopes and over nine experimental sessions are displayed. (Data from Deutsch, 1987.)

between pitch class and overall height. However, neither interaction was necessarily present, and even when an interaction was found, its influence in absolute terms was generally a minor one (Deutsch, 1987).

One way to demonstrate this effect is to attach a variable-speed device to a tape recorder. Find someone who consistently hears one of the patterns in a particular way (say, the D–G♯ pattern as ascending, or else as descending). Then speed the tape up so that everything is transposed up a half-octave, and the D–G♯ pattern becomes G♯–D instead. As a result solely of this manipulation, the listener who had heard the pattern as ascending now hears it as descending , and the listener who had heard the pattern as descending now hears it as ascending. And analogously, the same result is achieved by slowing the tape down, so that everything is transposed down a half-octave.[3]

So far, the results from a few selected subjects have been described. We may then ask whether the effect exists in a general population, and also how it might be distributed within this population. To examine this question, a group of subjects was selected on the sole criteria that they were undergraduates at the University of California, San Diego, that they had normal hearing and that they were able to determine reliably whether pairs of sine wave tones formed ascending or descending patterns. Twenty-nine subjects were thus selected, and they each participated in a single session (Deutsch et al., 1987).

For each subject, the percentage of judgments that a tone pair formed a descending pattern was plotted as a function of the first tone of the pair. Such individual judgments were again strongly influenced by the positions of the tones along the pitch class circle; and yet again, the direction of this influence varied considerably from one subject to another.

In order to evaluate the prevalence of this effect in the subject population as a whole, the following procedure was employed. First, it was determined for each subject's scores whether the pitch class circle could be bisected so that none of the scores in the lower half of the circle were higher than any of the scores in the upper half. This criterion was fulfilled by the data from 22 of the 29 subjects. Next, an estimate was obtained of the probability of producing this result by chance: The proportion of random permutations of the scores which could be so characterized was determined by computer simulation. When averaged across all the subjects, this was found to be .027 per subject; thus

[3] *Because changing the speed on a tape recorder has other effects, this procedure is not recommended for formal experimentation.*

the probability of producing the combined result by chance was shown to be extremely small. Putting it another way, we should have expected no more than 1 of the 29 subjects to produce this ordering by chance; however, 22 of them did so. We can see, then, that the phenomenon exists to a highly significant extent in this general population.

To examine the relationship between pitch class and perceived height in this population as a whole, the orientation of the pitch class circle was normalized across subjects,[4] and the normalized data were averaged. The resultant plot is shown in Figure 8.8. It can be seen that a remarkably orderly relationship between pitch and perceived height was obtained.

We may next ask whether the orientation of the pitch class circle varied haphazardly across the subjects, or whether it was distributed within this population in an orderly fashion. To examine this question, the two pitch classes which stood at the peak of the normalized circle were tabulated for each subject, and the distribution of peak pitch classes within this population was determined. The resultant plot is displayed in Figure 8.9. It can be seen that an orderly bell-shaped distribution was obtained, and for the most part the pitch classes between B and D♯ were heard as higher and those between F and A were heard as lower.

An Interpretation of the Tritone Paradox

Before proposing an interpretation of the tritone paradox, we should emphasize that the employment of multiple spectral envelopes controlled for any simple explanations in terms of differences in the relative amplitudes or loudnesses of the individual sinusoidal components. Recently, the profiles relating pitch class to perceived height for the tritone pattern have been shown to be unrelated to patterns of relative loudness for the sinusoidal components of the tones when these were compared directly (Deutsch, in preparation, a). It has also been shown that the phenomenon can be produced by presenting the odd-numbered components of the octave-related complexes to one ear and the even-numbered components to the other ear. However, when either the odd-numbered or the even-numbered components were presented alone to both ears, the phenomenon did not

[4] *The normalization procedure was as follows: For each subject, the pitch class circle was first bisected so as to maximize the difference between the averaged scores for the two halves. The circle was then oriented so that the line of bisection was horizontal. The data were then retabulated, with the leftmost pitch class of the upper half of the normalized circle taking the first position, its clockwise neighbor taking the second, and so on, for all 12 positions.*

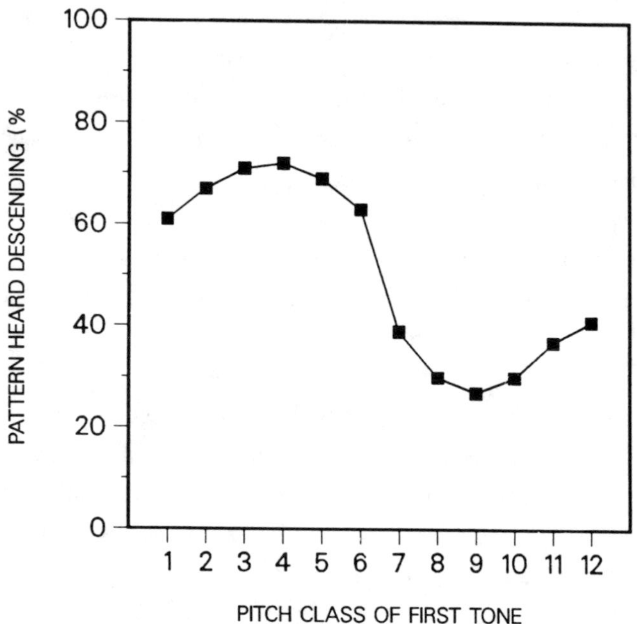

FIGURE 8.8 Percentages of judgments that a tone pair formed a descending pattern, averaged over a large group of subjects, with the orientation of the pitch class circle normalized across subjects. From "The Tritone Paradox: Its Presence and Form of Distribution in a General Population," by D. Deutsch, W. L. Kuyper, and Y. Fisher, 1987, *Music Perception, 5,* p. 86. Copyright 1987 by the Regents of the University of California. Reprinted by permission.

occur. Since the identical phenomenon can be produced by interactions between the inputs from the two ears, we may assume that it is not peripheral in origin (Deutsch, in preparation, b).

In another experiment, the distance between the sinusoidal components of each tone was stretched to a ratio of 2.01:1, so that the phase relationships between the components were constantly varying. This manipulation did not alter judgments of the tritone pattern, showing that the phenomenon cannot be attributed to the processing of phase

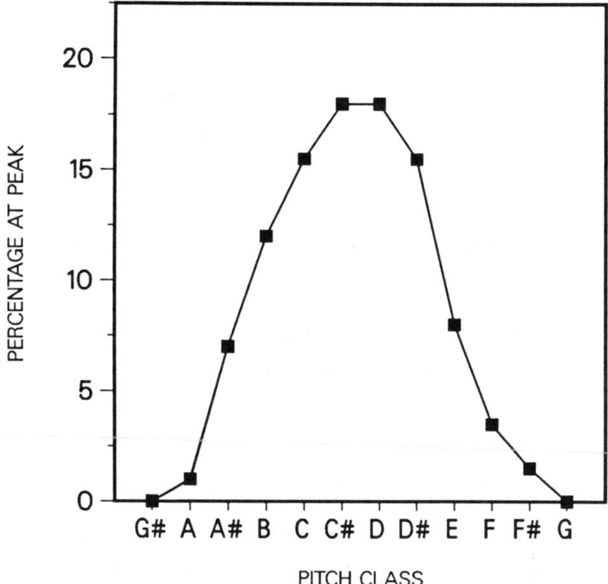

FIGURE 8.9 Distribution of peak pitch classes within a subject population. From "The Tritone Paradox: Its Presence and Form of Distribution in a General Population," by D. Deutsch, W. L. Kuyper, and Y. Fisher, 1987, *Music Perception, 5,* p. 88. Copyright 1987 by the Regents of the University of California. Reprinted by permission.

(Deutsch, 1988a). In yet another experiment, the tritone paradox was found to occur, at least for some listeners, with tones comprising full harmonic series, where the relative amplitudes of the odd and even harmonics were such as to produce ambiguities of perceived height. This phenomenon, therefore, is not confined to the use of tones that stand in octave or near-octave relation, but occurs also with tones that are closer in spectral composition to those of natural instruments (Deutsch, in preparation, c).

No correlate between the orientation of the pitch class circle with respect to height has been found with handedness or gender. Furthermore, no correlate with musical training has been found, either in terms of the size of the effect, or with its direction, or with the probability of obtaining it (see, for example, Deutsch et al., 1987). It would seem reasonable to hypothesize, therefore, that the phenomenon is extramusical in origin.

Recently, a study was undertaken to examine the hypothesis that perception of the tritone paradox may be related to the processing of speech sounds (Deutsch, North, & Ray, 1990). Specifically, it was conjectured that the listener develops a long-term representation of the range of fundamental frequencies of his or her speaking voice. This representation includes a delimitation of the octave band in which the largest proportion of these fundamental frequencies occurs, averaged over the long term. It was further conjectured that the pitch classes delimiting this octave band are taken by the listener as defining the highest position along the pitch class circle, and that this in turn determines the orientation of the circle with respect to height.

For example, consider a listener for whom the upper limit of the octave band for speech is between D4 and D♯4. According to the present hypothesis one would predict that the orientation of the pitch class circle, as manifested in judgments of the tritone paradox, would be such that the highest pitch classes would be close to D and D♯. Analogously, consider a listener for whom the upper limit of this speech band is between E3 and F3. One would predict that for this subject the pitch classes judged as highest would be close to E and F.

As a test of this hypothesis, nine subjects were selected who showed clear relationships between pitch class and perceived height for the tritone pattern. A 15-minute recording of spontaneous speech was taken from each subject. Fundamental frequency (F_0) estimates were then taken from these speech samples, and from these estimates the octave band containing the largest number of F_0 values was determined.[5]

Table 8.1 displays, for each subject, the pitch classes delimiting the octave band for speech, together with those defining the highest position along the pitch class circle as determined by judgments of the tritone paradox. As can be seen, for 8 of the 9 subjects, these two positions were separated by distances no greater than two semitones. Now since the largest possible unsigned distance between any two pitch classes is 6 semitones, there were 7 possible absolute distances, ranging from 0 to 6 semitones. The

[5]The following procedure was used: The samples were recorded into computer memory and band-pass filtered, with the low and high frequency cutoffs being 50 Hz and 1300 Hz for the female subjects, and 20 Hz and 650 Hz for the male subjects. F_0 estimates were then obtained, at 256 estimates per second, using the parallel processing scheme of Rabiner and Shafer (1978). Furthermore for each subject's speech samples the time-varying energy level of the signal was obtained. Only those F_0 estimates that were associated with levels no lower than 25 dB below the peak level were retained for further analysis. (This was to eliminate spurious F_0 estimates, such as those obtained during pauses in the flow of speech.) Finally, the F_0 estimates were allocated to semitone bins, with the center of each bin determined by the equal-tempered scale. Graphs were then made of the percentage occurrence of F_0 values in these semitone bins, and, thus, on a log frequency continuum.

TABLE 8.1
Pitch classes delimiting the octave band for speech, together with those defining highest position along the pitch class circle, tabulated by subject.

Subject	Limit of octave band for speech	Highest position along pitch class circle	Distance in semitones
AH	D♯–E	D–D♯	1
DM	D–D♯	D♯–E	1
DD	F–F♯	G–G♯	2
TT	D♯–E	D–D♯	1
MD	E–F	G♯–A	4
MC	A♯–B	C–C♯	2
MM			
ES	C–C♯	C–C♯	0
WB	D♯–E	D♯–E	0

Note. From "The Tritone Paradox: Correlate With the Listener's Vocal Range for Speech" by D. Deutsch, T. North, and L. Ray, 1990, *Music Perception, 7,* p. 381. Copyright 1990 by the Regents of the University of California. Reprinted by permission.

correspondence between the two sets of values was therefore statistically significant ($p = .04$, two-tailed, on a binomial test). A further representation of these findings is shown in Figure 8.10.

The results of this experiment are in accordance with the hypothesis that perception of the tritone paradox is based on a circular template which is related to the range of fundamental frequencies of the listener's own speaking voice. We may conjecture that such a correlate is acquired through learning: When presented with a series of pitch classes which are ambiguous with respect to height, the listener refers to an acquired circular template, in which the highest pitch classes are those at the upper end of his or her vocal range for speech.

Two versions of this hypothesis may be advanced. The more restricted version does not assume that the listener's vocal range for speech is itself determined by a learned template. The broader version assumes that such a template is acquired primarily for use in the generation and perception of speech itself. According to the second version, the statistical distributions of fundamental frequencies in speech should also be

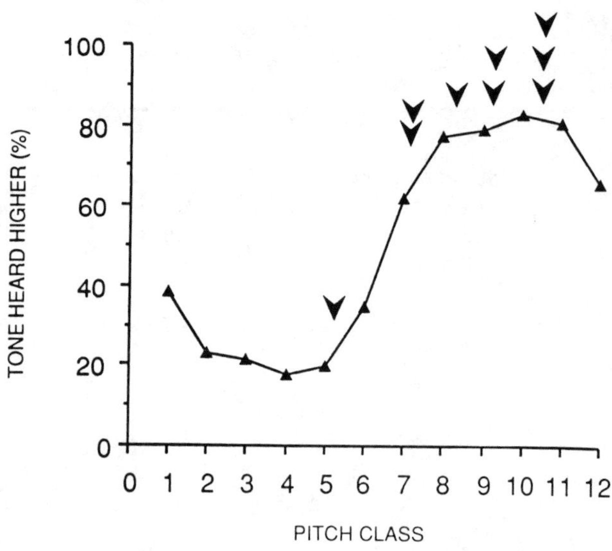

FIGURE 8.10 Percentage of judgments of a tone as the higher of a pair, with the orientation of the pitch class circle normalized across subjects.[4] The arrows indicate the position delimiting each subject's octave band for speech, in relation to the highest position along the pitch class circle. From "The Tritone Paradox: Correlate With the Listener's Vocal Range for Speech," by D. Deutsch, T. North, and L. Ray, 1990, *Music Perception, 7,* p. 382. Copyright 1990 by the Regents of the University of California. Reprinted by permission.

influenced by such a template, and might be expected to vary (in terms of pitch class) from one linguistic group to another. It also follows from this hypothesis that the distribution of peak pitch classes in perception of the tritone paradox should be orderly for any given linguistic group, but might be expected to vary across linguistic groups. Such an orderly distribution, implying a common template, was found by Deutsch et al. (1987) for a group of Californians (see Figure 8.9). Most recently, a significant difference in the distribution of peak pitch classes has been shown between a group of listeners who grew up in California and those who grew up in the south of England: Where the Californian group tended to hear the pattern as ascending the English group tended to hear it as descending, and vice versa. These findings indicated that the same, culturally acquired pitch template influences both speech production and perception of this musical pattern (Deutsch, 1991).[6]

Conclusions

The properties of the tritone paradox are highly unexpected on two grounds. First, the paradox provides a clear counterexample to the principle of invariance under transposition—a principle that has generally been considered to hold without exception. Second, it demonstrates that striking differences can occur between listeners in how even simple sound patterns are perceived.

Analogous findings have also been obtained with certain two-part patterns. When such patterns are transposed from one key to another, the relative heights of the different pitch classes are preserved, so that there results a perceived interchange of voices. Furthermore, when such patterns are presented in any given key, listeners differ radically in terms of which voice is heard as higher and which as lower, again reflecting different orientations of the pitch class circle with respect to height (Deutsch, Moore, & Dolson, 1986; Deutsch, 1988a).

The extent to which such effects occur in live musical situations remains to be documented. However, as described previously, these effects have been found to hold with other types of sound associated with registral ambiguities, including some whose spectra are considerably more similar to those of natural instruments than the octave-related complexes described here. It appears reasonable to assume, therefore, that phenomena such as these may occur in live musical situations, particularly in certain multi-voiced orchestral contexts.

The findings on the tritone paradox and related phenomena also have implications for the ways in which pitch structures are represented by the listener. Since for such patterns the relative heights of the different pitch classes remain unaltered in face of overall shifts in the frequency spectrum, they demonstrate that pitch class and perceived height are not orthogonal dimensions, as had been supposed. The findings

[6]*As a corollary, we should expect that, for a given linguistic group, the range of fundamental frequencies for male and female speakers should stand roughly in octave relation.*

therefore cannot be reconciled with the model of pitch as a geometrically regular helix as described earlier in this chapter.

For example, we can take a listener who perceives note G as higher and note C♯ as lower, regardless of the position of the spectral envelope. In Figure 8.11, the bracket on the right indicates a region along the height dimension which corresponds to a spectral envelope centered on F♯4. Within this region, note G should indeed be heard as higher and note C♯ as lower. But consider now the region along the height dimension indicated by the bracket on the left side of the figure, which corresponds to a spectral envelope centered on C5. According to this helical model, C♯ should now be heard as higher and G as lower. Yet the listener still hears G as higher and C♯ as lower, regardless of the shift in spectral region. Clearly, the model of pitch as a geometrically regular helix cannot accommodate this phenomenon (Deutsch, 1988b).

As a related point we can observe that the relative heights of two tones, as perceived by the listener, depend on the type of pattern presented. For example, with

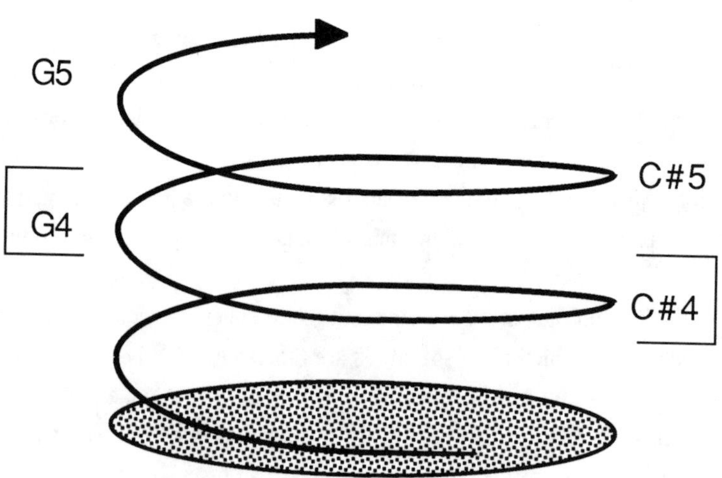

FIGURE 8.11 The relative heights of tones in different spectral regions, according to the model of pitch as a geometrically regular helix.

patterns of tones which stand in proximal relationships, such as those explored by Shepard and others, relative height is determined by proximity. However when proximity cannot be invoked, as with the tritone paradox, relative height instead depends on the absolute positions of the tones along the pitch class circle. Given this dependence on context, any representation of pitch as a rigid geometrical structure can be expected to run into difficulties as an explanatory device.

Another implication of the present findings for the representation of pitch structures is that although very few of us have absolute pitch, in the sense of being able to name notes that are presented in isolation, the large majority of us exhibit a form of absolute pitch in making judgments of this pattern, in that we hear notes as higher or as lower depending primarily on their pitch classes. Related work on key identification has been carried out by Terhardt and Ward (1982) and Terhardt and Seewann (1983). They found that musicians were able to judge whether or not a well-known passage was played in the correct key, even though most of the subjects denied having absolute pitch as conventionally defined. It appears, therefore, that absolute pitch is considerably more prevalent than had been assumed, at least in partial form.

Finally, the studies of Deutsch et al. (1990) and Deutsch (1991) provide what, to my knowledge, are the first demonstrations of correlates between the perception of a musical pattern on one hand and the listener's speech characteristics on the other. These correlates appear to account for differences between listeners in how certain aspects of music are perceived. Given that the differences obtained depended on linguistic dialect, we can assume that such differences are learned rather than innate. This may be contrasted with the strong handedness correlates that have been obtained with perception of the octave and scale illusions (Deutsch, 1974, 1975a, 1975b, 1983). These handedness correlates indicate that differences in music perception can also be based on innate differences at the neurological level.

The documentation of two distinct classes of musical pattern for which striking perceptual disagreements emerge leads us to wonder what other differences might also exist in music perception which have not yet been uncovered. Discourse concerning music is not precise enough for such differences to become manifest through normal communication, and it is only in laboratory situations that we can develop a clear idea of what the listener really hears. The possibility of genuine disagreement at the perceptual level should therefore be taken into account when considering the issue of communication between composer, performer, and listener.

References

Babbitt, M. (1960). Twelve-tone invariants as compositional determinants. *Musical Quarterly, 46,* 246–259.

Babbitt, M. (1965). The structure and function of music theory. *College Music Symposium, 5,* 10–21.

Bachem, A. (1948). Note on Neu's review of the literature on absolute pitch. *Psychological Bulletin, 45,* 161–162.

Bregman, A. S. (1978). The formation of auditory streams. In J. Requin (Ed.), *Attention and performance: VII* (pp. 63–76). Hillsdale, NJ: Erlbaum.

Burns, E. (1981). Circularity in relative pitch judgments for inharmonic tones: The Shepard demonstration revisited, again. *Perception and Psychophysics, 30,* 467–472.

Butler, D. (1979). A further study of melodic channeling. *Perception and Psychophysics, 25,* 264–268.

Charbonneau, G., & Risset, J. C. (1973). Circularité de jugements de hauteur sonore [Circularity in judgements of pitch height]. *Comptes Rendues de l'Académie des Sciences, Série B, 277,* 623.

Demany, L., & Armand, F. (1984). The perceptual reality of tone chroma in early infancy. *Journal of the Acoustical Society of America, 76,* 57–66.

Deutsch, D. (1969). Music recognition. *Psychological Review, 76,* 300–307.

Deutsch, D. (1973). Octave generalization of specific interference effects in memory for tonal pitch. *Perception and Psychophysics, 13,* 271–275.

Deutsch, D. (1974). An auditory illusion. *Nature, 251,* 307–309.

Deutsch, D. (1975a). Two-channel listening to musical scales. *Journal of the Acoustical Society of America, 157,* 1156–1160.

Deutsch, D. (1975b). Musical illusions. *Scientific American, 233,* 92–104.

Deutsch, D. (1982). The processing of pitch combinations. In D. Deutsch (Ed.), *The psychology of music* (pp. 271–316). NY: Academic Press.

Deutsch, D. (1983). The octave illusion in relation to handedness and familial handedness background. *Neuropsychologia,*Deutsch, D. (1986). A musical paradox. *Music Perception, 3,* 275–280.

Deutsch, D. (1987). The tritone paradox: Effects of spectral variables. *Perception and Psychophysics, 41,* 563–575.

Deutsch, D. (1988a). The semitone paradox. *Music Perception, 6,* 115–132.

Deutsch, D. (1988b). Pitch class and perceived height: Some paradoxes and their implications. In E. Narmour and R. Solie (Eds.), *Explorations in music, the arts, and ideas: Essays in honor of Leonard B. Meyer* (pp. 261–294). Stuyvesant: Pendragon Press.

Deutsch, D. (1991). The tritone paradox: An influence of language on music perception. *Music Perception, 8,* 335–347.

Deutsch, D. (in preparation, a). The tritone paradox in relation to patterns of relative loudness for the components of the tones.

Deutsch, D. (in preparation, b). The tritone paradox produced by central interactions.

Deutsch, D. (in preparation, c). The tritone paradox with tones comprising full harmonic series.

Deutsch, D., Kuyper, W. L., & Fisher, Y. (1987). The tritone paradox: Its presence and form of distribution in a general population. *Music Perception, 5,* 79–92.

Deutsch, D., Moore, F. R., & Dolson, M. (1986). The perceived height of octave-related complexes. *Journal of the Acoustical Society of America, 80,* 1346–1353.

Deutsch, D., North, T., & Ray, L. (1990). The tritone paradox: Correlate with the listener's vocal range for speech. *Music Perception, 7,* 371–384.

Drobisch, M. (1952). Über musikalische Tonbestimmung und Temperatur [Concerning perception of musical tones and temperature]. In S. Hirzel (Ed.), *Abhandlungen der Königlich sächsischen Gesellschaft der Wissenschaften zu Leipzig Vierter Band: Abhandlungen der mathematisch-physischen Classe* (pp. 3—121). Leipzig: Zweiter Band.

Forte, A. (1973). *The structure of atonal music.* New Haven: Yale University Press.

Humphreys, L. F. (1939). Generalization as a function of method of reinforcement. *Journal of Experimental Psychology, 25,* 361–372.

Meyer, M. (1904). On the attributes of the sensations. *Psychological Review, 11,* 83–103.

Nakajima, Y., Tsumura, T., Matsuura, S., Minami, H., & Teranishi, R. (1988). Dynamic pitch perception for complex tones derived from major triads. *Music Perception, 6,* 1–20.

Ohgushi, K. (1985). Circularity of the pitch of complex tones and its application. *Electronic Communications of Japan, Part 1, 68,* 1–10.

Pollack, I. (1978). Decoupling of auditory pitch and stimulus frequency: The Shepard demonstration revisited. *of speech signals.* Englewood Cliffs: Prentice Hall.

Revesz, G. (1913). *Zur grundlegung der Tonpsychologie* [On the foundations of the psychology of tones]. Leipzig: Feit.

Risset, J. C. (1971). Paradoxes de hauteur: Le concept de hauteur sonore n'est pas le meme pour tout le monde [Paradoxes of height: The concept of pitch is not the same for everyone]. In *Seventh International Congress of Acoustics* (p. 20). Budapest.

Ruckmick, C. A. (1929). A new classification of tonal qualities. *Psychological Review, 36,* 172–180.

Schroeder, M. R. (1986). Auditory paradox based on fractal waveform. *Journal of the Acoustical Society of America, 79,* 186–188.

Shepard, R. N. (1964). Circularity in judgments of relative pitch. *Journal of the Acoustical Society of America, 36,* 2345–2353.

Shepard, R. N. (1965). Approximation to uniform gradients of generalization by monotone transformations of scale. In D. I. Mostofsky (Ed.), *Stimulus generalization* (pp. 94–110). Stanford, CA: Stanford University Press.

Shepard, R. N. (1982). Structural representations of musical pitch. In D. Deutsch (Ed.), *The psychology of music* (pp. 344–390). New York: Academic Press.

Terhardt, E., & Seewann, M. (1983). Aural key identification and its relationship to absolute pitch. *Music Perception, 1,* 63–83.

Terhardt, E., & Ward, W. D. (1982). Recognition of musical key: exploratory study. *Journal of the Acoustical Society of America, 72,* 26–33.

Ueda, K., & Ohgushi, K. (1987). Perceptual components of pitch: Spatial representation using a multidimensional scaling technique. *Journal of the Acoustical Society of America, 82,* 1193–1200.

Van Noorden, L. P. A. S. (1975). Temporal coherence in the perception of tone sequences. Unpublished doctoral dissertation, Technische Hogeschoel, Eindhoven, the Netherlands.

Ward, W. D., & Burns, E. M. (1982). Absolute pitch. In D. Deutsch (Ed.), *The psychology of music* (pp. 431–452). New York: Academic Press.

Westergaard, P. (1975). *An introduction to tonal theory.* New York: Norton.

CHAPTER 9

Cognitive Interpretations of Functional Chromaticism in Tonal Music

Helen Brown

In the introduction to his elegant text, *Harmony in Western Music*, Goldman alerted the reader that his was not the mainstream approach:

> I differ (at times quite radically) from many commonly accepted theoretical positions or deductions, especially those concerning . . . the importance of time, and of temporal ambiguities, as determining factors in hearing. (It should be observed that I say *hearing* rather than *analysis*; although no one will deny that analysis from visible data is helpful to hearing, it is what one hears, rather than what one sees—or what one can prove in theory to be operative—that makes the sense of harmonic progression). (1965, p. xii)

Goldman's sentiment is reflected in Berry's (1985) critical test of an analysis, which is whether the analytic image of the piece makes sense when heard. But this is a difficult test to apply. The flexible time frame in which analysis operates can obscure differences between seeing and hearing music. As Narmour (1990) notes, "because we're always looking at the score, we tend to know how things turn out and not hear them for what they are." The ambiguity of the listening moment, so difficult to capture in models, is unique to the aural experience (Jones, 1976, 1981).

In this chapter, examples of stimuli from experimental studies in music are presented and considered from the differing perspectives of their notational appearance and their potential aural effect. The limited usefulness of the 12-tone equal-tempered set of pitches in capturing mental representations of tonal music is examined and a "tonal chromatic" collection, representative of common chromatic processes occurring in tonal music, is proposed.

When analytic interpretation is primarily a score-oriented activity, musical relationships are not always considered in the same way they would be if no score were at hand. Aural analysis is limited by constraints of musical experience and memory; the listener hears only the musical surface and must derive structural relationships from it. Hearing musical events for what they are and interpreting them for what they might be is part of the process of assigning tonal meaning to a passage.

Intervallic Content of Sets of Pitches

A listener's initial interpretation of the tonal meaning of the first two measures of Chopin's *Etude*, op. 25, no. 11 (Figure 9.1A), might be confirmed by the composer's harmonization that immediately follows, suggesting tonic and subdominant chords in a C major tonal context. It is the dominant seventh chord of the key of A minor on the last beat of the fourth measure that reveals the complexity of the situation.

In this *Lento* introduction to the A minor *Etude*, Chopin creates ambiguity by playing on tonal implications of two common melodic gestures involving the minor second interval between E and F as the third and fourth scale degrees in the key of C major and as fifth and sixth scale degrees in the key of A minor. Over the course of this work, implications of tonal possibilities introduced in the *Lento*, such as the imitation of the neighbor-note relationship between E and F on a larger scale (shown between the notes B and C, labeled n.n. in Figure 9.1B), are worked out on various levels with references overlapping in time and in tonal meanings. Schenker's (1935/1979) interpretation of the tonal relations of the *Etude* is a large-scale bass arpeggiation of the tonic triad (shown by the notes stemmed downward in Figure 9.1B). Secondary tonal levels are the composing-out of the ambiguity of the opening measures. In his view, the opening events are surface-level predictors of the fundamental tonal motion of the work and are retrospectively heard as such.

Schenker discusses the importance of psychological perception of unique tonal relationships. In *Harmony*, he writes that "if . . . the artist desires to define the situation

A

B

FIGURE 9.1 Chopin: *Etude in A Minor,* op. 25, no. 11. Figure 9.1A shows *Lento* introduction, mm. 1–4. Figure 9.1B illustrates the graphic analysis (no. 76/3), after Schenker (1935/1979), showing prolongation through neighbor-note motion (n.n.) over V in the B-section of the ternary form. Melodic descent from dominant to tonic with interruption is shown by notes stemmed upward and labeled by scale degree (^); large-scale bass arpeggiation of the A-minor tonic triad is shown with downward stems.

with precision and give us a sure perception of the key, he will resort to a univalent interval which, by its very nature, will exclude any other key" (1906/1954, p. 129). In spite of this, Schenker's major/minor diatonic system is reduced to notation by his categorization of it as "univalent," meaning interpretable as a diatonic event in one key only, the intervals of augmented second, augmented fourth, diminished fifth, and diminished seventh. But a listener needs more information to sort out enharmonic equivalents.

In Figure 9.2 it can be seen that univalence is exhibited by only the largest interval, the augmented fourth (the interval that spans the half-octave between scale degrees four and seven, inverts to the single diminished fifth, and is often referred to as the tritone), and only in the major mode. Harmonic minor contains an additional tritone between second and sixth scale degrees. By reading the notation, one can easily differentiate the

FIGURE 9.2 Interval vectors showing number of occurrences of interval classes (sizes measured by number of semitones spanned). Figure 9.2A represents interval classes in major set. Figure 9.2B represents interval classes in the harmonic minor set. The larger intervals up to the octave (fifths, sixths, and sevenths) can be generated by moving the lower note in each interval up by one octave, or the upper note down by one octave (inversion). The largest and rarest interval in the figure (the augmented fourth) spans one-half octave and thus inverts into another half-octave interval. When inverted, it is the smallest fifth and is called a *diminished fifth*; when neither spelling is specified, it is referred to as a *tritone*. Harmonic minor differs from major, not only in the number of intervals in each class but also by the combining of different intervals in class 3 (minor thirds and an augmented second) and class 4 (major thirds and a diminished fourth).

three-semitone interval (in interval class 3) that comprises the augmented second in minor from the several minor thirds that also comprise three semitones. Without more musical context, a listener could hear the augmented second as a minor third, an augmented fourth as a diminished fifth, or a diminished seventh as a major sixth. It is the potential for the listener's multiple interpretations of the multivalent interval of the minor second (in interval class 1) upon which Chopin plays in the *Lento*.

Intervals represent relationships in tonal music, not numbers of semitones; different intervals that share the same number of semitones (enharmonics) represent different relationships in music. None of these crucial tonal relationships can be reflected in interval vectors (which are merely lists of numbers of occurrences of interval sizes within designated sets of pitches). In order for a listener to place any interval in its tonal setting, each interval needs to be disambiguated. Because the tritone occurs only once in each major set but inverts into itself, one additional tone is needed to determine the set to which it belongs. There are also minimal patterns from which tonal contexts can readily be determined in music in the minor mode, but a little more information is required because its intervallic makeup does not exhibit the same unique number of occurrences of each interval size that the major set does. Conversely, it is possible for listeners to interpret pitch patterns that reduce to no single scale as tonal. Because virtually all but the simplest Western tonal music uses chromaticism between degrees of the scale of its key and incorporates elements from both major and minor modes, listeners acquire skills in interpreting tonal centers in the presence of chromaticism and mixing of modes.

Examples From Experimental Literature

Because listening to music and studying musical scores can involve very different mental activities, one cannot assume that music will be interpreted aurally as it is notated. Sometimes the differences go unrecognized; sometimes artificial differences are imposed. Both oversights have inhibited ways experimental research on tonality is designed and interpreted and the resulting ways in which tonal relationships are represented in descriptions of cognitive processes. Stimuli from the experimental literature are useful in comparing aural and visual aspects of tonal relationships.

The left half of Figure 9.3 contains examples of melodic patterns used in music perception studies. Zenatti (1985) categorized the first pattern as "atonal." Cross, Howell, and West (1985) labeled the second pattern as "nonscale-conformant." "Atonal melodies" were derived from an "atonal scale" in the third pattern, which Dowling (1988) created by lowering the second, fifth, and sixth steps of a major scale. Used by Cuddy and Badertscher (1987), the fourth pattern did not yield "a profile that could be considered tonal" (p. 618). Taylor's (1976) subjects rated the fifth pattern as more atonal when they viewed it while hearing it than when they heard it without viewing it.

The first melodic pattern is quite angular and the third and fifth patterns make fairly strange-looking scales, but each can be regarded as tonal. This is not to say that they could not occur in atonal contexts. The key word here is *context.* Tonal context is supplied by the renotation in the box on the right side of Figure 9.3, illustrating that each pattern (except the third) can be diatonic, as well as the ease with which each of the

FIGURE 9.3 Examples of melodic patterns used in music perception studies. Figure 9.3A (1a–5a) represents stimuli categorized as atonal. Figure 9.3B (1b–5b) represents renotation of each stimulus to illustrate possible tonal interpretations. Figure 9.3A(2a) is from *Musical Structure and Cognition* (p. 133) by I. Cross, P. Howell, and R. West, 1985, Orlando: Academic Press. Copyright 1985 by Academic Press. Reprinted by permission. Figure 9.3A(5a) is from *Perception of Tonality in Short Melodies* by Jack A. Taylor, 1976. Copyright 1976 by Music Educators National Conference. Used by permission.

patterns can be interpreted tonally. In Figure 9.3B(1b), simply respelling C as B♯, the leading tone in C♯, yields a distillation of harmonic motion from dominant to tonic in harmonic minor. The same tones, the tritone and its resolution in C♯ minor, are included at the far right in what Mitchell (1962)—noting that the tritone "plays a critical role in directing the harmonic motion toward the final tonic chord" (p. 7)—calls the "diatonic 'key defining' progression." It is not always clear that either minor mode or implied harmony is considered in experimental studies using pitch patterns. The minor mode, as Meyer (1956) points out, differs from the major in that it is "quasi-chromatic and changeable." He observes that the "listener practiced in the perception of and response to this music is well aware of the ever present possibility of chromaticism [because] tendencies of tones as they approach substantive tones are stronger in minor than in major" (p. 224).

Meyer also refers to additional "leading tones" in minor mode that occur above the substantive tones, those provided by the half step above the dominant (the F above E, for example, in the Chopin excerpt in Figure 9.1) and by the Phrygian half step above the tonic. The third stimulus could be explained through incorporation of mixing pitches from parallel modes (here upper leading tones that are a semitone above dominant and tonic, A♭–G and D♭–C), and through "tonicization," incorporating chromatic tones a semitone below scale degrees other than tonic in order to give them the most important characteristic of a tonic—a semitone or leading tone below it—to heighten their effect. Here the raised fourth scale step of F♯ could function as the leading tone of the dominant.

Enharmonic respelling as a Phrygian scale (or a major scale beginning and ending on the third scale degree) provides a diatonic pattern for the fifth stimulus. The second and fourth stimuli are diatonic as notated. The second is shown on the right side of Figure 9.3(2b) with a possible harmonization in D minor. To understand why the fourth stimulus might have been considered nontonal and to explain the reason for its enharmonic renotation on the right, it will be examined briefly in its experimental setting and related to the powerful effect of temporal ordering in tonal interpretation of pitch patterns.

Temporal Context

In a study in which listeners were asked to give their "subjective evaluations of how well the final note of each pattern provided a musical completion for the pattern," Cuddy and Badertscher's (1987) subjects heard the arpeggiation, notated in Figure 9.3B(4a), of a diminished triad 12 times, each time followed by a different probe tone out of the 12 tone chromatic set. Because the "tonal profile" gleaned from these ratings (shown in Figure 9.4A) did not correlate well with the tonal hierarchy (Krumhansl, 1979) in which tonic (pitch class 0 in figure 9.4A) of the major mode outranks other choices, it was concluded that "the diminished triad pattern did not recover a profile that could be considered tonal" (p. 618).

Other studies (Brown, 1988; Brown & Butler, 1981, 1988, 1989) have produced results in which diminished triads were interpreted as powerful tonal indicators in certain

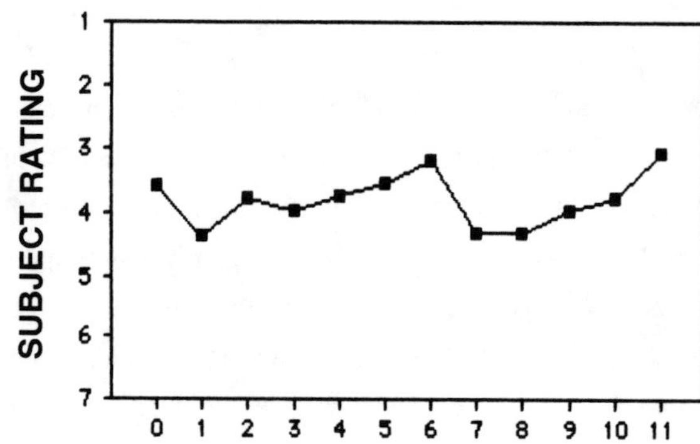

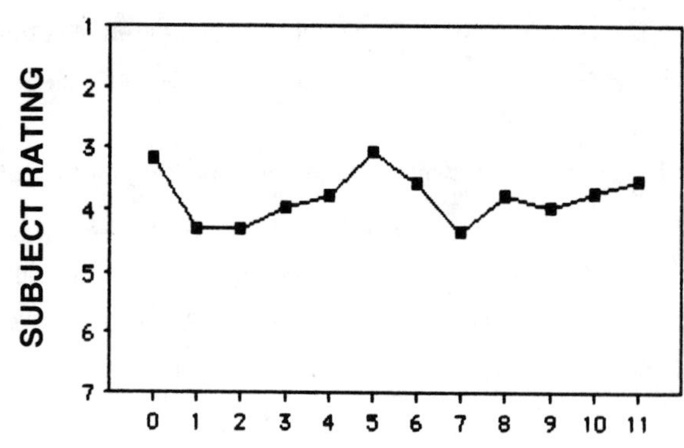

FIGURE 9.4 Figure 9.4A represents the tonal profile reported by Cuddy and Badertscher (1987) in response to subjects' ratings of probe tones for diminished triad stimulus shown in Figure 9.3 (4a). A subject rating of 1 is high and a subject rating of 7 is low. Ratings for the stimulus are interpreted in C major (C = pitch class 0). Figure 9.4B represents a six semitone transposition of the same tonal profile (in response to the same stimulus in the same study) from the key of C to F♯, reflecting a possible interpretation of the pattern as renotated in Figure 9.3 (4b). Here, F♯ = pitch class 0. Figure 9.4A is from "Recovery of the Tonal Hierarchy: Some Comparisons Across Age and Levels of Musical Experience," by L. L. Cuddy and B. Badertscher, 1987, *Perception and Psychophysics, 41*(6), p. 617. Copyright 1987 by L. L. Cuddy. Reprinted by permission.

contexts and produced tonal confusion in others. The tritone, the rarest interval in the diatonic set, is the interval between the root and fifth of the diminished triad; in Figure 9.3B, it is notated as a diminished fifth between the B and F (4a) and as an augmented fourth between the B and E♯ (4b). The tritone is the best interval with which to identify a tonal center when its context allows tonal interpretation in the temporal ordering of fourth followed by seventh scale degrees. Simple reversal of the ordering greatly reduces its power in aural identification of that tonal center and increases the likelihood of its enharmonic interpretation in another key.

Analyses of responses in these studies have also revealed listeners' tendencies to interpret the last tone heard in a pattern as part of a dominant function, implying continuation. It was found that when the last tone is the subdominant or is interpreted by the listener as subdominant, then tonal confusion is greatest. This has become so predictable that such an ordering purposely has been used to create tonal ambiguity (Brown, 1988). An interpretation of Cuddy and Badertscher's subjects' ratings to the B diminished triad in the key of C major means that the last tone in the pattern was heard as the subdominant. The single ordering they chose to test the key-defining power of the diminished triad has been shown to be the very one least likely to produce a strong tonal profile for C as tonic. Although subjects' ratings yielded what Cuddy and Badertscher considered a poor tonal response in their study, those ratings might indeed be a clear indication of tonal reasoning among listeners. If the B–F tritone were interpreted by subjects as B and E♯—that is, if its enharmonic interpretation were considered—then scale degrees four and seven would exchange tonal meanings and the key a tritone away would be suggested as a plausible tonal interpretation.

This exchange and enharmonic respelling between the major scale of each key are shown in Figure 9.5. Notice, in Figure 9.4A, the high ranking of the raised fourth scale degree (pitch class 6), which is a semitone above the last tone heard in the pattern, in the tonal profile of the diminished triad pattern as interpreted in the key of C. When the diminished triad profile is transposed by that tritone interval to a tonal center of F♯—an ordering that suggests an arpeggiation of the leading-tone seventh chord in F♯ minor, ending with its leading tone, E♯—the semitone above the last tone heard is a logical completion for the pattern. Indeed, that tonal profile (shown in Figure 9.4B) more closely correlates with the tonal hierarchy.

A particular triad, when heard, is not an idealization that can be taken as representative of all tonal meanings of the triad. Subjects in the Cuddy and Badertscher experiment, of course, were not limited by the notation of the stimulus they did not see, nor

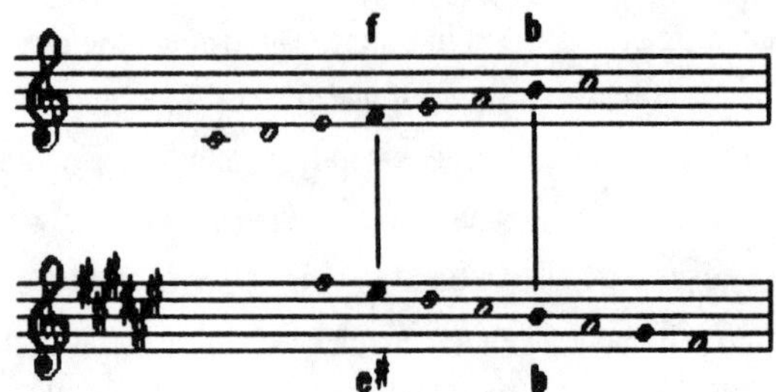

FIGURE 9.5 Enharmonic interpretation of the tritone-related pitches in major scales on C and F♯. Between these two scales, F/E♯ and B are the only two pitches shared.

were they instructed to restrict their completion ratings to major mode or diatonic interpretations, although the multiple tonal and modal possibilities of this pattern seem to have a complicated interpretation of the tonal profiles resulting from their probe-tone ratings. It was assumed that presentation of a diminished triad in the single melodic pattern of B–D–B–F, as in Figure 9.3A (4a), should elicit the best completion rating for the key of C major and that such results should represent a fair demonstration of the tonal implications of all diminished triads. This assumption underestimates the power of temporal context as well as the richness of tonal processes in music.

Chromaticism and Temporal Context

It has been well established that a context of musical tonality enhances perception of relationships among tones for listeners in recall and reproduction tasks and that tonal context enhances musical learning (e.g., Buttram, 1969; Francès, 1958/1972; Deutsch, 1982; Shatzkin, 1984; Wittlich, 1980). But beyond this point, working definitions of the term tonality and assumptions about tonal context can be problematic. Diatonicism does not ensure tonality; chromaticism (or randomness) does not equal atonality.

Zenatti reports that "perceptual discrimination of a melodic change is significantly easier" when the melodic patterns correspond to those "most often used in the tonal system" (1985, p. 400). She composed patterns for a study and categorized them as tonal or as atonal. Through enharmonic respelling (see Figure 9.6), examples from the study have been reclassified, reduced to their pitch classes, and given possible "tonal" contexts.

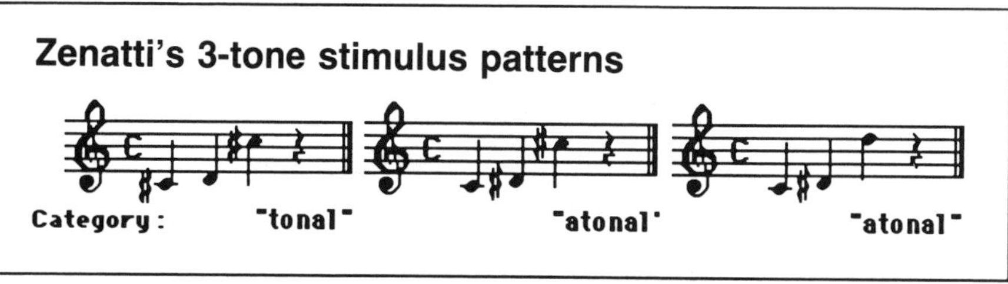

Renotation

Reduction

A possible tonal context

Renotation

FIGURE 9.6 Patterns composed by Zenatti (1985) are shown first as notated and interpreted by Zenatti; second, as enharmonically respelled and reinterpreted; and third, in a possible tonal context. From "The Role of Perceptual-Discrimination Ability in Tests of Memory for Melody, Harmony, and Rhythm" by A. Zenatti, 1985, *Music Perception, 2*(3), p. 400. Copyright 1985 by The Regents of the University of California. Adapted by permission.

A priori classifications of which patterns are tonal or atonal can affect interpretations of results in music perception experiments that are used as foundations for larger psychological models that are in turn taken to represent how we hear tonal relationships in music. Chromaticism is assumed to weaken tonality in studies when discussion includes no incorporation of concepts of mixture of modes and tonicization of scale degrees other than tonic, both of which are chromatic processes common in diatonic tonality that can easily function to enrich and reinforce a single tonal center.

A Tonal Chromatic Collection

It is possible for each pitch in a chromatic set to possess a unique meaning that suggests relationships to a tonal center. It takes more than the usual chromatic scale to represent this because tonal music has more than 12 functional pitches per octave. In Mitchell's words:

> The ordering force of diatonicism becomes a dispersing force of the chromatic scale. Where each degree of the diatonic major scale is imbued with a single meaning, due to its characterizing interval set and its distance from a tonic degree, the tones of the chromatic scale have multiple meanings. (1962, p. 8)

There have been various representations of this concept in notations of chromatic scales (e.g., Marra, 1986; Mitchell, 1962). In Figure 9.7, a distinction is shown among multiple meanings that result from the two chromatic processes of mixture and tonicization in what Proctor (1977) terms "diatonic tonality—a product of the interaction of different diatonic scales" (p. iv). This means that although there can be abundant chromaticism, the asymmetry of the diatonic basis with its unique pitch relationships (see Figure 9.2) is preserved. This is distinguished from symmetrical structures in chromatic tonality, where an equal-tempered 12-pitch-class collection is appropriate and where enharmonicism is a tonal, as well as a notational, phenomenon; for example, in Chopin's E Major *Prelude*, op. 28, no. 9, key relationships represent a symmetrical division of the octave into major thirds: E, C, A♭/G♯, E.

Common chromaticism in diatonic tonality resulting from mixture incorporates elements from parallel modes (see Figure 9.7B). Added to the diatonic tones in C major shown in Figure 9.7A, E♭, A♭, and B♭ are derived from the parallel minor (Aeolian) and D♭ from the parallel Phrygian. Tonicizations temporarily elevating scale degrees two, three, five, and six to the status of tonic are shown in Figure 9.7C. Schenker describes every tone as "aspiring to be the tonic." Other tones can be tonicized, or can acquire

A

B

Chromaticism from mixture

2̂ 3̂ 6̂ 7̂

C

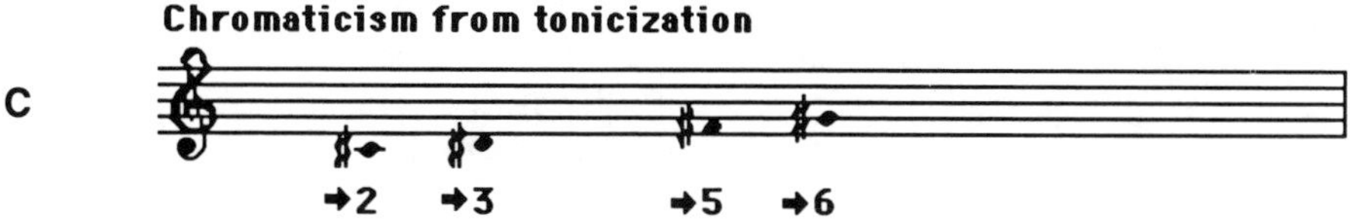

Tonal chromatic collection

D

FIGURE 9.7 A tonal chromatic collection is shown as (A) C major scale, (B) additional pitches derived from process of modal mixture, (C) additional pitches derived from tonicization, and (D) the combined collection.

characteristics of the tonal center, by adding a leading tone below and the perfect fourth above. Notice that the combined tonal chromatic collection in Figure 9.7D contains three pitches more than the 12-tone chromatic scale in order to represent the differing tonal functions of pitches that are enharmonically the same. For example, D♯ is shown as a temporary leading tone of the third scale degree and is distinguished from E♭ as the lowered third scale degree in the parallel mode of C minor. Notice also that the tonal chromatic collection does not comprise merely two spellings of the five chromatic pitches: There are pitches that do not occur (G♭ and A♯) because the lowered fifth and raised sixth scale degrees do not commonly occur in diatonic tonality.

Experimental Support for the Tonal Chromatic Collection

In a study designed to investigate aspects of chromaticism in listeners' apprehension of tonal centers (Brown, 1985), subjects demonstrated flexibility of tonal interpretations. Tonal centers were revealed or concealed in identical pitch sets on the basis of contextual manipulations of temporal relationships of the same pitches within the sets. For example, subjects thought the tonal implications of each of the three six-tone stimuli (shown as black noteheads in Figure 9.8) were clear, as indicated by the majority response in the case of each for the key it was temporally ordered to elicit: In (A) 67% of subjects vocalized A♭ after hearing the pattern; in (B) 69% sang the pitch B, even though it was not a tone heard in the stimulus; and in (C) 81% sang F, also not included in the stimulus. Temporal manipulations of the tritone and two minor seconds evidently contributed strongly to their tonal interpretations.

The melodic pattern in Figure 9.8A incorporates mixture and tonicization, providing upper and lower leading tones for the dominant. Although the F♭ to D might initially be heard as a major second, rather than as the much less common diminished third, the arrival of E♭ suggests the latter interpretation. The tritone was thus interpreted as the interval between second and sixth scale degrees in harmonic minor. In Figure 9.8B, tonicization of the sixth scale degree is followed by a key-defining progression suggesting the tonal center of B. Figure 9.8C features an enharmonic reinterpretation of the tritone as spelled in Figure 9.8B, which functioned well as a suggestion of the tritone-related key. The respellings reflect logical tonal interpretations based on the temporal ordering of tones in each stimulus. Yet, according to the a priori classifications in relation to the stimuli in Figure 9.3, discussed above, each of these could have been regarded as atonal.[1]

Musical Support for the Tonal Chromatic Collection

Snyder (1990, p. 127) found that realignments of Knopoff and Hutchinson's (1983) a priori assumptions about tonal relationships revealed critical flaws in their quantitative study of chromaticism as a determinant of musical style. Snyder considered their

[1] *For ease of comparison, pitch patterns are shown here as the same pitch class sets. In the experimental setting, the patterns were randomly transposed.*

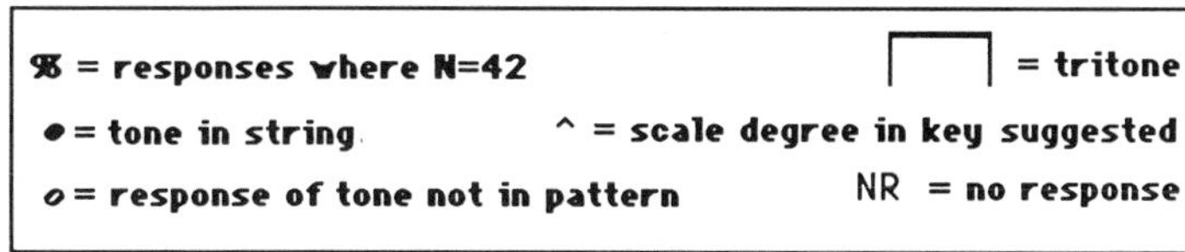

A

To suggest A♭

B

To suggest B

C

To suggest F

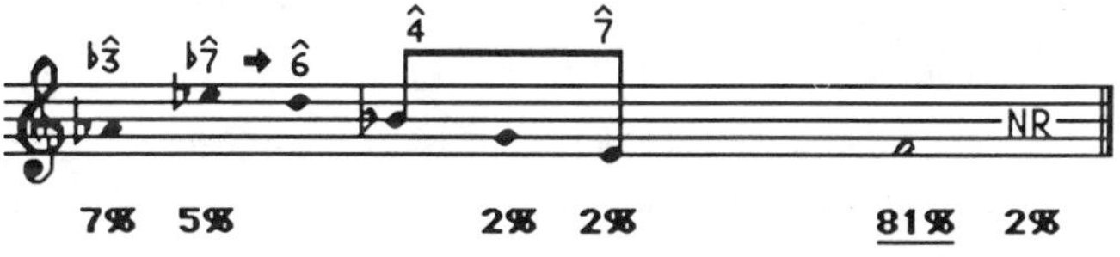

FIGURE 9.8 Sample of a group of melodic stimuli from Brown (1985), related in that they are temporal arrangements of the same pitch collection ordered to suggest tonal implications of the keys (A) A♭, (B) B, and (C) F. Results showed that subjects responded to the temporal reordering in each of the three stimuli, to which they vocalized their choice of tonic, by choosing the suggested key (those response percentages are underlined) significantly more than other choices, even when the suggested key was not heard in the pattern.
Note. Temporal rearrangements of pcs 2 3 4 7 8 10; pitch patterns were arranged melodically to promote major tonic responses. Interval vector = ⟨3,2,2,3,3,2⟩.

results to be at odds with his own experience of the music and suspected that they had not measured pitch usage as practiced by the composers whose harmonic styles they were evaluating. Upon investigation, he found that Knopoff and Hutchinson's assumption of a 12 pitch-class octave and use of notated key signatures as indicators of tonal level (among other problems) led to distortion of their data, thereby "obliterat[ing] evidence of the very expansions of tonality their studies were ... intended to measure." When he corrected the errors resulting from these visual misinterpretations of tonal relationships, Snyder found that composers' styles were significantly realigned and much better distinguished.

Two musical excerpts serve to illustrate how a tonal concept enlarged from the 12-tone equal-tempered set can be useful because it is reflective of compositional and listening strategies. In his song *Morgen*, Richard Strauss systematically uses spellings of D♯/E♭ and A♯/B♭ in contexts differing in musical meaning. Pitch class 3 is notated several times as D♯, the raised first scale degree in D major. Each time it occurs, it resolves to the second scale step, as a tonicization of the supertonic (e.g., Figure 9.9A, m. 14). In other words, the second scale degree has acquired its tritone of D♯–A. In Schenker's anthropomorphic terminology, E has momentarily realized its aspiration to become tonic. Later, in Figure 9.9B, at m. 36, pitch class 3 is notated as E♭—flat second scale degree—in the context of mixture of Phrygian mode. The effect of this change in function and musical meaning of the same pitch class is smooth, but stunning. Similarly the flat sixth scale degree descending to the dominant had been introduced enharmonically in *Morgen* as sharp fifth scale degree in a tonicization of six. Except for the lowered seventh scale step, at a change of texture in m. 31, this is the extent of chromaticism in the song. This is shown in the tonal chromatic collection of *Morgen* in Figure 9.10. In a more detailed analysis of *Morgen*, the musical meaning of the chromaticism can also be interpreted in relation to the meaning of the text of the song.

Chromaticism in an instrumental work, however, has solely musical meaning. The *Adagio* of Schubert's String Quintet in C illustrates the usefulness of the concept of a tonal chromatic collection in analyzing chromatic events even in much more tonally complex contexts.

The formal/tonal structure of the *Adagio*, which is in the key of E major, involves keys related through double mixture—the parallel minor of Phrygian II:

Formal Division	A	B	A	Coda
Keys	E Major	F Minor	E Major	E Major

FIGURE 9.9 Excerpts from *Morgen*, op. 27, no. 4, by Richard Strauss. Figure 9.9A, m. 14, shows tonicization of E (second scale degree) provided by D♯. Figure 9.9B, m. 36, shows the same pitch class respelled as E♭ providing an upper leading tone to the "substantive tone" of D, the tonic.

The last few measures of the movement, notated in Figure 9.11, feature several chromatic events, which can be interpreted as reinforcing and enriching tonal processes:

- mixture of tones from the parallel minor (C♮, the lowered six, in the minor iv and diminished ii°6 chords in m. 90, and in the VI in m. 91),
- double mixture (in m. 92, A♭ as the mediant in F, the parallel Phrygian of the prevailing key of E major),

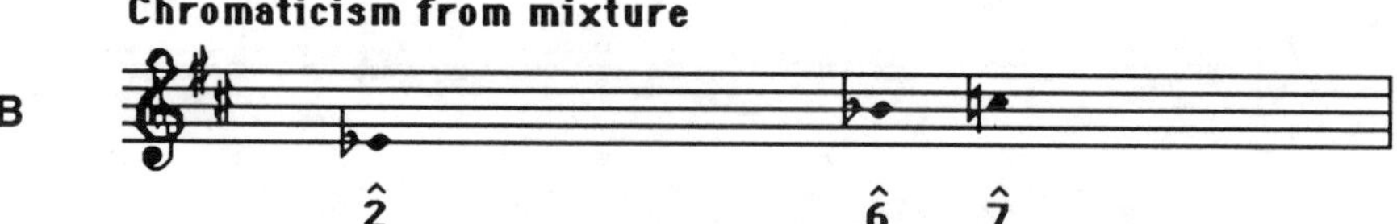

Tonal chromatic collection

FIGURE 9.10 Tonal chromatic collection from the *Morgen* excerpt.

- linear embellishing seventh chord emphasizing the dominant (m. 90),
- microtonicization of scale degree three (provided by the F𝄪 in m. 89),
- tonicization of scale degree six (in the augmented triad in m. 89), in an altered dominant in which B♯ functions to strengthen the resolution to IV, and
- German augmented sixth chord (m. 92) whose double interpretation as the dominant seventh chord of F minor (which would be spelled with a B♭ instead of the A♯ that creates the augmented sixth with the C in the bass) recalls the key of the middle section.

FIGURE 9.11 *Adagio* from String Quintet in C, D.956, by Franz Peter Schubert, mm. 88–94.

At the structural close (the cadence in m. 91) the coda summarizes the tonal activity of the movement by relating these two keys in a small-scale gesture that is a distillation of the overall tonal plan. In these six measures the entire tonal chromatic collection (notated in Figure 9.12), save tonicization of the second scale degree, is encapsulated.

Conclusions

Listeners learn through their associations with tonal music to have particular expectations. According to Kramer (1988), we habitually listen "linearly" to the goal-directed

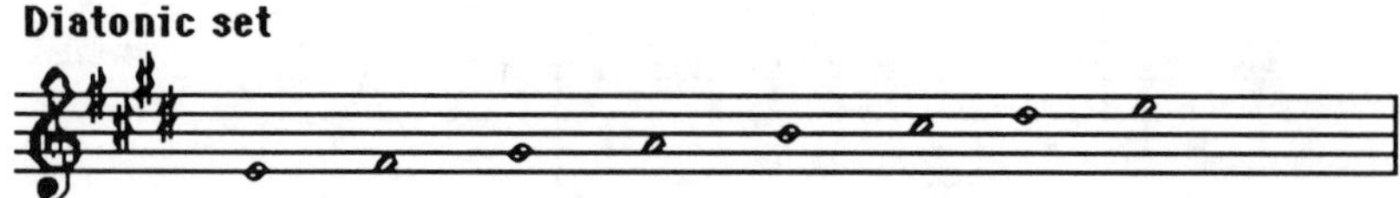

Tonal chromatic collection

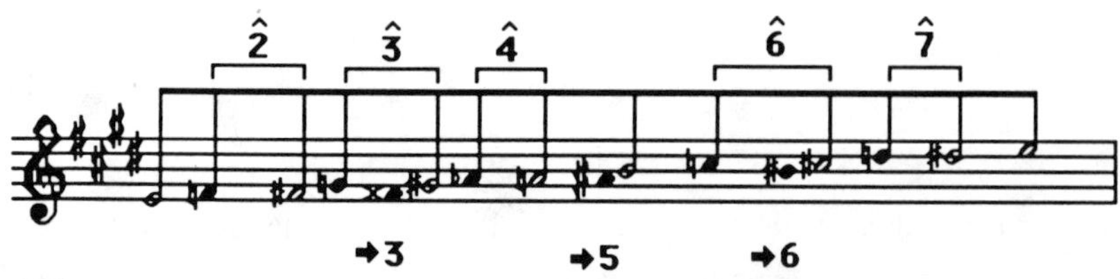

FIGURE 9.12 Tonal chromatic collection from Schubert's String Quintet, II, mm. 88–94.

motion of harmonies in tonal music. Composers control these implications in their music through their manipulations of tones in particular combinations and temporal relationships. Analysis of listeners' mental representations of tonal meanings of music is enhanced by the concept of the tonal chromatic collection, because it is more reflective of these cognitive processes than is the 12-tone chromatic scale, reliance on which has limited both the design and interpretation of some experimental research on tonality, and has thus constrained ways in which tonal relationships are represented in descriptions of cognitive processes.

References

Berry, W. (1985). Sense and sensibility: What can we know about music? (What do we want to know?) *College Music Society Proceedings: The National and Regional Meetings.* Boulder: The College Music Society.

Brown, H. (1985). *The influence of chromaticism in set content and temporal context on tonic judgments.* Unpublished study.

Brown, H. (1988). The interplay of set content and temporal context in a functional theory of tonality perception. *Music Perception, 5*(3), 219–250.

Brown, H., & Butler, D. (1981). Diatonic trichords as minimal tonal cue-cells. *In Theory Only, 5*(6/7), 39–55.

Brown, H., & Butler, D. (1988, October). *Temporal effects on tonal hierarchies.* Paper presented at the College Music Society National Meeting, Santa Fe, NM.

Brown, H., & Butler, D. (1989). Tonal hierarchies and musical time. In P. Pravica (Ed.), *Proceedings of the XIIIth International Congress on Acoustics* (III) (pp. 19–22). Belgrade: SAVA CENTAR.

Browne, R. (1981). Tonal implications of the diatonic set. *In Theory Only, 5*(6/7), 3–21.

Buttram, J. (1969). The influence of selected factors on interval identification. *Journal of Research in Music Education, 17*(3), 309–315.

Cross, I., Howell, P., & West, R. (1985). Structural relationships in the perception of musical pitch. In P. Howell, I. Cross, & R. West (Eds.), *Musical structure and cognition* (pp. 121–142). Orlando: Academic Press.

Cuddy, L., & Badertscher, B. (1987). Recovery of the tonal hierarchy: Some comparisons across age and levels of musical experience. *Perception and Psychophysics, 41*(6), 609–620.

Deutsch, D. (1982). *The psychology of music.* New York: Academic Press.

Dowling, W. (1988). Tonal structure and children's early learning of music. In J. Sloboda (Ed.), *Generative processes in music* (pp. 113–128). Oxford: Clarendon Press.

Francès, R. (1958). *La perception de la musique* [The perception of music]. Paris: Librarie Philosophique J. Vrin. (2nd ed., with an English summary, 1972).

Goldman, R. (1965). *Harmony in Western music.* New York: W. W. Norton & Company.

Jones, M. R. (1976). Time, our lost dimension: Toward a new theory of perception, attention, and memory. *Psychological Review, 83,* 323–355.

Jones, M. R. (1981). Only time can tell: On the topology of mental space and time. *Critical Inquiry, 7,* 557–576.

Knopoff, L., & Hutchinson, W. (1983). Entropy as a measure of style: The influence of sample length. *Journal of Music Theory, 27*(1), 75–98.

Kramer, J. (1988). *The time of music.* New York: Schirmer.

Krumhansl, C. (1979). The psychological representation of musical pitch in a tonal context. *Cognitive Psychology, 11*, 346–374.

Marra, J. (1986). The tonal chromatic scale as a model for functional chromaticism. *Music Perception, 4*(1), 69–84.

Meyer, L. B. (1956). *Emotion and meaning in music.* Chicago: University of Chicago Press.

Mitchell, W. (1962). The study of chromaticism. *Journal of Music Theory, 6*, 2–31.

Narmour, E. (1990, April). *Melodic hierarchies as systems of aesthetic communication.* Presentation at The Ohio State University Symposium on the Cognitive Bases of Musical Communication, Columbus, OH.

Proctor, G. (1977). *Technical bases of nineteenth century chromatic tonality: A study in chromaticism.* Doctoral dissertation, Princeton University.

Schenker, H. (1954). *Harmony.* E. M. Borgese, Trans.; O. Jonas, Ed. Cambridge, MA: MIT Press. (Original work published in 1906)

Schenker, H. (1979). *Free composition.* E. Oster, Ed. and Trans. New York: Longman. (Original work published in 1935)

Shatzkin, M. (1984). Interval recognition in minimal context. *Journal of Research in Music Education, 32*(1), 5–14.

Snyder, J. (1990). Entropy as a measure of musical style: The influence of a priori assumptions. *Music Theory Spectrum, 12*(1), 121–160.

Taylor, J. (1976). Perception of tonality in short melodies. *Journal of Research in Music Education, 24*(4), 197–208.

Wittlich, G. (1980). Developments in computer–based music instruction and research at Indiana University. *Journal of Computer-Based Instruction, 6*(3), 62–71.

Zenatti, A. (1985). The role of perceptual-discrimination ability in tests of memory for melody, harmony, and rhythm. *Music Perception, 2*(3), 397–403.

CHAPTER 10

On Pitch-Set Properties and Perceptual Attributes of the Minor Mode

David Butler

It should not be necessary at this point to iterate the relative merits and weaknesses of the competing perceptual theories of pitch relations in Western tonal music (for background, see Krumhansl, 1979, 1983, 1990; Brown & Butler, 1981; Brown, 1988; and Butler, 1989, 1990). I think it does bear repeating, however, that static models of pitch relations are not able to account for tonal ambiguities even at extremely simple levels. By "static," I mean models that do not regard the temporal and registral relations of pitches that we hear and/or conceive as crucial cues that help us form our mental representations of pitch relations in tonal music. Among these are models based on mental geometries of pitch space (e.g., Krumhansl, 1979; Shepard, 1982a, 1982b).

Pitch Relations in Tonal Music

The importance of such temporal and registral relations was examined in a casual study I conducted recently, in which two pitch strings were presented to nine music students. The strings were: (a) $D\flat_4$–$A\flat_4$–$D\flat_4$–$A\flat_3$–$D\flat_4$; and (b) G_4–C_5–G_4–C_4–G_4. Six of the nine music students who heard these strings felt that the tone that began and ended the first pattern better represented the tonal center for that pattern, while the tone in the middle of the pitch register of the second pattern (that is, the second and fourth tones in the serial order) stood as the better tonic. Yet, the same pitch intervals made up the so-called "pitch structure" of the two patterns: octaves, fifths, and fourths. Clearly, then, it is risky business to base a perceptual theory of tonal pitch relations on nothing more than an inventory of intervals—especially these particular intervals, although octaves and fifths typically are considered the most consonant, the most "tonal" intervals to be found in music.

Babbitt (1960) gave a precise depiction of the structural properties of sets that could be derived from the equal-tempered 12th-octave pitch gamut, and on the foundation of Babbitt's work, Browne (1981) formulated a perceptual theory of pitch relations in tonal music based on the characteristic unique multiplicity of intervals in the major diatonic set. Unique multiplicity means that each class of interval is found a unique number of times within the pitch set. The property of unique multiplicity of interval classes within the major diatonic set is illustrated in Figure 10.1.

Intervals in the Major Set

The bracketed numbers <2,5,4,3,6,1> in Figure 10.1 are simply a count of the interval classes present in the major diatonic set (shown here in scalar order), listed from smallest to largest. Interval class (ic) 1, comprising minor seconds and their enharmonic equivalents, octave complements, and octave compounds, can be found twice among the members of the major set, while ic2 (major seconds, enharmonic equivalents, and so on) can be found among five different pairs of notes in the set. Each interval occurs a different number of times within the pitch set—not necessarily within tonal musical compositions, but within the set. The rarer intervals in the set, Browne reasoned, should establish for the listener a clearer impression of tonality than the more common intervals. Minor

FIGURE 10.1 Differing levels of frequency (rare and common) among interval classes found in the major diatonic set.

seconds are common melodic events, while tritones (ic6) typically occur as simultaneities (more explicit harmonic entities). Yet, tritones often do appear in melodies, their presence usually veiled by intervening tones.

A number of studies (e.g., Brown, 1988; Brown & Butler 1981; Butler, 1983, 1989) have amassed experimental evidence that supports Browne's assertions. We can quickly get our tonal bearings by the harmonic implications of an amazingly small number of tones presented melodically and find our mental positions in this tonality without hearing the complete pitch set or a tonic chord. We have also found that the clarity of the tonal messages that these tones convey can be altered markedly by varying the time-orders of the stimulus tones. When I asked the nine music students from my study group to sing, hum, or whistle the tonal center they felt was most appropriate for each of the melodies notated in Figure. 10.2, there was little hesitation.[1] The almost unanimous choices are represented by the tones notated to the right of the melodies in the figure.

FIGURE 10.2 Major-mode melodies used in the key identification experiment; (A) the March from Handel's *Judas Maccabeus*; (B) the third theme from Movement 4 of the Schumann *Quintet in E♭* op. 44; and (C) the second theme from Movement 4 of the Brahms *Quartet in A Minor,* op. 51. The tonal center produced by most of the listeners is notated to the right of each melody.

[1] *The method of testing was straightforward. Listeners were tested individually, and each was instructed to listen to just as much of each unaccompanied melody as he or she felt was necessary to become confident of the key implied by that melody. Melodies were realized by a MIDI-controlled synthesizer, producing tones with a nearly square waveform. As soon as listeners were sure that they could identify the key implied by the melody, they immediately sang, hummed, or whistled a tone to identify their choice of most appropriate tonal center. Prior to the test session, listeners were instructed that they would be rewarded each time they identified the tonal center of a melody upon hearing it only once. Listeners were told also that they would be paid nothing for*

FIGURE 10.3 Differing levels of frequency (rare and common) among interval classes found in the minor diatonic set.

Listeners in this informal study—and in many (but not all) of the earlier "rare intervals" studies—were told to interpret the melodic patterns that they heard solely in relation to the major diatonic set; that is, they were instructed to disregard possible chromatic implications, and were told not to interpret the patterns within the mental context of minor mode. Browne (1981) pointed out that the minor diatonic set had intrinsically more ambiguous intervallic properties, because the most common intervals in the major set became less common in minor and the rare intervals became less rare. In this chapter I elaborate on that remark, and then propose that the rarer intervals in the minor diatonic set evoke a clear sense of key in the tonally enculturated listener after the listener has been given little more tonal context than is needed for the major set.

Intervals in the Minor Set

The array of more and less common intervals found in the minor diatonic set[2] is illustrated in Figure 10.3. As Browne (1981) pointed out, frequency values of interval classes in minor begin to retreat toward the middle, to become more similar: None is represented fewer than two times or more than five times in the set. We find, also, that two pairs of interval classes appear an equal number of times. Forget unique multiplicity. And yet, although there is no interval class that occurs only once, there are intervals that occur only

an incorrect response. Thus, listeners were given an incentive to respond quickly and accurately. Of course, listeners were given no visual cues. Responses were tape recorded and response accuracy was monitored by two independent evaluators.

[2]The minor diatonic set is typically regarded as the unordered pitch collection found in the "harmonic" form of the minor scale, illustrated in ascending form in Figure 10.3. Melodies and chords derived from the "pure" (or "natural") form of the minor scale (formed by the pattern of half-steps [H] and whole-steps [W] W–H–W–W–H–W–W) would more nearly resemble the modal idiom—specifically, the Aeolian mode—than the tonal idiom. The "melodic" form of minor, in which the upper four notes form the ascending pattern W–W–H, and the descending pattern W–W–H, represents the attempt to represent in a scalar abstraction common melodic patterns that may be superimposed over chords derived from the harmonic minor.

once—two of them, in fact. These are marked with asterisks in Figure 10.3: the augmented second (enharmonic with the minor third) and the diminished fourth (enharmonic with the major third). At this point it makes sense to set aside the concept of interval class and to begin, instead, to think of intervals with specific tonal meanings. Just as a pitch class designation can be indifferent to important tonal meanings invested in specific pitch names (e.g., the neutral designation "pc8" disregards the important difference in tonal reference between G♯ and A♭), neutral interval-class labels can miss important tonal references contained in specific intervals. When these intervals are heard and not seen, they are context dependent: We cannot distinguish a minor third from an augmented second (given equal temperament) when the interval is presented out of context. But it is certainly possible to provide tonal context (and not much context at that) sufficient to remove all ambiguity. This is shown in Figure 10.4.

The tonal clarity resulting from the tonal context illustrated in Figures 10.4B, 10.4D, and 10.4E is very likely to arise because the rarest intervals in the set are positioned within unique, context-providing configurations of semitones, much as the single tritone is nested within the two semitones in the major set (see Figure 10.5A). Similarly in the minor set, the two rarest intervals are framed by unique arrangements of semitones. The augmented second (see Figure 10.5B) is set off both above and below by semitones, while the diminished fourth (Figure 10.5C) encircles two semitones. Each of these intervals is the only member of its interval class to be set off in just that way by semitones, and it seems interesting that both of these rare intervals are situated around the leading tone of the minor set; thus, that part of the semitonal context for both intervals involves the relation of leading tone and tonic. Although the examples in Figure 10.5 illustrate the tritone, augmented second, and diminished fourth in a scalar context, it should be emphasized here that it is not scalar pitch relations, but rather compositional pitch relations

FIGURE 10.4 The rare intervals of the C minor diatonic set (notated in whole notes): the augmented second shown (A) out of context and (B) within a common harmonic context, the leading-tone seventh chord; the diminished fourth shown (C) out of context and (D, E) within typical melodic and contrapuntal contexts.

FIGURE 10.5 The rare intervals of the minor set, in context: (A) the tritone (tt) shown within the context of the semitones (st) in the C Major set; (B) the augmented second (a2), the only member of ic3 positioned within semitones, shown for the C Minor set; and (C) the diminished fourth (d4), the only member of ic4 that encompasses two semitones, also shown for the C Minor set.

that inform the listener. This means at least two things: (a) tones need not be in strictly scalar configurations to provide intervallic context for one another, and (b) composers are free to create tonally clear or tonally ambiguous pitch combinations by using or avoiding these pitch relations.

Let's put it another way: The listener's indecision as to how to interpret interval classes 3 and 4 may be resolved by the context provided by conventional arrangements of other tones across time. Temporal arrangements must be considered because of common melodic versus harmonic arrangements of the tones. For example, in Figure 10.4B, A♭ and B♮ can relate harmonically as members of the leading-tone seventh chord, but the B♮ and E♭ that form the diminished fourth (Figure 10.4C) are not found together in any commonly used chord; rather, they are found more typically in nonharmonic relations or in a melodic context, as shown in Figures 10.4D and 10.4E.

The intervallic characteristics of both the major and minor diatonic sets are compared in Table 10.1. Although the minor set is not characterized by the unique multiplicity of component intervals that we find in the major diatonic set, it may be that this characteristic is not as critical to a perceptual theory of minor-mode tonality as is the fact that the minor set does contain intervals sufficiently unambiguous in their context-enriched sound to serve as cues for the listener.

In an informal test of this proposal, I selected several minor-mode melodies from the tonal literature; within the first several tones, these examples contained the rare intervals of the augmented second and the diminished fourth, composed within a context that

TABLE 10.1
Interval index for major and harmonic minor diatonic sets; intervals are listed in order of increasing frequency of occurrence in both the major and harmonic minor sets.

Interval[a]	Occurrences, Major	Occurrences, Harmonic Minor	Total
Aug 2[b]	0	1	1
Dim 4[b]	0	1	1
Tritone	1	2	3
Min 2	2	3	5
Maj 3	3	3	6
Min 3	4	4	8
Maj 2	5	3	8
Per 4	6	4	10

[a]Octave complements and compounds are assumed to be equivalent. Octaves and unisons are not considered.
[b]Note that the Aug 2 and Dim 4 are enharmonic with fairly common intervals (the minor 3 and major 3, respectively). This means that neither of these rarest intervals in the harmonic minor set can be recognized as such without sufficient context.

ruled out enharmonic interpretations of the rare intervals. It was not considered necessary that the rare intervals be positioned between adjacent melodic tones; in some cases there were intervening contextual tones. On the other hand, I did consider it necessary that the melodies neither contain sequentially presented members of the tonic triad nor contain an intact scalar represention of the pitch set. These constraints were added to determine whether listeners could reliably identify tonal centers without hearing these tonal patterns, which are usually regarded as indispensable cues to tonal center in experimental studies of the tonal hierarchy (e.g., Krumhansl, 1979; Krumhansl & Kessler, 1982; Cuddy & Badertscher, 1987). I asked the music students (the same group as discussed earlier) to respond exactly as they had before: to identify the keys of the melodies that they heard, as soon as they felt sure that they recognized them. The minor-mode melodies are shown in Figure 10.6. I predicted that if listeners heard melodies containing the rarest intervals of the minor diatonic set within a tonal context that logically prevented enharmonic interpretations of those intervals, then listeners would be able to identify the minor-mode tonal centers as accurately as they had the major-mode tonal centers in the earlier study. Again, the tonic reponses given by almost all of the listeners are notated to

FIGURE 10.6 Melodies used in the second key identification experiment: (A) from the third movement of Brahms' Quartet in A Minor, op. 51; (B) from the Incidental Music to Sibelius's *Pelléas et Mélisande*, op. 16; and (C) from Beethoven's Piano Concerto No. 3 in C Minor, op. 37. The tonal center produced by most of the listeners is notated to the right of each melody.

the right of each melody in the figure. The students' accuracy levels and speeds of response virtually matched those given for the major-mode melodies.

Conclusions

The study reported here was very small and informal, but it offers some evidence that musical listeners can make systematic inferences of minor-mode tonality in much the same way as with the major mode, even when they are exposed to only meager pitch information. Of course, actual musical listening typically involves much richer fare, and this fuller, more explicit tonal context makes the key-identification task much less demanding. Still, we can (and apparently do) make tonal assumptions on a best evidence basis for music in both the major and minor modes. The best evidence, regardless of mode, is carried by the intervals most easily identified because they stand out from the pack. And the augmented second and diminished fourth stand out from the pack only when they are set in the context of leading-tone motions, resolutions to and from the dominant harmonic level, across musical time.

References

Babbitt, M. (1960). Twelve-tone invariants as compositional determinants. *The Musical Quarterly, 46*(2), 246–259.

Brown, H. (1988). The interplay of set content and temporal context in a functional theory of tonality perception. *Music Perception, 5,* 219–250.

Brown, H., & Butler, D. (1981). Diatonic trichords as minimal tonal cue-cells. *In Theory Only, 5*(6, 7), 37–55.

Browne, R. (1981). Tonal implications of the diatonic set. *In Theory Only, 5*(6, 7), 3–21.

Butler, D. (1983). The initial identification of tonal centers in music. Paper presented to the NATO Conference on the Acquisition of Symbolic Skills, University of Keele, England, July 6–9, 1982. In J. Sloboda and D. Rogers (Eds.), *Acquisition of symbolic skills* (pp. 251–261). New York: Plenum Press.

Butler, D. (1989). Describing the perception of tonality in music: A proposal for a theory of intervallic rivalry. *Music Perception, 6,* 219–241.

Butler, D. (1990). Response to Carol Krumhansl. *Music Perception, 7,* 325–338.

Cuddy, L., & Badertscher, B. (1987). Recovery of the tonal hierarchy: Some comparisons across age and levels of musical experience. *Perception & Psychophysics, 41*(6), 609–620.

Krumhansl, C. (1979). The psychological representation of musical pitch in a tonal context. *Cognitive Psychology, 11,* 346–374.

Krumhansl, C. (1983). Perceptual structures for tonal music. *Music Perception, 1,* 28–62.

Krumhansl, C. (1990). Tonal hierarchies and rare intervals in music cognition. *Music Perception, 7,* 309–324.

Krumhansl, C., & Kessler, E. (1982). Tracing the dynamic changes in perceived tonal organization in a spatial representation of musical keys. *Psychological Review, 89,* 334–368.

Shepard, R. (1982a). Geometrical approximations to the structure of musical pitch. *Psychological Review, 89,* 305–333.

Shepard, R. (1982b). Structural representations of musical pitch. In D. Deutsch (Ed.), *The psychology of music* (pp. 343–390). New York: Academic Press.

CHAPTER 11

Pitch-Space Journeys in Two Chopin Preludes

Fred Lerdahl

Ray Jackendoff's and my Generative Theory of Tonal Music (henceforth GTTM) relies on the distinction between a tonal hierarchy, a nontemporal schema in long-term memory, and an event hierarchy, a pitch reduction assigned in response to a musical sequence (Bharucha, 1984). The four main components of the theory—grouping, meter, time-span reduction, and prolongational reduction—concern event hierarchies. The tonal hierarchy appears as the "stability conditions" that are central in determining the hierarchical importance of pitch structures as they unfold in rhythmically structured time. Figure 11.1 summarizes the form of the theory from this perspective.

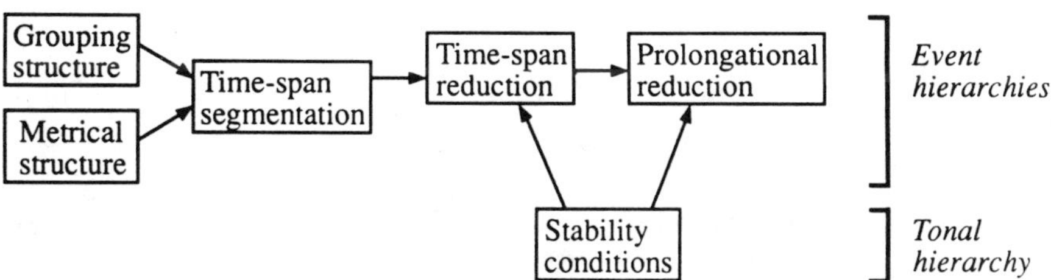

FIGURE 11.1 The form of generative music theory.

GTTM's treatment of the stability conditions is very sketchy (see Lerdahl & Jackendoff, 1983, pp. 117–118 & 224–225). To flesh out this part of the theory, and in response to pitch-space traditions in music theory and music psychology (Krumhansl, 1983; Longuet-Higgins, 1962; Schoenberg, 1954; Shepard, 1982; Weber, 1821; Werts, 1983), I recently proposed a pitch-space model of the common practice tonal hierarchy that derives geometric representations from an arithmetic foundation (Lerdahl, 1988). Increasing distance from a given point of stability in the model (a tonic) means increasing instability in relation to that point.

This model incorporates the distinct levels of pitch, chord, and region (or key) within one framework. Figure 11.2A illustrates its "basic space," a group-theoretic (mod 12) structure comprised of hierarchically organized "alphabets." (The seeds of this approach lie in Deutsch & Feroe, 1981; also see Simon & Sumner, 1968.) This and other figures in this chapter use the following orthographic conventions: C = 0, C♯ (D♭) = 1, D = 2, . . . , B = 11; chords and regions are represented by letters or Roman numerals (chords in nonbold type and regions in boldface); large-case letters or Roman numerals indicate major chords or regions; small-case letters or numerals indicate minor chords or regions; and **I** and **i** are arbitrarily set at **C** and **c**, respectively.

Octave space:	0											
Fifth space:	0							7				
Triadic space:	0				4			7				
Diatonic space:	0		2		4	5		7		9		11
Chromatic space:	0	1	2	3	4	5	6	7	8	9	10	11

A

		2									
		2							9		
		2			5				9		
0		2		4	5		7		9		11
0	1	2	3	4	5	6	7	8	9	10	11

B

							7				
		2					7				
		2					7				11
0		2		4		6	7		9		11
0	1	2	3	4	5	6	7	8	9	10	11

C

FIGURE 11.2 Classical pitch space, oriented to (A) I/**I**, (B) ii/**I**, (C) I/**V**. © 1988 by the Regents of the University of California. Reprinted from *Music Perception* Vol. 5 No. 3, (Spring 1988), pp. 315–349, by permission.

From any given numerical configuration of the basic space, the psychological distance of any other chord or region is calculated by a formula whose variables issue from the psychoacoustically significant top two levels, octave space (shared common pitch classes) and fifth space (movement along the circle of fifths). In Figure 11.2A, the orientation is to I/**I**, or a C major chord in the region of **C** major. The formula shifts the space so that, for example, Figure 11.2B represents ii/**I** (ii in **C**) and Figure 11.2C represents I/**V** (I in **G**). More specifically, ii/**I** indicates a d minor triad (2 5 9) within a C diatonic collection (0 2 4 5 7 9 11), and I/**V** shows a G major triad (2 7 11) within a G diatonic collection (0 2 4 6 7 9 11). Regional space is implicit in the diatonic level: Proceeding from Figure 11.2B to Figure 11.2C, 5 (F) is replaced through a circle-of-fifths operation by the adjacent 6 (F♯), which is just the difference between a **C** and a **G** tonic orientation.

Repeated applications of a variable produce closed cycles. For example, continuing the circle-of-fifths procedure on the diatonic level yields the chromatic circle of fifths: (0 2 4 5 7 9 11), (0 2 4 6 7 9 11), (1 2 4 6 7 9 11), . . . , (0 2 4 5 7 9 10). (Add 7 mod 12 to each number in a collection and reorder from the lowest value.) For progressions within a given region, chordal cycles move by regular slotting along a stationary diatonic level. For example, on the diatonic collection (0 2 4 5 7 9 11), chords moving two diatonic steps to the right yield the cycle (0 4 7), (4 7 11), (2 7 11), . . . , (0 4 9) in algebraically equidistant intervals.

It is useful to map such cycles geometrically, where a given axis represents a particular cycle. It turns out that at both the chordal and regional levels the closest distances occur along a fifths axis and a thirds axis. When these two axes combine the result is a four-dimensional torus, which then can be partially visualized on a two-dimensional page. Figure 11.3A shows the "core" of chordal space and Figure 11.3B shows a portion of regional space. In Figure 11.3A, the diatonic level of Figure 11.2A does not change, and all of the structures stay within the given diatonic set. In Figure 11.3B the diatonic level also shifts, yielding the chromatic circle of fifths on the vertical axis and relative/parallel major-minor relations on the horizontal axis.

Space forbids my going into more details concerning how these distances are derived (see Lerdahl, 1988). I will mention, however, that the model connects in fruitful ways with earlier music theories. For example, Figure 11.3A accords with Riemann's (1893) theory of harmonic function, and Figure 11.3B corresponds to Schoenberg's (1954) chart of regions. This model also correlates with the relevant experimental literature (Krumhansl, 1990; Krumhansl, Bharucha, & Kessler, 1982; Krumhansl & Kessler, 1982).

iii	V	vii°
vi	I	iii
ii	IV	vi

A

B	b	D	d	F
E	e	G	g	B♭
A	a	C	c	E♭
D	d	F	f	A♭
G	g	B♭	b♭	D♭

B

FIGURE 11.3 Figure 11.3A represents the "core" of chordal space. Figure 11.3B represents a portion of regional space.

That is, the derived distances (whether in arithmetic or geometric format) correspond to listeners' sense of pitch, chord, and key distance. The relation here between theory and experiment is different from, for instance, Deliège's (1987) testing of GTTM's local grouping rules. That was a typical case of experiment confirming theory. This is a case of theory providing an ex post facto explanatory framework for experimental results. I do not claim that listeners "really" carry around in their heads the numerical representations or their geometric mappings, although I would not be surprised if in some sense they do. My lesser claim is that the pitch-space theory rather accurately models, according to plausible formal, musical, and psychological principles, an empirically robust dimension of musical understanding. On that assumption, let us take some pitch-space journeys.

Paths through the E Major Prelude

Figure 11.4 presents the score of Chopin's E Major Prelude. Figure 11.5 supplies its hierarchical event analysis in a notation that differs somewhat from the GTTM format. Only the soprano-bass skeleton is given. A regular metrical grid is implicit in the diminution of note values from the quarter note to the 16th note; a full measure in Figure 11.5 corresponds to a 4-bar hypermeasure in Figure 11.4. The phrase structure is conveyed by the three grouping slurs immediately beneath. The time-span reduction (TSR), which embeds pitch events in the rhythmic structure and is a derivational step in constructing the prolongational analysis, appears in musical notation in the middle of the graph. The prolongational reduction (PR) is represented both in the tree and, alternatively, in the note/slur

FIGURE 11.4 Chopin: E Major Prelude, op. 28, no. 9.

notation at the bottom of the figure. The function of the prolongational component is to model perceived hierarchical patterns of tension and relaxation in the flow of pitch events: A dissonant note resolves, a harmonic progression tenses, a modulation turns toward the tonic region, and so on. Right branches in the tree stand for a tensing motion (or departure), left branches for a relaxing motion (or return). The three kinds of branching connection are strong prolongation, in which an event repeats; weak prolongation, in which an event repeats in an altered form (such as triadic inversion); and progression, in which an event connects to a completely different event. Strong prolongation is indicated by a node with an open circle, weak prolongation by a filled-in circle, and progression by no circle. A dashed branch in the tree provides an alternative branching at a point of

FIGURE 11.5 Prolongational analysis of Chopin's E Major Prelude.

relative maximal tension and reversal. The slurs at the bottom correspond precisely to tree branchings, with dashed slurs reserved for strong prolongations.

The prolongational analysis in Figure 11.5 essentially says that the piece projects strong prolongations from the opening to the beginning of the second phrase and from there to the beginning of the third phrase. Within each phrase there is a tensing-to-relaxing pattern (right branches move to left branches), with the final relaxation resolving to a point of global stability. There are stimulating details and alternative descriptions to ponder along the way, particularly with respect to the voice-leading and the melodic line, but these would lead us away from the topic at hand. Look at the first and third phrases, and consider how alike they begin yet how dissimilar their overall effects are. The first phrase is almost wholly diatonic, while the third modulates to a distant place, returning home at the last possible moment. No reductional analysis, Schenkerian or otherwise, can truly capture this difference. To express this dimension of musical experience, we must evoke another analytical component, not a replacement for prolongational analysis but something complementary to it, a component that conveys the space within which the music resides and the path the music takes through that space. Although others have developed such approaches (e.g., Krumhansl & Kessler, 1982; Werts, 1983), the present effort is distinguished by (a) its employment of multiple spatial models, each derivable from the basic space of Figure 11.2A and capable of highlighting particular intuitions, and (b) the correlation of pitch-space paths with prolongational analysis.

Pitch-Space Journeys

As a first attempt at modeling pitch-space journeys, let us adopt the regional space of Figure 11.3B and plot the path of the second and third phrases. (The first phrase is omitted, because it remains resolutely in the tonic region; Chopin is setting us up for the adventure to follow.) Figure 11.6 shows only the relevant portions of the space from Figure 11.3B. For present purposes, the passage from region to region can be thought of informally as in Roman numeral analysis, although in fact this theory calculates the numerical shifts in the basic space from event to event and then abstracts the regional shifts from these data. Regions that are passed through are circled or squared and connected by arrows. The squares around a region (as opposed to circles) denote each graph's beginning and ending points, and coincide with the E major tonics that are the framing events in the prolongational analysis of Figure 11.5. The solid arrows specify paths between events

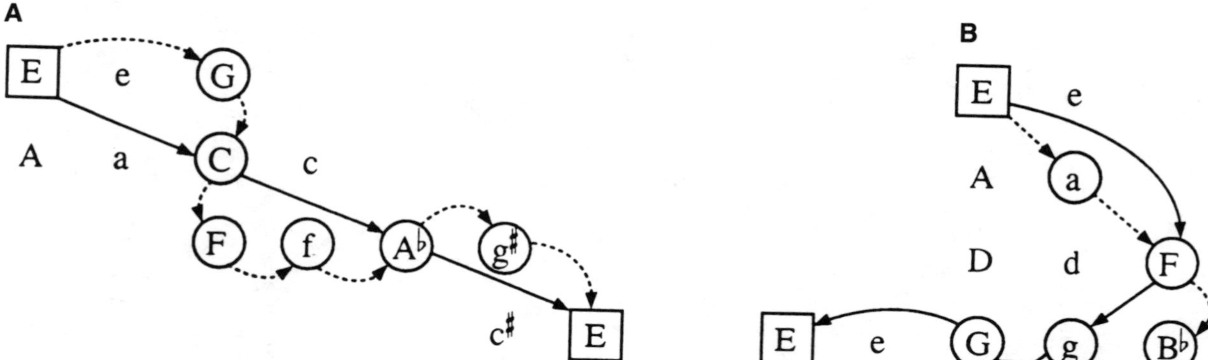

FIGURE 11.6 The journey in regional space. Figure 11.6A represents the second phrase. Figure 11.6B represents the third phrase.

of intermediate prolongational importance, the dashed arrows subsidiary paths that include prolongationally still more subordinate events. Thus the notation in Figure 11.6 conveys a degree of hierarchy. In a complete analysis there would be a pitch-space representation for each level in the corresponding prolongational reduction. (Alternatively, one can imagine prolongational branchings extending down not to events in music notation but to events in pitch space itself.)

Some interesting patterns emerge in Figure 11.6. The primary regions of the second phrase subdivide the octave into equal intervals (in this case, major thirds), a common 19th-century technique that Chopin pioneered. (It does not matter, incidentally, whether a tonal return ends up at the same point in the toroidally unfolded space; **E** is **E**, regardless of where it appears.) In the third phrase, observe the leap in the space from **G** to the final **E**, which corresponds to the almost visceral sense that the progression has jumped over into the final cadence. It is useful at this level of abstraction to appropriate the distinction (usually reserved for surface melodic phenomena) between a step and a skip. Until this point, the regional shifts have been stepwise: Each (local) arrow moves to a vertically, horizontally, or diagonally adjacent region in the space. But here there is a decided regional skip, for **G** must pass over **e** in order to reach **E**.

Figure 11.6 is hierarchically inadequate in that it collapses the distinction between chord and region. In the second phrase, for example, the G major triad (m. 5) is hardly a region, but is represented as **G** because there is no G available in the representation; on the other hand, **F** stands for a region (m. 6) traversed without any statement of its tonic chord. To capture such distinctions, we must invoke a more complex model, chordal/regional space. Fragments of this space are given for the same two phrases in Figure 11.7. Each six-chord unit represents the chordal space of Figure 11.3A. The regional designation at the center of each unit doubles for its tonic (I or i), and the regions are arrayed to form the regional space of Figure 11.3B. Parallel lines in the graph symbolize "pivots," entities that are single events at the musical surface but reinterpreted in the course of listening as two equivalent entities in different parts of the space. The path through this space is charted as before, but down to the detail of individual progressions. Although the "square" designation is retained for superordinate points, only local arrows (local progressions) are included, so as not to clutter up the graph. Now the G chord (m. 5) becomes a harmonic borrowing from the parallel tonic minor, **e**, reinterpreted as V/♭**VI** (V of **C**), to which region it subsequently progresses. **F** and **f** (mm. 6–7) are properly represented as regions passed through without local tonic realizations. Similarly, the mediant pivot chords in the third phrase (a and B♭) do not have to pretend to be regions.

A

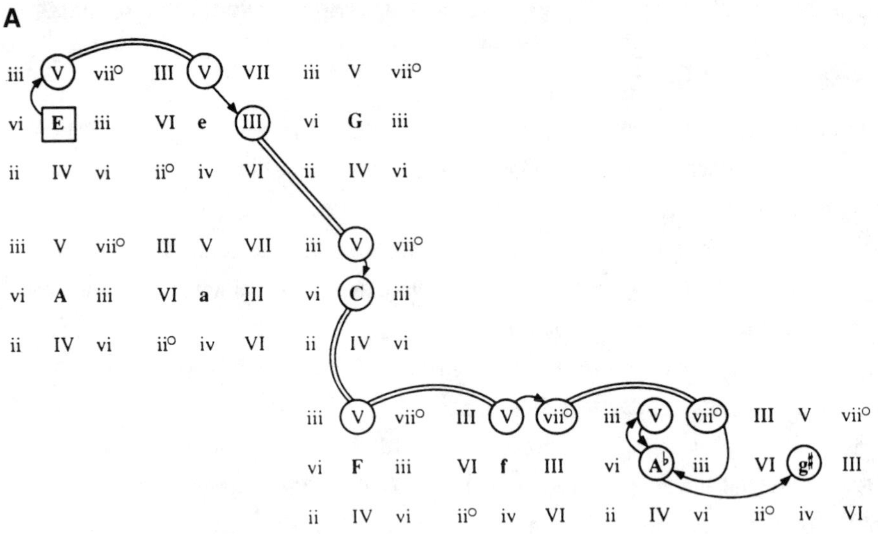

B

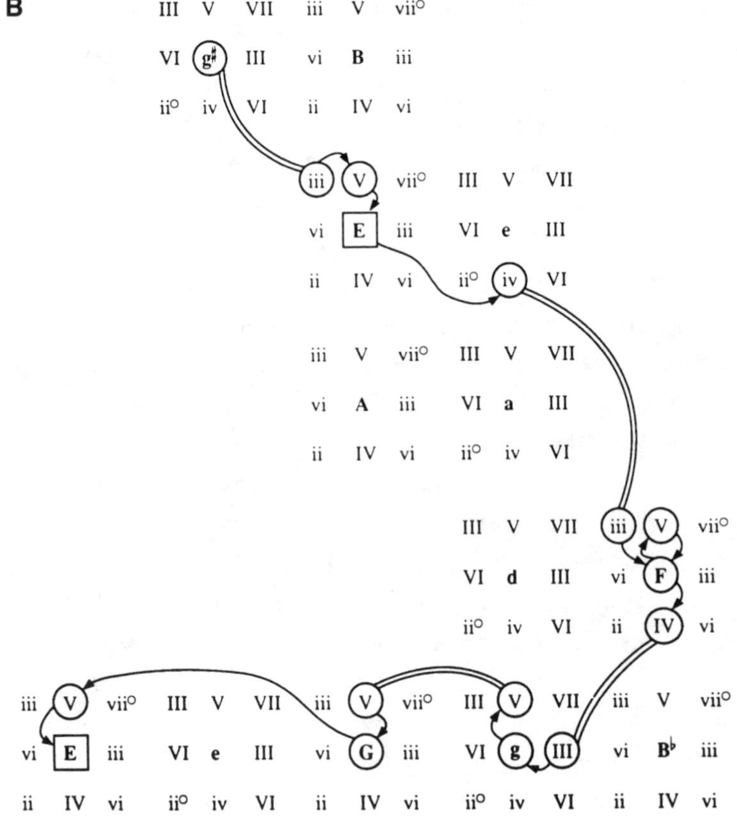

FIGURE 11.7 The journey in chordal/regional space. Figure 11.7A represents a plot of the second phrase. Figure 11.7B represents a plot of the third phrase.

Figure 11.7 falls short in one important respect. It does not show that the piece revolves around different forms of the mediant. There are four possible mediant harmonies: g♯ and G, directly available from **E** and **e**, respectively; and G♯ and g, accessed from the intermediate locations of **g♯** and **G**, respectively. The piece exploits all four possibilities: The first chromatic event is a G chord (m. 5); the climax resolves to I/**G♯** (**A♭**), followed by a transitional g♯ (m. 8); and the stepwise regional progression of the third phrase reaches **g–G** (m. 11) before the final resolution. But, as can be seen in Figure 11.8, regional space splits the four mediant regions into two clusters, **G♯** and **g♯**, and **G** and **g**. Should all of these chords and regions be proximate in the space to reflect the generalization that they are all forms of the abstraction we call the mediant? Is another axis needed to accomplish this?

The solution to this difficulty lies elsewhere. Figure 11.9 reveals a correspondence between the chordal and regional spaces. Vertically and horizontally, parallel major/minor regions clump together to form the same ordering as at the chordal level. Thus iii moves vertically down to vi and ii, just as **III–iii** do to **VI–vi** and **II–ii**; iii moves horizontally to V and vii°, just as **III–iii** do to **V–v** and **♭VII–♭vii**; and so on. This overall correspondence is due to both levels being generated by fifths and thirds axes. On the basis of this relation, let us propose a transformation that maps the regional and chordal spaces onto scale-degree space, as shown in Figure 11.10. The psychological claim for this representation is that listeners are able to hear units of tonal chords and regions as variants on a diatonic scale-degree schema. The mapping fixes the diatonic level and thereby reduces all chromaticisms to a diatonic base, a step that is implicit in Roman numeral notation, which assigns a diatonic scale degree to harmonic roots. However, since a scale degree is an abstraction rather than a specific pitch configuration (Schenker, 1906/1980), Figure 11.10 symbolizes scale degrees by Arabic numerals with carets (the Schenkerian symbol for scale degree) rather than by Roman numerals, which retain specific chordal or regional meanings. The dashed square encloses the part of the space that corresponds to Figure 11.9, but once again the fifth and third axes generate closed cycles.

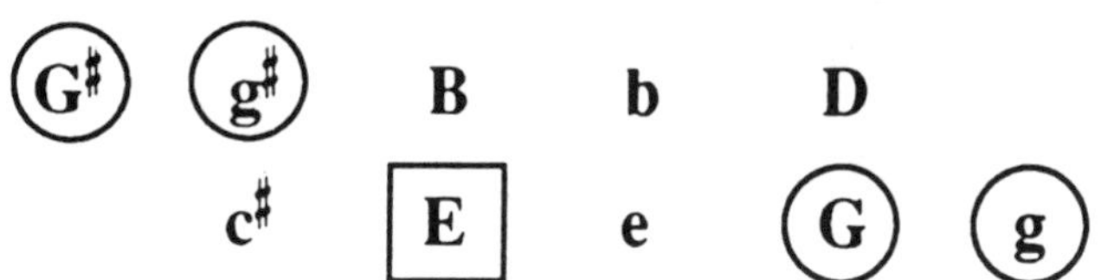

FIGURE 11.8 Nonproximity in regional space of different forms of region III.

iii	V	vii°
vi	I	iii
ii	IV	vi

III	**iii**	**V**	**v**	**♭VII**	**♭vii**
VI	**vi**	**I**	**i**	**♭III**	**♭iii**
II	**ii**	**IV**	**iv**	**♭VI**	**♭vi**

FIGURE 11.9 Correspondence between the chordal and regional tori.

$\hat{3}$	$\hat{5}$	$\hat{7}$	$\hat{2}$	$\hat{4}$	$\hat{6}$	$\hat{1}$
$\hat{6}$	$\hat{1}$	$\hat{3}$	$\hat{5}$	$\hat{7}$	$\hat{2}$	$\hat{4}$
$\hat{2}$	$\hat{4}$	$\hat{6}$	$\hat{1}$	$\hat{3}$	$\hat{5}$	$\hat{7}$
$\hat{5}$	$\hat{7}$	$\hat{2}$	$\hat{4}$	$\hat{6}$	$\hat{1}$	$\hat{3}$
$\hat{1}$	$\hat{3}$	$\hat{5}$	$\hat{7}$	$\hat{2}$	$\hat{4}$	$\hat{6}$

FIGURE 11.10 Scale-degree space.

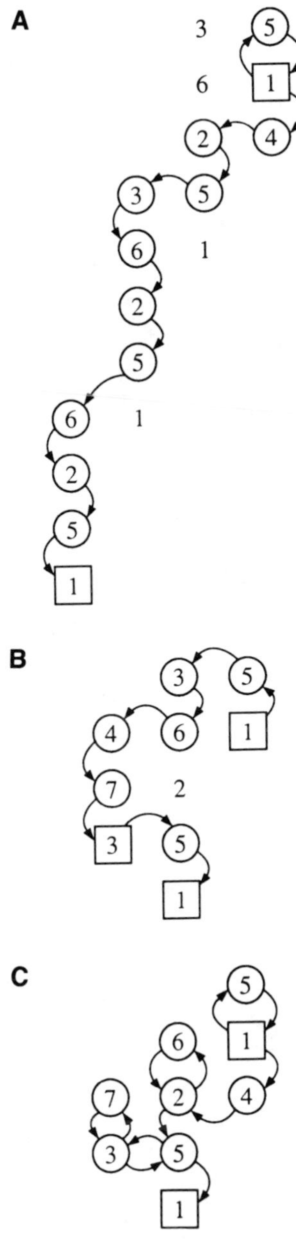

FIGURE 11.11 Three phrases in scale-degree space. Figure 11.11A represents the first phrase in scale-degree space. Figure 11.11B represents the second phrase in scale-degree space. Figure 11.11c represents the third phrase in scale-degree space.

Figure 11.11 gives the scale-degree representation for the Prelude. The arrows from number to number must take the shortest distance possible, a constraint that has been implicit all along but must be specially noted here, since the scale-degree numbers duplicate at short intervals. This constraint relies on the gestalt assumptions that the perceiver seeks simple patterns and that proximity is an important principle in organizing them.

The first phrase in Figure 11.11 requires an extensive unfolding of the space because its structural V arrives early and is drawn out by "deceptive" moves; that is, 5 moves twice to 6 rather than to 1. (Compare the twice-prolonged dominant in the first phrase of the prolongational analysis in Figure 11.5.) The second and third phrases are spatially more compact. Of course much of their musical interest is ironed out at this level of abstraction. However, that the representation has intuitive validity is shown by Figure 11.12, which recomposes the second and third phrases (simplifying the figuration) with all but a few local chromaticisms taken out. (Purists can realize a full diatonic version by ignoring the remaining accidentals.) This recomposition makes syntactic sense, so it seems reasonable to assert that listeners hear the highly chromatic music that Chopin wrote as a transformation of this underlying structure. Among other things, there is now one mediant harmony. Another telling detail in the unmodified version concerns the A major chord at the downbeat of m. 7, which Aldwell and Schachter (1979) interpret as an incidental consequence of the voice-crossings in mm. 5–7. Figures 11.5 and 11.7 in effect

FIGURE 11.12 Diatonic version of the second and third phrases of Chopin's E Minor Prelude.

agree and sweep it under the rug, but there is also a sense in which this event shines through, as it were, from the diatonic substrate that otherwise has been painted over at the chromatic surface. Figure 11.12 shows how smoothly the A major chord fits into the diatonic transform. When music cannot plausibly be reduced to scale-degree space, it is truly chromatic.

The three spatial models that have been invoked are not contradictory but, rather, are three ways of looking at and using the same essential structure. All derive from the basic space of Figure 11.2. Regional space is useful for finding and representing modulational patterns in a piece at various hierarchical levels correlated with prolongational reduction, but it is limited in its lack of chordal representation. Chordal/regional space rectifies this omission and in many repects provides an adequate simulation of pitch-space journeys, but at the price of a notational complexity that makes it difficult to convey hierarchically organized paths. Scale-degree space is useful in conjunction with the other representations, as a means of illuminating the diatonic substrate that underlies much chromatic music. A brief consideration of Chopin's E Minor Prelude suggests a fourth and rather different kind of representation.

Regional Prolongations in the E Minor Prelude

The score and prolongational analysis of the E Minor Prelude appear in Figures 11.13 and 11.14. In the latter (except for the registrally complex mm. 15–18) I have taken the shortcut of moving directly to the two-bar level in the time-span derivation. To bring out particular features, the note/slur prolongational notation at the bottom of the graph is cast in three levels. Level (c) in Figure 11.14 gives some linear shape to the descending chromatic harmonies, level (b) reveals their stepwise diatonic underpinnings, and level (a) displays the skeleton of the antecedent-consequent period that constitutes the form of the piece.

Although the harmonies are a product of voice leading, they are also objects that move through pitch space. Let us look at the first phrase (mm. 1–12) from this angle. Figure 11.15A shows the journey up to m. 8, just before the unambiguous emergence of the dominant preparation. Figure 11.15B resumes and completes the phrase. As Figure 11.15A shows, the regions of **iv**, **i**, and **III** are passed through (mm. 3–4, 5–6, and 7, respectively) without any arrival on their tonics. Not to capture these regional references would be to miss an important part of the phrase's meaning. Just as the melody is frozen, so the harmonies are unresolved; everything is implication.

FIGURE 11.13 Chopin: E Minor Prelude, op. 28, no. 4.

FIGURE 11.14 Prolongational analysis of Chopin's E Minor Prelude.

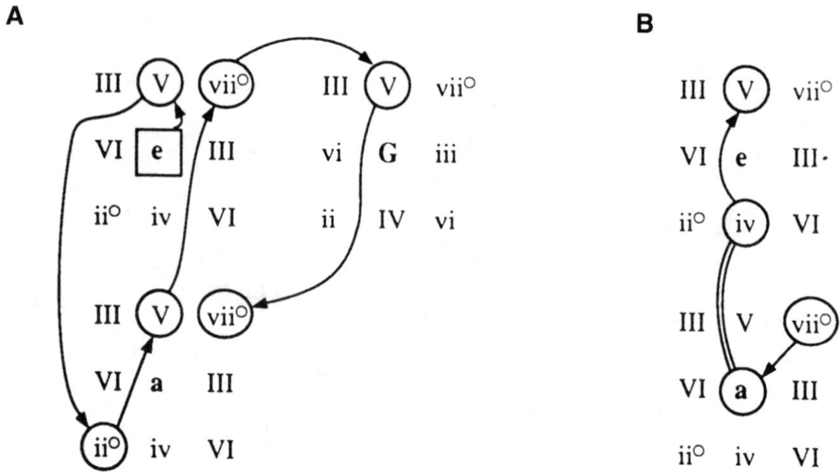

FIGURE 11.15 The path of the first phrase in chordal/regional space. Figure 11.15A represents mm. 1–8. Figure 11.15B represents mm. 8–12.

This is an embryonic instance of a technique that later became pervasive in such composers as Wagner and Debussy. Analytic discussions of Wagner's harmony (e.g., Bailey, 1977; Lewin, 1984; McCreless, 1982) habitually refer to key areas as being of primary importance, regardless of the presence or absence of tonic resolution. Indeed, regions in chromatic music often acquire a vividness far beyond the individual events and linear connections that instantiate them. In a reduction of a Classical tonal passage, the remaining event at an underlying level is normally the tonic to which the subordinate events refer; thus the reduction reflects the frame of reference. But an event reduction is of limited help in cases where, at various levels of detail, no tonic event is available to emerge as superordinate. Mitchell's (1967) well-known Schenkerian analysis of the Tristan Prelude fails on this ground alone.

These considerations suggest the need for a level of analysis that assigns hierarchical structure directly to regions, beyond the level of the pitch event. Figure 11.16 illustrates a regional prolongational analysis for the two Chopin preludes. The leaves of the trees are not events but regions. Whole notes designate regions whose tonics are stated, black notes regions whose tonics are not stated. Notes in parentheses indicate regions that are referred to marginally. Strong prolongations are obtained between whole notes, leaving weak prolongations for connections involving implied tonics. Once again, the slurs

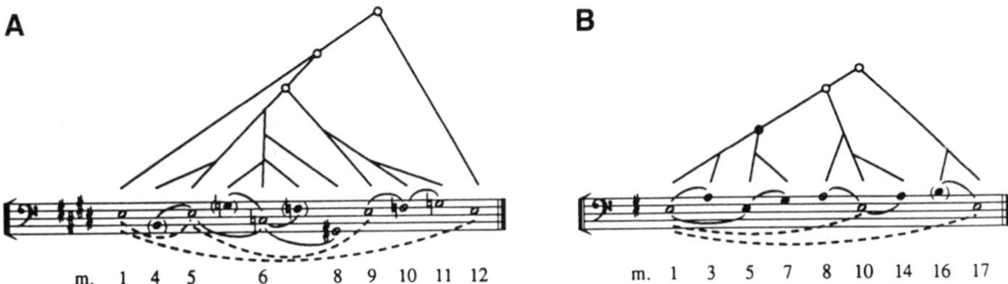

FIGURE 11.16 Regional prolongational analyses. Figure 11.16A represents Chopin's E Major Prelude. Figure 11.16B represents Chopin's E Minor Prelude.

correspond to branchings, with dashed slurs reserved for strong prolongations. The tree for the E Major Prelude conforms to a global level of the corresponding event prolongational analysis (see the superordinate branchings in Figure 11.5), but such cannot be the case for the E Minor Prelude with its unstated tonics. In particular, the return to **i** in mm. 5–6, treated as passing in the event analysis (Figure 11.14), is elevated to the status of a prolongation of the opening **i** in Figure 11.16, and **iv** (mm. 3–4) and **III** (m. 7) are given explicit representation as passing regions.

The graphs in Figure 11.16 complement the event prolongational analyses of Figures 11.5 and 11.14. Regional prolongational analyses register the significance of regions and their connections in the listener's comprehension and are indispensable when tonics are implied rather than realized.

Conclusions

With regional prolongational analysis we have reached a degree of theoretical abstraction that is at the same time experientially concrete. This suggests that the GTTM idealization of the pitch event as the leaf of a tree is an oversimplification. The GTTM conception of the pitch event (any discretely sounding sonority, hence any single pitch or vertical combination of pitches) includes only two of the three levels of pitch space, pitch and chord. The notion of regional prolongational analysis adds the third level, region, completing a correspondence between the levels of pitch space and the leaves of event reduction.

More generally, the pitch event is but one stage in the listener's organization of the musical signal. At lower levels, the perceptual processing that forms the event from the signal is quite complex (Bregman, 1990; Handel, 1989). At higher levels, events coalesce into regions and other abstract entities. The pitch event is merely a stable and theoretically useful point in the perceptual/cognitive flux we call music.

What is the psychological validity of the constructs advanced in this chapter? Although they are supported in general by the empirical literature, it remains to be seen how well they help model specific listening experience. The path representations, particularly that of chordal/regional space, may offer a precise means for investigating certain dynamic aspects of musical processing (along the lines of Krumhansl & Kessler, 1982). In any case, this study has been an exercise in theoretical rather than experimental music psychology. It is, in fact, only a first step toward a larger theoretical exploration of pitch-space journeys that must include a full treatment of prolongational analysis, pitch space, and the mappings from one to the other. Once that theoretical program is accomplished, it will be interesting to consider the relation of these musical structures to broader psychological issues. For example, this chapter treats music in terms of events and paths. Questions can be posed regarding what features and constraints musical events and paths must have in order to yield optimal intelligibility and to what extent, at an abstract level, they transfer to nonmusical experience.

References

Aldwell, E., & Schachter, C. (1979). *Harmony and voice leading: Vol. 2.* New York: Harcourt Brace Jovanovich.

Bailey, R. (1977). The structure of the Ring and its evolution. *19th-Century Music, 1,* 48–61.

Bharucha, J. J. (1984). Event hierarchies, tonal hierarchies, and assimilation: A reply to Deutsch and Dowling. *Journal of Experimental Psychology: General, 113*(3), 421–425.

Bregman, A. (1990). *Auditory scene analysis.* Cambridge, MA: MIT Press.

Deliège, I. (1987). Grouping conditions in music listening: An approach to Lerdahl and Jackendoff's grouping preference rules. *Music Perception, 4,* 325–360.

Deutsch, D., & Feroe, J. (1981). The internal representation of pitch sequences in tonal music. *Psychological Review, 88,* 503–522.

Handel, S. (1989). *Listening.* Cambridge, MA: MIT Press.

Krumhansl, C. L. (1983). Perceptual structures for tonal music. *Music Perception, 1*(1): 28–62.

Krumhansl, C. L. (1990). *Cognitive foundations of musical pitch.* New York: Oxford University Press.

Krumhansl, C. L., Bharucha, J. J., & Kessler, E. (1982). Perceived harmonic structure of chords in three related musical keys. *Journal of Experimental Psychology: Human Perception and Performance, 8*, 24–36.

Krumhansl, C. L., & Kessler, E. (1982). Tracing the dynamic changes in perceived tonal organization in a spatial representation of musical keys. *Psychological Review, 89*, 334–368.

Lerdahl, F. (1988). Tonal pitch space. *Music Perception, 5*(3), 315–350.

Lerdahl, F., & Jackendoff, R. (1983). *A generative theory of tonal music.* Cambridge, MA: MIT Press.

Lewin, D. (1984). Amfortas' prayer to Titurel and the role of D in Parsifal: The tonal spaces of the drama and the enharmonic C♭/B. *19th-Century Music, 7*, 336–349.

Longuet-Higgins, C. H. (1962). Two letters to a musical friend. *The Music Review, 23*, 244–248, 271–280. (Reprinted in H. C. Longuet-Higgins, *Mental Processes: Studies in Cognitive Science*, 1987, Cambridge, MA: MIT Press)

McCreless, P. (1982). *Wagner's* Siegfried: *Its drama, history, and music.* Ann Arbor, MI: UMI Research Press.

Mitchell, W. J. (1967). The *Tristan* prelude: Techniques and structure. In W. J. Mitchell & F. Salzer (Eds.), *The music forum: Vol. I.* New York: Columbia University Press.

Riemann, H. (1893). *Vereinfachte Harmonielehre, oder die Lehre von den Tonalen Funktionen der Akkorde.* London, Augener.

Schenker, H. (1906/1980). *Harmony.* (E. M. Borghese, Trans.). Chicago: University of Chicago Press.

Schoenberg, A. (1954). *Structural functions of harmony* (rev. ed.). New York: Norton (Reissued in 1969)

Simon, H. A., & Sumner, R. K. (1968). Pattern in music. In B. Kleinmuntz (Ed.), *Formal representation of human judgment.* New York: Wiley.

Shepard, R. (1982). Geometrical approximations to the structure of musical pitch. *Psychological Review, 89*, 305–333.

Weber, G. (1821). *Versuch einer Geordeneten Theorie.* Mainz, Germany: B. Schotts Söhne.

Werts, D. (1983). *A theory of scale references.* Unpublished doctoral dissertation, Princeton University, Princeton, NJ.

PART FOUR

Acquisition and Representation of Musical Knowledge

Introduction

As we have seen, persisting musical knowledge has often been described in terms of an acquired symbolic mental representation that listeners use to encode relevant aspects of a particular piece of music. The details of this acquired representation are the subject of much theoretical debate, but typically they are taken to reflect some elementary aspects of tonal, melodic, and/or metrical structure. But this general approach raises a number of questions. One of these is "What is elementary?" Carol Krumhansl in chapter 12 considers the importance of surface features in mental representations. Other questions concern the acquisition of musical knowledge—for instance, "How do listeners come to represent the structure of a musical event in a particular way?" Jamshed Bharucha (chapter 13) and Robert Gjerdingen (chapter 14) tackle this question and, curiously, their approach, which is connectionist in flavor, poses a challenge to the very notion of symbolic representations of knowledge.

Krumhansl juxtaposes iconic representations with symbolic ones. She reviews a wide range of evidence that points to the possibility of musical representation being both iconic, as visual representations are said to be, and symbolic, in the linguistic sense. She explores the possible modes of representation of four "psychological properties" of music (pitch, duration, loudness, timbre) as they may enter into larger organizational units in highly constrained, normative ways. The existence of these "stylistic norms" is important for musical memory, but Krumhansl describes a recent study which demonstrates that features of the musical surface also afford accurate memorial encoding.

Theories of acquisition of musical knowledge are hard to come by, and the two contrasting approaches represented by Bharucha and Gjerdingen are thought provoking. They both rely on the increasingly popular neural network modeling techniques to describe categorical learning of musical information of various sorts.

Bharucha has turned his attention to possible mechanisms for the spontaneous emergence of schematic structures for chord relations, assuming a listener's exposure to sequences of chords. Employing a connectionist network with an initial fixed architecture of tone, chord, and key units, he shows that the network can learn by the progressive maturation of units into feature detectors for increasingly higher level tonal patterns involving chords and their parent keys.

Neural networks may also be useful in the identification and categorization of high- and low-level *melodic* schemata that appear in musical compositions. Using self-organizing nets, Gjerdingen has demonstrated that surface-level events, which constitute simple grammatical features, can enter into identifiable relationships that impart a richness to the musical whole. Networks which are sensitized to the periodicities inherent in the acoustic signal, and those which are enabled to select preferences among embedded chord sequences, produce more "musical" memories.

CHAPTER 12

Internal Representations for Music Perception and Performance

Carol L. Krumhansl

As even a casual reading of the literature shows, the past decade has witnessed a phenomenal increase in the body of empirical knowledge about musical behaviors. Thus, it may be an appropriate time to step back somewhat from the specific observations to consider their bearing on traditional theoretical concerns within psychology, especially a psychology embedded within the broader context of the developing cognitive sciences. The nature of internal representations is perhaps the fundamental problem shared by all cognitive scientists. Observations bearing on this question depend on the disciplinary methodology with which the question is approached—whether, for example, insights come from behavioral measurements or computational models. However, there appears to be a general commitment to the idea that different approaches will converge on a common notion of appropriate representational formats.

Different domains of intelligent behavior may employ different kinds of representations. Studies of vision, for example, suggest that some internal representations have a continuous, perceptual character (that can be called "iconic"), with dimensions and operations that are analogous to physical dimensions and operations. In contrast, studies of language suggest more abstract, rule-governed representations (that can be called "symbolic"), with arbitrary mappings between discrete symbols and objects or events in the world. Music, as a domain of complex human behavior, suggests other kinds of representations or, at least, suggests ways in which our notions of representation can be broadened or sharpened. In this chapter I describe the experimental results from studies in music perception and production that seem suggestive about the nature of internal representations for music. Let me make clear in advance that I have no special convictions as to whether the evidence weighs toward iconic representations or symbolic representations. Rather, I present results supporting both kinds, suggesting that some aspects of music may be more iconic while other aspects may be more symbolic.

The Nature of Music: Some Preliminaries

Let us begin with the kinds of questions that immediately come to mind when first considering a domain from a cognitive science point of view. The answers suggested here are tentative and necessarily brief, clearly simplifying very complex issues. First, is music universal? Music is universal in the sense that all known cultures have some form of music. This may seem surprising to many at first because in our own culture we tend to leave the business of making music to a few individuals and consider it a special ability restricted to those individuals. Our culture may, in fact, be one of the most extreme in the degree to which musical participation is limited.

Second, why do we have music anyway? Does it serve any obvious adaptive function? I would say no single function seems to be served, but rather, different cultures emphasize diverse, possible functions to a variety of degrees. In addition to the aesthetic function, music is used to mark social groups or hierarchies within groups. It is used in ritual and religion, as well as for communication and commercial purposes. It produces strong emotional effects and engages intricate perceptual and cognitive processes. With regard to the latter, studying music enables us to expand our understanding of human thought. Lewis Thomas (1974/1980) suggests: "Instead of using what we can guess at about the nature of thought to explain the nature of music, start over again. Begin with music and see what this can tell us about the sensation of thinking. Music is the effort we make to explain to ourselves how our brains work" (p. 127). If he is right, then it may be that music is the most appropriate domain to study in the cognitive sciences.

Third, are there structural universals in music, cross-culturally and historically? Music varies widely, and although there are no absolute invariants, some general tendencies can be identified. In the rhythmic domain, ratios of durations such as 2:1 or

3:1 tend to dominate. In the pitch domain, most music selects from the continuous dimension of pitch frequency a small subset of discrete pitches that will make up the scale. With a few exceptions, musical cultures use an octave such that scale pitches repeat at the octave interval with frequency ratios of 2:1. Beyond these generalizations, the ways the dimensions of music are elaborated (melodically, harmonically, rhythmically, timbrally), and the ways it is performed (whether vocal or instrumental, solo or ensemble), vary tremendously.

The fourth question is what does music mean? Does music signify anything outside itself? There are different, sometimes widely divergent, opinions on this topic, some of which are summarized by Kraut (chapter 2), Raffman (chapter 3), and Sloboda (chapter 4) in this volume. Some commentators have suggested that music has iconic functions in that it simulates objects or events in the world, such as birds singing, brooks babbling, and so on. Others have suggested that music simulates in some way emotional states such as joy and sorrow. For the most part, studies (e.g., Brown, 1981) that have looked at listeners' associations to music have not found high levels of agreement—which seems a reasonable criterion for communicated meaning. So, it would seem that the meaning of music resides primarily in the relationships between musical events themselves rather than between musical events and nonmusical entities (see also Meyer, 1956).

This brings us to the fifth question, which is whether there is something like a musical syntax or grammar. Here, I would say the general consensus is yes. Within stylistic traditions, there are conventions concerning the way in which musical elements are combined into patterns. Examples would be metrical organization of events in time, sequences of harmonic progressions, and mechanisms for establishing rhythm and phrasing. These regularities can be explicitly codified as collections of rules (i.e., counterpoint and harmony in Western music, and harmony in jazz) in some cases. Other aspects are more difficult to describe in this way. Even in the clearer cases, however, I would point to two important differences from what is meant by grammar in linguistics. First, in music the distinction between what is grammatical and what is ungrammatical is not clear. One can judge whether a sequence fits norms of well-formedness, but intentional deviations may serve artistic purposes. In other words, these rules are meant to be broken. Second, the role of ambiguity in music seems much larger. For example, a chord may be heard simultaneously in its multiple roles in different keys, with the effect that modulations between closely related keys are easily assimilated. The role of a chord need never be disambiguated; no single, final parsing is required.

The sixth and final question is whether processes of logical reasoning, like deduction, induction, and problem solving, occur in the domain of music, and the general answer seems to be no. One pattern can suggest or imply another pattern, and, indeed, dynamically changing expectations are central to the experience of music. Moreover, in composition or improvisation certain problems of organization need to be worked out. Performers have to devise a plan for how to play a piece so as to convey their interpretation (see Palmer, chapter 15, this volume). However, none of these examples appears to fit what is generally meant by logical reasoning as studied in other domains.

Events in Music

With these preliminaries aside, I would like to turn now to some more concrete and specific observations about music. It is important to remember that the physical stimulus for music is the sound-pressure wave, that is, the changes in sound pressure over time. The ear analyzes this physical stimulus into component frequencies over a wide range, from approximately 20 to 20,000 cycles per second. Most tones produced by musical instruments contain a number of component frequencies that are harmonically related, that is, with frequencies that are simple integer ratios. These harmonics, however, are heard as coming from the same source. When two instruments are playing at the same time, the problem of separating the acoustic information into the two sources becomes much more complex.

A great deal of early processing must go on to transform the acoustic signal into the elementary events that are perceived. What we experience are musical instruments playing certain notes for certain durations at certain dynamic levels. Various principles of a gestalt nature help segment the auditory information as described in Bregman's (1990) book *Auditory Scene Analysis.* The harmonics of an instrument tend to begin and end together in time, tend to undergo the same frequency and amplitude modulation, come from the same location in space, and (as has already been mentioned) tend to have simple frequency ratios. These principles yield the elementary events (the musical tones) that then go into the formation of larger melodic, harmonic, rhythmic, and metrical units.

We come now to the central question about internal representations in music: What kind of information about the musical stimulus is internalized, in what form(s) is it stored, and how is it interpreted and recognized? With regard to visual perception, Kosslyn and Pomerantz (1977) warned against thinking of visual representations as pictures in the head. Similarly, I would warn against thinking of perceived or imagined music as auditory tapes in the head which record sound-pressure variations continuously over time. Visual representations are organized at early levels of processing into objects, properties of objects, and spatial relations between objects; music is organized at early levels of processing into events, properties of events, and temporal relations between events. These early processes are assumed to be automatic and not under attentional control.

For purposes of discussion, let us adopt the following formalism for musical events: $\text{Event}_{\text{time}}$ (pitch, duration, loudness, timbre). The subscript notation is used to indicate that musical events are indexed in time. This mathematical convention is adopted as a way of specifying a value (time) for each event with respect to which it is ordered relative to other events. This index would be analogous to spatial location for objects in visual space. Each event has four (not necessarily independent) psychological properties: pitch, duration, loudness, and timbre. To these four, one might also add the location of the source, although various results (Bregman, 1990) indicate this property may be relatively weak. Each of the other terms of the formalism will be examined in light of whether it is better considered a continuous, iconic attribute (perhaps directly analogous to some external, physical attribute) or whether it is better considered a discrete, symbolic attribute (coded in terms of a cognitive category abstracted from any physical attribute).

The Attributes of Music

The indexing attribute of time is best considered to be a continuous dimension that corresponds fairly closely to veridical (objective or clock) time. My primary reason for believing this comes from the very precise and regular measurements of timing in performances. For example, Shaffer, Clarke, and Todd (1985) measured the durations of each note in the opening theme and two of its repeats in three performances of a Satie piano piece (*Gnossienne* No. 5). The correspondences between the performances were striking, suggesting that the performed events were controlled by a mechanism having an accurate index of time. This is not to suggest, however, that timing in musical performance conforms to notated values. Rather, as indicated later and discussed in detail by Palmer and Shaffer (chapters 15 and 16, this volume, respectively) studies of performance timing show systematic deviations from mechanical regularity.

Perceptual observations also suggest that time is the indexing dimension for music. For example, the unidirectional aspect of time (progressing forward) is reflected in the fact that, although possible, it is difficult to recognize a melody played backwards, whereas other transformations such as transposition in pitch range, change of tempo, change of dynamics, and change of instrument, leave the melody recognizable. Also suggesting that musical representations are coded with respect to time is Halpern's (1988) result showing something analogous to mental scanning of visual images. She presented one word from the lyrics of a song, and then another word from the same song. Subjects had to compare the pitch height of the corresponding notes. Reaction time to do this task increased as a function of the distance in beats between the two words in the actual song, suggesting the listeners temporally scanned an image of the melody. In the sense of there being a continuous indexing dimension to musical representations corresponding fairly closely to veridical time, then, we might say that music is iconic.

However, some of the perceived attributes of music appear to be more of a discrete, categorical nature. Pitch is one such attribute, and I will say more later about how pitch structures are formed. As indicated earlier, musical cultures select from the continuous dimension of pitch frequency a small subset of pitch values from which the music will be constructed. Listeners tend to perceive musical pitch in terms of pitch categories, with focal values within categories. Some studies have even suggested that there are circumstances in which musical pitch is perceived categorically by musicians. The study of Burns and Ward (1978), for example, found a typical pattern of categorical perception: sharp boundaries between interval labels (of minor third, major third, and perfect fourth) and an inability to distinguish intervals within categories. This may, in part, account for the degree to which we accept poor intonation in performance, notably string and vocal performance. However, there may be systematic deviations from focal pitch values used for expressive purposes, although this aspect of musical performance has not been studied as systematically as have timing variations.

Musical notation indicates discrete values for note durations. Usually, the majority of durations in a composition are one value, setting a kind of durational unit, and there is a secondary value that is two or three times this durational unit (Fraisse, 1982). For example, the majority of notes might be quarter-notes, and most of the remaining notes might be half-notes, with a 1:2 ratio. Povel's (1981) study of imitation timing of simple durational patterns showed a strong bias to simplify the ratios to a 1:2 value, suggesting that for simple patterns there may be a kind of categorical perception of durations or, at least, an assimilation to simple ratios. The situation with real musical performances, however, is far more complicated. As has been shown by Gabrielsson (1987, 1988), Palmer (1989; chapter 15, this volume), Shaffer (1981, chapter 16, this volume), Todd (1985), and others, there are systematic deviations from mechanical regularity. The general view is that these deviations sharpen durational contrasts at local levels of temporal structure and highlight structural properties at higher levels. For example, rubatos (slowings of tempo) signal phrase endings. These deviations (it is assumed) are interpreted against the background of regular temporal units, which are discrete and categorical.

Less is known about how loudness is used in performance and how it is perceived. Musical notation indicates approximately seven discrete dynamic levels, as well as continuous increases in dynamics (crescendos) and continuous decreases in dynamics (decrescendos). Nakamura (1987) recently studied how well listeners can judge the performer's intended dynamics, and found this information is communicated fairly well. However, physical measurements of intensity did not correspond to either the intended or the perceived dynamics, suggesting context is important. For example, rising pitch enhances the impression of crescendos, while falling pitch enhances the impression of decrescendos. In sum, this attribute of music appears to interact in perception with other attributes and, in some instances, to vary along a continuous dimension (from soft to loud or loud to soft).

The final attribute is timbre, which is defined as the way in which musical tones differ once they are equated for pitch, loudness, and duration. For example, it is the difference between a violin and an oboe playing the same note for the same duration at the same loudness. Scaling studies, such as those done by Grey (1975), show that at least three continuous dimensions underlie perceived differences between instrumental tones: (a) how much energy is concentrated in the higher harmonics, (b) how rapid or percussive the attack portion is, and (c) whether the harmonics evolve synchronously or not. I suspect that even this three-dimensional description is an oversimplification (Krumhansl, 1989b). Unique qualities also mark different instruments, and the identification of the source is at least one part of the perceptual experience. Thus, timbre is perhaps the most clearly iconic of musical attributes in the sense of resisting simple categorical description. As with dynamics, timbre appears to interact with pitch (Iverson & Krumhansl, 1989).

Thus, in describing music it seems useful to talk about elementary musical events that are indexed with respect to the continuous dimension of time. Each event has four attributes. The first two, pitch and duration, appear to be more discrete and categorical in nature, with variations around focal values. The last two, loudness and timbre, are more continuous. Given this, it may be that the first two attributes enter more naturally into larger organizational units whose construction is rule governed. Indeed, the primary organizational attributes of longer musical sequences are pitch and duration, and the remainder of my chapter will be concerned with these.

Musical Syntax

With the increased interest in considering music more from a cognitive than a purely perceptual point of view came a concern with describing the kinds of knowledge listeners have about the rules governing the way the elementary events are combined. Within stylistic traditions, certain regularities can be identified concerning the formation of melodic, harmonic, rhythmic, and metrical units. These regularities, internalized by listeners through experience, are presumed to affect the way individual sequences are encoded and remembered. They provide a basis for interpreting the functions of the elementary events within the broader context and generating expectations for subsequent events. The term *schema* is often used to refer to knowledge of this sort and has proved useful in connection with music.

In studies of Western tonal-harmonic music, experimental investigations have shown that tonal schemas include knowledge of scale structure, the functions of tones and chords in keys, and the relations between different keys. These results conform well to music–theoretical descriptions. For example, music theorists (Lerdahl, 1988, chapter 11, this volume; Meyer, 1956) describe a hierarchy of tones in tonal contexts which has been experimentally verified using the probe-tone technique (Krumhansl & Kessler, 1982; Krumhansl & Shepard, 1979). The listeners' probe-tone ratings correspond to the frequency with which the tones are sounded in tonal compositions (Krumhansl, 1990), suggesting that the tonal hierarchy is internalized through experience with music in this style. The tonal hierarchy also affects the degree to which different tones are heard as being related to one another (Krumhansl, 1979, 1990). Moreover, Krumhansl and Kessler (1982) showed that the experimentally quantified tonal hierarchy can be used to generate a musically interpretable map of musical keys (in which the 24 major and minor keys are located on the surface of a torus), which was then used to trace how the sense of key develops and changes over time.

This kind of schematic knowledge is known to have a variety of consequences for how events are encoded and remembered (summarized in Krumhansl, 1990). For example, tonal schemas affect the perceived relations between tones and between chords, as well as temporal-order preferences for tones and chords. Regular key-distance effects on perceived tonal and harmonic relations have also been found. Tonal schemas have been shown to influence memory for individual tones and chords within sequences, and also memory for entire tone and chord sequences. Key distance also affects memory for melodic and harmonic sequences. Finally, effects of schemas are also evident in expectations for tonal and harmonic continuations (Schmuckler, 1989) and improvised continuations (Schmuckler, 1988). The emerging picture, at least for Western tonal-harmonic music, is one in which listeners have knowledge about the structural functions of three kinds of elements (tones, chords, and keys) and their interdependencies.

In addition, various commonalities between music and language have been identified. In comparing these two communication systems, it is important to keep in mind that there are undoubtedly highly developed characteristics specific to each. However, because at an early level of processing they utilize the same sensory system and probably are subject to the same principles of perceptual organization, there may also be commonalities. Bregman (1990) and Handel (1990) suggest similar factors operate in speech and music at early levels of processing to organize the complex acoustic signal into events that make up extended rule-governed patterns.

At more abstract structural levels, parallels can also be identified. Music, like language, can be described in terms of hierarchically embedded temporal units. A short segment constitutes a unit at one level and then joins with other segments to form longer units at higher levels of the hierarchy. One way of characterizing this is Lerdahl and Jackendoff's (1983) time-span reduction. This representation not only describes the hierarchical embedding of events of different lengths, but also indicates which events are dominant and which are subordinate. Some support for this representation comes from two studies by Palmer and myself (1987a, 1987b). We stopped the music (a Bach fugue and the opening theme from the Mozart A Major Piano Sonata) at various points and asked listeners to rate the sounded segment in terms of how good or complete a phrase it formed. These phrase-ending judgments correlated significantly with the position of the last-sounded event in the time-span reduction tree. Krumhansl and Jusczyk (1990) recently showed that infants are sensitive to phrase structure in music and may depend on some of the same cues as those found in speech (drops in pitch and longer durations).

Musical Surface

The research cited in the last section has been useful for demonstrating that musical schemas (i.e., knowledge of stylistic norms for forming larger well-formed sequences) are used to interpret the sounded events. However, it may have underestimated listeners' ability to remember surface, stylistic characteristics of particular pieces. Intuitively, it seems that we may have a very large memory capacity for musical detail. I tested this in a recognition memory study (Krumhansl, 1989a, 1991). For this study, it seemed important to use music written in an unfamiliar style, so that the memory judgments would necessarily be based on memory for surface characteristics rather than on a representation interpreted in terms of stylistic norms. The piece used was Messiaen's *Mode de valeurs et d'intensités*, written in 1949. It is notated in three lines, and conforms to a unique compositional principle. Within each line, all 12 chromas appear. Moreover, every time a particular chroma appears it is always sounded in a particular octave, for a specified duration, and at a specified dynamic. This is to say that these dimensions are perfectly correlated in the music.

Figure 12.1 shows the procedure used in the experiment. Listeners heard just the first half of the piece, which is about 2 minutes long. This was followed by six test segments of six types. The first segment type was from the part of the piece they had heard, called Original (old). The second was from the part of the piece they had not heard, called Original (new). The third was a transformation in which six chromas were changed in the top line, each by one semitone so as to preserve contour. The fourth was a transformation in which the chromas used in the bottom line were substituted for those used in the top line and vice versa. This transformation also preserved contour, but changed the majority of melodic and harmonic intervals. The fifth segment type was an inversion of each line around its midrange, inverting contour in all cases. The sixth was a transformation in which the top line was moved to the range of the bottom line and vice versa.

The listeners' task was to judge the likelihood that each excerpt came from the piece (whether or not it came from the part of the piece they had heard). A correct "Yes" answer would thus be given to the first two kinds of segments. They were told that the piece was very homogeneous throughout; it contained no exact repetitions, however. For this task, listeners used a rating scale on which 1 was designated "very sure the segment is not from the piece" and 8 was designated "very sure the segment is from the piece." After hearing the first half of the piece and the six test segments in random order, listeners heard the first half of the piece again and six more test segments. This process was

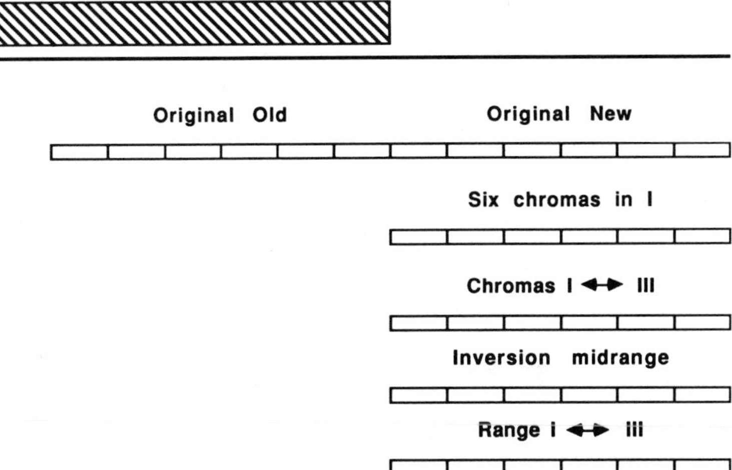

FIGURE 12.1 Outline of the design of the memory study of Messiaen's *Mode de valeurs et d'intensités*. The entire duration of the piece is indicated by the horizontal line. Listeners heard the first half of the piece (indicated by the hatched segment). The six types of test segments were: Original (old)—from the part of the piece the listeners had heard; Original (new)—from the part of the piece the listeners had not heard; and four transformations of materials from the second half of the piece. From "Memory for Musical Surface," by C. L. Krumhansl, 1991, *Memory and Cognition*. Copyright (1991) by the Psychonomic Society, Inc. Reprinted by permission.

repeated a total of six times. The listeners were undergraduate music majors, none of whom knew the piece in advance.

The results appear in Figure 12.2. A number of features are striking. First, even after just one hearing listeners very accurately recognized segments from the section of the piece they had heard, and performance did not improve with repeated listenings. Second, they were able to generalize to the rest of the piece, judging these test excerpts to be from the piece with above chance accuracy. The higher accuracy for the Original (old) segments than for the Original (new) segments indicates some memory for precise surface detail. The ability to generalize to the rest of the piece indicates that listeners have also abstracted something about the stylistic characteristics of the piece as a whole. However, listeners frequently made false alarms to the transformation in which only six chromas in the top line were changed, preserving contour (consistent with Dowling's,

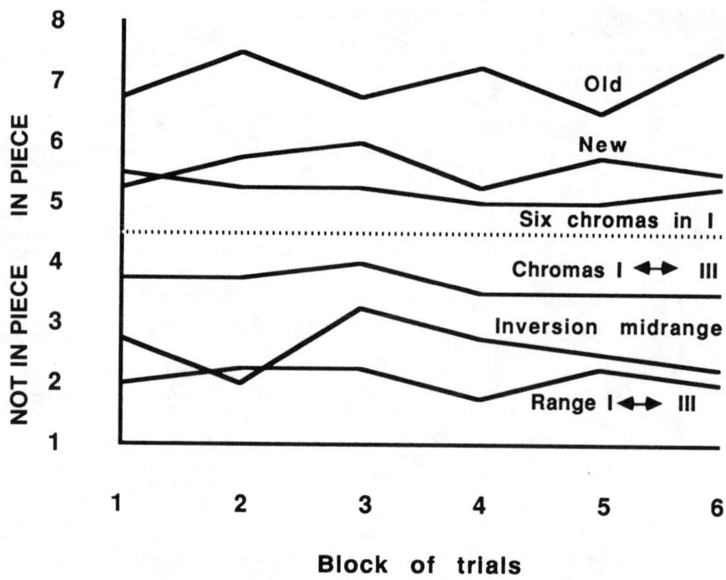

FIGURE 12.2 Results for the six types of test segments. After hearing the first half of the piece, listeners heard six test segments (one of each of the six types). These were judged in terms of whether or not they came from the piece, either from the part of the piece listeners had heard or the part of the piece they had not heard. This process was repeated, for a total of six blocks of trials. From "Memory for Musical Surface," by C. L. Krumhansl, in press, *Memory and Cognition*. Copyright (in press) by the Psychonomic Society, Inc. Reprinted by permission.

1978, results showing the importance of contour). Apparently, listeners do not remember the precise intervals or the correlations between chroma and the other dimensions. The other transformations were easier to reject.

Thus on the negative side, this study found certain transformations of the music were difficult for the listeners to reject. However, on the positive side, listeners were surprisingly accurate in recognizing segments from the part of the piece they had heard only a few times, and they were able to extend a sense of the style to the part of the piece they had not heard. This suggests that studies of musical memory, which have typically looked at recognition of short, artificially constructed sequences, may have underestimated long-term memory capacity for surface characteristics of particular pieces. Although musical schemas (which tend to reduce the sounded events to discrete categories) may significantly affect musical memory, they are not apparently necessary for fairly accurate memory encoding of surface (perceptual or iconic) attributes.

Conclusions

The intensive empirical effort to understand musical behaviors over the last decade has yielded some preliminary notions about the nature of internal representations for music. It is an interesting domain to compare with the more studied domains of vision and language. Like visual representations, there is a continuous indexing dimension—space for vision and time for music. In both cases, however, the stimulus is encoded as discrete subunits, each with distinctive attributes. In vision, for example, objects are identified with attributes of color, texture, form, and so on. In music, events are identified with attributes of pitch, duration, loudness, and timbre. These events enter into larger structural units of melody, harmony, meter, rhythm, and phrasing. These larger structural units appear to be more rule governed and to share some abstract structural principles with the syntactic aspect of language. Thus, music appears to be a case requiring both iconic and rule-governed (or symbolic) representations.

References

Bregman, A. S. (1990). *Auditory scene analysis.* Cambridge, MA: MIT Press.

Brown, R. (1981). Music and language. In *Documentary report of the Ann Arbor symposium: Applications of psychology to the teaching and learning of music.* Reston, VA: Music Educators National Conference.

Burns, E. M., & Ward, W. D. (1978). Categorical perception-phenomenon or epiphenomenon: Evidence from experiments in the perception of melodic musical intervals. *Journal of the Acoustical Society of America, 63,* 456–468.

Dowling, W. J. (1978). Scale and contour: Two components of a theory of memory for melodies. *Psychological Review, 85,* 341–354.

Fraisse, P. (1982). Rhythm and tempo. In D. Deutsch (Ed.), *The psychology of music.* New York: Academic Press.

Gabrielsson, A. (1987). Once again: the theme from Mozart's Piano Sonata in A Major (K.331). In A. Gabrielsson (Ed.), *Action and perception in rhythm and music* (Publication No. 55). Stockholm: Royal Swedish Academy of Music.

Gabrielsson, A. (1988). Timing in music performance and its relations to music expression. In J. A. Sloboda (Ed.), *Generative processes in music.* Oxford: Oxford University Press.

Grey, J. M. (1975). *Exploration of musical timbre.* Doctoral dissertation, Stanford University, Stanford, CA. (Department of Music Report STAN-M-2)

Halpern, A. R. (1988). Mental scanning in auditory imagery for songs. *Journal of Experimental Psychology: Learning, Memory, and Cognition, 14,* 434–443.

Handel, S. (1990). *Listening.* Cambridge, MA: MIT Press.

Iverson, P., & Krumhansl, C. L. (1989). Pitch and timbre interaction in isolated tones and in sequences. *Journal of the Acoustical Society of America, 86,* S58.

Kosslyn, S. M., & Pomerantz, J. R. (1977). Imagery, propositions, and the form of internal representations. *Cognitive Psychology, 9,* 52–76.

Krumhansl, C. L. (1979). The psychological representation of musical pitch in a tonal context. *Cognitive Psychology, 11,* 346–374.

Krumhansl, C. L. (1989a, November). *Memory for compositional style in music.* Paper presented at the meeting of the Psychonomic Society, Atlanta, GA.

Krumhansl, C. L. (1989b). Why is musical timbre so hard to understand? In S. Nielzen & O. Olsson (Eds.), *Structure and perception of electroacoustic sound and music.* Amsterdam: Elsevier.

Krumhansl, C. L. (1990). *Cognitive foundations of musical pitch.* New York: Oxford University Press.

Krumhansl, C. L. (1991). Memory for musical surface. *Memory & Cognition, 19,* 401–411.

Krumhansl, C. L., & Jusczyk, P. (1990). Infants' perception of phrase structure in music. *Psychological Science, 1,* 70–73.

Krumhansl, C. L., & Kessler, E. J. (1982). Tracing the dynamic changes in perceived tonal organization in a spatial representation of musical keys. *Psychological Review, 89,* 334–368.

Krumhansl, C. L., & Shepard, R. N. (1979). Quantification of the hierarchy of tonal functions within a diatonic context. *Journal of Experimental Psychology: Human Perception and Performance, 5,* 579–594.

Lerdahl, F. (1988). Tonal pitch space. *Music Perception, 5,* 315–350.

Lerdahl, F., & Jackendoff, R. (1983). *A generative theory of tonal music.* Cambridge, MA: MIT Press.

Meyer, L. B. (1956). *Emotion and meaning in music.* Chicago: University of Chicago Press.

Nakamura, T. (1987). The communication of dynamics between musicians and listeners through musical performance. *Perception & Psychophysics, 41,* 525–553.

Palmer, C. (1989). Mapping musical thought to musical performance. *Journal of Experimental Psychology: Human Perception and Performance, 15,* 301–315.

Palmer, C., & Krumhansl, C. L. (1987a). Independent temporal and pitch structures in perception of musical phrases. *Journal of Experimental Psychology: Human Perception and Performance, 13,* 116–26.

Palmer, C., & Krumhansl, C. L. (1987b). Pitch and temporal contributions to musical phrase perception: Effects of harmony, performance timing, and familiarity. *Perception & Psychophysics, 41,* 505–518.

Povel, D. J. (1981). Internal representation of simple temporal patterns. *Journal of Experimental Psychology: Human Perception and Performance, 7,* 3–18.

Schmuckler, M. A. (1988). *Expectation in music: Additivity of melodic and harmonic processes.* Unpublished doctoral dissertation, Cornell University, Ithaca, NY.

Schmuckler, M. A. (1989). Expectation in music: Investigation of melodic and harmonic processes. *Music Perception, 7,* 109–150.

Shaffer, L. H. (1981). Performances of Chopin, Bach, and Bartok: Studies in motor programming. *Cognitive Psychology, 13,* 326–376.

Shaffer, L. H., Clarke, E. F., & Todd, N. P. (1985). Rhythm in piano performance. *Cognition, 20,* 61–77.

Thomas, L. (1974/1980). *The medusa and the snail.* Toronto: Bantam.

Todd, N. P. (1985). A model of expressive timing in tonal music. *Music Perception, 3,* 33–59.

CHAPTER 13

Tonality and Learnability

Jamshed J. Bharucha

How are perceptual schemata for tonality acquired? This chapter is an attempt to demonstrate how a schematic structure for simple chord relationships can develop as a consequence of exposure to a musical environment in which these relationships are pervasive.

A tonal context influences the perception of tones (Cuddy, Cohen, & Miller, 1979; Dowling, 1978; Krumhansl, 1979) and chords (Bharucha & Krumhansl, 1983; Bharucha & Stoeckig, 1986, 1987; Krumhansl, Bharucha, & Castellano, 1982). Effects of this sort have been attributed to acquired mental schemata (e.g., Dowling, 1978). A schema is a mental representation that encodes abstract patterns in the environment. Once acquired, it generates expectations for patterns that are similar to those encountered before. These schematic expectations establish an internalized cultural baseline that is presupposed by what Meyer (1956) and others have considered to be a central aspect of musical aesthetics, namely, the fulfillment and violation of expectancies.

There is strong evidence that Western listeners have schemata for typical chord relations. A triad is processed more quickly, its intonation is judged more accurately, and it is heard as more consonant if it follows a triad with which it is commonly associated (Bharucha & Stoeckig, 1986, Experiments 2 and 3). These facilitative effects do not depend on formal musical training and occur even when associates have no probability advantage in the

This work was supported by a grant from the National Science Foundation (BNS–8910778). I thank Mari Riess Jones, Susan Holleran, Robert Gjerdingen, and Peter Todd for comments on this chapter.

proximal context (Bharucha & Stoeckig, 1986). They are automatic, persisting in spite of explicit knowledge of whether to expect an associate or not (Bharucha & Stoeckig, 1989). They persist when acoustic factors that favor associated chords are removed (Bharucha & Stoeckig, 1987). They mirror data from expectation judgments (Schmuckler, 1988), relatedness judgements and memory confusions (Bharucha & Krumhansl, 1983; Krumhansl, Bharucha & Castellano, 1982) and are in accord with music theoretic descriptions of musical structure, suggesting a common underlying process. Since these effects cannot easily be explained solely by acoustic, psychoacoustic, or distributional factors that depend only on the proximal musical context, one is compelled to conclude that they reflect the prior schematic encoding of chord relations as a result of long term exposure.

The goal of this chapter is to show specifically how such a schematic representation might be acquired and to provide support for both the genre of representation as well as the learning mechanism it supports. The model, called MUSACT, has been described in earlier papers after learning was presumed to have occurred. Bharucha (1987a, 1987b) has proposed a learning mechanism that bootstraps MUSACT's particular connectivity. It falls under the broad category of mechanisms that have been proposed to enable networks of neurons to self-organize in response to regularities in the environment (Fukushima, 1975; Grossberg, 1972, 1976; Kohonen, 1984; Rumelhart & Zipser, 1985; von der Malsberg, 1973).

MUSACT is a computational neural net model that accounts for the patterns observed in the studies cited above on the basis of a hierarchical organization of pitch classes. It exhibits, as an emergent property, abstract harmonic relations such as the circle of fifths. An "emergent property" is taken to mean a global property that the model exhibits as a consequence of multiple local constraints acting in tandem. The local constraints are the grouping of tones to form chords and the grouping of chords to form keys. These local constraints are learned by the corresponding physical grouping of tones and chords in Western music. As such, there is nothing surprising about the pattern of connectivity in the network: Units representing pitch classes are connected to units representing their parent chords, and these in turn are connected to units representing their parent keys. What is interesting is how much can be derived from so little. Nothing needs to be represented or learned explicitly about diatonicity or key relationships, which are emergent properties. Although these properties may be demonstrated formally, without recourse to a neural net, MUSACT is intended to be a processing model of how the properties emerge from a neurologically plausible system that learns through passive exposure to the environment.

MUSACT makes two general assumptions. The first assumption concerns the initial architecture of the network. This involves the specification of how units are initially interconnected and what units, if any, have prior tuning characteristics. The second assumption concerns the learning algorithm—that is, the determination of which connections should change their strengths and by how much. Each assumption is discussed in the following sections.

Initial State

The initial architecture of the network is a hierarchy of units, such that each unit in a layer is connected to each unit in the next layer. The weights (the strengths of the connections) are initially random.

Tuning Characteristics of the Input Units

Units in the input layer are tuned to pitch classes; that is, they are feature detectors for pitch classes. Feature detectors are cells that respond selectively to the presence of specific features. In the visual system, for example, there are cells that respond to selected wavelengths bands of light (e.g., cones), and cells that respond only to edges or bars at specific orientations (Hubel & Wiesel, 1979). In the auditory system, there are cells that respond selectively to narrow bands of audible frequencies. The frequency continuum is thus represented by an array of such specialized cells whose receptive fields collectively span the audible range.

The input units of the model are pitch class units rather than frequency units. They represent octave equivalent pitch categories that are assumed to receive their input from frequency units. In an early neural model, Deutsch (1969) indicated how this might be accomplished.

Pitch class units have receptive fields that are broad enough to account for the range of acceptable tunings in music. Support for the existence of such units comes from the study of a stroke patient, MS (Tramo, Bharucha, & Musiek, in press). MS exhibited a neurological dissociation of processes responsible for schematic tonal expectancies from processes responsible for fine-grained pitch perception. Slight mistunings, although noticeable, will thus not appreciably affect the behavior of the network.

The known tonotopic mapping of frequency in the auditory system supports the presence of an input layer that is not relational. Cells that respond to selected bands of the frequency continuum can be found at most levels of the auditory system. This means that information about absolute pitch levels is at least potentially available at all levels of the auditory system, the rarity of absolute pitch notwithstanding. Although models of musical processing must be able to account for invariance under pitch transposition (see Bharucha, 1988, for how this can be done), they need not employ pitch-invariant representations throughout. Indeed, models that abandon absolute pitch information at early stages and retain only interval or other relational information at later stages are at odds with neuroscientific data as well as the growing body of data on latent absolute pitch abilities (see Deutsch, 1991; Terhardt & Seewann, 1983). Nevertheless, MUSACT can be reconstrued so as to respond to normalized rather than absolute pitch classes at the chord and key level.

Hierarchical Organization of Units

Units in higher layers initially have no meaningful tuning characteristics but later become feature detectors for entire patterns whose primitives are pitch classes. The hierarchical arrangement of feature detectors in the model is supported by a growing consensus in neuroscience (mostly from work on the visual system) that the brain is organized hierarchically, with cells that respond to elementary features at the lowest levels and cells that respond to increasingly complex patterns at the highest levels (Hubel & Wiesel, 1979; Marr, 1982). There is some evidence of hierarchically organized feature detectors in the auditory system as well. Although frequency-tuned neurons can be found at both sensory and cortical levels, the cortex also contains neurons with more complex response characteristics. For example, Weinberger and McKenna (1988) report the existence of neurons in the cat that respond selectively to very specific contours of tonal sequences. Contour patterns must thus be extracted by the set of connections through which frequency-tuned neurons feed into other neurons. Whereas the tuning characteristics of a sensory neuron are determined by its transducing properties, the tuning characteristics of a higher order neuron are determined by the particular set of neurons that feed into it and the strengths of these connections.

Development of Abstract Feature Detectors Through Learning

Whereas the tuning characteristics of feature detectors at early stages of processing can be innately specified, the tuning characteristics of feature detectors at later stages of processing may become defined incrementally by perceptual learning. Their tuning characteristics are determined by the weights of the connections that feed them, and these weights are initially random. During learning, weight changes transform the initially agnostic units into feature detectors. For example, von der Malsberg (1973) suggests that the ability of cells in striate cortex to respond selectively to certain orientations can be learned. Linsker (1986) makes the startling observation that even elementary feature detectors in the visual system, such as edge and bar detectors, can acquire their specialization as a necessary consequence of simple constraints on neural connectivity. In the auditory system, there is clear evidence that some cortical neurons show response plasticity during associative learning (Weinberger & Diamond, 1988). Plasticity of this sort (in which a neuron begins to respond selectively to a pattern to which it formerly did not respond) would be expected if neurons at this level adapt their response characteristics to the prevailing regularities of the auditory environment.

Several algorithms have been proposed to accomplish the maturation of available cells into feature detectors (Fukushima, 1975; Grossberg, 1972, 1976; Kohonen, 1984; von der Malsberg, 1973). The learning mechanism formalized in these algorithms is essentially Hebbian; the strength of a synapse changes as a function of the states of the units connected by that synapse (Hebb, 1949).

The algorithm employed in the simulations reported in this chapter is a variant of "competitive learning," described by Rumelhart and Zipser (1985). Consider a network with two layers of units, called input and output, such that each input unit is linked to each output unit and the weights at these links are initially random. A pattern in the environment activates the input units that are tuned to the features that constitute the pattern. The activation at each output unit is a weighted sum of the activation received from the input units. The output layer is a winner-take-all layer. The winner succeeds in shutting down all other units in the layer (this can be achieved by mutual inhibition and self-excitation of units in the output layer; see Grossberg, 1976). The links to the winner are strengthened if they fed the winner activation and are weakened otherwise. The winner, which was selected at random because of the random weights, is now more likely to win in response to the same pattern presented subsequently, and is less likely to win in response to a different pattern. In this way it can develop into a feature detector for the set of features that constitutes that pattern.

An Illustrative Simulation of Learning in MUSACT

Competitive learning was used to simulate the development of chord units in MUSACT. Figure 13.1 shows the initial configuration of a network with two layers of units. The

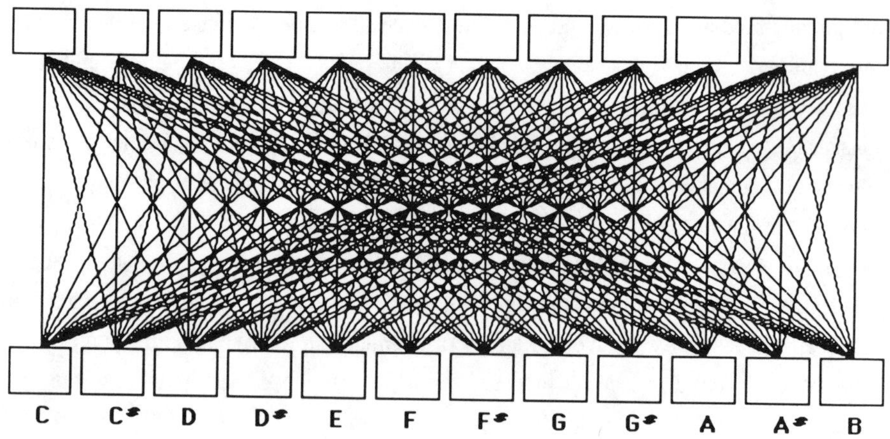

FIGURE 13.1 The network before learning. The input units (bottom layer) are tuned to pitch classes. The output units (top layer) have no initial specialization because the links (represented by the lines connecting the units) have random weights.

input (bottom) layer consists of pitch class units that correspond to chromatic pitch classes. The output (top) layer consists of units with no particular specialization, because they receive activation from the input layer and the weights are initially set at random. Given that major triads are the most common tone combinations in the Western musical environment, the learning sequence illustrated here is limited to major triads, though it generalizes easily to other chords.

A chord is picked at random. Figure 13.2 depicts the presentation of a G major triad; the G, B, and D pitch class units are activated. In the simulation, these units are each given activation values of 1. At each output unit, the total activation is a weighted sum of the activations received from all connected pitch class units, as indicated numerically on the output units. Because the weights are initialized to be random numbers within a given range, some arbitrary output unit will be the most strongly activated of all units in that layer. In Figure 13.2 the activation of the winning unit is shown in bold.

Figure 13.3 shows, in exaggerated form, the consequence of this experience on the weights. Links to the winner that fed it activation are strengthened (shown in bold), and links to the winner that did not feed it activation are weakened (shown as having disappeared). This winning output unit is thus more likely to win in response to another G major chord and is less likely to win in response to any other chord. Normally, weight changes are assumed to be incremental; no single chord presentation would result in the

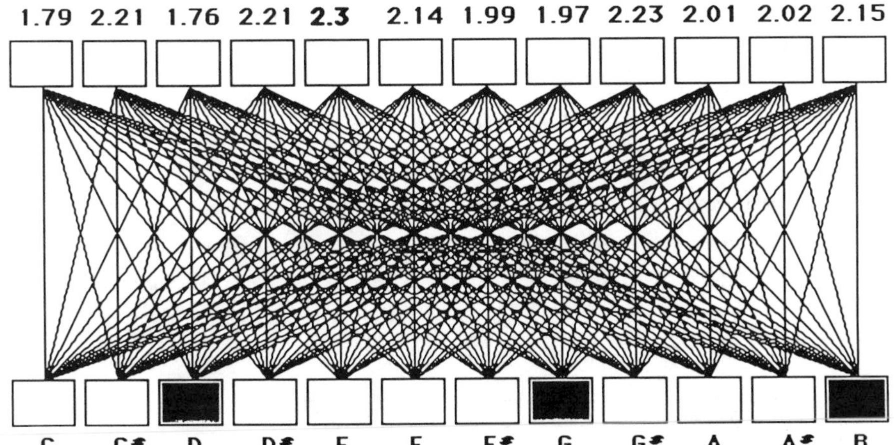

FIGURE 13.2 A chord is picked at random, in this case G major. The sounded tones (G, B, D) activate the input units that are tuned to them. The resulting activation at the output units is shown numerically, with the winner in bold.

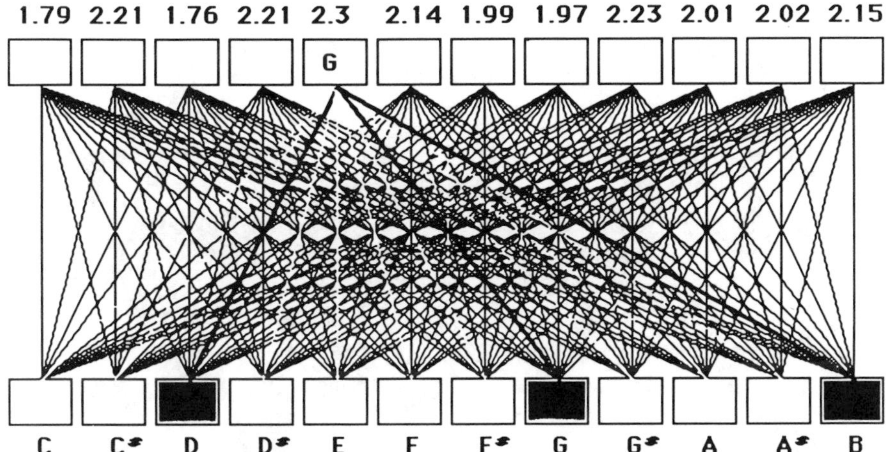

FIGURE 13.3 The links to the winner from the activated input units are strengthened (shown in bold lines), and the other links to the winner drop out. An output unit thus becomes a detector for the G major chord.

formation of a chord detector, but repeated presentations would. For purposes of demonstration, however, the learning in this simulation is radical: Links to the winner that did not feed it activation drop out altogether. If the initial random weights are within an appropriate range, the same unit will never become specialized for two different chords, and each new chord will be assured a dedicated unit.

Figures 13.4 and 13.5 show the same process after another chord (C♯ major), picked at random, is presented, leading to the formation of a feature detector for this chord. As other chords are presented, feature detectors develop for them too, leading to the final state of the network in Figure 13.6. At this point the mapping of pitch class units onto chord units is exactly that of MUSACT. Note that the arrangements of chord units from left to right is arbitrary. Repeated simulations employing different initial random assignments of weights will result in different arrangements from left to right, but the effective pattern of connectivity will be the same.

After the chord layer has matured, key units can develop at a higher layer using the same algorithm. This can be accomplished if the activation of chord units is assumed to persist over time, decaying slowly. All or most of the chord units corresponding to chords within a key would then be active simultaneously during learning, leading to the formation of the key units in MUSACT. A slowly decaying memory of chords that have been recently sounded can be implemented either as a property of the chord units or by the

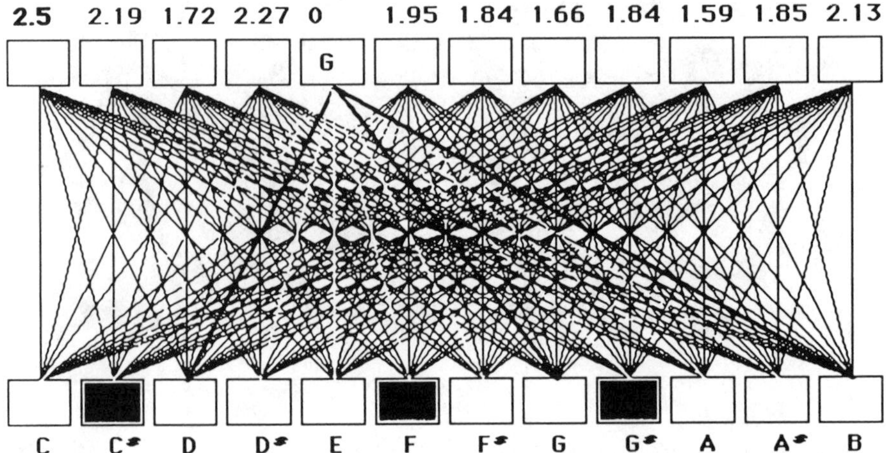

FIGURE 13.4 Another chord, picked at random (in this case, C♯ major), is sounded. The resulting activation at the output units is shown numerically, with the winner in bold. Note that the G major unit receives 0 activation.

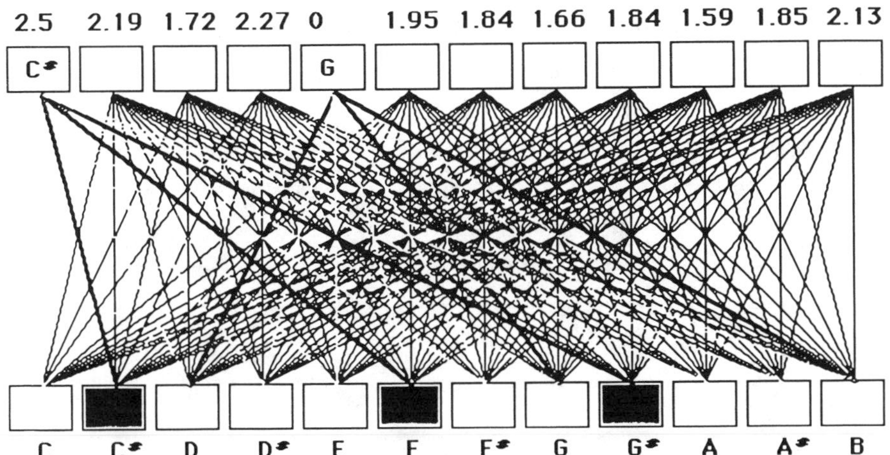

FIGURE 13.5 The links to the winner from activated input units are strengthened (shown in bold lines), and the others drop out. An output unit becomes a detector for the C♯ major chord.

use of recurrent links (links through which units keep themselves active; see Bharucha & Todd, 1989; Todd, 1989).

Conclusions

Given plausible neurophysiological assumptions, a structure that is at least functionally equivalent to a hierarchy of feature detectors for tones, chords, and keys is likely to de-

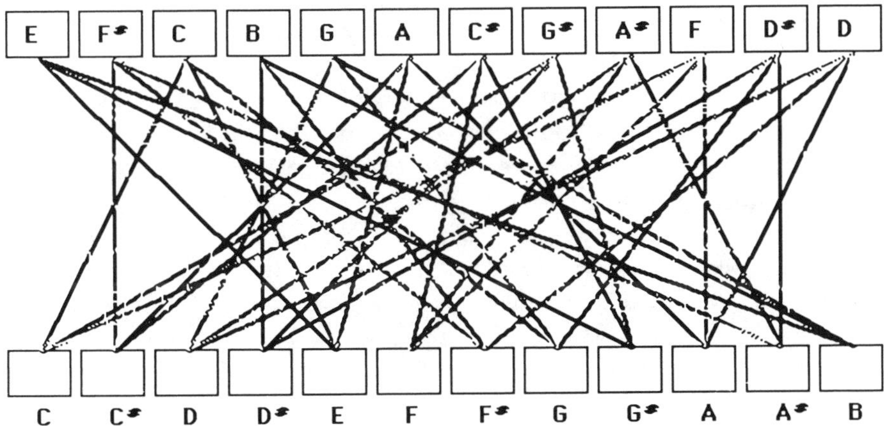

FIGURE 13.6 After hearing all 12 major triads, the network has developed a unit for each.

velop as a consequence of exposure to the Western musical environment. Indeed, given the proposed representation and learning mechanism, and given that the grouping of pitch classes is so highly and consistently constrained in the Western musical environment, one can scarcely escape acquiring the proposed schema, if only inadvertently. Although the model is undoubtedly simpler than the mental structure it is intended to model, it captures some central aspects of the corpus of psychological data and music theoretic descriptions of tonality. The model can, in principle, be expanded to learn other kinds of chords or to learn the pitch organizations of other actual or hypothetical musical environments or cultures.

References

Bharucha, J. J. (1987a). MUSACT: A connectionist model of musical harmony. In *Ninth Annual Conference of the Cognitive Science Society* (pp. 508–517). Hillsdale, NJ: Lawrence Erlbaum Associates, Inc.

Bharucha, J. J. (1987b). Music cognition and perceptual facilitation: A connectionist framework. *Music Perception, 5,* 1–30.

Bharucha, J. J. (1988). Neural net modeling of music. In *Proceedings of the First Workshop on Artificial Intelligence and Music* (pp. 173–182). St. Paul, MN: American Association of Artificial Intelligence.

Bharucha, J. J., & Krumhansl, C. L. (1983). The representation of harmonic structure in music: Hierarchies of stability as a function of context. *Cognition, 13,* 63–102.

Bharucha, J. J., & Stoeckig, K. (1986). Reaction time and musical expectancy: Priming of chords. *Journal of Experimental Psychology: Human Perception and Performance, 12,* 403–410.

Bharucha, J. J., & Stoeckig, K. (1987). Priming of chords: Spreading activation or overlapping frequency spectra? *Perception & Psychophysics, 41,* 519–524.

Bharucha, J. J., & Stoeckig, K. (1989). *Chord priming: The automaticity of schematic expectancies.* Paper presented at the meeting of the Psychonomic Society, Atlanta, GA.

Bharucha, J. J., & Todd, P. (1989). Modeling the perception of tonal structure with neural nets. *Computer Music Journal, 13,* 44–53.

Cuddy, L. L., Cohen, A. J., & Miller, J. (1979). Melody recognition: The experimental application of musical rules. *Canadian Journal of Psychology, 33,* 148–157.

Deutsch, D. (1969). Music recognition. *Psychological Review, 76,* 300–307.

Deutsch, D. (1991). The tritone paradox: An influence of language on music perception. *Music Perception, 8,* 335–347.

Dowling, W. J. (1978). Scale and contour: Two components of a theory of memory for melodies. *Psychological Review, 85,* 341–354.

Fukushima, K. (1975). Cognitron: A self-organizing multilayered neural network. *Biological Cybernetics, 20,* 121–136.

Grossberg, S. (1972). Neural expectation: Cerebellar and retinal analogs of cells fired by learnable or unlearned pattern classes. *Kybernetic, 10,* 49–57.

Grossberg, S. (1976). Adaptive pattern classification and universal recoding: Part I. Parallel development and coding of neural feature detectors. *Biological Cybernetics, 23,* 121–134.

Hebb, D. O. (1949). *The organization of behavior.* New York: Wiley.

Hubel, D., & Wiesel, T. N. (1979). Brain mechanisms of vision. *Scientific American, 241,* 150–162.

Kohonen, T. (1984). *Self-organization and associative memory.* Berlin: Springer-Verlag.

Krumhansl, C. L. (1979). The psychological representation of musical pitch in a tonal context. *Cognitive Psychology, 11,* 346–374.

Krumhansl, C. L., Bharucha, J. J., & Castellano, M. A. (1982). Key distance effects on perceived harmonic structure in music. *Perception & Psychophysics, 32,* 96–108.

Linsker, R. (1986). From basic network principles to neural architecture. *Proceedings of the National Academy of Sciences, USA, 83,* 7508–7512, 8390–8394, 8779–8783.

Marr, D. (1982). *Vision.* San Francisco: Freeman.

Meyer, L. (1956). *Emotion and meaning in music.* Chicago: University of Chicago Press.

Rumelhart, D. E., & Zipser, D. (1985). Feature discovery by competitive learning. *Cognitive Science, 9,* 75–112.

Schmuckler, M. A. (1988). *Expectation in music: Additivity of melodic and harmonic processes.* Unpublished doctoral dissertation, Cornell University, Ithaca, NY.

Terhardt, E., & Seewann, M. (1983). Aural key identification and its relationship to absolute pitch. *Music Perception, 1,* 63–83.

Todd, P. (1989). A connectionist approach to algorithmic composition. *Computer Music Journal, 13,* 27–43.

Tramo, M. J., Bharucha, J. J., & Musiek, F. E. (1990). Music perception and cognition following bilateral lesions of auditory cortex. *Journal of Cognitive Neuroscience, 2,* 195–212.

von der Malsberg, C. (1973). Self-organizing of orientation sensitive cells in the striate cortex. *Kybernetic, 14,* 85–100.

Weinberger, N. M., & Diamond, D. M. (1988). Dynamic modulation of the auditory system by associative learning. In G. M. Edelman, W. E. Gall, & W. M. Cowan, *Auditory function, neurobiological basis of hearing.* (pp 485–512). New York: Wiley.

Weinberger, N. M., & McKenna, T. M. (1988). Sensitivity of single neurons in auditory cortex to contour: Toward a neurophysiology of music perception. *Music Perception, 5,* 355–390.

CHAPTER 14

Revisiting Meyer's "Grammatical Simplicity and Relational Richness"

Robert O. Gjerdingen

The *Garland Library of the History of Western Music* sets aside the last of its 14 volumes for "Approaches to Tonal Analysis" (Rosand, 1982), an anthology of 50 years of important articles in the field of music theory. Among the many analyses reprinted, the longest is not William Mitchell's detailed study of Wagner's vast Prelude to *Tristan und Isolde* or Donald Francis Tovey's thorough discussion of all four mammoth movements of Beethoven's Ninth Symphony. No, by far the longest article is Leonard Meyer's discussion of the tiny Trio of Mozart's G Minor Symphony (Meyer, 1975). A mere 42 measures of light, graceful music provide the point of departure for 69 pages of closely argued, heavily footnoted text. That "Grammatical Simplicity and Relational Richness," as it is titled, dwarfs its neighbors is due largely to Meyer's approach, to his analysis not of a fixed musical object but of a dynamic musical experience.

Meyer's emphasis on things multiform, frequently unrealized, culturally conditioned, open ended, and evolving runs counter to a long and deeply embedded tradition of music-theoretical discourse, one that took its modern form in the early eighteenth century with the writings of Jean-Philippe Rameau. *A Treatise on Harmony Reduced to Its Natural Principles* (Rameau, 1722) was an acknowedged attempt to establish the science of music along Newtonian lines. Rameau reduced the welter of eighteenth-century chords to just one "perfect" type (a neat stack of thirds, e.g., C–E–G or G–B–D–F) and reinterpreted all traditional sequences of chords as nothing but rule-governed progressions of a "fundamental bass." The belief that a bold reductionist program could both reveal the true bodies of the musical cosmos and explicate the laws governing their orbits did not pass away with the early eighteenth-century society that fostered it. Reductionism lives on wherever the elements of musical experience are treated as inanimate objects. Lifeless musical bodies can be described in the concise, clinical language of the postmortem—"a Mozart trio, age 203, double-reprise form, key of G." But the densely textured, lively experience communicated by Mozart's music can be described only through a discourse that recognizes the important contribution made by the listener.

The root vocabulary for this discourse already exists thanks to Meyer's identification, definition, and interdisciplinary expropriation of a wealth of refreshingly unsystematized interpretive categories. "Grammatical Simplicity" treats the parameters of melody, harmony, counterpoint, and rhythm from the perspective of how a listener first intuits what musical continuations are implied by previous events and then evaluates how subsequent events either frustrate or fulfill those expectations. Particularly rich are Meyer's descriptions of melodic processes, of melodic gaps with their ensuing fillings in, and of melodic relationships based on similarity. Narmour (1977, 1990) has extended the range of what might be called Meyer's listener-response melodics to the point where one can now begin to discuss the basic constituents of melodic perception—those fundamental melodic shapes and processes assumed to be detected and evaluated during the processing of melodic information. "Grammatical Simplicity" explains the listener's interpretation of melodic/harmonic/contrapuntal/metric complexes in terms of a listener's repertory of style-specific, learned musical schemata. My own studies of the roles that learned musical schemata play in the composition and perception of music (Gjerdingen, 1988a, 1988b) have all been directly influenced by Meyer's approach.

Sixteenth Century Counterpoint

One study (Gjerdingen, 1988b) explored the possibility of reformulating the presumed rules of sixteenth century counterpoint in terms of learned musical schemata. Counterpoint treatises are thick volumes of rules—prescriptions and proscriptions that purport to describe a musical style. But style is usually the first victim of a student's efforts to write counterpoint according to a list of rules. The high degree of technical perfection demanded in writing Renaissance counterpoint can sometimes pose insuperable problems for the modern student. Yet in the sixteenth century, the type of two-voice counterpoints taught today were considered trifles suitable for practice in improvisation.

To demonstrate both the feasibility and efficiency of a schema-based approach to sixteenth-century counterpoint, I wrote a small computer program named Praeneste. Praeneste's ability to improvise counterpoint depends on its rich memory of the melodic/contrapuntal utterances known to characterize this musical style—patterns defined by melodic contours, consonances and dissonances, strong and weak beats, and relative durations. In making a counterpoint, the program first selects those memories that match the low-level schemata governing the immediate contrapuntal environment. For example, if the next tone in the counterpoint will fall on a strong beat, Praeneste will select only those utterances with a matching strong beat. The program then evaluates the selected utterances on the basis of their goodness of fit to what can be termed a topology of five higher-level musical constraints. These constraints are: (a) a preference for filling in melodic gaps (Meyer, 1989); (b) a preference for continuing melodic lines (Meyer, 1989); (c) a preference for an archlike overall melodic contour (Jeppesen, 1935); (d) a preference for pitch variety (Dahlhaus, 1990); and (e) a weak preference for the important pitches in each modal scale (Dahlhaus, 1990). After the utterance with the best fit is chosen for performance, the cycle of matching and evaluation begins again in preparation for the next choice. (Praeneste cannot back up and try again—it improvises a counterpoint in a single pass.) Figure 14.1 shows three examples of counterpoints written to go with the same given melody (in whole notes). The first two counterpoints were penned by Knud Jeppesen (1935), one of this century's great authorities on Renaissance musical style. The third was produced by Praeneste. The computer program took only about 2 seconds to write its counterpoint. Yet by knowing numerous appropriate utterances, it was able to piece together a counterpoint that bears comparison with the elegant work of Jeppesen.

Musical Schemata

In spite of its success at improvising counterpoint, Praeneste embodies a simplistic view of musical schemata. The type of contrapuntal melody it cobbles together is composed of rigid, tinker-toy-like segments that cannot overlap each other or recombine in new forms. By contrast, the musical schemata used by human composers are flexible, readily transformed, and easily overlaid upon each other. For example, the beginning of the Mozart Trio analyzed by Meyer (1975) simultaneously presents at least two standard thematic

FIGURE 14.1 Three counterpoints to the same melody (shown in whole notes). Two were written by Knud Jeppesen (1935), a famous authority on Renaissance music. The third was written by Praeneste, a computer program.

schemata. He terms the first and more salient one the "changing-note archetype" (Figure 14.2). This pattern, a stock opening gambit for the inner movement of a larger work, features a combined melodic and harmonic move away from, and then back to, the tonic harmony, with the melody circling above and below a central pitch (B4 in Figure 14.2). Mozart presents the core tones of the schematic melody on the downbeats of the first four measures: B4–A4 . . . C5–B4.

During the same measures, the first and last tones of each half of the phrase hint at a different thematic schema (Figure 14.3), one whose melody rises from scale degrees 1 to 2, and then from 2 to 3: G4–A4 . . . A4–B4. Prototypical presentations of that schema, where the central melody is reinforced by meter and cued by upward leaps from the fifth scale degree, occur in two movements from Mozart's Horn Concertos No. 1, in D Major, and No. 2, in E♭

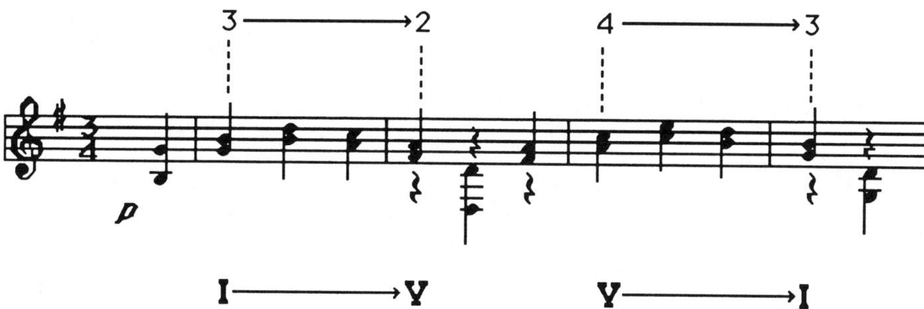

FIGURE 14.2 The opening measures of the Trio from Mozart's G Minor Symphony, presenting an instance of the "changing-note archetype" (Meyer, 1975): a combined melodic and harmonic move away from, and then back to, the tonic harmony, with the melody circling above and below a central pitch (B4).

Major (Figure 14.4). And one can find the same pattern in hundreds of other eighteenth-century works. In his Trio, Mozart arranges for these two schemata to converge fully in measure four. But their copresence up to that point has already communicated to knowledgeable listeners a sense that relational richness will be the order of the day.

The La–Sol–Fa–Mi Schema

After inserting a stock cadential schema, Mozart continues his Trio with what I call the "la–sol–fa–mi" schema, a simple example of which can be found in Mozart's well-known C Major Keyboard Sonata, K. 545, written at the time of his Trio (Figure 14.5). In the major mode, the la–sol–fa–mi descending intervallic pattern of whole step, whole step, and half step is shared not only by scale degrees 6–5–4–3 but also by 3–2–1(=8)–7. For instance, the tones E5–D5–C5–B4 are both 6–5–4–3 in the key of G major and 3–2–1–7

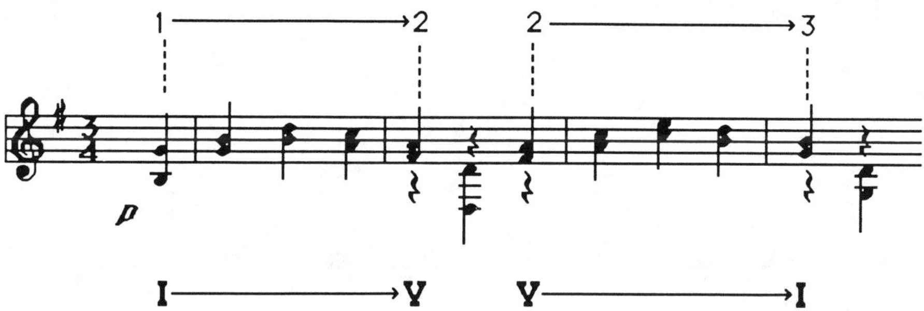

FIGURE 14.3 Opening measures of the Trio from Mozart's G Minor Symphony with an alternate eighteenth-century musical schema highlighted.

FIGURE 14.4 Prototypical instances of the schema shown in Figure 14.3, melodies taken from Mozart's Horn Concertos No. 1, in D Major, and No. 2, in E♭ Major.

in the key of C major. Eighteenth-century composers often exploited this similarity to effect a smooth transition to the dominant key. That is, they would begin the 3–2–1–7 melodic descent in the home key but would then change the harmonic context so that the listener was led to reinterpret the melody as 6–5–4–3 in the key a fourth below (the dominant).

If we take the opening movements of Mozart's first 10 violin sonatas as a sample repertory, 7 of the 10 movements employ the la–sol–fa–mi schema immediately after the opening thematic statement(s). And 5 of the 7 instances use the la–sol–fa–mi schema to

FIGURE 14.5 An example of the la–sol–fa–mi schema as it appears in Mozart's Keyboard Sonata in C Major, K. 545.

effect a modulation to the dominant key. Figure 14.6 shows these five modulating instances with the la–sol–fa–mi melody marked above the staff (small notes in parentheses indicate tones in the bass that are important to the schema; some have been raised an octave or two in order to fit onto the treble staff). When each example is heard in its full context, the tone marked "la" is first interpreted as the third scale degree of the home key but soon reinterpreted as the sixth scale degree of the dominant key.

FIGURE 14.6 Modulatory instances of the la–sol–fa–mi schema as they appear in Mozart's early violin sonatas.

The la–sol–fa–mi schema was not Mozart's invention. It was, in fact, a commonplace used by every composer. An eighteenth-century listener would have heard such a schema in piece after piece. And a composer might, in the course of a long career, employ such a useful pattern hundreds of times. The overt conventionality of the pattern allowed both listener and composer to concentrate on the subtleties of its individual instantiations. What was aesthetically significant was not the bare presence of the la–sol–fa–mi schema but the inventive, witty, elegant, noble, wise, or playful manner of its presentation. When Mozart selected the modulatory form of the la–sol–fa–mi schema for his Trio, he could draw on more than 20 years of experience in determining how to dress it for presentation at the court of musical opinion. The phrase he produced, shown in Figure 14.7, would have been familiar to nearly all his listeners, although perhaps only the more discerning among them would have fully appreciated its high degree of refinement. Of course the single staff of Figure 14.7 conveys neither the rich context of subsidiary patterns into which this schema is embedded nor the subtleties of its musical references to other passages in Mozart's G Minor Symphony. These issues have already been addressed by Meyer (1975).

The notion that a listener simultaneously applies multiple frames of reference to each of the levels in the hierarchy of musical patterns correlates well with Meyer's argument that the simplicity of a musical object in no way limits the relational complexity that one may appreciate in hearing it performed. There are, however, practical limits to how much complexity we can systematically investigate by the ordinary means of careful observation and comparison. On reaching that limit, one may either turn back in despair or press on with the aid of computers. I have chosen the latter course, though it is fair to say that computers come with some measure of despair built in.

FIGURE 14.7 The la–sol–fa–mi schema composed by Mozart for the Trio of his G Minor Symphony.

Neural Networks

In a series of experiments (Gjerdingen, 1989a, 1989b, 1990), I have used computer simulations of self-organizing neural networks, networks inspired by Stephen Grossberg and his associates (Carpenter & Grossberg, 1987; Grossberg, 1978), to study how large numbers of diverse musical schemata can be abstracted, interrelated, and applied to music-perceptual tasks. The first experiment (Gjerdingen, 1989a) tested how a network can abstract melodic/harmonic/contrapuntal schemata through repeated exposures to the patterns of melodic and bass scale degrees, melodic and bass contours, inner-voice scale degrees, and certain dissonances in Mozart's six earliest keyboard works. Figure 14.8 shows the

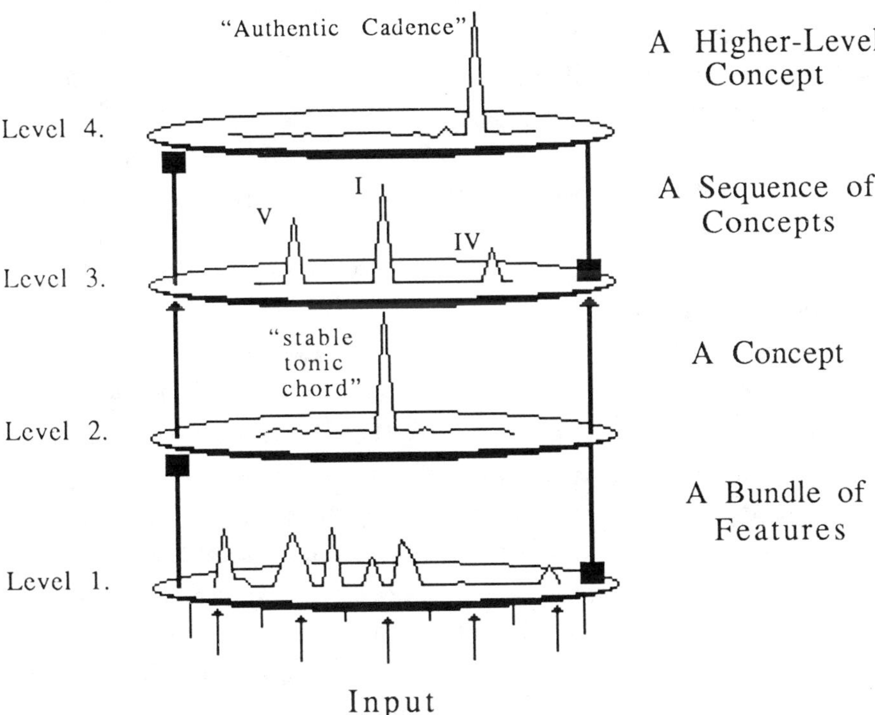

FIGURE 14.8 The basic design of a four-level, self-organizing neural network trained to categorize musical patterns in Mozart's early keyboard works. Levels 1 and 3 are dynamic short-term memories; Levels 2 and 4 are cooperative-competitive neural fields that categorize the spatio-temporal patterns at Levels 1 and 3, respectively.

network's basic design. Input from musical feature detectors enters Level 1 of the network, a level that functions as a dynamic short-term memory. For the purpose of illustration, let us assume that these features represent various aspects of the final tonic chord in one of Mozart's pieces. The complex spatiotemporal pattern registered in short-term memory is categorized by Level 2 and stored in long-term memory as a pattern of synaptic strengths—a pattern we can label as the "stable tonic chord." Category nodes activated in Level 2 send their output to Level 3, another short-term memory. And the resulting temporal pattern of recent categorizations—shown in Figure 14.8 as the three-chord sequence IV–V–I—is itself categorized by Level 4 and stored in long-term memory as the concept that music theorists term an "authentic cadence."

The actual categorizations derived by the network were somewhat more complex than those just described. For example, Level 2, instead of abstracting individual chords, generally abstracted common pairings of chords. Figure 14.9 shows how Level 2 categorized (and consequently parsed) an authentic cadence written by Mozart. Each of the eight memories excited by the playing of this cadence represents the abstracted trace of a small musical gesture important to Mozart's musical syntax—a type of melodic/harmonic/contrapuntal gestalt. Number 3, for example, is the memory of moving from a tonic chord in first inversion to a subdominant chord in root position (I^6–IV). And number 6 is the memory of a dissonant fourth (C4) resolving to a consonant third (B3) over the fifth scale degree in the bass (V^{4-3}).

The actual Mozartian musical schemata discussed earlier were melodic/harmonic/contrapuntal/*metric* complexes, not just melodic/harmonic/contrapuntal gestalts. Can a neural-network simulation have a sense of musical meter? A second study (Gjerdingen, 1989b) modeled meter as the periodic modulation of attention (i.e., musical inputs coinciding with strong beats had a greater impact on short-term memory than those coinciding with weak beats because the network's sensitivity to input oscillated in synchrony with the musical meter). A comparison of memories developed by twin networks—one with oscillating attention levels and one without—showed that memories in the metrically sensitive network were more "musical." That is, it appears that the phenomenon of meter, defined as temporally focussed attending, may heighten sensitivity to the more important musical events while filtering out incidental or subsidiary events.

Internal Neural Oscillators

This view of meter, which seemed quite original until I discovered that Mari Riess Jones had been discussing the general subject for some years (Jones, 1976, 1986), suggests the

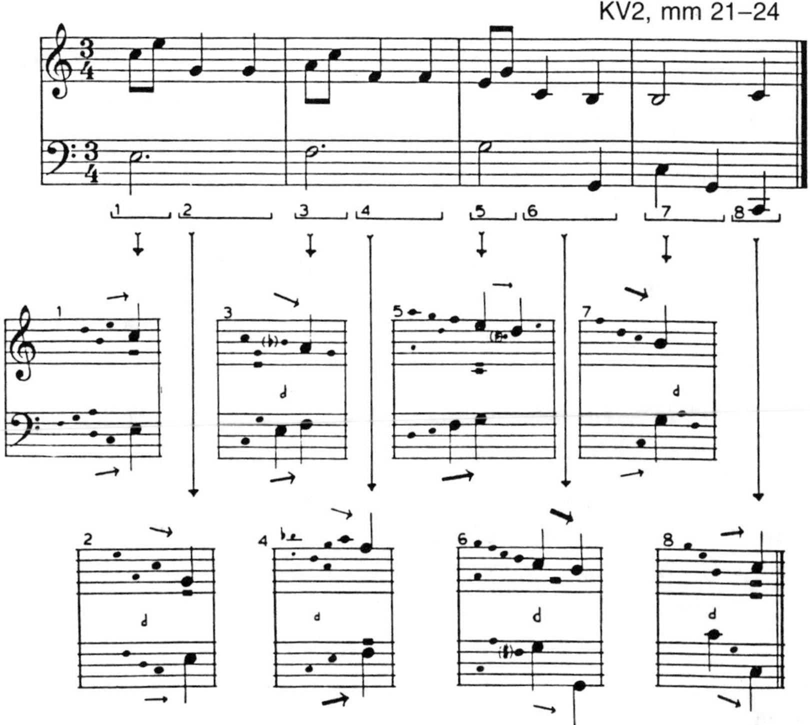

FIGURE 14.9 As this cadence by Mozart is played to the network of Figure 14.8, eight of the network's Level 2 memories respond to the bracketed sections of music. The memories are not of this music alone but of stock gestures shared by several compositions. For each memory, the large notes with stems indicate the strongest memory trace of melody and bass; inclined arrows above and below the staff indicate a memory trace of melodic and bass contour; square noteheads indicate a memory trace of inner voices; and the letter "d" indicates a memory trace of dissonance. From "Using Connectionist Models to Explore Complex Musical Patterns," by R. O. Gjerdingen, 1989, *Computer Music Journal, 13*(3), p. 74. Copyright 1989 by MIT Press. Reprinted by permission.

presence in the brain of oscillatory assemblages of neurons that can entrain themselves to musical meters. Preliminary simulations of such oscillatory neural circuits demonstrate that the simple periodicities of musical meters are not difficult to induce. Figure 14.10, for example, shows the output from a circuit of three neural populations (they are interconnected so that population A excites population B, B excites C, C inhibits B, and B inhibits A; interpopulation signals are sigmoidal functions of activation levels; and activations decay in the absence of new excitation). External input pulses initially stimulate population A at a simulated 390-ms interval. As marked above the graph, a longer 1,170-ms period (390×3) was an emergent property of this neural circuit and survived intact when the input pulses were slowed to 600 ms (note: $600 \times 2 = 1{,}200 \approx 1{,}170$). In musical terms one might say that the circuit performed a hemiola: the smooth shift from the triple to the duple division of a constant measure.

Real listeners, in order to synchronize their internal neural oscillators with music being heard, may be able to detect reliable metric cues from periodicities in the music's loudness. Figure 14.11 shows a simplified Fourier transform of the time series of amplitudes

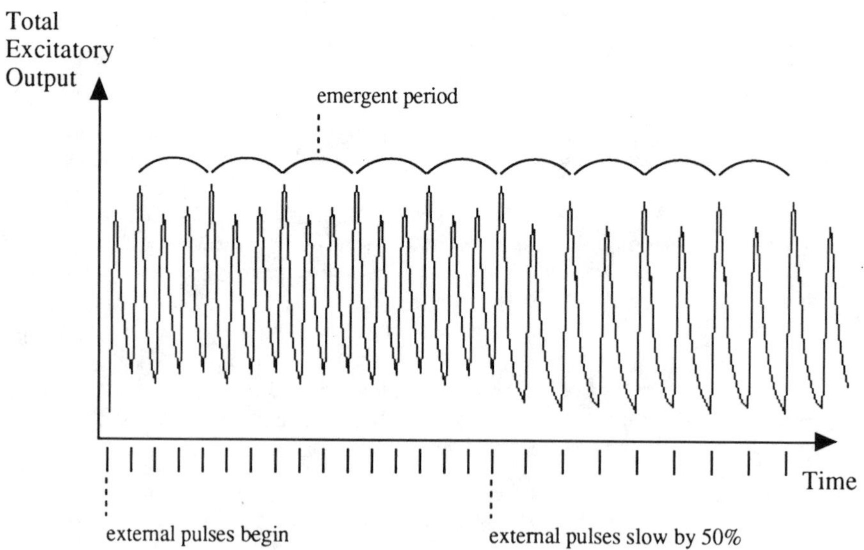

FIGURE 14.10 A graph of the output from a circuit of three interconnected neuronlike populations. External input pulses stimulate one of the populations at time intervals marked below the horizontal axis. A larger period extending over first three, and later two, external pulses is an emergent property of the excitatory and inhibitory interactions of these populations.

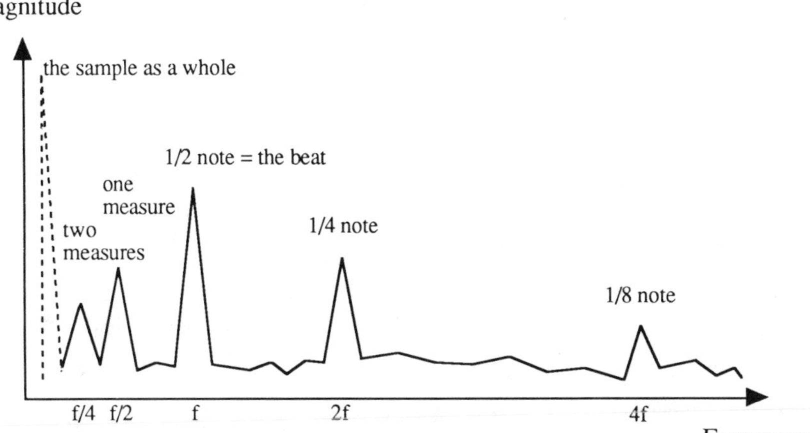

FIGURE 14.11 A simplified Fourier transform of the time series of amplitudes sampled from a commercial recording of eight measures of a Mozart string quartet (K. 575). The analysis outlines a metric hierarchy, with a salient beat both subdivided by faster note values and grouped into one- and two-measure units.

sampled from a commercial recording of eight measures of a Mozart string quartet (K. 575). Discounting the narrow dashed peak at the left of the figure (which indicates the eight-measure sample as a whole), the graph depicts the strongest periodicity at the frequency of the perceived beat, with additional periodicities at both subdivisions and multiples of the beat. In the music analyzed, the beat was a half note, with subdivisions into quarters and eighths, and groupings of beats into one- and two-measure units. Thus, the outline of a metrical hierarchy, usually assumed to be a product of high-level music cognition, is present in the raw acoustic signal and could be used by any listener, even one completely unfamiliar with Mozart, to synchronize his or her neural oscillators. From this perspective, meter may be a very low-level psychological construct both separate from, and transparent to, the perception of rhythmic groupings.

Even with a sense of meter, the type of self-organizing network shown earlier in Figure 14.8 remains oblivious to much of the relational complexity experienced in listening to real music. The discussion of Mozart's Trio, for example, made mention of melodic references to other parts of the symphony, and the discussion of the Praeneste program for Renaissance counterpoint emphasized the importance of memories of stock melodic utterances. Both cases suggest that listeners are adept at recognizing and comparing melodic figures—or what a musician would term motives and themes. Indeed one can hardly imagine what a Palestrina motet or a Mozart symphony would mean to someone who could not recognize motives and themes.

Motives and Themes

Because musical motives and themes undergo many transformations in a typical composition, their core identities are often best defined in relative terms. For example, the famous opening motive from Beethoven's Fifth Symphony is more than just the exact pitches G4–G4–G4–E♭4. When later transformations are taken into account, the motive emerges as an abstract figure: three relatively short iterations of a single pitch followed by a leap down to a relatively long tone. A neural network capable of this kind of abstraction requires for its input a rich set of features describing many aspects of melody. In a recent unpublished experiment, I took a self-organizing network similar to just Levels 1 and 2 of Figure 14.8 and gave it 77 inputs that convey information about the various types of musical microfeatures described by Narmour (1990, in press) and Meyer (1989):

1. simple melodic contour (up or down);
2. silence;
3. relative duration (short-long, long-short, same-same; these are registered only when such information becomes available, that is, often only after a third event occurs to mark the end of the second duration);
4. melodic returns and near returns (e.g., C–D–C or F–D–E);
5. registral process or reversal (up-up vs. up-down, down-down vs. down-up);
6. intervallic process or reversal (small-small vs. small-large, large-large vs. large-small, etc.);
7. interval size (small, medium, or large); and
8. exact semitone interval size (modulo 12).

The number of inputs was so large because information about exact semitone interval size requires 12 separate inputs (one for each semitone) and because that information, as well as information about melodic contour and melodic returns, was calculated at all four levels of a metric hierarchy similar to that shown in Figure 14.11. For example, imagine a melodic figure in 2/4 time that begins on a downbeat with four eighth-notes followed by a half note: |–C–D–E–D–|–C———|. When the half-note C sounds, the network receives not only information about the immediate transition from the weak eighth-note D to the strong half-note C, but also information about the implicit transitions from the metrically stronger E to the final C and from the metrically even stronger initial C to the final C. Thus the C that ends this small melodic motive is simultaneously the terminus of a three-tone stepwise descent (E–D–C), a melodic return (C–E–C), and a repeat of the opening tone (C–C). As a melody is played, each new tone evokes a complex cluster of microfeatures that reflects both proximate and remote relationships.

From the one piece that has been taught to this network—the third of Mozart's Variations on *Ah, je vous dirai maman,* or what we call "Twinkle, Twinkle, Little Star"—the network abstracted 15 simple melodic figures. Six of them are shown in Figure 14.12 above a segment of Mozart's melody. Note that on the last eighth-note of each of the first two measures the network recognized the completion of two concurrent figures—both an ascending triad and what might be called a "large ascent after repetition." This is another instance of multiple frames of reference being applied to the musical patterns or, as Meyer might say, an example of relational richness generated from simple musical materials. Furthermore, the fact that the sequence of figures in the first measure repeats itself

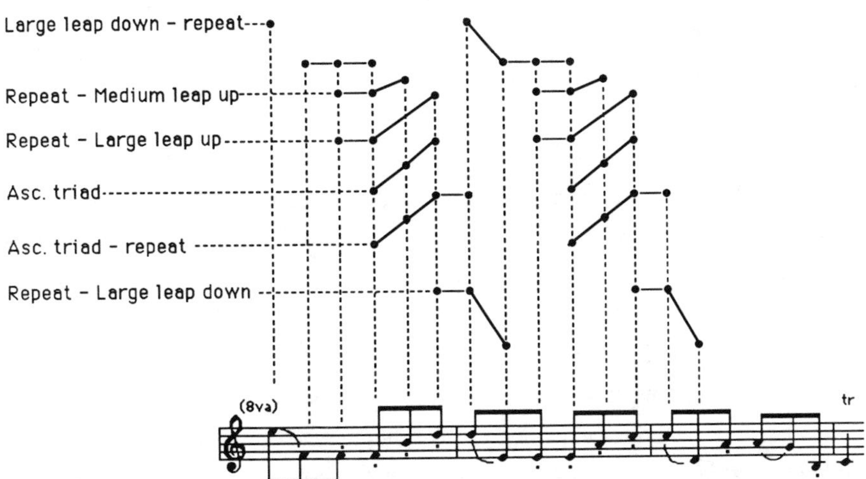

FIGURE 14.12 A neural-network analysis of basic melodic figures in the melody of Mozart's variations on *Ah, je vous dirai maman.*

in the second measure implies that a higher-level neural network, if given this patterned sequence of primitive figures as input, could learn the profiles of the types of complex musical figures that serve as characteristic motives and themes.

Harmonic Syntax

As a final problem in the network modeling of relational richness, let us consider the case of harmonic syntax. In the sequence of chords I–IV–V–I–V–I–IV–I–vi–ii–V–I, how is a network supposed to learn on its own that certain two-, three-, or four-chord chunks ending in a I chord are harmonically well formed? Or how is it to know that V–I, when preceded by a I chord, is a self-sufficient two-chord unit but that the same V–I pair, when preceded by the chords vi-ii, becomes part of a four-chord unit? The ability to be equally sensitive to chunks of different lengths and yet to mask embedded subsequences (the way the word "harmony" masks the word "arm" embedded within it) is possessed by a complex network architecture known as a "masking field" (Cohen & Grossberg, 1987; Grossberg, 1978). In general terms, a masking field can be described as a network of interconnected subnetworks. Each subnetwork receives input only from a subset of all inputs—its "subfield." The inhibitory interactions between subnetworks (interactions that are central to the operation of a masking field) vary directly with the overlap in these subfields. In a musical analogy, one might note that while all musicians compete for an audience, they compete most directly and most intensely with others who play the same instrument in the same style.

In the simulation described below, 480 subnetworks were given random subfields of from 0 to 8 inputs. Because each subnetwork had the same probability of connecting to each input (.53), the probabilities of a subnetwork developing connections to *n* inputs approximate a Poisson distribution, as shown in Figure 14.13. Thus most subnetworks had subfields with three, four, or five inputs, fewer with two or six, and hardly any with zero, one, seven, or eight. As a result, even before learning began, the subnetworks naturally tended to chunk input sequences into groups of about four, "plus or minus two."

To test this masking field, I first chose eight different chords (I, IV, V, vi, vii^6, V^6, I^6, and V^2) and arranged them in a 70-chord series that incorporated a variety of traditional patterns and followed the accepted norms of harmonic syntax. I then taught the series to the masking field three times, "playing" it as a series of eight abstract musical events occurring at regular half-note intervals. No other information was provided apart from

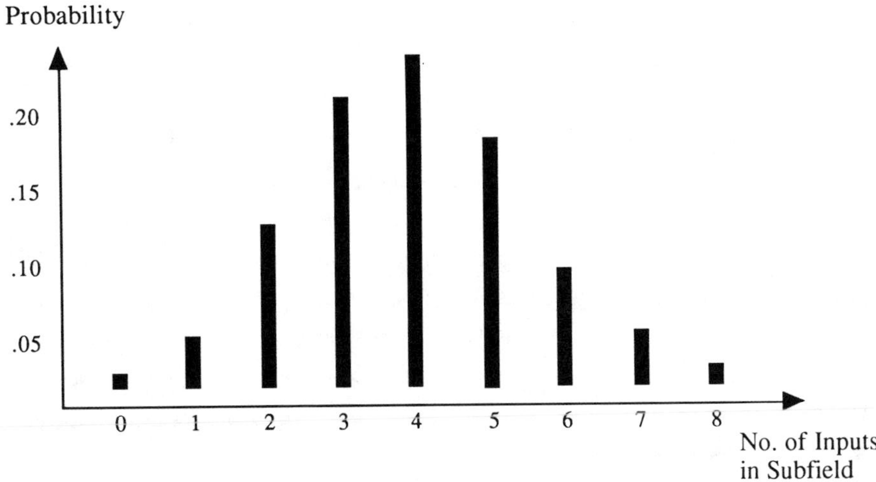

FIGURE 14.13 The probabilities that a "masking field" subnetwork will have n inputs in its subfield, where $0 \leq n \leq 8$ (masking fields are described in the text). These probabilities approximate a Poisson distribution.

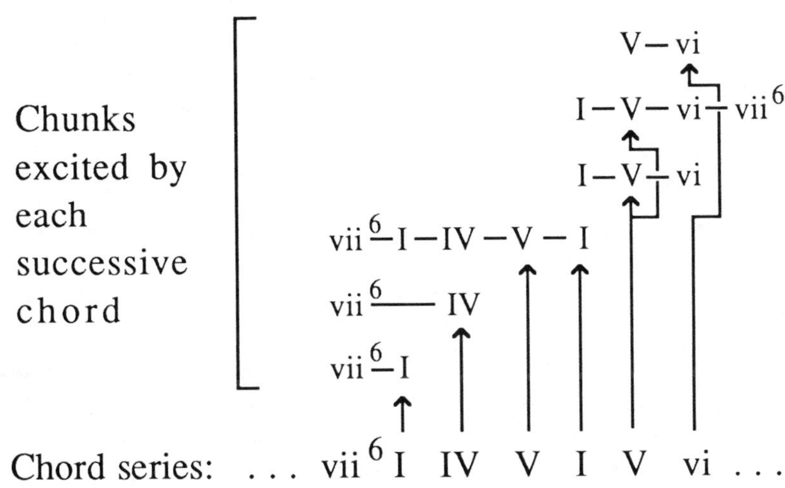

FIGURE 14.14 A neural-network analysis of significant chunks in a long series of chords. Individual chunks are listed horizontally above the chord series. Vertical arrows point to which chunk or chunks in the network's memory are excited by each new chord in the series.

that contained in the series itself. Figure 14.14 shows preliminary results for a small section of the 70-chord series. The shorter chord sequences shown above the chord series list the appropriate two-, three-, four-, and five-chord chunks abstracted by the masking field, and the vertical arrows show which input chord excited which chunk or chunks. Without going into detail, a few observations can nonetheless be made. First, the three chords that musicians would immediately recognize as a "strong progression" (IV–V–I) are all in the same chunk, and the subnetwork responsible for that chunk becomes highly excited even before the I chord is played. Second, the two-chord chunk vii^6–I is masked when it precedes the IV–V–I sequence. Third, the second of the input V chords causes two subnetworks with similar subfields to become excited. And fourth, the masking field appears to recognize the role of a I chord preceded by a strong cadence as both the end of some patterns and the beginning of others.

Conclusions

Self-organizing neural networks have yet to show that they can simulate the full richness of even the simplest of musical experiences. Yet they are already contributing to the study of musical patterns by suggesting new ways to conceptualize such patterns. In particular, the ways in which these networks apply multiple frames of reference to the interpretation of each new musical event—even a grammatically simple one—seem to provide the best computational model of Leonard Meyer's compelling vision of relational richness.

References

Carpenter, G. A., & Grossberg, S. (1987). ART 2: Self-organization of stable category recognition codes for analog input patterns. *Applied Optics, 26,* 4919–4930.

Cohen, M. A., & Grossberg, S. (1987). Masking fields: A massively parallel neural architecture for learning, recognizing, and predicting multiple groupings of patterned data. *Applied Optics, 26,* 1866–1891.

Dahlhaus, C. (1990). *Studies on the origin of harmonic tonality* (R. O. Gjerdingen, Trans.). Princeton, NJ: Princeton University Press. (Original work published 1967)

Gjerdingen, R. O. (1988a). *A classic turn of phrase: Music and the psychology of convention.* Philadelphia: University of Pennsylvania Press.

Gjerdingen, R. O. (1988b). Concrete musical knowledge and a computer program for species counterpoint. In E. Narmour & R. Solie (Eds.), *Explorations in music, the arts, and ideas* (pp. 199–227). New York: Pendragon Press.

Gjerdingen, R. O. (1989a). Using connectionist models to explore complex musical patterns. *Computer Music Journal, 13,* 67–75.

Gjerdingen, R. O. (1989b). Meter as a mode of attending: A network simulation of attentional rhythmicity in music. *Intégral, 3,* 64–92.

Gjerdingen, R. O. (1990). Categorization of musical patterns by self-organizing neuronlike networks. *Music Perception, 8,* 339–370.

Grossberg, S. (1978). A theory of human memory: Self-organization and performance of sensory-motor codes, maps, and plans. In R. Rosen & F. Snell (Eds.), *Progress in theoretical biology: Vol. 5* (pp. 233–374). New York: Academic Press.

Jeppesen, K. (1935). *Kontrapunct.* Leipzig: Breitkopf & Härtel.

Jones, M. R. (1976). Time, our lost dimension: Toward a new theory of perception, attention, and memory. *Psychological Review, 83,* 323–335.

Jones, M. R. (1986). Attentional rhythmicity in human perception. In J. R. Evans & M. Clynes (Eds.), *Rhythm in psychological, linguistic, and music processes* (pp. 13–40). Springfield, IL: Charles Thomas Publishers.

Meyer, L. B. (1975). Grammatical simplicity and relational richness: The trio of Mozart's G Minor Symphony. *Critical Inquiry, 2,* 693–761.

Meyer, L. B. (1989). *Style and music: Theory, history, and ideology.* Philadelphia: University of Pennsylvania Press.

Narmour, E. (1977). *Beyond Schenkerism: The need for alternatives in music analysis.* Chicago: University of Chicago Press.

Narmour, E. (1990). *The analysis and cognition of basic melodic structures: The implication-realization model.* Chicago: University of Chicago Press.

Narmour, E. (in press). *The analysis and cognition of melodic complexity: The implication-realization model.* Chicago: University of Chicago Press.

Rameau, J. P. (1722). *Traité de l'harmonie réduite à ses principes naturels* [A treatise on harmony reduced to its natural principles]. Paris.

Rosand, E. (Ed.) (1982). *The Garland library of the history of Western music: Vol. 14. Approaches to tonal analysis.* New York: Garland.

PART FIVE

Communicating Interpretations Through Performance

Introduction

Prior to the advent of the computer age, people listened primarily to music composed and performed by other people, and they were without the technical means of scientifically studying this sort of communication. With the development of computers, we now have the technical means to scientifically study musical communications, but paradoxically computers themselves are often found in the role of composers and performers.

Much of this research on musical communication falls into one of two categories: (a) studies concerned with perception and memory of computer-produced musical events, and (b) theories concerned with the grammatical structure of music that are based on analyses of musical scores. Until recently, these two areas of research dominated the field and seemed to be mutually reinforcing with theoretically important structural features of some grammar prominently figuring in what listeners perceive and remember.

But there were nagging concerns. Subjects serving in listening experiments routinely complained that computer-generated music did not "express" real musical meanings. And various theories about musical grammars did not always agree on what was important in a given score. Many musical events seemed, on paper at least, ambiguous. Yet most music lovers do not experience marked interpretive confusions when they attend the symphony or listen to a recording of their favorite performer. What is it about music performed by people, rather than computers, that conveys meaning?

This is the question addressed by a very small group of pioneering researchers who have created a third research category: live performance studies. Among these pioneers are Johan Sundberg, Henry Shaffer, and Caroline Palmer, all of whom participated in our conference. This final section contains the papers presented by Shaffer and Palmer.

Caroline Palmer's research directly explores the ways performing artists interpret a score (chapter 15). Using expert pianists whom she can "instruct" in various ways, she cleverly manipulated their interpretive performances of a score which, on paper, is ambiguous, lending itself to two different phrasing interpretations. In many ways, Palmer presents findings which converge with research on computer synthesis of music elaborated by scholars such as Sundberg which show that timing is an important variable for understanding communicative expression in music. In particular, Palmer makes a compelling case that a performer literally shapes the dynamics of a sound pattern to communicate an artistic vision of the score.

Henry Shaffer is another pioneer in this field. His ongoing research, some of which is reported in chapter 16, also deals with live performance but from it he draws a broad picture of its meaning. He is concerned with "what" is expressed through expressive timing and his answer involves the novel idea that expressive timing has a narrative quality. Defining a narrative in this context to consist of an event plus a protagonist, Shaffer maintains that only the event is a direct function of the score. The protagonist is the character or mood communicated by a performer's interpretation of that score. Ultimately, his perspective differs from that of others in performance studies (e.g., Sundberg, Palmer) in suggesting that expressive timing does more than simply parse a sound stream to recover a scored interpretation: Its narrative quality supplements an interpretation with mood.

CHAPTER 15

The Role of Interpretive Preferences in Music Performance

Caroline Palmer

One goal of music cognition is to specify mental representations for the musical knowledge shared by listeners, composers, and performers that allows communication of musical ideas and emotions. An important assumption underlying this goal is that the same mental representations determine how we perceive and comprehend, as well as perform, music. I will concentrate on the mental representations underlying skilled piano performance and I will argue that performance, rather than perception, is the most important source of evidence for mental representations of musical knowledge. The strong version of this claim is that theories of musical knowledge based on listeners' intuitions or on analyses of the compositional score *must* be incomplete, because the particular emphasis given in each performance guides our musical understanding. Instead of arguing for this strong version now, I will present evidence supporting a weaker version that embodies the necessary conditions for the strong claim: First, mental representations are retrieved and organized according to each performer's interpretive preferences. Second, mental representations of musical structure *can* be signaled through expressiveness in performance. Once these conditions are established, we can address whether interpretive preferences are sufficient to account for mental representations of musical knowledge.

This research was supported by an Ohio State University Seed Grant and by NIMH grant 1 R29 MH45764-01 to the author. Thanks are due to the members of the Music Cognition Group at the MIT Media Lab, where some of this research was conducted.

One theory of music perception that incorporates the notion of preferences is that of Lerdahl and Jackendoff (1983), who model an idealized listener's musical intuitions for Western tonal music. Their theory predicts the relative importance of musical events, based on a combination of well-formedness rules that specify the set of possible structural descriptions and preference rules that choose, from among these descriptions, the most coherent or preferred interpretation. This theory represents a common approach in music cognition: to model the intuitions of an idealized listener in terms of what is notated in the musical text, usually predicting one derivation per piece of music. This undertaking has met with some success in predicting listeners' judgments of grouping structure (Deliège, 1987) and metrical structure and the relative importance of musical events (Palmer & Krumhansl, 1987).

There are problems with the theory's application to music performance, however—problems shared by most current theories of musical knowledge. It is not clear how preferences resolve among alternative interpretations of ambiguous musical passages. Because the theory is based only on the musical score, it does not reflect the structural information introduced in performance, such as different expressive phrase markings of the same musical passage, which may resolve an ambiguity problem. In fact, the application of this theory to music performance may be inappropriate because of the different theoretical goals: Lerdahl and Jackendoff's (1983) goal is to model the idealized listener's knowledge, whereas my goal is to model the successful communication of ideas in each performance (not only in an idealized performance). Thus, current theories do not weight performers' preferences heavily in mental representations for music.

Previous studies of music performance (Palmer, 1989a, 1989b; Shaffer & Todd, 1987) have examined the role of interpretations by comparing different performances of the same music. By interpretations I mean the musicians' modeling of a piece according to their own choices of appropriate musical structure for emphasis, such as melody, phrasing, and dynamics (Apel, 1972). The function of interpretation is to highlight particular structural content relative to other content (Clarke, 1987). The question addressed here is: How does an individual performer's interpretation influence mental representations of music? I will argue that each performer's interpretive preferences determine structural descriptions, which subsequently determine expressive performance.

This chapter will focus on interpretive preferences for phrasing in music performance. Phrasing is a good candidate for several reasons: Phrases are considered an important element of interpretation, and they are often defined as units of musical meaning

(Cogan & Escot, 1976). There are well-documented effects of pausing and increasing durations at phrase boundaries that support the notion of phrase as constituent structure in both music (Todd, 1985) and speech (Grosjean, Grosjean, & Lane, 1979). Algorithms have been developed to predict pausing and duration-lengthening in speech and music by an amount proportional to the hierarchical level or depth of phrase embedding (Grosjean et al., 1979; Todd, 1985). However, the same problem arises with these algorithms as with other theoretical applications to music performance: The algorithms predict temporal changes based on information in the compositional score or text and thus tend to result in one prediction per text.

I will describe two sources of evidence for interpretive preferences determining phrase structure in music performance. The first source is from expressive timing variations in skilled piano performance and the second is from errors in performance. All of the performances were recorded on a computer-monitored acoustic grand piano that contains optical sensors and solenoids (see Palmer, 1988, for details). This instrument allows precise measurement, recording, and playback of timing and hammer velocity (loudness) parameters of a performance, without affecting the touch or sound of the acoustic instrument.

Evidence From Expressive Timing Variations

The first goal is to define the relationship between interpretive preferences for phrasing and expressive timing in music performance. In a previous study (Palmer, 1988) professional pianists were asked to perform the same musical excerpt, a piano Prelude in D♭ Major by Chopin, op. 28, no. 15, and then notate their phrasing interpretations on an unedited musical score. The pianists had studied the piece extensively. With the exception of a few bars, the notated interpretations of melody and phrasing did not differ across the performers. The goal of this study was to find a correspondence between the intended phrasing and the timing variations (changes in tempo) in each performance.

Figure 15.1 shows the timing variations in a section of one pianist's performance. The phrasing interpretation of the pianist is marked by the lines above the musical score, and the phrase boundaries are marked by the gaps in the figure. The amount of change in onset-to-onset durations is expressed on a note-by-note basis in percent deviation from a mechanically regular performance (the zero line is a strictly mechanical performance).

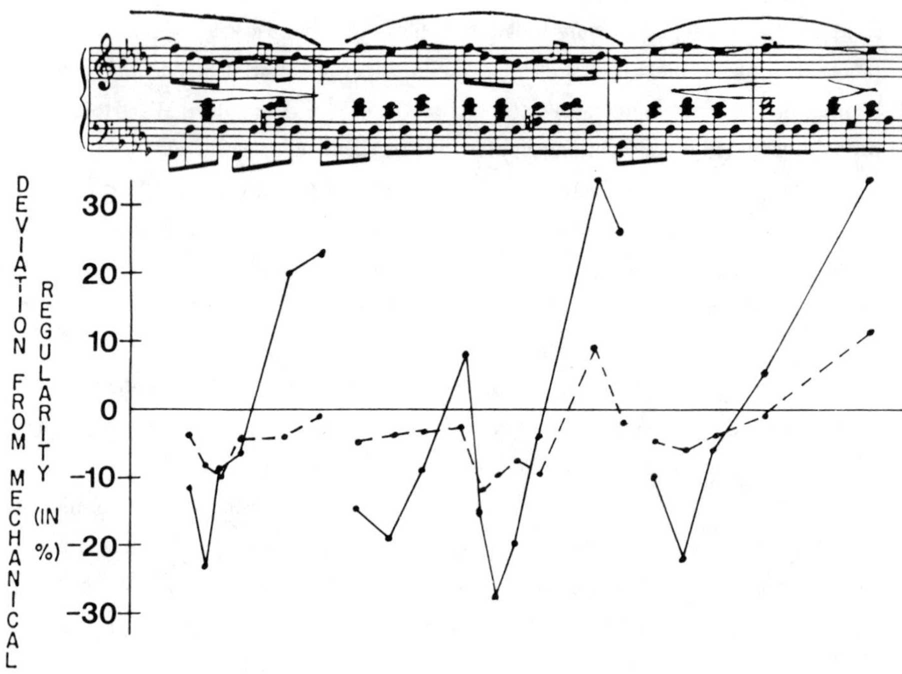

FIGURE 15.1 Excerpt from a pianist's performance of Chopin's Prelude in D♭ Major. Notated phrasing of pianist is shown above the score, and temporal deviations from mechanical regularity of the score are shown below. From "Structural Representations of Music Performance," by C. Palmer, in *Proceedings of the Cognitive Science Society* (p. 351), 1989, Hillsdale, NJ: Lawrence Erlbaum Associates, Inc. Copyright 1989 by Lawrence Erlbaum Associates, Inc. Reprinted by permission.

The deviations are calculated relative to each pianist's mean tempo or rate. The correspondence between amount of tempo change and intended phrasing is most evident at phrase boundaries (indicated by gaps). Tempo changes occurred at each phrase boundary notated by each performer (Palmer, 1988).

After performing the musical excerpt, the pianist was asked to play it again, this time in a flat and mechanical manner, without adding any expressive interpretation to the musical score. The dashed line in Figure 15.1 represents the timing of the mechanical performance; the differences in tempo change at notated phrase boundaries decrease in the mechanical performance, suggesting that the use of expressive timing is part of the performer's intention to emphasize phrase structures.

The next example includes a musical passage with more ambiguous phrasing. In this study (Palmer, 1988), Brahms' Piano Intermezzo, op. 118, no. 2, was chosen because pianists suggested different choices of phrasing for it. Two of the phrasing interpretations (suggested by different pianists) are shown in Figure 15.2.

To study whether the mapping from phrasing interpretation to timing variations is unique, a single pianist was asked to perform the piece in terms of each phrasing interpretation. The timing in each performance was then analyzed in terms of the different interpretations. By asking the same pianist to perform the different interpretations, we can also address the flexibility with which the same musical material can be restructured in performance.

The graphic notation in Figure 15.3 demonstrates the timing variations in the pianist's two performances. The nontraditional notation allows increased resolution of the temporal and hammer velocity (loudness) information. As in traditional music, pitch height increases on the *y*-axis, time on the *x*-axis. Each rectangle denotes the temporal onset and offset of key presses, and the shadowing of the boxes denotes the loudness of each event (black denotes loud, white denotes quiet musical events). This figure displays the first six notes in the melody for each performance. The intended phrasing is marked with lines.

FIGURE 15.2 Two phrasing interpretations of the opening section of Brahms' Piano Intermezzo, op. 118, no. 2. From "Structural Representations of Music Performance" by C. Palmer, in *Proceedings of the Cognitive Science Society* (p. 352), 1989, Hillsdale, NJ: Lawrence Erlbaum Associates, Inc. Copyright 1989 by Lawrence Erlbaum Associates, Inc. Reprinted by permission.

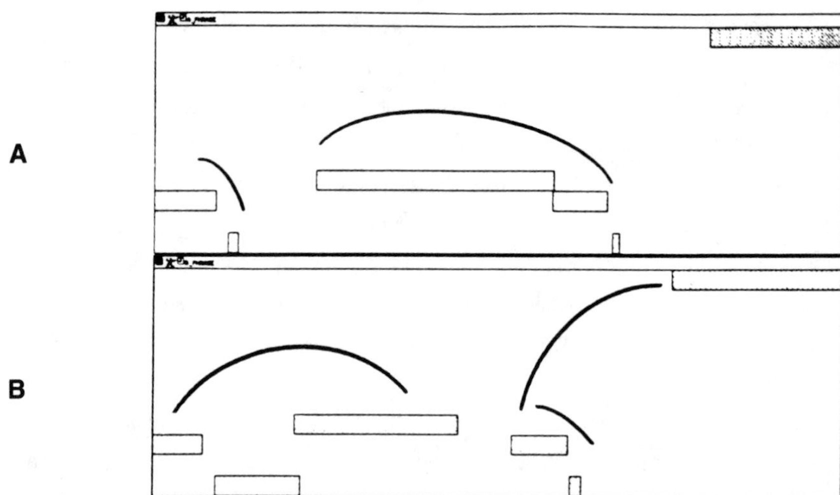

FIGURE 15.3 Graphical notation of two piano performances of opening melody in Brahms' Piano Intermezzo, op. 118, no. 2. Time is represented on the abscissa, pitch height on the ordinate. The pianist's intended phrasing is indicated by lines. From "Structural Representations of Music Performance," by C. Palmer, in *Proceedings of the Cognitive Science Society* (p. 353), 1989, Hillsdale, NJ: Lawrence Erlbaum Associates, Inc. Copyright 1989 by Lawrence Erlbaum Associates, Inc. Reprinted by permission.

The gaps between the lines indicate an increase in expressive timing coincident with the intended phrase boundaries. An analysis of the expressive timing for each performance indicated that tempo changes (defined as the absolute change in percent deviations) were significantly larger at, rather than within, intended phrase boundaries in each performance. Only the pianist's intended phrasing for each performance characterizes the timing accurately.

In summary, expressive timing accommodates different phrasing interpretations by the same performer and decreases in the absence of interpretation (as evidenced in the mechanical performance). These findings indicate that individual preferences for phrase structure directly affect both the units to be marked and the amount of marking by expressive timing.

Evidence From Errors in Performance

Evidence from performance errors also suggests that interpretive preferences play an important role in mental representations of performance. Errors, or breakdowns resulting in unintended output, are fairly common in many skilled behaviors, such as speech and typing, and often result from competition among possible actions, thoughts, or plans. An analysis of the types and amounts of errors in music performance may suggest what kinds of mental processes compete. If phrases are basic constituents of mental representations, then performance errors may reflect competition among different musical elements, determined by phrase preferences. Specifically, the likelihood with which errors occur in different locations may be influenced by the intended phrasing. If the relative importance or strength of musical events is lower within phrases than at phrase boundaries, then intended phrasing may differentially affect error rates at these locations. I will describe three error types in piano performance and how they reflect the relative importance of musical events determined by each performer's phrasing preferences.

Twenty performances of the Chopin excerpt and 14 performances of the Brahms excerpt are described here; half of the Brahms performances were of each phrasing interpretation shown in Figure 15.2. The pianists had studied the pieces extensively, and the performances were collected on the computer-monitored piano. Because errors often result from competition among similar alternatives, musical errors may go unnoticed by listeners because they may be similar in sound to the intended events. The computer-monitored piano allows us to avoid potential problems in error detection.

Musical errors in piano performance can involve elements of pitch, duration, or both. I will describe three types of pitch errors and their relations with the phrase structure indicated by each performer's interpretation. Pitch errors provide an unambiguous starting point in measurement of errors because the intended pitches are fixed by the compositional score. These are errors of planning (rather than perceptual or memory errors) that reflect processes from the time the intent to emphasize some particular structure is formed to the time the fingers move toward the keys. The errors do not result from perceptual (musical score reading) or memory problems, because (a) the piece has been well-learned and is usually played from memory and (b) the errors differ in each performance and the same error rarely occurs more than once.

The three error types described here are deletions, perseverations, and substitutions. Although there were other errors as well, including additions, anticipations, and exchanges, these three error types were most frequent. Figure 15.4 contains examples of each error type from performances of the Brahms excerpt. Deletion errors occur when an intended musical event is dropped or missing from the performance. Perseveration errors occur when an intended musical event is inappropriately repeated later in the performance. Substitution errors occur when an intended musical event is replaced or substituted by an unintended

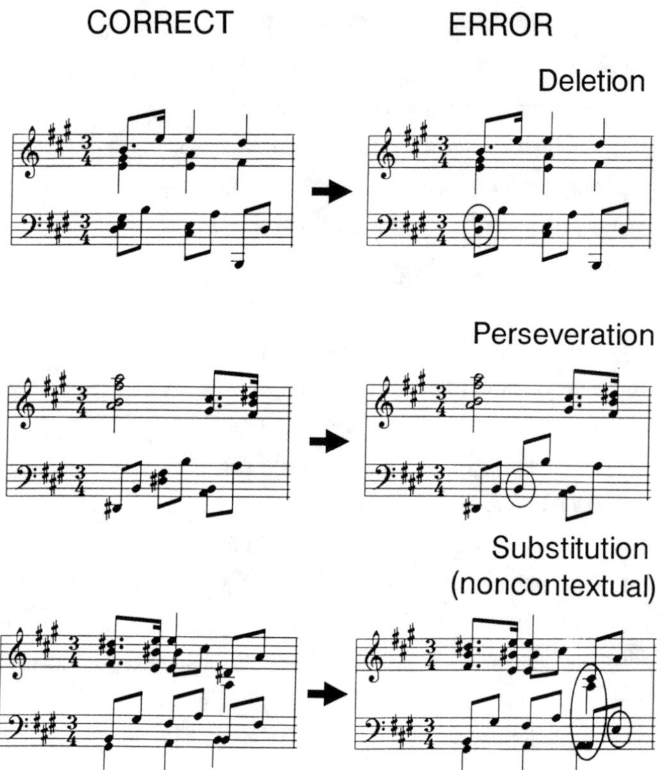

FIGURE 15.4 Examples of deletion, perseveration, and substitution errors in performances of Brahms' Piano Intermezzo, op. 118, no. 2.

event not from the musical context (noncontextual). Perseverations can take the form of substitutions or additions; only perseverations that are substituting for an intended event are described here (there were no addition-perseverations).

Figure 15.5 illustrates how each error type is influenced by interpretive phrasing preferences. The deletion error at the top of the figure of a note from a chord occurred when the chord was *within* the phrase according to the intended interpretation (shown by the solid line), not when the chord was at a phrase boundary as in the alternate interpretation (shown by the dashed line). The opposite effect of phrase boundary locations occurred with perseveration errors. The middle of Figure 15.5 shows a musical event repeating or perseverating *at* a phrase boundary according to the intended interpretation, after the phrase was successfully completed and before the next phrase was begun. Finally, the bottom of Figure 15.5 shows a substitution error, with two notes in the first chord substituting for the intended notes and a note in the second chord substituting for the intended note.

FIGURE 15.5 Effects of intended phrasing on deletion, perseveration, and substitution errors in piano performances.

Table 15.1 displays the relative frequency with which each error type occurred in the Chopin performances. At first glance, it appears that intended phrase locations affected only the number of deletion errors. However, the proportion of musical events that occur at these locations must be considered. Estimates of the likelihood of obtaining errors within or at phrase boundaries were created, based on the proportion of musical events that occur at these locations in the musical score. These estimates were used to generate expected values (shown in Table 15.1) which reflect the fact that there are, on average, more musical events within than at phrase boundaries in this musical excerpt. When these estimates are taken into account, both the deletion and perseveration error rates show a significant difference between the two phrasing interpretations (deletion errors: two-tailed binomial test, $p < .05$; perseveration errors: two-tailed binomial test, $p < .05$). Thus, the locations of both deletion and perseveration errors were significantly influenced by the performers' intended phrasing, with deletions occurring within phrases and perseverations occurring at phrase boundaries.

Table 15.1 also displays the error rates from the Brahms performances. Again, the same three patterns emerged. Deletion errors were more likely to occur within than at

TABLE 15.1
Performance Errors by Phrase Location

		Within Phrases		At Phrase Boundaries		
Chopin's Prelude for Piano						
(20 performances, n=40)						
Deletions		28	(20)	0	(8)	*
Perseverations		2	(6)	6	(2)	*
Substitutions		2	(3)	2	(1)	
Chords:	4					
Notes within chords:	0					
Brahms' Piano Intermezzo						
(14 performances, n=27)						
Deletions		15	(9)	2	(8)	*
Perseverations		0	(3)	5	(2)	*
Substitutions		2	(2)	2	(2)	
Chords:	3					
Notes within chords:	1					

NOTE. Numbers in parentheses are expected values, based on proportion of events within and at phrase boundaries.
* $p < .05$, two-tailed binomial test.

phrase boundaries. This is similar to phonemic slippage effects in speech, in which a phoneme is deleted more often within a word than at word boundaries (Cole, 1973). In the context of a musical phrase, events within phrases appear to be most susceptible to deletion; this coincides with some music-theoretic explanations of phrases defined by the relatively important events at boundaries (Cogan & Escot, 1976). The notion of relative importance is also found in various tests of musical memory, where deletions of unimportant events are most common.

In contrast, perseveration errors were more likely to occur at than within phrase boundaries. Some models of language production predict that perseveration occurs when the relative strength or activation of intended elements is lower than that of unintended elements (Dell, 1986). The more strongly activated (perseverating) elements dominate the intended elements. The present results suggest that intended elements at phrase boundaries are stronger or relatively more important than elements within phrases, and thus unintended (stronger) elements are more likely to perseverate at phrase boundaries.

One explanation of these phrasing effects on error rates is that errors result from a disposition to attend more carefully to events at phrase boundaries; however, not all errors reflect effects of phrase locations, as this explanation would predict. Table 15.1 indicates that substitution errors, although fewer in number, appear to be unrelated to phrase locations (they were just as likely within as between phrases). Instead, they appear to be related to form: Chords, or simultaneous note events, were substituted more often for each other than were single elements within chords. In the first substitution error shown in Figure 15.5, the multiple notes being substituted within a chord are harmonically related to each other. This suggests a possible explanation for why substitutions involve groups of notes, rather than single notes within chords. The result of a single substitution of a note within a chord in many cases would create harmonically dissimilar or discordant combinations of elements. Instead, musical elements appear to be retrieved and organized for performance in a form closest to their intended harmonic content and/or finger movements. In other words, the distance of the intruding event from the intended event may constrain the error, as the examples in Figure 15.5 suggest, but it is not the only constraint. The resulting error tends to be harmonically acceptable and in these musical examples, tends to incorporate multiple events, rather than individual parts of the intended event. Thus, these substitutions seem to reflect operations on elements of similar form, rather than operations on phrase preferences.

The deletion and perseveration errors suggest that the planning processes underlying performance operate on phrase structures, determined by individual performers' preferences. These errors may be understood in terms of the relative strengths of musical events in phrases; musical parameters interact to create phrases whose beginnings and endings tend to exhibit larger degrees of strength or stability than the midpoints (Narmour, 1989). Effects of phrasing on relative strengths of musical events may explain the tendency for deletions to occur in the middle of a phrase, where events contain the least stability or relative strength, and for perseverations to occur at phrase boundaries, where events contain the most stability or strength (occasionally more strength than upcoming events). Thus, interpretive phrasing preferences influence error rates by altering the relative strengths of musical events and their chances for successful retrieval and organization in performance.

Conclusions

Both expressive timing and performance errors support the notion of phrasal preferences in mental representations for music performance. These two sources of evidence converge on the same mental structures determined by individual choices of musical constituents, not by the musical score. This evidence suggests that the mental representations, as well as their retrieval and organization in performance, are strongly affected by interpretive preferences.

Interpretive preferences form a necessary component of theories of musical knowledge because they can determine the content of mental representations for music. Preferences can distinguish among different possible constituent structures in ambiguous musical cases, as evidenced by the use of expressive timing and by the likelihood of performance errors. Also, interpretive preferences affect listening to music, our primary method of exposure to music (rather than score reading). Therefore, the performer's preferences are likely to influence the particular structural description a listener assigns to a musical piece, reinforcing the communication of musical constituents. The structural description underlying a musical piece may be one that is maximally coherent not in terms of the compositional score, as suggested by some theories (Lerdahl & Jackendoff, 1983), but instead in terms of the performer's interpretive preferences.

Preferences provide a powerful theoretical component because they apply across multiple levels of musical description. For example, consider theories that posit distinct levels or stages of musical knowledge. One proposal distinguishes bottom-up and top-down levels of processing in music perception (Narmour, 1989), with distinct mental manipulations at each level (the bottom-up level having to do primarily with innate Gestalt laws and the top-down having to do with experiential knowledge of musical forms or idioms). Another division into levels of processing rests on the basis of classes of musical content: the canonical, discrete information in the musical score (i.e., notated pitches and durations) versus the continuous structural information (i.e., note-by-note intensity or timing changes) (Clarke, 1987). These approaches assume that different processes operate on the information at each level. For example, the retrieval of an E in a C-major chord requires cognitive processes separate from those necessary to determine the right amount of expressive timing to apply at the phrase boundary containing that chord. This assumption of different processes implies that the two types of information, the content and the strength of a phrase boundary, are determined separately.

In contrast to level or stage theories, the present findings suggest that preferences affect the content and form of all types of musical knowledge. If expressive timing variations and performance errors provide evidence for an event's relative strength or importance, then the present findings suggest that the same mental processes operate on phrase cadences and chord content. Both expressive timing and failures to retrieve a chord's content are influenced by the same interpretive phrasing preferences, reflecting the relative importance of musical events. Thus, instead of separate mental processes operating on distinct levels or types of information, the present findings suggest that preferences are powerful enough to influence the relative importance of events at the lowest levels of individual notes and chords as well as the highest levels of major phrase divisions.

I have tried to establish support for a weak claim of the role of music performance in theories of musical knowledge—namely, that performers' interpretive preferences influence mental representations for music. Evidence was provided for the following conditions: (a) Interpretive preferences can influence the retrieval and organization of musical events, indicated by changes in error rates relative to musicians' phrasing choices; and (b) preferences influence the locations and amounts of expressive marking used to signal structural content, reflected by timing changes relative to individual phrasing choices. The establishment of these conditions is a necessary step toward the strong claim—that theories of musical knowledge are incomplete without the powerful component of interpretive preferences.

References

Apel, W. (1972). *Harvard dictionary of music.* (2nd ed). Cambridge, MA: Harvard University Press.

Clarke, E. F. (1987). Levels of structure in the organization of musical time. *Contemporary Music Review, 2,* 211–238.

Cogan, R. D., & Escot, P. (1976). *Sonic design: The nature of sound and music.* Englewood Cliffs, NJ: Prentice-Hall.

Cole, R. A. (1973). Listening for mispronunciations: A measure of what we hear during speech. *Perception & Psychophysics, 13,* 153–156.

Deliège, I. (1987). Grouping conditions in listening to music. An approach to Lerdahl and Jackendoff's grouping preference rules. *Music Perception, 4,* 325–360.

Dell, G. S. (1986). A spreading-activation theory of retrieval in sentence production. *Psychological Review, 93,* 281–321.

Lerdahl, F. & Jackendoff, R. (1983). *A generative theory of tonal music.* Cambridge, MA: MIT Press.

Grosjean, F., Grosjean, L., & Lane, H. (1979). The patterns of silence: Performance structures in sentence production. *Cognitive Psychology, 11,* 58–81.

Narmour, E. (1989). The "genetic code" of melody: Cognitive structures generated by the implication-realization model. *Contemporary Music Review, 4,* 45–63.

Palmer, C. (1988). *Timing in skilled music performance.* Unpublished doctoral dissertation, Cornell University, Ithaca, NY.

Palmer, C. (1989a). Structural representations of music performance. *Proceedings of the Cognitive Science Society* (pp. 349–356). Hillsdale, NJ: Lawrence Erlbaum Associates, Inc.

Palmer, C. (1989b). Mapping musical thought to musical performance. *Journal of Experimental Psychology: Human Perception & Performance, 15,* 301–315.

Palmer, C., & Krumhansl, C. L. (1987). Temporal and pitch structures in determination of musical phrases. *Journal of Experimental Psychology: Human Perception & Performance, 13,* 116–126.

Shaffer, L. H., & Todd, N. P. (1987). The interpretive component in musical performance. In A. Gabrielsson (Ed.), *Action and perception in rhythm and music* (pp. 139–152). Stockholm: Royal Swedish Academy of Music.

Todd, N. (1985). A model of expressive timing in tonal music. *Music Perception, 3,* 33–58.

CHAPTER 16

How to Interpret Music

L. Henry Shaffer

It has been drolly observed that linguists are unable to provide a convincing description of the grammar of a language, yet young children can quickly master it. It also seems true that performers and listeners can understand music even though musicologists cannot agree what music means. The drollery is perhaps misplaced since there are many examples in physics, biology, and psychology of self-organizing systems which can converge on stable solutions to problems that defy formal analysis. Thus it should not be surprising that we do not yet understand the basis of many human skills. The history of ideas has shown that failures of understanding often arose from a poor initial perspective of the problem and that it can be a useful tactic to try opening up the inquiry at the empirical level (even in an abstract system such as music), if only to improve the perspective. The present study of musical performance has been undertaken in this spirit. If music is something that people play, dance to, and listen to, then it can be fruitful to approach it from the viewpoint of the participants.

This chapter looks at the performances of pianists asked to provide multiple interpretations of a given piece of music in order to assess the kinds of constraints a score imposes on performances. If interpretation involves understanding and conveying musical meaning, then multiple interpretations are possible only if the musical score is ambiguous. Finding out how it is ambiguous thus offers a way of exploring musical meaning.

I would like to thank Rachel Kirby for her programming assistance in the research for this chapter, Nick Marston for helping with the musical analysis of WoO 60 and Eric Clarke for comments on a first draft of the chapter.

Musical Meaning

We need look only briefly at current ideas of musical meaning, since these have already been well rehearsed elsewhere. Some theorists identify meaning with musical structure, which in Western music can be analyzed in terms of harmony, rhythm, timbre, melody, repetition, sequence, and counterpoint. These structures are seen as creating a play between tension and relaxation over the large scale forms of sonata, fugue, rondo, and so forth. The descriptions of this play of tension and of the structures that create it are considered sufficient to characterize the music (Lerdahl & Jackendoff, 1983).

This view of musical meaning has a pleasing appearance of objectivity, and it can have the desirable effect of making audiences (and players) listen more carefully to the sound patterns. However, it may not be sufficient. Listeners tend to hear moods and emotions expressed in the music, performers feel they are conveying these moods and emotions, and composers may conceive these moods and emotions as part of the musical intention. Form and feeling are not readily separable in mental activity. Although the expression players use in a performance can be objectively described in terms of deformations of notated values of pitch and time, doing so may miss the point that the sounds shaped by these gestures often seem related to the gestures people make when they feel emotion.

Two further observations bear on the expressive aspects of musical meaning. If a musical pattern can be exhaustively described in terms of sets of relations, then tempo, which only alters temporal relations by a scale factor, should not affect its meaning. Yet apparently it does, and it seems important for the performer to observe tempo markings in the score.

Expressive Markings

Up to and including much of the writing of Mozart, scores contained few expressive markings, but from then on the number of such markings tended to grow. One might think of these as being redundant, merely duplicating musical information already implicit in the notations of pitch, duration, and articulation. This seems unlikely, given the nature of these markings: They seem relevant to a different dimension of the music. This can be tested empirically by removing them from the score. For if it turns out that they genuinely contribute to the performer's perception of musical meaning, then it becomes interesting to explore them, and to ask what historical changes in the ways composers understood musical meaning led them to include these marks.

Expression, including the choice of tempo, seems relevant to conveying mood as an aspect of musical meaning. If we further suppose that music can convey an abstract narrative, then we can think of the musical structure as describing an implicit event, and the gestures of musical expression as corresponding to the emotional gestures of an implicit protagonist who witnesses or participates in the event. Thus, the performer's interpretation can be viewed as helping to define the character of the protagonist. This in turn determines the patterning of mood over the event. Although it is convenient to speak of the character of the music, the point made here is that the details of expression can be more fully understood if they are seen as corresponding to the gestures of an implicit protagonist. Using this conception as a way of relating structure and mood in the music also allows us to see that, in principle, a performer can be faithful to its structure and at the same time have the freedom to shape its moods. An interesting question in musical aesthetics then is whether it matters if the moods perceived by the performer and the listener diverge from those intended by the composer.

In natural language there are many rhetorical devices that take meaning beyond the literal meanings captured by logic. These include the uses of metaphor, allusive reference, ellipsis, and the prosodic modulations of tone and rhythm in speech. Expression in speech has a function similar to that in musical performance: It can convey moods and attitudes underlying an utterance and so shape its meaning. If I say that George Bush has a moral stature rivalled only by Margaret Thatcher, the real fact my voice may convey is that I have a low opinion of the morals of both. Understanding the character of the speaker helps us to interpret these subtler aspects of meaning. In the theatre the effective speaker is not the actor but the persona projected by the actor. The roles of a pianist playing Schubert and an actress playing Chekhov thus seem to be similar: Both are involved in creating a persona or character that can add a depth of meaning to the "literal" surface of the music or speech.

If the structures in the music, particularly those governing tension and relaxation, define the implicit event, then structure should be the primary determinant of the patterning of expressive gesture over the musical surface. On the other hand, the shaping of expression and the choice of expressive features—timing, dynamics, timbre, and articulation—is a function of the musical character, and is, at least partly, created by the performer. The concept of an underlying narrative takes the study of musical expression beyond recent studies that relate expression only to local properties of music structure (Sundberg, Askenfelt, & Fryden, 1983), or that concentrate on a single expressive feature, such as slowing at a phrase boundary (Shaffer & Todd, 1987). It emphasises the sensitivity to context of expressive devices, where context may extend over the whole piece of music, and it shifts the focus of theoretical attention from local expressive device to overall expressive form.

A Pilot Study

For the purpose of this study it was desirable to find a piece of music with the following properties: (a) It should be short enough to make data analysis manageable; (b) it should have enough musical quality to engage the pianists' interest; and (c) it should be unfamiliar to the pianists so that they would not have preconceptions of how it should be played. The piece chosen was a *Klavierstück* by Beethoven. It is described by Dunsby (1984) as one of Beethoven's late masterpieces; it does not have an opus number and is catalogued only as WoO 60. Because of this, because of its brevity (it lasts only 39 measures) and because it does not belong to a group like the sets of *Bagatelles*, it seems to be little known even among concert pianists. Dunsby provides a structural analysis of the piece, some of which has been adapted here (Figure 16.1). Two versions of the score were used in the study, the one shown and another in which all of the expressive markings (including the tempo marking, *Ziemlich lebhaft*, and the fermata signs in bars 9, 34, and 39) were deleted.

Four pianists, all of them professional musicians, took part in the study. Clearly this is too small a number to make this a full-scale exercise. Each was given a copy of the score and was asked independently to prepare performances for a future date. Three were given the full score and the other one was given the edited score. They were told they would be asked to give their preferred interpretation of the piece, together with any other interpretations they thought were musically valid.

The performances were given on a Bechstein grand piano, specially adapted to provide digital information about the timing and dynamic of performance. The data were then stored and analyzed on a computer (Shaffer, 1981).

On the occasion of performance, the pianists were asked to give two or three playings of their preferred version, followed by any other versions that had occurred to them. In fact, the number of alternative versions offered ranged between two and four. The total number of recordings obtained in this manner was 21. Graphs of timing and dynamic

FIGURE 16.1 Beethoven: *Klavierstück* WoO 60.

were obtained from the performances; these could be displayed separately or superimposed from different performances. Pedal information is normally available in piano recordings, but because of a technical oversight they were not obtained here.

The Music

In order to understand the performers' attempts to characterize the music, it is necessary to have a description of its structure. There is not a unique way of doing this, the one given here is based on traditional ideas of harmony, rhythm, and melody.

Despite its brevity, WoO 60 has much of the structure of the sonata form. A nine-measure exposition (mm. 1–9) introduces two subjects, at m. 1 and m. 5. A development section (mm. 10–25) makes free use of the motivic material introduced in those subjects, and a recapitulation section (mm. 26–39) brings the two subjects together, ending with a miniature coda in the last measure.

The piece is in B♭, but it moves around its tonal center in rather unusual ways. The first subject is stated in dominant rather than tonic harmony; the second subject is in the fairly distant key of D♭, on the subdominant side of B♭, and this too is stated mainly in the dominant harmony. The new tonality persists in the development section up to a perfect cadence in m. 17. In a bridging phrase (mm. 18–20) the harmony seems to slip briefly into E♭ minor, marking a further shift on the subdominant side of B♭, and then, with an enharmonic note change, it crosses the circle of fifths to D, on the dominant side of B♭. One effect of this is that the four-measure melody in the upper voice in mm. 14–17 reappears a semitone higher in mm. 22–25. At the end of the development section, again with minimal preparation (dropping from F♯ to F), the music returns to B♭ in the recapitulation. Tonic harmony in the home key is established for the first time in m. 30, leading to a dominant climax in m. 34 with progression to a perfect cadence over the remaining measures and a summary coda.

A conspicuous rhythmic feature is that the piece makes asymmetric use of phrase lengths, the number of measures in each phrase being (4 5)(4 4 3 5)(4 5 5). The brackets mark the major sections and the last measure includes the coda.

Another rhythmic feature of significance is the frequent use of syncopation. In particular, the long-short rhythm of the opening subject changes to a short-long rhythm in the closing measures of the exposition.

The latter reappears in the climax of the recapitulation and makes a final appearance in the last measure in which the long of the short-long rhythm has nested within it the original long-short. Thus the coda is a compact summary of both the tonality and rhythm of the piece.

In his analysis of the piece, Dunsby (1984) draws attention to the carefully crafted use of motivic developments of the opening phrases. One striking use of melodic reference worth mentioning is the way the downward flowing melody that ushers the change from the tonic B♭ to D♭ (mm. 5–6) is reflected in inversion by the melody in the bass preceding the return to B♭ from D (mm. 24–25).

If analysis reveals a highly crafted structure, the abrupt and radical changes in harmony and rhythm give the musical surface an almost throwaway appearance. It is as if Beethoven was intent on concealing the craft, and making the piece seem arbitrary. The style of the piece is further brought out in the exposition. Its opening subject has a dotted rhythm and ends with a brief eighth-note, suggesting a lively mood that is reinforced by the tempo marking, "fairly lively." Yet the second subject signals a shift to a more dramatic mood in a number of ways:

1. It modulates from B♭ to D♭, with the association of moving to the "dark" side of the home key.
2. It shifts from a long-short rhythm to a more angular short-long rhythm.
3. The melodic opening gives way to a series of spaced chords, marked with sforzandos.
4. The last of these chords extends the expected four measure phrase into a five measure phrase, and the chord is marked to be sustained.
5. There is an opening up of register by an octave in each successive chord, such that the chord ending the first subject in m. 2 is extended by three octaves in m. 9.

These structural devices create a rise of tension over the nine measures of the exposition, and the expressive markings indicate something of the composer's intentions of mood change, but it is up to the performer to determine the quality of the moods and their change. The way in which the performer chooses these moods and shapes their transition affects the character of the exposition and of the whole piece.

Another major, expressive decision that the performer has to make is the handling of the modulation in the development section from D♭ to D, which can be thought of as the pivot of the whole piece. The expression used here affects the balance achieved between the opening and closing sections. If it is interpreted as a shift from a "dark" to a "bright" mood then it can serve to restore the levity of the opening phrase. Here, if anywhere, the performer must choose between pursuing the playful or the dramatic elements in the exposition.

These remarks indicate possible focal points in analyzing the performance data, rather than expressive commitments identified by the pianists. In fact, one of the pianists did spontaneously remark on the pivotal importance of the modulation at m. 21. What is not clear, and this is a weakness of the study, is how much the performers understood the musical structure. They were not asked to annotate the score with their own analyses (see Palmer, chapter 15, this volume) and in a fuller study this should be done.

The Performances

The first question of interest is on the consistency of shape of the expressive profiles of timing and dynamic across the performances by each performer. Shape can be examined at different levels of detail, and the first level explored is that of the measure. The duration of a measure can be obtained directly; the dynamic of a measure is less easily defined, and can be chosen arbitrarily as an average over all notes in the measure or as the most salient note dynamic. The latter method may better represent how the dynamics of the measure is perceived and so this was the method chosen for our study.[1]

An immediate picture of the consistency and variety of expression is obtained by superimposing the graphs of these variables for each performer (see Figure 16.2). It is apparent that three of the performers, DC, MG, and PM, produced patterns of timing and dynamic that kept their shape across a variety of tempi and were in major agreement whereas RE showed no such consistency, either among her performances or with the others. What is interesting is that it was RE who played from an edited score, with expressive markings deleted. This could be a coincidence, since with only four players there is no question of statistical significance, but it offers a suggestive lead for further study.

It is possible that RE had less control of her playing than the others. This can be checked by superimposing the performances in which performers were trying to keep to the same interpretation. This can be seen in Figure 16.3. This figure shows that RE's precision of control was of the same order as the others. The occasional discrepancies of

[1] Arbitrary decisions had to be made about the timing of a few measures. Measures 8 and 9 begin with rests and do not have well defined moments of onset. The solution adopted was to suppose that there was no tempo change within m. 7, and so give the half-note twice the time value of the quarter-note. The value of the following rest inferred in this way was propagated to m. 9. Also, the half-note straddling m. 33 and m. 34 was allocated equal time in each measure. It should be added that these decisions had a minor effect on the shape of the timing graphs.

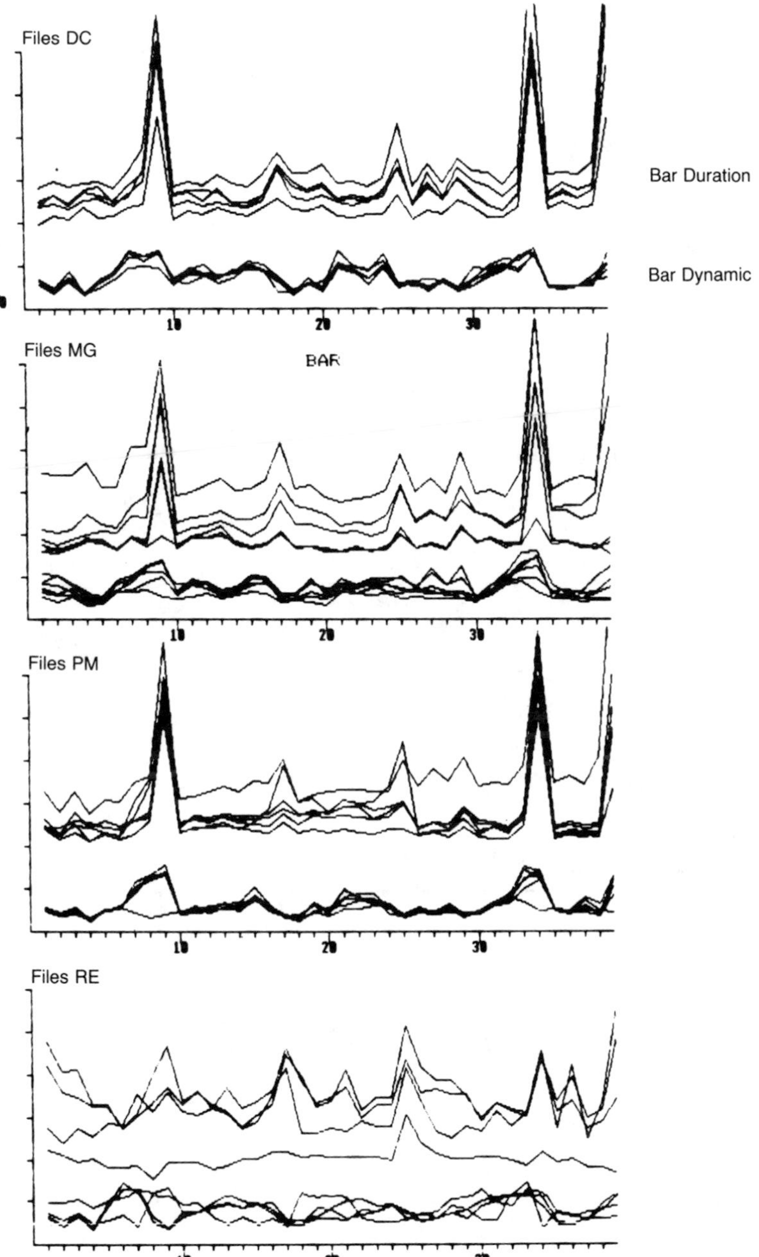

FIGURE 16.2 Graphs of measure duration and measure dynamic superimposing the different performances for each pianist. The vertical scales have arbitrary units but a true zero.

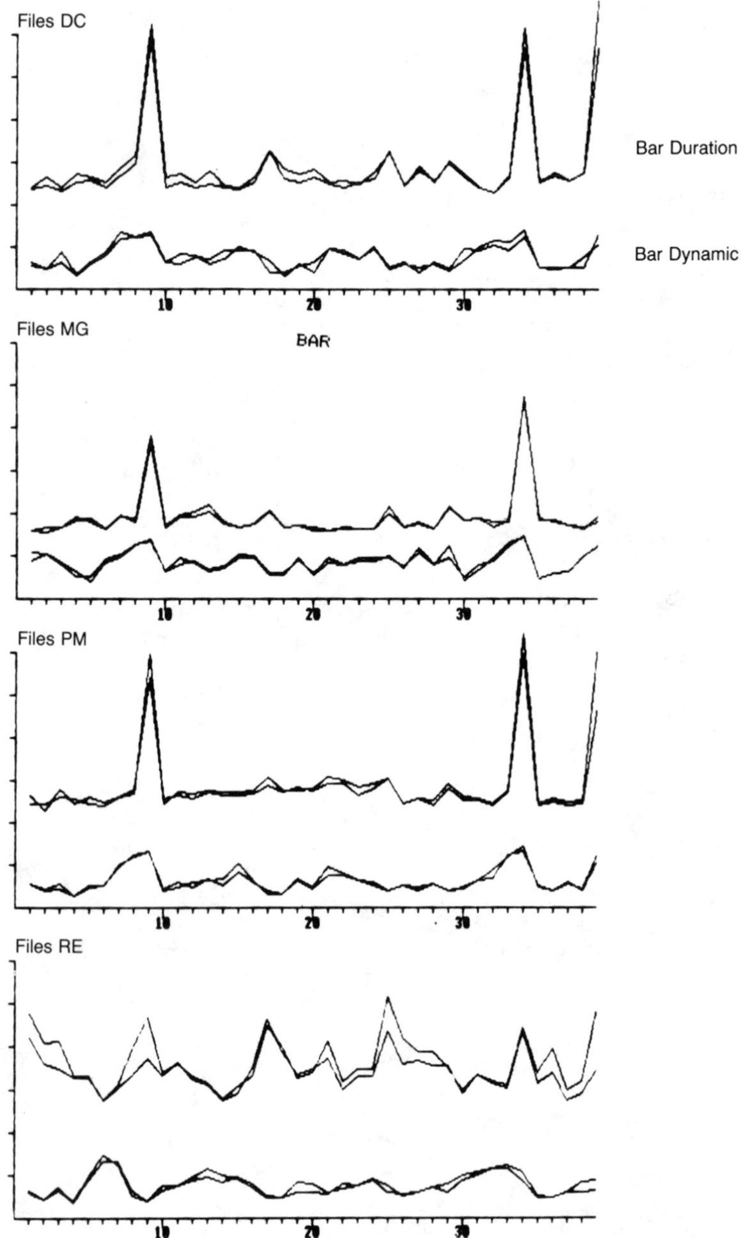

FIGURE 16.3 Measure duration and measure dynamic superimposing the first two performances for each pianist. The pianists were asked to keep the same interpretation in these.

tempo may reflect the fact that in her first performance she set a very slow tempo, slower than that attempted by any other performer, and she may have regarded this extreme as inappropriate.

Discussion

If these results are valid, then the contrast in consistency between RE and the others indicates the power of expressive markings, despite their ambiguity, to constrain an interpretation. In terms of the concept of musical narrative, one might say that these markings help to crystallize a narrative for the piece, and this would be supported by the amount of agreement of expression among the other performers. To say that RE had more freedom to invent different narratives, however, raises difficulties for the concept of narrative as it has been discussed.

If narrative = event + protagonist, and event is determined by musical structure, then the only aspect of narrative free to change in different interpretations is the character of the protagonist. Thus there is scope for altering mood and hence the quality of expressive gesture, but since the event is invariant, then, by hypothesis, the expressive form should change in detail rather than in overall shape. This is largely true for DC, MG, and PM, as the graphs for their performances indicate. But it should also be true for RE, and it is not.

A possible, rather uninteresting explanation for the lack of consistency by RE is that she may have spent less time than the others analyzing the score and relied on improvising on a rather superficial reading. There is no way of arguing around this possibility other than by getting data from more pianists, half shown the edited score and half the normal score. Preferably, too, as already indicated, the pianists should be asked to annotate the score with their analyses. If the result turns out to be robust, this still leaves two distinct hypotheses: (a) Expressive markings provide redundant information about structure and offer a shortcut in determining that structure; and (b) These markings can contribute something to a narrative event that is not defined by structure.

It is possible that none of the pianists made a full analysis of the piece, but that those who saw the unedited score were able to reconstruct aspects of structure from the expressive markings. An example from the data is consistent with this idea. There are two climaxes marked in the score, occurring on the first beats of measures 16 and 24. They are structurally similar points in their respective phrases and they represent cadential 6–4 chords preparing perfect cadences, and at these points tension moves to its resolution. It can be seen in Figure 16.2 that DC, MG, and PM often reached a dynamic climax earlier in the phrase, suggesting that they were responding not to the cadential preparation as such but to the vicinity indicated by the marked crescendo and decrescendo. Thus it is feasible (based on the present data) to accept the first hypothesis.

Of the three pianists who saw the full score, it was MG who introduced the most variety across her performances, as Figure 16.2 shows. DC maintained an almost invariant dynamic profile, and his timing, at the level of the measure, was more or less scaled by tempo across performances. PM too showed little exploration of dynamic across performances, except in one when (on a hint by the experimenter, the only occasion on which this was done) he ignored the sforzando markings and played the chords very softly, with exaggerated pause. However, he made more exploration of timing. In one performance, he kept the tempo almost constant, except at the chords marked with a fermata; in another he slowed the tempo from the phrase marked "tenderly" up to the end of the development section; in the slowest performance he made the tempo get progressively slower throughout.

The preferred performances of DC and PM had similar tempi, both performers starting at around 110 quarter-notes per minute. Those of MG had the much higher starting tempo of nearly 170 quarter-notes per minute. Perhaps relevant to this, her rhythms were more dotted in the opening subject and its later recapitulation. Greater dottedness gives the music a more dance-like character and this is consistent with a faster tempo. Also, consistent with that character, she sometimes ignored the "p dolce" marking in the opening phrase. Her slowest performance, on the other hand, was slower than any by DC or PM, its rhythms became less dotted, and was played more quietly, with less use of dynamic contrast, suggesting that this was a more song-like approach to the music. In one of the faster performances, she too aimed at an unvarying tempo, even to the extent of barely prolonging the chords marked with a fermata. Figure 16.2 also shows that in one performance she allowed the tempo to become progressively slower.

These remarks indicate the variety of expression used by the pianists, but the more interesting question here is whether it could be said that they explored different characters in the music. To answer this we need to look for evidence of an expressive unity within a performance, beyond merely playing the piece quietly or slowly. The following is an attempt to indicate how such an analysis might proceed.

Two of the performances by MG (MG_3 and MG_5) depicted in Figure 16.4 are of immediate interest. MG_3 was played at a tempo of 125 quarter-notes per minute, closer to that preferred by DC and PM. This tempo seemed optimal for making a contrast between the light and dark moods of the piece: At faster speeds the dramatic moments are weakened, and at slower speeds the lighter moments become ponderous. MG_5 began faster but gradually and progressively became slower. Let us try to extract some of the different characteristics of these two performances.

Looking again at the exposition, the opening subject ends in an eighth-note chord with a rising note in the melody, whereas its imitation ends in a quarter-note chord and with a falling melody note. If the opening subject is jaunty, its imitation seems to hint at something more dramatic ahead, which duly unfolds in a sixteenth-note downward run in octaves (in a different key) followed by a sequence of detached chords in a syncopated rhythm. In m. 6 the rhythm is ambiguous. A performer wishing to make a strong contrast between a light opening and a dark ending in the exposition has an opportunity for shaping this transition in this measure.

MG_3 introduces a pause in m. 4 following the imitation, and in the sixteenth-note run in m. 6 both builds a crescendo and accelerates, giving an urgency to the downward run. In contrast, MG_5 does neither, so the sforzando chords enter almost unprepared. Yet they are much louder in MG_5 than in MG_3. MG_3 slows progressively over the chord sequence; MG_5 slows less but pauses longer on the last chord (m. 9). Thus MG_5 seems to portray in the exposition a less subtle character, which fails to anticipate changes in the music but reacts more strongly when they occur. Looking back, one can already see a relative unsubtlety portrayed in the rather fast and loud statement of the opening subject.

In the second half of the development, MG_3 anticipates the modulation from D♭ to D with an acceleration over the bridging phrase (mm. 18–20). Keeping a quiet dynamic in this phrase, it builds a slow crescendo over the following measures, allowing the semitone-raised melody to sing out. MG_5, in contrast, accelerates less in the bridging phrase, reacts to the upward leap in the melody in m. 19 by raising the dynamic level, and maintains this level through to the end of the development section. It misses a sense of wonder in the modulation and a feeling of uplift in the semitone-raised melody. Thus MG_3 restores a levity to the music in the recapitulation in a way that MG_5 does not. Instead, the latter gradually loses its impetus. It reacts to the upwardly moving counterpoint of the melody in mm. 30–34 by building a crescendo that climaxes on the dominant seventh chord, with a massive slowing on that chord. There is a similar slowing on the dominant

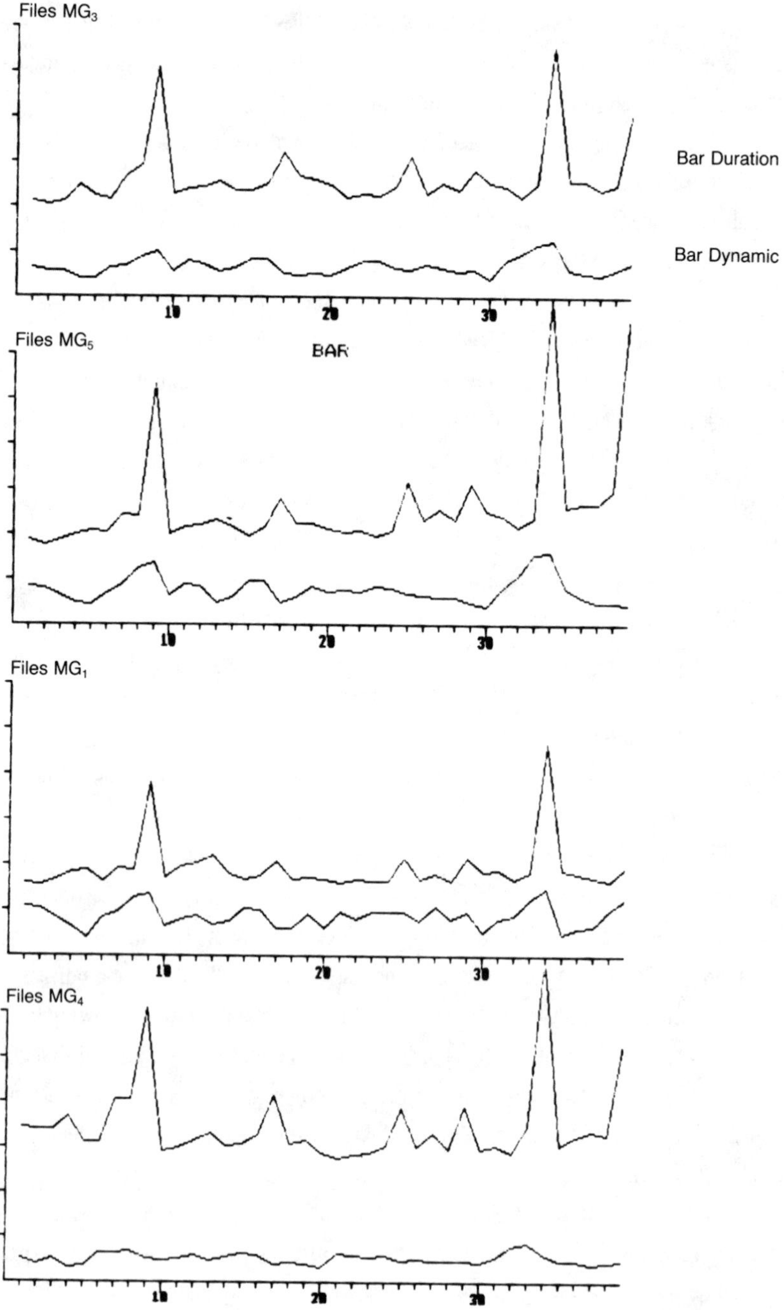

FIGURE 16.4 Measure duration and measure dynamic for four performances by MG.

chord in the coda (m. 39). If the purpose of the fermata in the coda is to gently underline the nesting of a long-short rhythm within the short-long rhythm of the measure, this touch of rhythmic wit caught in MG_3 is lost in MG_5.

It is also worthwhile to compare MG_5 with MG_1, which was fast throughout, and MG_4, which was slow throughout (see Figure 16.4). MG_1 gives a dance-like character to the piece, making the opening subject and the various climaxes fairly loud and tending to underplay the dramatic nature of the chords in m. 9 and m. 34 by sustaining them less. Because it makes less dramatic contrast between the subjects in the exposition, it has less need to resolve a dramatic conflict. MG_4 has a quieter, song-like character, with more sustained pauses at climaxes and phrase endings, but little use of dynamic contrast, even taking the chords quietly. Again, there is little need to resolve a dramatic contrast, but the quickening of pace approaching m. 21 and the rising volume in that measure helps preserve the song-like quality up to the end.

The purpose here is not to evaluate the performances but to exemplify ways of describing their character. It would be interesting to ask separately which of them was appropriate to the musical structure. It should also be apparent that the descriptions here are provisional and need to be superseded by a language better suited to the task of analyzing expression.

Conclusions

This chapter makes a case for considering expression as a contributor to musical meaning. It also presents an empirical problem and a paradigm for its solution. The problem is to find descriptors of expression powerful enough to (a) discriminate between performances of a piece and (b) reveal a unity of character within an expressive performance. The paradigm is to obtain multiple performances of the same piece of music, by the same or by different performers. A possible tactic within the paradigm, only informally explored here, is to manipulate the expressive markings within the score and so assess their contributions in determining expression.

The idea of an implicit narrative in the music is fairly benign and may have some heuristic value in opening up the empirical study of expression. One can think of the narrative event in terms of musical structures: There seems to be no need to suppose more literary representations. The utility of the idea of a protagonist within the narrative hinges on whether one accepts mood or feeling as an aspect of musical meaning.

There are three reasons for introducing the concept of musical narrative. One is to emphasize that expression cannot be fully mapped onto descriptors of musical structure by local context-free rules: Rather it is determined within a characterization of the piece of music. The second is to draw attention to the role of the performer as a creator of musical character, rather than as someone presenting only what is implicit in the notated music. The third reason arises from the second: It seems sufficient to talk of the character of the music and dispense with the concept of a protagonist in a narrative. The point of this anthropomorphic step, however, is to make the claim (still untested) that the performer, perhaps unconsciously, uses the physical gestures of emotion as models for shaping the gestures in the musical sound.

References

Dunsby, J. (1984). A bagatelle on Beethoven's WoO 60. *Music Analysis, 3*, 57–68.

Lerdahl, F., & Jackendoff, R. (1983). *A generative theory of tonal music.* Cambridge, MA: MIT Press.

Shaffer, L. H. (1981). Performances of Chopin, Bach, and Bartok: Studies in motor programming. *Cognitive Psychology, 13*, 327–376.

Shaffer, L. H., & Todd, N. P. (1987). The interpretive component in musical performance. In A. Gabrielsson (Ed.), *Action and perception in rhythm and music* (pp. 139–152). Stockholm: Royal Swedish Academy of Music.

Sundberg, J., Askenfelt, A., & Fryden, L. (1983). Musical performance: A synthesis-by-rule approach. *Computer Music Journal, 7*, 37–43.

Index